CRITICS SALUTE <u>RAMSES</u>

"HE DIED THREE THOUSAND YEARS AGO. BUT HE IS STILL THE LITERARY STAR OF THE YEAR. THE RAMSES II SAGA . . . IS A MUST-READ BESTSELLER."
—*Paris Match*

"Officially, Christian Jacq was born in Paris in 1947. In fact, his real birth took place in the time of the pharaohs, along the banks of the Nile, where the river carries eternal messages. . . . Who could ever tell that Christian Jacq, Ramses' official scribe, was not writing from memory?"
—*Magazine Littéraire*

"With hundreds of thousands of readers, millions of copies in print, Christian Jacq's success has become unheard of in the world of books. This man is the pharaoh of publishing!"
—*Figaro Magazine*

"In 1235 B.C., Ramses II might have said: 'My life is as amazing as fiction!' It seems Christian Jacq heard him. . . . Christian Jacq draws a pleasure from writing that is contagious. His penmanship turns history into a great show, high-quality entertainment."
—*VSD*

"It's *Dallas* or *Dynasty* in Egypt, with a hero (Ramses), beautiful women, plenty of villains, new developments every two pages, brothers fighting for power; magic, enchantments, and historical glamour."
—*Libération*

"He's a pyramid-surfer. The pharaoh of publishing. His saga about Ramses II is a bookselling phenomenon."
—*Le Parisien*

RAMSES

VOLUME III

THE BATTLE OF KADESH

CHRISTIAN JACQ

Translated by Mary Feeney

WARNER BOOKS

A Time Warner Company

Originally published in French by Editions Robert Laffont, S.A. Paris, France.

Warner Books Edition
Copyright © 1996 by Editions Robert Laffont (Volume 3)
All rights reserved.

Warner Books, Inc., 1271 Avenue of the Americas, New York, NY 10020

Visit our Web site at
http://warnerbooks.com

W A Time Warner Company

Printed in the United States of America

First U.S. Printing: July 1998
10 9 8 7 6 5 4 3 2

Library of Congress Cataloging-in-Publication Data

Jacq, Christian.
   [Bataille de Kadesh. English]
   The battle of Kadesh / Christian Jacq.
      p. cm. — (Ramses ; v. 3)
   ISBN 0-446-67358-7
   I. Title. II. Series: Jacq, Christian. Ramsès. English ; v. 3.
   PQ2670.A2438B3813   1998
   843'.914—dc21   98-5227
                                                      CIP

Book design and composition by L&G McRee
Cover design and illustration by Marc Burkhardt

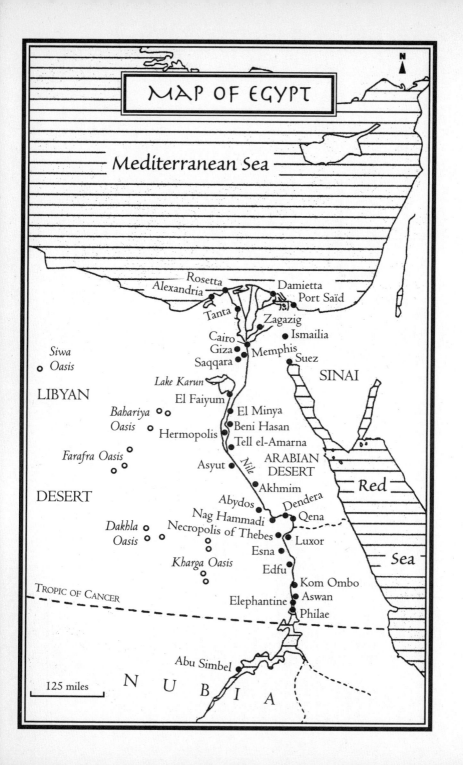

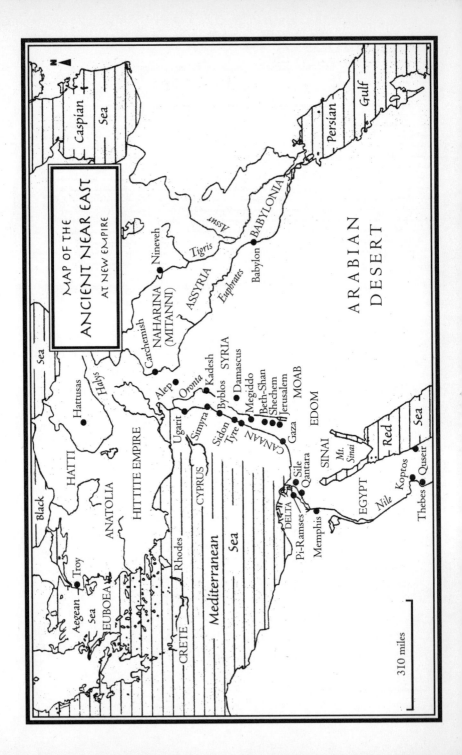

MAP OF THE
ANCIENT NEAR EAST
AT NEW EMPIRE

N

Caspian Sea

Persian Gulf

ARABIAN DESERT

Nineveh

NAHARINA (MITANNI)

Tigris

Assur

ASSYRIA

BABYLONIA

Babylon

Euphrates

Carchemish

Sea

Halys

Black Sea

Hattusas

HATTI

ANATOLIA

HITTITE EMPIRE

Alep

Ugarit

Oronta

Kadesh

SYRIA

Byblos

Damascus

Megiddo

Beth-Shan

Shechem

Jerusalem

MOAB

Smyrna

Sidon

Tyre

CANAAN

Gaza

EDOM

CYPRUS

Rhodes

Troy

Aegean Sea

EUBOEA

CRETE

Mediterranean Sea

SINAI

Mt. Sinai

Sile

Qantara

DELTA

Pi-Ramses

Memphis

EGYPT

Nile

Koptos

Thebes

Quseir

Red Sea

310 miles

ONE

Danio's horse galloped down the overheated track leading to the Abode of the Lion, a settlement in southern Syria founded by the illustrious Pharaoh Seti. Egyptian on his father's side and Syrian on his mother's, Danio had chosen the honorable profession of postman, eventually specializing in priority dispatches. The government furnished the horse, along with food and clothing; Danio also qualified for housing in Sile, an outpost on the northeastern frontier, as well as free lodging in post houses. In short, a good life; constant travel and romances with Syrian girls who were ready and willing, if sometimes too interested in settling down. The moment things started getting serious, the postman was gone.

It was in his stars. Shortly after his birth, Danio's parents had the village astrologer cast his horoscope, which showed he would be a wanderer. He hated feeling tied down, even by an enticing mistress. He lived for the open road.

Reliable and efficient, he received excellent performance reviews, never having misplaced a single piece of mail and often making an extra effort to expedite an urgent message. The postal service was truly his calling.

When Ramses assumed the throne after Seti's death, Danio had misgivings. Like many of his countrymen, he feared the young Pharaoh had the makings of a warlord and might try to reassert Egypt's regional dominance. Ramses had spent the first four years of his reign on an ambitious round of projects—enlarging the temple of Luxor, completing the gigantic colonnade at Karnak, breaking ground for his Eternal Temple, and building a new capital, Pi-Ramses, in the Delta. Yet he had not veered from his father's foreign policy, the centerpiece of which was a mutual nonaggression pact with Egypt's archenemy, the Hittites. This warlike people from the windswept plateaus of Anatolia seemed less intent than usual on conquering Egypt and challenging their claim to Syria.

The future was looking rosy until Danio noted a dramatic increase in the military correspondence between Pi-Ramses and the fortresses along the Way of Horus. He had asked his supervisors about it and quizzed the officers he met; no one knew anything, but there was talk of unrest in northern Syria and even the Egyptian-controlled province of Amurru.*

Evidently the messages Danio delivered were intended to alert frontier post commanders along the Way of Horus.

Thanks to Seti's military ability, Canaan,† Amurru, and Syria now formed a vast buffer zone between the warring empires. Of course, the local overlords bore careful watching and required the occasional reminder. Nubian gold was the remedy of choice when loyalties shifted with the winds of change. The presence of Egyptian troops and their military parades on state occasions was another effective means of preserving the fragile peace.

---

*The site of modern-day Lebanon.
†Canaan included Palestine and Phoenicia.

In times past, the forts along the Way of Horus had more than once barred their doors and sealed off the northeastern border. The Hittites had never ventured this far south, and by now the fear of hard fighting had dissipated.

So Danio remained hopeful; the Hittites had respect for the Egyptian army, and the Egyptians feared their enemy's violence and cruelty. Neither party would emerge unscathed from direct confrontation. It was therefore in the best interest of both to maintain the status quo and confine themselves to a war of words. Ramses, absorbed in his grandiose building program, had no intention of provoking a fight.

Danio thundered past the marker that showed he was entering the Abode of the Lion's dependent farmland. Suddenly he pulled up short and retraced his path: something looked wrong.

The postman dismounted next to the marker.

He noted indignantly that the point of the stone slab had been damaged and several hieroglyphs defaced. The magical inscription, no longer legible, had lost the power to protect the site. The vandals would be severely punished; tampering with a royal stela was punishable by death.

The postman realized that he was the first to stumble upon the desecration. He would lose no time reporting it to the regional commander, who would bring it to the Pharaoh's immediate attention.

A brick wall surrounded the complex, with two sphinxes guarding the main entrance. The postman froze in his tracks: the ramparts lay in ruins, the sphinxes lay on their sides, mutilated.

The Abode of the Lion had been attacked.

No sound issued from the settlement, usually so animated with infantry drills, horse training, discussions around the fountain in the center of town, noisy children, braying donkeys . . . the eerie silence caught at Danio's throat. He uncorked his drinking gourd and took a cooling swig.

Curiosity won out over fear. He should have turned back and alerted the nearest garrison, but he had to see for himself. Danio knew almost everyone in town, from the commander to the innkeeper. He had friends here.

Danio's horse whinnied and bucked; stroking his neck, the postman soothed him. Still, the beast refused to take one step forward.

Danio made his way toward the silent town on foot.

Grain bins slashed, jars shattered. Nothing was left of the stores of food and drink.

The small two-story houses lay in ruins; not a single one had escaped the attackers' fury, not even the governor's residence.

Not one wall of the town's small temple stood intact. The divine likeness had been hacked at and beheaded.

And still the thick, oppressive silence.

Dead donkeys floated in the well; by the fountain, the remains of a bonfire where furniture and documents had been piled and burned.

The smell.

A clinging, sickening stench sent him in the direction of the meat market, on the north side of the complex, beneath a broad, shaded portico, where animals were butchered, carcasses cooked in a huge cauldron, fowl roasted on spits. A busy place where the postman liked to eat lunch once his messages were delivered.

When he saw them, Danio stopped breathing.

They were all there: soldiers, tradesmen, craftsmen, old people, women, children, babies. Heaped on top of each other, their throats slit. The governor had been impaled, the three officers hung from the crossbeams.

On a wooden pillar, Hittite script proclaimed: *Victory to the army of Muwattali, powerful sovereign of Hatti. Thus shall all of his ene-mies perish.*

Hittite commandos—a typical bloodthirsty raid, leaving no survivors. But this time they had pushed past their sphere of influence and struck close to the border of Egypt's north-eastern provinces.

A sick panic swept over him. What if the Hittite strike force was still on the prowl?

Danio backed away, still staring dumbly at the horrid spec-tacle. Such cruelty—taking human life without a thought for a decent burial—was beyond comprehension.

The postman staggered toward the main gate and the top-pled sphinxes. His horse had disappeared.

He anxiously scanned the horizon for any sign of the Hittite raiders.

Chariots . . . chariots heading in his direction!

Wild with terror, Danio ran as fast as his feet would carry him.

TWO

P i-Ramses, the Pharaoh's new capital deep in the Delta, already had a population of more than one hundred thousand. The Nile looped around it in two branches, the Ra and the Avaris, keeping the climate pleasant even in summer. A network of canals facilitated transport, an artificial lake was delightful for boating, and ponds teemed with prize catches.

The lush countryside provided ample food for the "Turquoise City," as Pi-Ramses was dubbed because of the shiny tiles that graced its buildings.

The town was a strange blend of pleasure dome and military base, with an army division headquartered in each quadrant and a weapons depot close to the palace. For months now, workers had been there day and night to manufacture chariots, armor, swords, spears, shields, and arrowheads. The central foundry boasted a specialized section for bronze work.

A war chariot, sturdy but light, was just rolling out of the factory. It stood at the top of the ramp leading to the courtyard where such vehicles were stored under a portico. As a woodworker checked the fittings, the overseer tapped him on the shoulder.

"Look, at the bottom of the ramp, there he is!"

"Who?"

The woodworker squinted and saw for himself: the Pharaoh, Lord of upper and lower Egypt, the Son of Light, Ramses.

At twenty-six, Seti's successor enjoyed the love and admiration of his people. Tall and athletic, a magnificent head of red-gold hair topped his square-jawed countenance with its broad, high forehead; thick brows arching over deep, sparkling eyes; long, slightly hooked nose; rounded, delicately rimmed ears; and full lips. Ramses radiated strength which some were apt to call supernatural.

His father had trained him in the art of kingship by testing his mettle. Over a span of years, Ramses had earned the right to his glorious predecessor's mantle of authority. Even without his ritual garments, his mere presence inspired respect.

The king climbed the ramp and inspected the chariot. The awestruck overseer and joiner braced themselves for his opinion. A surprise visit to the factory showed Pharaoh's personal interest in the quality of their product.

Ramses did far more than glance at it casually. He inspected each piece of wood, prodded the shaft, tapped the wheels to make sure they were solid.

"Nice work," he said, "but how do we know it will hold up in battle?"

"We have a plan, Your Majesty," the overseer ventured. "Spare parts will be sent along for on-the-spot repairs."

"Have there been many incidents?"

"No, Your Majesty. We log all problems so that design flaws can be corrected."

"Keep up the good work."

"Majesty . . . may I ask a question?"

"Go ahead."

"How soon will it be?"

"Afraid of war, are you?"

"We're gearing up for it, but yes, we're frightened. How many Egyptian men will die, how many women will be widowed, how many children left fatherless? May the gods spare us from such a conflict!"

"May they hear your prayer! But what would our duty be if Egypt were under threat?"

The overseer hung his head.

"Egypt is our mother, our past and our future," Ramses reminded him. "She gives unstintingly, a constant bounty . . . Are we to respond with ingratitude, selfishness, and cowardice?"

"We want to live, Majesty."

"If need be, Pharaoh will give his life for Egypt. Work in peace, my good man."

What a thriving place his capital was! Pi-Ramses was a dream come true, where the sun seemed always to shine. The former site of Avaris, despised stronghold of earlier Asian invaders, had been transformed into a charming and elegant city, where rich and poor alike could bask in the shade of the sycamore and the acacia.

The king liked to walk in the countryside with its luxuriant vegetation, flower-lined paths, and canals perfect for swimming. He stopped to taste a sweet apple, then a plump onion, crossed the vast olive groves that produced an unending flow of oil, and savored the fragrance of garden flowers. His outing would end at the dockyards, which grew busier by the day, crammed with storehouses where the city's wealth of precious metal, rare woods, and grain was kept.

For the past few weeks, however, Ramses had had little time to stroll country lanes or the streets of his Turquoise City. Most of his time was spent on base, with commanding officers, charioteers, and infantrymen, all quite content with their fine new installations.

The members of the standing army, which included a number of mercenaries, were delighted with their wages and excellent rations, but grumbled about the constant drilling. They were sorry they had joined during peacetime when they were convinced it would last. Even the most hardened veterans blanched at the prospect of passing from training, however intensive, to a full-blown war with the Hittites. The Anatolians had a reputation for cruelty and were undefeated in recent memory.

Ramses had sensed the fear gradually infiltrating his troops and tried to quell it by visiting each of the four bases, leading the various units through their drills. He must appear serene and keep the men's confidence high, although his soul was in torment.

How could he feel at ease in the city he had built with the help of Moses, his boyhood friend, when Moses was gone? Wanted for the murder of Sary, the king's disgraced brother-in-law, Moses had fled soon after his teams of Hebrew brick-makers finished the Turquoise City. Yet Ramses still found the accusation hard to believe, since Sary, his onetime tutor, had been an inveterate plotter who badly mistreated the brick-makers. The murder must simply have been an argument gone terribly wrong.

When his long-lost friend was not on his mind, the king spent long hours with his older brother and secretary of state, Shaanar, and Ahsha, head of the Secret Service. Shaanar had done everything in his power to keep Ramses off the throne, but now he seemed to have learned his lesson and took his new role quite seriously. As for Ahsha, the rising star of the Foreign Service, he was a brilliant schoolmate of Ramses and Moses whom the king trusted implicitly.

Each day the three men reviewed the intelligence from Syria and tried to assess the situation. At what point would Egypt be forced to check the Hittite advance?

Ramses was obsessed with the huge map of the Near East and Asia on view in his office. To the north was the kingdom of Hatti. The capital, Hattusa, was in the heart of the Anatolian plateau. Farther south lay Syria, a vast stretch bordering the Mediterranean. He traced the Orontes River, which flowed through it. The country's main stronghold was Kadesh, under Hittite control. South of that was the province of Amurru and the ports of Byblos, Tyre, and Sidon, controlled by Egypt. Next was Canaan, also faithful to the Pharaoh.

Pi-Ramses was a world away from Hattusa, home of King Muwattali. A mountain ridge ran from the northeastern border of Egypt through central Syria, protecting the Two Lands from any attempted invasion.

But the Hittites were growing restless, and Seti was no longer alive. Pushing beyond their territory, the fierce Anatolians had moved as far south as Damascus, the Syrian capital.

Or so claimed Ahsha, based on reports from his intelligence network. Ramses had to be sure before he marched out at the head of his army to drive the enemy back into the north. Neither Shaanar nor Ahsha could advise him to do so; Pharaoh, and Pharaoh alone, could weigh the decision and take action.

Ramses' impulse had been to counterattack the moment he learned of the Hittite ploy, but readying his troops after their transfer from Memphis to Pi-Ramses would take several more weeks, if not months. The wait might have been for the best,

though it tried the king's patience: for the past ten days, no
further alarming news had come out of central Syria.

Ramses headed for the aviary where hummingbirds, jays,
titmice, hoopoes, lapwings, and a multitude of other birds led
a charmed existence amid the shady sycamores and lotus-
studded ponds.

He was sure he would find her there, plucking the notes of
an ancient air on her lute.

Nefertari, his queen and consort, the love of his life. While
not of noble descent, she was the loveliest woman in the land.
Her sweet voice never uttered a wasted word.

As a girl, Nefertari had aspired to a cloistered life as a
temple musician in some remote spot. Then Prince Ramses
had fallen madly in love with her. Neither of them had fore-
seen that he would become Pharaoh and she his Great Royal
Wife, together holding Egypt's fate in their hands.

With her glossy black hair, blue-green eyes, and her love of
silence and meditation, Nefertari had won the hearts of the
nobility. Deft and discreet, she worked at her husband's side,
miraculously blending the roles of queen and helpmate.

Their daughter, Meritamon, resembled her. Nefertari
could bear the king no more children, but this sorrow seemed
to sit no more heavily on her than a spring breeze. The love
she and Ramses had built through nine years of marriage
seemed to her a source of happiness for the people of Egypt.

Ramses watched her in secret as she conversed with a
hoopoe. It fluttered, sang a few bright notes, and landed on
her wrist.

"Come out, wherever you are," Nefertari called. As usual,
she had sensed his presence and read his thoughts. He came
forward.

"The birds are restless today," she remarked. "A storm is
brewing."

"What's the palace gossip?"

"Loose tongues make jokes at the expense of the Hittites and brag about the size of our army. Then there's the usual matchmaking and favor seeking."

"What are they saying about the king?"

"That he's more like his father every day and will keep the country from harm."

"If only their opinion could be proven true . . ."

Ramses took Nefertari in his arms. She laid her head on his shoulder.

"Bad news?"

"No, all quiet to the north."

"The Hittites have stopped advancing?"

"Ahsha hasn't heard anything dire."

"Are we ready to fight?"

"No soldier is eager to march into battle against this particular enemy. The more experienced men see no hope of victory."

"Is that what you think?"

"Leading a war on this scale is beyond my experience. Even my father decided not to wage all-out war against the Hittites."

"The fact that they've changed their tactics must mean they think they can win," commented Nefertari. "The queens of Egypt have always fought to maintain their country's independence. Much as I despise the thought of violence, I'll be at your side if war is the only solution."

A sudden commotion stirred the aviary. Nefertari's hoopoe flew to the top of a sycamore. Birds whirled in all directions.

Ramses and Nefertari glanced up to see a homing pigeon straggle in, searching uncertainly for its destination. The king reached out in welcome, and the pigeon landed in front of him.

Tied to its right leg was a miniature scroll. The message was in tiny but legible hieroglyphs, signed by an army scribe.

Scanning it, Ramses felt a sword was running through him.

"You were right, Nefertari. A storm was brewing . . . and just broke."

THREE

The great audience chamber at Pi-Ramses was one of the wonders of Egypt. It was at the top of a monumental stairway, lined with scenes of slain enemies, a representation of the ever present forces of evil that only Pharaoh could subjugate. They must be brought in line with Ma'at, the principle of harmony and justice with the queen as its living face.

Around the entryway, the monarch's coronation names were painted in blue on a white background, enclosed in an oval symbolizing the cosmos over which Pharaoh ruled as the creator's son and earthly representative.

Its serene beauty stunned all who crossed the threshold of Ramses' domain. The glazed floor tiles danced with painted scenes of fountains and gardens. A duck floated on a blue-green pond; a bolti fish darted through lotus blossoms. On the walls, pale green, dark red, light blue, golden yellow, and off-white animated the plumage of frolicking waterfowl; water lilies, poppies, daisies, and cornflowers were painted on captivating friezes.

The room was a hymn to nature in the hands of men, yet for many its most memorable scene was the face of a young woman meditating by a hedge of hollyhocks. The resemblance to Nefertari was so striking that the king had clearly intended it as a tribute to his wife.

Climbing the steps to his golden throne, Ramses did not pause to look at the lion carved in its base, closing its jaws around a threatening demon. Instead, he glanced at the hollyhocks, an import from Syria. Now Syria was the threat.

Every member of the court was present, yet the silence was total.

Cabinet officials and their assistants, ritualists, royal scribes, magicians and scholars versed in ancient lore, priests in charge of daily offerings, keepers of secrets, grand ladies with a role in the royal household, and everyone else admitted by Romay, the jovial yet vigilant chief steward.

It was rare for Ramses to call such a large assembly, which would quickly broadcast the content of his speech to the nation. The crowd held its breath, fearing some dreadful announcement.

The king wore the twin crown of red and white, representing the crucial union of upper and lower Egypt. He held the sekhem, the sacred scepter, to his breast; it symbolized Pharaoh's dominance over the elements, over life itself.

"A Hittite war party has destroyed the Abode of the Lion, an outpost in lower Syria established by my father. The barbarians massacred every living soul, women and children included."

An indignant murmur rose. No soldier, no army had the right to act that way.

"A postman happened upon the outrage," the king continued. "Frightened out of his wits, he was found wandering by one of our patrols, which relayed the news to me. In addition to the slaughter, the Hittites destroyed the settlement's temple and defaced the stela Seti had placed on the outskirts."

A fine-looking old man, visibly upset, came forward and bowed to the Pharaoh. Ramses recognized the Keeper of Secrets, in charge of the palace archives.

"Your Majesty, do we have proof that this crime was perpetrated by the Hittites?"

"They left their signature: '*Victory to the army of Muwattali, powerful sovereign of Hatti. Thus shall all of his enemies perish.*' And there's more: the princes of Amurru and Palestine have now sworn allegiance to the Hittites. Egyptian residents have been slaughtered, according to the survivors who fled to our fortresses."

"But Your Majesty, that means . . ."

"War."

Ramses' office was huge and sunlit. Windows framed in blue and white ceramic tile allowed the king to watch the changing seasons and smell the scents of his garden. Bouquets of massed lilies sat on gilded stands; a long acacia table served for studying papyrus scrolls. In one corner of the room was a diorite statue of Seti seated on his throne, eyes raised toward the great beyond.

Ramses had convened his closest advisers: Ahmeni, his friend and private secretary, plus Shaanar and Ahsha.

Slight, pale, and balding at twenty-four, with long, slender hands, Ahmeni had devoted his life to serving Ramses. He was hopeless at sports and suffered from back problems, yet he was famed as a workhorse who practically lived in his office, rarely slept, and accomplished more in an hour than his staff of highly competent scribes managed to do in a week. Ahmeni could have named his own job in the government, but he preferred to remain in the background, with the title of sandal-bearer to the pharaoh.

"The magicians have been doing their part," he reported. "They've made waxen images of Hittites and other Asiatics and burned them, scratched the enemy's names into earthenware vessels and smashed them. I'll have them keep at it until the army leaves for battle."

Shaanar shrugged his shoulders. Ramses' older brother, short and pudgy, had a moon face (close-shaven except when he had been in mourning for their father), thick lips, small, dark eyes, and a reedy voice.

"We can't depend on magic," he advised. "As secretary of state, I propose that we recall our ambassadors to Syria, Amurru, and Palestine. They're simpletons who couldn't spot the inroads the Hittites were making in our protectorates."

"I've taken care of that," said Ahmeni.

"You could have consulted with me," said Shaanar in a hurt tone.

"The point is that it's been done."

Unconcerned with their verbal jousting, Ramses pointed to a spot on the map spread in front of them on the acacia table.

"Have the garrisons on the northwest border been put on alert?"

"Yes, Majesty," replied Ahsha. "No Libyan will be allowed entry."

The only son of a wealthy noble family, Ahsha had the bearing of a thoroughbred. Beautifully groomed and smartly dressed, he had a fine-boned face, sparkling eyes, and a slightly haughty air. He spoke several languages and had shown a passion for the Foreign Service for as long as anyone could remember.

"Our patrols are monitoring the Libyan coastal zone and the desert along the Delta. Our forts are on high alert and could easily contain an attack, in the unlikely event one was attempted. At the moment, there seems to be no leader capable of rallying the desert tribes under a single banner."

"Is that conjecture, or for certain?"

"Certain."

"Finally, some positive news!"

"That's all there is, unfortunately. My operatives have just forwarded appeals from the mayors of Megiddo, at the end of the caravan route, as well as Damascus and the Phoenician ports where so much shipping activity takes place. The Hittite raids and the destabilization of the region are already interfering with trade. If we don't act quickly, the Hittites will isolate us from our trading partners and then wipe them out. The world Seti and his predecessors built up will be destroyed."

"Do you think for a moment I'm not aware of that, Ahsha?"

"We can never be too aware of a mortal danger, Majesty."

"Has every diplomatic avenue really been exhausted?" queried Ahmeni.

"An entire settlement has just been wiped out," admonished Ramses. "No negotiation is possible in the face of such slaughter."

"Thousands will die if we go to war."

"Is your secretary recommending capitulation?" asked Shaanar with a sneer.

Ahmeni clenched his fists. "Take that back, Shaanar."

"Finally ready to fight, Ahmeni?"

"Enough," proclaimed Ramses. "Save your energy for defending Egypt. Shaanar, are you in favor of direct and immediate retaliation?"

"I wonder . . . wouldn't it be better to wait and strengthen our defenses?"

"The Supply Corps needs ample warning," protested Ahmeni. "Marching off unprepared could only lead to disaster."

"The longer we stall, though," offered Ahsha, "the farther revolt will spread through the provinces. We need to stop it short in Canaan and restore the buffer zone between the Hittites and us. Otherwise, they'll have a convenient base for launching their offensive."

"Pharaoh shouldn't risk his life without due consideration," Ahmeni said testily.

"Are you questioning my judgment?" snapped Ahsha.

"You don't know the state our troops are in! They're still underequipped, even though the foundries have stepped up production."

"In spite of the obstacles, we have to bring the protectorates back in line without delay. Egypt's survival depends on it."

Shaanar tactfully refrained from entering the two old friends' debate. Ramses, valuing their opinion equally, had listened attentively.

"Leave me," he commanded.

When he was alone again, the king regarded the sun, the source of light from which he had sprung. As the Son of Light, he was able to stare into it with impunity.

"Bring out the best in each person around you. Use it to help you," his father had counseled. "But each decision will be yours alone. Love Egypt more than your life, and the way will be clear."

Ramses considered each of the three men's positions.

Shaanar was uncertain, eager not to displease; Ahmeni wanted to keep the country as a sanctuary, turning his back on what was happening outside; Ahsha had a broad perspective on the situation and did not try to deny how serious it was.

Other worries nagged at him: had Moses been caught in the upheaval? Ahsha had searched high and low for him, to no avail. His agents had nothing to offer. If his Hebrew friend had found his way out of Egypt, he would have headed either for Libya, the lands of Edom and Moab, or else for Canaan or Syria. In calmer times, he would have been spotted by now. As it was, if Moses was still alive, discovering his whereabouts would be a stroke of luck.

Ramses left the palace and went to call on his generals. His only concern must be getting his army ready to leave as soon as possible.

FOUR

Shaanar pulled the two wooden bolts locking the door to his State Department office, then checked the windows to make sure no one was outside in the courtyard. He had cautiously ordered the guard in the outer office to the far end of the hallway.

"No one can hear us," he told Ahsha.

"Still, we could have met somewhere a bit more private."

"It has to look as if we're working night and day for national security. Ramses has made unexcused absences grounds for immediate firing. We're at war, my dear Ahsha!"

"Not yet."

"It's obvious the king has already made up his mind. You've convinced him!"

"I hope so, but let's be cautious. You know how unpredictable Ramses is."

"Our little game was perfect. My brother thought I was unsure and didn't dare commit myself for fear of displeasing him. You, on the other hand, were firm and decisive, making me look even more spineless. How could Ramses suspect that we're in league?"

Satisfied, Shaanar filled two cups with a white wine from the town of Imau, famous for its vineyards.

The secretary of state's decor formed a marked contrast to the stark simplicity of the Pharaoh's office. It was full of chairs with lotus-blossom fabric, brocaded cushions, bronze-footed plant stands, murals of waterfowl-hunting scenes, and, most notably, vases from all over the world—Libya, Syria, Babylon, Crete, Rhodes, Greece, and Asia. Shaanar loved vases and had paid dearly for most of the unique pieces in his office. His passion only continued to grow, and his collection was overflowing his villas at Thebes, Memphis, and Pi-Ramses.

At first the new capital had seemed like another unbearable triumph for Ramses, but it had turned out to be a godsend, bringing Shaanar closer geographically to his Hittite backers, as well as to the lands where his prized vases were crafted. Seeing, touching his treasures, recalling their exact provenance, was a source of inexpressible pleasure.

"Ahmeni worries me," confessed Ahsha. "He's sharp . . ."

"Ahmeni is an imbecile, a weakling who clings to Ramses' tunic. He sees and hears only what serves his purpose."

"He did speak out against me, though."

"The miserable little scribe thinks that Egypt is the only country in the world, that we can hide behind our fortresses, close our borders, and keep out every possible enemy. He's dead set against the military, convinced that the only chance of peace is in isolationism. A clash between the two of you was inevitable, but it can only help us."

"Ahmeni is Ramses' closest adviser," objected Ahsha.

"In peacetime, yes; but the Hittites have declared war, and your reasoning was forceful. And don't forget Tuya and Nefertari!"

"Are they in favor of war?"

"They hate the idea, but the queens of Egypt have always been staunch fighters for their country; some have gone to remarkable lengths to safeguard the Two Lands. Remember how the noblewomen of Thebes reorganized the army and sent it to clear the Hyksos invaders out of the Delta? My revered mother and the enchanting Nefertari will be no exception to the rule. They'll urge Ramses to go on the offensive."

"Let's hope you're right." Ahsha sipped at the fruity, full-bodied wine; Shaanar guzzled his.

The prince, no matter how expensively dressed, never seemed as well turned out as the diplomat.

"I know I'm right!" he said heartily. "Look, you're the head of our spy network, one of Ramses' oldest friends, the only man he trusts on foreign policy. He's bound to listen to you!"

Ahsha nodded.

"We're nearing our goal," Shaanar continued, with growing excitement. "Ramses will be killed in battle or else come home defeated and be forced to step down. In either case, I'll look like the only one who can negotiate with the Hittites and save Egypt from disaster."

"Peace will have a price," Ahsha cautioned.

"I haven't forgotten our plan. I'll shower the princes of Canaan and Amurru with gold, give fabulous presents to the Hittite emperor, and make even more fabulous pledges! The treasury may be depleted for a time, but I'll be king. And Ramses will soon be forgotten. The people are like sheep. Whom they love today, they hate tomorrow. Their stupidity will be my secret weapon."

"Have you given up on the idea of an immense empire stretching from the heart of Africa to the Anatolian plateau?"

A faraway look came over Shaanar's face.

"A dream of mine, true, but only in trade terms . . . once we're at peace again, we'll open new ports, develop the caravan routes, and form economic ties with the Hittites. Then Egypt will be too small for me."

"And if your empire were also . . . political?"

"I don't follow."

"Muwattali governs the Hittites with an iron hand, but even he can be challenged. Court gossip in Hattusa mentions two possible successors—the emperor's son, Uri-Teshoop, and his brother, Hattusili. The son makes no secret of his ambitions; Hattusili has stayed in the background, a priest of the goddess Ishtar. If Muwattali died in battle, one of them would take over. Now, the two men hate each other, and their supporters are primed for a fight."

Shaanar rubbed his chin. "More than simple palace feuds, you think?"

"Much more. The Hittite empire could fall to pieces."

"And if someone were there to pick them up . . . and add them on to Egypt . . . what an empire that would be, Ahsha!

Babylonia, Assyria, Cyprus, Rhodes, Greece, and the northern lands, all under my banner!"

The young diplomat smiled.

"The pharaohs have lacked ambition because they were only concerned with their people's welfare and Egypt's prosperity. You, Shaanar, have a broader outlook. That's why Ramses must be eliminated, one way or another."

Shaanar felt no guilt about betraying his brother. If Seti's mind hadn't been weakened by illness, he, Shaanar, the elder son, would have been the successor. He had been treated unfairly; he would fight to regain what was his by right.

He eyed Ahsha inquisitively. "Of course, you haven't told Ramses everything."

"Of course not, but he has access to any message I receive from my operatives. They're logged and filed here. Not a single one could be spirited away or destroyed without attracting attention and exposing me to charges of wrongdoing."

"Has Ramses ever called for an accounting?"

"Up to this point, no, but now that we're on the brink of war, I'd better take care not to arouse suspicion and have him come looking more closely."

"You have a plan, then?"

"As I've said, every report from the field is open and aboveboard, nothing has been cut."

"If that's the case, Ramses knows all there is to know!"

Ahsha's finger traced a slow circle around the rim of the alabaster goblet.

"There's a certain art to espionage, Shaanar. The facts are important, but the interpretation even more so. My job is to summarize the facts and provide a basis for the king's future actions. In the present situation, he can't say that I've refused to take a position. You heard me urging him to launch a counteroffensive."

"Whose side are you on?"

"Ramses will respond in kind to the Hittite aggression," Ahsha said coolly. "Who can blame him? But look beyond the facts for a moment."

"What do you mean?"

"Moving the main military base from Memphis to Pi-Ramses has involved countless logistical problems that remain unsolved. The more we pressure Ramses into action, the more the army suffers; that's the first point in our favor. They're underequipped and poorly supplied, putting the troops at a distinct disadvantage."

"What else is there in our favor?"

"The terrain itself and the extent of the defection in the provinces. While I haven't hidden that from Ramses, I haven't stressed the scope of the conflagration. The savagery of the Hittite raids and the massacre at the Abode of the Lion have terrorized the princes of Canaan and Amurru and the governors of the port cities. Seti respected the ability of the Hittite warriors—that's not the case with Ramses. Most of the local chieftains would rather be Muwattali's vassals than face his wrath."

"They don't think Ramses will come to their rescue, so they've decided to have first crack at Egypt, to please their new master . . . am I right?"

"That's one possible interpretation."

"Well, what's yours?"

"It's a bit more complicated. The fact that there's been no word from certain of our fortresses may mean that they're in the enemy's possession. If so, the resistance Ramses encounters may be much stiffer than expected. What's more, the Hittites have probably been busy shipping arms to the insurgents."

Shaanar licked his lips. "Some nice surprises in store for the Egyptian battalions! Ramses may be defeated the first time he faces them, even before he meets the Hittites!"

"We mustn't rule out the possibility," Ahsha agreed.

FIVE

At the end of a trying day, the Queen Mother Tuya was relaxing in the palace gardens. She had celebrated the rites of dawn at a shrine to the goddess Hathor, the feminine face of the sun. She had ironed out protocol problems, granted an audience to disgruntled courtiers, and been briefed by the secretary of agriculture, at Ramses' request. Finally, she had spent time talking with Nefertari, the Great Royal Wife.

Tuya was slender. She had huge, almond-shaped eyes that were harsh and piercing, a thin, straight nose, and a firm chin. Her moral authority was uncontested. The twisted plaits of her wig flowed over her ears and down her back. She wore a long, knife-pleated linen gown, a collar with six strands of amethysts around her neck, and golden bracelets on her wrists. No matter what the hour, Tuya was flawlessly groomed.

She missed Seti more each day. Time made her husband's absence even harder to bear, and she longed for the release that would allow her to join him for eternity.

Still, she took great pleasure in the new generation. Ramses had the makings of a great ruler, Nefertari a great queen. They loved their country passionately, as she and Seti had. They were willing to die for Egypt.

The moment she saw Ramses approaching, Tuya realized her son had arrived at a serious decision. The king gave his mother his arm; they strolled down a sandy path between two rows of flowering tamarisks. The air was heavy and fragrant.

"It will be a hot summer," she said. "Luckily, your secretary of agriculture serves you well. The dikes will be kept in good repair and the irrigation reservoirs dug wider. If the inundation is as good as last year's, the harvest will be plentiful."

"My reign may be a long and happy one."

"Is there any reason it won't be? The gods have blessed you and nature smiled upon you."

"We're heading for war."

"I know, son. It's the right decision."

"I needed your approval."

"No, Ramses. You and Nefertari act as one."

"My father signed a pact with the Hittites."

"Because they stopped attacking Egypt. If they'd broken their word, Seti would have responded without delay."

"Our troops aren't prepared."

"Are you telling me they're afraid?"

"Who can blame them?"

"You."

"The combat veterans are telling horror stories about the Hittites."

"Bad enough to frighten Pharaoh?"

"If I only knew what I was facing . . ."

"You'll face it on the battlefield, when your courage will save the Two Lands."

Meba, the former secretary of state, detested Ramses. Convinced that the king had unjustly dismissed him, his only thought was of revenge. Like several members of the court, he was waiting for the young Pharaoh to falter after four years of success.

Rich and sophisticated, with a broad face and proud bearing, Meba was exchanging local gossip with his ten dinner guests, the cream of Pi-Ramses society. The food was first-rate, the ladies charming. He lived for the day Shaanar pulled off his coup, but in the meantime, why not enjoy himself?

A servant murmured a few words in Meba's ear. The diplomat immediately rose to his feet.

"My friends, the king is about to honor us with his presence."

Meba's hands shook. Ramses was not in the custom of appearing at private gatherings.

The entire party rose and bowed as one.

"Your Majesty, we hardly . . . Would you like to sit down?"

"No need. I've come to announce war."

"War!"

"Have you been too busy feasting to hear that Egypt's enemies are at the gate?"

"We've all been concerned, of course," said Meba reassuringly.

"Our soldiers have been worried that conflict was inevitable," said a veteran scribe. "They know they'll have to march in the sun, heavily laden, down difficult roads. Impossible to quench their thirst, since water will be rationed. Even if their legs give out, they'll have to keep going, forget their aching backs and growling stomachs. A rest in camp? Their hopes will be dashed—too many chores to be done before they can hit their bedrolls. In case of an alarm, they'll stagger to their feet, half awake. Food? Don't ask. Medical attention? Minimal. But plenty of danger to go around—enemy arrows and spears in the air and death always on the prowl."

"Nice rendition," proclaimed Ramses. "I was a scribe, so I also know that old text by heart. But today, we're not talking about literature."

"We have confidence in our valiant soldiers, Majesty," Meba proclaimed, "and we know our forces will be victorious, no matter what hardships they must endure."

"I appreciate the sentiment, but it doesn't go far enough. I know what patriots you and your noble guests are, and I therefore welcome you all as volunteers."

"Your Majesty . . . perhaps professionals could better handle—"

"The army needs men of quality to supervise new recruits. Shouldn't the rich and noble set an example? You're all expected at headquarters first thing in the morning."

The Turquoise City was frantic with activity. Transformed into a military base, cavalry and infantry command post, and naval launching site, it rang with maneuvers and drills from dawn to dusk. Ramses spent his days at the foundry or on base, delegating the day-to-day business of government to Nefertari, Tuya, and Ahmeni.

The monarch's presence reassured and encouraged the men. He checked the quality of spears, swords, and shields, inspected the new recruits, talked with officers as well as enlisted men, and held out the prospect of generous rewards for valor in battle. The mercenaries would receive fat bonuses if they led Egypt to victory.

The king paid great attention to the care of the horses. The outcome of any battle greatly depended on keeping them in top physical condition. In the center of each stable yard, paved with cobblestones and crisscrossed with gutters, stood a holding tank used both to water the horses and for cleaning purposes. Each day Ramses inspected a different set of stalls, examined the horses, and dealt severely with signs of neglect.

Ramses' joint forces were beginning to work like a large body, its governing head constantly on call. The king always responded swiftly, spelling out his requirements and settling disputes on the spot. Confidence solidified. Each soldier felt that orders were given advisedly and that the Egyptian military had coalesced into a real war machine.

Being able to see the Pharaoh up close, even talk to him on occasion, was an amazing privilege for the men and their officers. Many a courtier would have envied their access to the king. His attitude gave the troops an unaccustomed energy, a new strength. Even so, Ramses the man remained aloof. He was Pharaoh, unique on earth, driven by a force beyond himself.

The sovereign was attending to business in the stables when he saw Ahmeni approaching, much to his surprise. Years earlier, Prince Ramses had rescued his friend from forced labor in just such a setting; ever since, Ahmeni had studiously avoided horses.

"Reporting for duty?"

"Our friend the poet has arrived in Pi-Ramses. He's asking to see you."

"As soon as he's settled."

"He won't have any trouble. His villa here is a copy of his house in Memphis."

Seated beneath a lemon tree, his favorite, Homer was drinking wine spiced with anise and coriander, and smoking dried sage leaves tamped in the thick snail shell he used as a pipe. His skin glistening with olive oil, the old poet greeted the king with his customary gruffness.

"Don't get up, Homer."

"I can still manage a bow to the Lord of the Two Lands."

Ramses sat down on a stool beside Homer. The bard's black and white cat, Hector, hopped in the king's lap and began to purr as he petted it.

"Does my wine suit Your Majesty?"

"A bit rough, but the nose is delicious. How have you been doing?"

"My bones ache, my sight keeps dimming, but the climate does wonders for me."

"Satisfied with your house here?"

"It's perfect. The cook, housekeeper, and gardener came up from Memphis. Good people; they know how to pamper me without getting in the way. They were as eager as I was to discover this new capital of yours."

"Wouldn't your life be quieter in Memphis?"

"Nothing's happening in Memphis anymore! This is where the fate of the world is decided. And no one's better qualified than a poet to tell about it. Remember this passage? *'From the peaks of Olympus, Apollo descends, furious, carrying the bow on his shoulder and the quiver well closed: he is full of rage, and on his back, when he leaps, the arrows rattle. Like dark night he approaches, shooting men . . . innumerable pyres must light to burn the corpses.'* "

"The first book of your *Iliad?*"

"Yes, but it's more than merely the story of Troy. This Turquoise City, a lovely maze of gardens and canals, is turning into a military camp!"

"I have no choice, Homer."

"War is the scourge of humanity, the proof that we're a degenerate species, manipulated by unseen forces. Every verse of the *Iliad* is an exorcism. My hope is to purge the heart of man of violence—though sometimes I doubt my magic."

"Still, you have to keep on writing. And I have to rule my country, even if it becomes a battlefield."

"This will be your first great war, won't it? *The* great war, perhaps."

"The thought frightens me as much as it does you, but I have neither the time nor the right to be afraid."

"There's no way out?"

"None."

"Then I pray that Apollo may guide your sword arm, Ramses. May death be your ally."

SIX

Over the years, Raia had become the richest Syrian merchant in Egypt. He fit in well, with his average build, lively dark eyes, and trim, pointed goatee. From his chain of shops in Thebes, Memphis, and Pi-Ramses he sold choice preserved meats and collectible vases imported from Syria and other Near Eastern lands. His wealthy and cultured clientele gladly paid top prices for the work of master craftsmen from abroad, which they showed off at social gatherings.

Courteous and discreet, Raia enjoyed an excellent reputation. Thanks to the rapid expansion of his business, he had acquired a dozen-odd boats and three hundred donkeys, enabling him to ship his foodstuffs and objets d'art all over Egypt with admirable dispatch. He was a purveyor to the court and the nobility, with connections in the government, the army, and the police.

No one suspected that the mild-mannered Syrian was also a secret agent for the Hittites, receiving coded messages inside specially marked vases, and funneling information through an informant in southern Syria. Pharaoh's major enemy was thus kept closely informed of political developments and public opinion in Egypt, as well as the nation's economic situation and military capabilities.

When Raia appeared on the doorstep of Shaanar's plush villa, the steward seemed flustered.

"My master is in conference. He can't be disturbed."

"We have an appointment," Raia pointed out.

"I'm sorry."

"Can't you at least tell him I'm here and that I've brought an exceptional vase, the masterpiece of a potter who's now retired?"

The steward hesitated. Knowing how passionate Shaanar was about his collection, he decided to risk ignoring his master's orders.

A quarter of an hour later, Raia observed the exit of a young female, heavily made up, with tousled hair and a tattoo on her exposed left shoulder. She could only be one of the foreign beauties imported to work at the new capital's most elaborate tavern.

"My master will see you now," announced the steward.

Raia crossed the magnificent garden, its vast central pond shaded by date palms.

Shaanar, looking exhausted, sat back on a chaise longue.

"The young are so demanding," he sighed. "Beer, Raia?"

"Please."

"All the women at court are after me, but I have no inclination to marry. When I become king, I can settle down with someone suitable. Meanwhile variety is the spice of life, don't you agree? Or has some woman got you under her thumb?"

"The gods forbid, Sir Prince! At any rate, my business never leaves me much free time."

"You've saved a splendid find for me, my steward says?"

From a canvas sack stuffed with wadded cloth, the merchant carefully extracted a minuscule porphyry vase, the handle formed into the body of a doe. The sides of the vase were covered with hunting scenes.

Shaanar caressed the piece, scrutinizing each detail. He got up and studied it from every angle, fascinated.

"What a marvel . . . and one of a kind!"

"Reasonable, too."

"Have my steward settle with you." He lowered his voice. "And there's no telling what the message from my Hittite friends is worth."

"Ah, Sir Prince! They're more firmly behind you than ever. They already consider you Ramses' successor."

On the one hand, Shaanar was using Ahsha to mislead Ramses; on the other, he was making plans for his future thanks to Raia, the Hittite go-between. Ahsha was unaware of Raia's role, just as Raia was of Ahsha's. Shaanar was the grand master, moving the game pieces and sealing his secret allies off from each other.

The only unknown was a daunting one: the Hittites.

Piecing together Ahsha's intelligence reports and the information Raia would provide, Shaanar would eventually form a clear picture without taking undue risks.

"How far-reaching is the offensive, Raia?"

"Hittite commandos have led deadly raids in central Syria, southern Syria, the Phoenician coast, and the province of Amurru, to terrorize the natives. The boldest stroke so far was wiping out the Abode of the Lion and destroying Seti's marker, which resulted in unhoped-for reversals of allegiance among local princelings."

"Are Phoenicia and Palestine under Hittite control now?"

"Even better, they're up in arms against Ramses! The local leaders have occupied the fortresses and forced Egyptian troops out. Pharaoh has no idea he's about to run into a wave of resistance that will sap his strength on the way north. As soon as Ramses' losses are serious enough, the Hittite army will swoop down and destroy him. That will be your chance, Shaanar; you'll take over and forge a lasting alliance with the victors."

Raia's predictions were markedly different from Ahsha's. In either scenario, Shaanar became Pharaoh, replacing the dead or defeated Ramses. Yet Raia saw him ending up as the Hittites' vassal, whereas in Ahsha's version he took control of their empire. Everything would depend on the magnitude of Ramses' defeat and the damage he inflicted upon the Hittite army. It would be a close call, but still, it might work, and his primary goal remained the throne of Egypt. From that base, further conquests could be planned in time.

"How have the trade centers reacted?"

"As usual, they're siding with whoever looks stronger at the moment. Aleppo, Damascus, Palmyra, and the Phoenician ports have already gone over to Muwattali."

"Bad news for our economy," Shaanar said with a frown.

"Not at all! The Hittites are the world's greatest warriors, but not as strong on trade. They're counting on you to help them develop the international market . . . and share in the profits. Don't forget I'm a merchant. I mean to stay in Egypt and keep on prospering. The Hittites will bring us the stability we need."

"You'll head my Treasury Department, Raia."

"We'll both make our fortune, God willing. The war will last only a time. The trick is to stay on the sidelines and gather the windfalls."

The beer was delicious, the garden shade refreshing.

"My brother's activities worry me," confided Shaanar.

The merchant grew somber. "What is he up to?"

"Constantly prowling the bases, pumping up his soldiers. Before long he'll have them believing they're invincible!"

"What else?"

"The foundries are turning out weapons day and night."

Raia tugged at his goatee. "Not to worry. He's so far behind the Hittites that he'll never catch up. And morale will plummet the moment the troops see battle. The Hittites will send them packing, mark my word."

"You may be underestimating our army."

"If you've ever watched a Hittite attack, you understand why brave men tremble at the very thought."

"I can name one who won't."

"Ramses?"

"No, the captain of his bodyguard, a hulking Sard named Serramanna. A pirate, no less, who's won the Pharaoh's trust."

"I know him by reputation. Why single him out?"

"Because Ramses has put him in charge of an elite regiment, in large part mercenaries. He may turn them all into swashbucklers! I shudder to think what they might do in battle."

"A pirate and a mercenary . . . surely he can be bought?"

"That's just the trouble. He's grown devoted to Ramses and guards him like a faithful old watchdog. A dog's love is one thing no riches can buy."

"Then he can be eliminated."

"I've considered it, my dear fellow, but it's preferable not to try anything too sudden or violent. Serramanna is ruthless and extremely wary. He's fought off other attempts on his life, and even if we succeeded, Ramses would be hot on our trail."

"Do you see another option?"

"Yes. We need to find some way to sideline Serramanna without implicating ourselves."

"I know how to stay out of trouble, Sir Prince. One possibility does occur to me . . ."

"It has to be foolproof. The Sard has a nose for danger."

"I'll make sure that he's out of the way."

"It will be a blow to Ramses. There's a bonus in it for you, Raia."

The merchant rubbed his hands together. "I have more good news, Sir Prince. Do you know how Egyptian troops stationed across the border communicate with Pi-Ramses?"

"Relay riders, signals, and carrier pigeons."

"But when trouble is brewing, only the birds can be used. And the army's main supplier is no incorruptible like Serramanna; I got him to name his price. It will be easy for me to destroy outgoing messages and intercept or switch the incoming ones. Without their knowing it, the army's communications system will be in complete disarray."

"Excellent initiative, Raia. But don't forget to keep finding me vases like this one."

SEVEN

Serramanna took a dim view of the war. He had left the pirate's life behind to head Ramses' personal guard detachment, and by now was accustomed to Egypt, his splendid residence, and the local beauties that brightened his leisure hours. Lilia, his current flame, was the best to date. Their last bout of lovemaking had left him exhausted—unthinkable for a Sard!

He cursed the circumstances that would take him away from what he considered a charmed life, even though keeping the Pharaoh safe was no easy job. The young monarch consistently ignored his pleas for caution. But Ramses was a great king, and Serramanna admired him. If keeping him on the throne meant spilling some Hittite blood, then spill it he would. He even hoped his own sword might slit the throat of Muwattali, whose soldiers called him the "Great Chief." The Sard snorted: a "great chief" leading a pack of bloodthirsty savages! Once his mission was accomplished, Serramanna would wax his mustache and return to his amorous conquests.

When Ramses had put him in charge of an elite detachment, entrusted with dangerous missions, Serramanna had felt a reinvigorating surge of pride. Since the Lord of the Two Lands demonstrated such confidence in him, the Sard would make sure it was well placed. His training program had already weeded out the underqualified and overfed; he would keep only the toughest soldiers, who could fight one against ten and suffer multiple wounds without complaint.

No one knew exactly when the army was marching out, but Serramanna's instincts told him it would be soon. The atmosphere in the barracks was tense. At the palace, the high command met more and more frequently. Ramses was often closeted with Ahsha, his intelligence chief.

Rumors swirled though the capital: the revolt was spreading like wildfire, prominent Egyptian loyalists had been executed in Phoenicia and Palestine. Yet the messages arriving by carrier pigeon maintained that the fortresses were holding strong and thwarting enemy attacks.

Pacifying Canaan should present no problem. Ramses would probably decide to continue northward, toward the province of Amurru and on to Syria, where the inevitable confrontation with the Hittite army would come. According to army intelligence, the commando troops had now withdrawn from southern Syria.

Serramanna was not afraid of the Hittites. In spite of their deadly reputation, he was itching for a fight with the barbarians. He'd mow down as many as he could before they ran off with their tails between their legs.

There was one item he must take care of before he left for the fields of glory, however. It was a short walk from the palace to the craftsmen's workshops close by the storehouses. The maze of streets buzzed with activity as cabinetmakers, garment workers, sandal makers plied their trade. A bit farther on, toward the docks, stood the Hebrew brickmakers' humble dwellings.

The giant's arrival caused a stir among the workers and their families. In Moses, the Hebrews had lost an outstanding leader, who had defended them against all forms of authoritarianism and restored their pride. The sudden appearance of a well-known figure like the Sard did not augur well.

Serramanna nabbed a fleeing boy by the kilt.

"Stop wiggling and tell me where Abner the brickmaker lives."

"I don't know."

"If you know what's good for you . . ."

The boy registered the threat and started talking. He even agreed to show Serramanna the way to Abner's house, where they found the brickmaker huddled beneath some covers in one corner of the main room.

"Come along with me," ordered the security chief.

"You can't make me."

"What are you afraid of, man?"

"I've done nothing wrong."

"Then you have nothing to fear."

"Please leave me be."

"The king is asking to see you."

Abner clung to his covers until the Sard was forced to lift him with one hand and set him on the back of a donkey that calmly made its way back to the royal palace.

Abner was terrified.

Prostrated before the Pharaoh, he dared not meet his gaze.

"I'm not satisfied with the inquest into Sary's death," said the king. "I want to know what really happened, and I think you can tell me, Abner."

"Your Majesty, I'm only a humble brickmaker . . ."

"Moses is charged with killing my sister's husband. If he admits to the crime, he should face the punishment. But why on earth would he do it?"

Abner had hoped that no one would question his own role in the affair too closely. He should have known that Ramses would refuse to believe the worst of his old friend Moses.

"He must have gone mad, Your Majesty."

"And you must take me for a fool, Abner."

"Majesty!" he gasped.

"There was no love lost between you and Sary."

"That's hearsay."

"No, I have sworn statements. Get up, Abner."

Trembling, the Hebrew rose hesitantly. He hung his head, unable to meet Ramses' gaze.

"Are you a coward, Abner?"

"A simple brickmaker who wants to live in peace, Your Majesty—that's what I am."

"Wise men don't believe in chance. What was your role in this tragedy?"

Abner knew he should stick to his story, but the Pharaoh's deep voice broke through his defenses. "Moses was a hero to the Hebrews. We all respected him. Sary was our overseer, and he resented the challenge to his authority."

"Did Sary mistreat you?"

Abner muttered a few incomprehensible words.

"Speak up," the king demanded.

"Sary"—he cleared his throat—"Sary was not a good man, Your Majesty."

"Yes, I'm aware that he'd become abusive and dishonest."

Abner was reassured enough to continue. "Sary threatened me and demanded a kickback."

"Extortion. So that was his game! Why did you give in to him?"

"I was afraid, Your Majesty. So afraid! Sary would have beaten me, taken everything."

"Why didn't you file a grievance?"

"Sary had connections with the police. No one dared cross him."

"No one but Moses."

"Just look where it got him!"

"With your help, Abner."

The brickmaker wished he could burrow underground, away from this powerful man who seemed to tap directly into his thoughts.

"You confided in Moses, didn't you?"

"Moses was a good man, a brave man."

"Out with it!"

"Yes, Your Majesty, I told him about my trouble with Sary."

"And what did he say?"

"He agreed to help me."

"How?"

"Ordering Sary to leave me alone, I suppose. He never told me exactly."

"Stick to the facts."

"I was at home after work when Sary showed up that night, mad as a hornet. 'Miserable Hebrew cur!' he was shouting. 'I told you to keep your mouth shut!' He struck me. I put my hands over my face and tried to stay clear of him. Then Moses came running in. They struggled, and Sary went down. If Moses hadn't been there, I would have been the one who ended up dead."

"In other words, it was self-defense. Thanks to your testimony, Abner, Moses could be cleared of the charges against him and regain his place in Egyptian society."

"I had no idea . . ."

"Why didn't you come forward, Abner?"

"I was afraid."

"Of what? Sary is dead. Was there anyone else who threatened you?"

"Uh, no . . ."

"What has you so worried, then?"

"The courts, the police . . ."

"Lying under oath is a grave offense, Abner. But perhaps you don't believe that Osiris will weigh our souls in the next world."

The Hebrew bit his lips.

"You didn't speak up," continued Ramses, "because you were afraid of calling attention to yourself. You didn't care about helping Moses, the man who saved your life."

"Your Majesty!"

"The truth is, Abner, that you wanted to keep a low profile because you've been demanding kickbacks, too. Serramanna had a little talk with some of the brickmakers junior to you. The way you exploit them is shameful."

The Hebrew knelt before the king.

"I find them work, Your Majesty. It's only a sort of commission."

"You're only a petty crook, Abner, but you're worth a great deal to me, because you could clear Moses' name."

"You mean you're letting me go?"

"Serramanna will have a scribe take your sworn statement. Make sure you include every detail. And let this be the last I hear of you, Abner."

EIGHT

The Bald One, a dignitary of the House of Life at Heliopolis, inspected every bit of food the local suppliers brought him. He painstakingly examined each piece of fruit, each vegetable, each fish. The farmers and fishermen feared yet respected him, for he paid them fairly; still, they realized they would never attain the comfortable position of official purveyor, since he refused to play favorites, relying instead on his high standards. Every item he selected to be blessed and placed on the altars, then redistributed to the community, must be perfect.

Once his selections were made, the Bald One routed them toward the House of Life's kitchens, called the "pure place," reflecting the strict cleanliness in which it was maintained. The priest relied on frequent unannounced inspections, sometimes followed by a wave of demotions.

Now it was time for a routine check of the dried and salted fish. Only he and the steward in charge of the storeroom knew how to work the wooden latch.

The latch had been tampered with.

Stunned, he pushed open the door. Inside it was silent and dark as ever.

He entered the room uneasily, but sensed no one else around. Somewhat relieved, he stopped to inspect each earthenware vessel, fingering the tags that spelled out the contents. Then, near the door, he found an empty spot.

A vessel had been stolen.

Every noblewoman's dream was to become a member of the queen's household. Yet when Nefertari chose her attendants, she was more concerned with ability and maturity than fortune and rank. A number of her appointments had been unconventional, like Ramses' choices when forming his government.

Thus the enviable position of wardrobe mistress had gone to a pretty brunette from a rather ordinary Memphis family. Her role was caring for Nefertari's favorite garments; though her wardrobe was extensive, the queen was particularly fond of soft old dresses and a worn shawl she liked to drape around her shoulders at nightfall. While it protected her from the chill night air, it also reminded her of the day she first met Ramses, how she had worn it that evening gazing at the stars and thinking of the brash yet gentle young prince, how she had kept him at arm's length for months, unable to admit even to herself that the attraction was mutual.

Like the other ladies-in-waiting, the wardrobe mistress virtually worshiped her sovereign. Nefertari managed her household smoothly, gave orders with a smile. She considered even the humblest task worth doing well, demanded that all be done promptly and thoroughly. When a problem arose, she preferred to discuss it directly with the parties involved, giving their explanations serious consideration. Like Tuya before her, she won the admiration of all around her. It was little wonder that she had grown so close to Tuya.

The wardrobe mistress was airing garments, sprinkling them with flower essences, and carefully repacking them in the wooden chests and cupboards. As dusk gathered, she went to fetch the queen's old shawl for her to wear as she performed her nightly devotions.

The young woman's face drained of color. The shawl was gone.

"Impossible," she thought. "I must be looking in the wrong place." She tried another chest, then another, then the cupboards.

Still nothing.

The wardrobe mistress questioned the other ladies-in-waiting, the queen's hairdresser, the laundry maids . . . None of them had the slightest idea.

Nefertari's favorite shawl had been stolen.

The war council met in the audience chamber of the royal palace. The generals heading the four army divisions had answered the summons of their supreme commander. Ahmeni took notes for the report he would later compile.

The generals were middle-aged scribes, well educated, masters of great estates, excellent managers. Two of them had seen combat with the Hittites under Seti, but the engagement had been brief and limited. In reality, none of the commanding officers had experienced full-scale war with an outcome in question. The closer real war came to breaking out, the more apprehensive they became.

"The state of our arsenals?"

"Good, Your Majesty."

"Arms production?"

"Still at full capacity. According to your directives, the foundry workers and fletchers are being paid double for overtime. But there's still a shortage of swords and daggers for close combat."

"Chariots?"

"We're within weeks of being on target."

"Horses?"

"They'll depart in peak condition."

"Morale?"

"That's the sore spot, Your Majesty," offered the youngest general. "Your presence has done wonders, but there's been no end of wild tales about the Hittites. Despite our repeated denials and prohibitions, this sort of rubbish can still have an influence."

"Even on some of my generals?"

"No, of course not, Your Majesty . . . though there are some questions we haven't been able to answer."

"Such as?"

"Well, will we be outnumbered?"

"First we'll settle matters in Canaan. That ought to give us an idea."

"Are the Hittites already entrenched there?"

"No, their army hasn't ventured that far from their bases. A few commandos struck out, then headed north again. They've bribed the local overlords in the hope that we'll tire ourselves out in the effort to win them back. We won't give them the satisfaction. We'll put down the rebellions as we go, giving our soldiers the confidence to march north and win a decisive victory."

"Some of the men are concerned about our fortresses."

"They needn't be. Yesterday and the day before, a dozen

carrier pigeons arrived at the palace with positive messages. Not one fortress has fallen into enemy hands. They have all the supplies and weapons they need to resist any possible attacks until we arrive. We haven't another moment to waste, though."

Ramses' wishes were the generals' commands. They bowed and hurried back to their barracks, firmly resolved to speed preparations along.

"They're useless," grumbled Ahmeni, setting down the chiseled reed he used for writing.

"You're hard on them," Ramses replied.

"Just look at them: too rich, too settled, too scared! They've spent more time in the shade of their gardens than in the heat of battle. And war is the Hittites' national sport, you know it! Your generals are as good as dead—provided they don't desert at the first hint of fighting."

"So you think I should replace them?"

"Too late, and what good would it do? Your officers are all cut from the same cloth."

"Are you suggesting that we shouldn't go to war?"

"That would be a deadly mistake. You have to take action, of course, but one thing is clear. Our ability to win depends on you, Ramses. On you alone."

Ahsha came to see Ramses late at night. The king and the head of his intelligence network were both working almost nonstop; the atmosphere in the capital grew tenser by the day.

At one of the windows of the Pharaoh's office, side by side, the two men gazed at the night sky, its soul made of thousands of stars.

"Do you have news for me, Ahsha?"

"The situation is stalled: the rebels on one side, our line of fortresses on the other. Our supporters are depending on your help."

"I'm eager to get under way, but I have no right to risk my soldiers' lives. The lack of preparedness, the arms shortages . . . we've been living in a dreamworld for far too long, Ahsha. This comes as a rude awakening, and we needed it."

"May the gods be with us."

"Do you doubt that they'll help us?"

"No, but are we ready to help ourselves?"

"The men who fight under me will be risking their lives to defend Egypt. If the Hittites have their way, dark days are ahead, my friend."

"Have you considered that you may be risking your own life?"

"Nefertari will be named my regent, to rule in my stead."

"Such a lovely night . . . why are men so intent on killing one another?"

"I hoped for a peaceful reign. Since it's not to be, I won't shirk my destiny."

"Your destiny may not be favorable, Ramses."

"Are you losing faith in me?"

"Maybe I'm afraid. It's in the air."

"Have you found any trace of Moses?"

"It seems he's vanished into thin air."

"No, he hasn't."

"How can you be so sure?"

"Because I know you haven't started looking."

Ahsha was cool as ever.

"You refused to have your agents track Moses down," Ramses continued, "because you don't want him brought back to Egypt and sentenced to death."

"Is that what you want? I thought Moses was our friend."

"He won't be convicted of murdering Sary."

"What? You may be Pharaoh, but even you can't put friendship above the law."

"I won't have to. Moses may be tried, but he'll be acquitted."

"But he did kill Sary, didn't he?"

"In self-defense, according to a sworn witness."

"That's the best news I've heard in quite a while."

"Send your men after Moses. Track him down for me."

"It won't be easy. With all that's been going on in the border states, he may have ended up somewhere we can't follow."

"Find him, Ahsha."

NINE

Glowering, Serramanna strode among the brickmakers' dwellings. Four young Hebrews, new arrivals from middle Egypt, had willingly cooperated in accusing Abner. Yes, he'd helped them get work, but at what a price!

The police inquest had been a slipshod affair. Sary, while still influential, had become a dubious character, and Moses had never been easy to deal with; the police seemed to think his disappearance and Sary's death were all for the best. There was no telling how many important clues they missed.

The Sard had been gathering information in the neighborhood before he once again appeared on Abner's doorstep.

The brickmaker was studying a wooden tablet covered with figures as he munched on bread rubbed with garlic. As soon as he caught sight of Serramanna, he slid the tablet beneath his haunches.

"Doing your accounts, Abner?"

"I swear I'm innocent!"

"The next time you try to shake someone down, you'll answer to me."

"I'm under the king's protection."

"That's a laugh."

The Sard reached for a sweet onion and took a bite. "Anything to drink around this dump?"

"Yes, in the chest . . ."

Serramanna lifted the lid. "By Bes, the god of wine, you've got enough for a crowd here! And plenty of beer . . . you earn a good living, Abner."

"They were, well, gifts."

"It's nice to be popular."

"What do you want from me? I gave my statement."

"I can't help it. I just enjoy your company."

"I've told you all I know."

"I don't believe it. When I was a pirate, I questioned all my captives. A lot of them couldn't recall where they'd hidden their treasure. With a little persuasion, they finally remembered."

"I'm not hiding any treasure!"

"Your little bundle doesn't interest me."

Abner seemed relieved. As the Sard opened up another amphora of beer, the Hebrew slipped his tablet under a reed mat.

"What were you writing on that piece of wood, Abner?"

"Nothing, nothing . . ."

"The sums you've squeezed out of your fellow Hebrews, I'll bet. A sturdy bit of evidence, if it went to court."

Frightened out of his wits, Abner found no reply.

"We can come to an agreement, my friend. Remember, I'm not a judge, not even a policeman."

"You have a proposition?"

"I'm interested in Moses, not in you. You knew him pretty well, didn't you?"

"No better than anyone else . . ."

"Don't lie, Abner. You wanted his protection, so you watched him to find out what kind of man he was, how he behaved, who his friends were."

"He spent all his time working."

"So most of his contacts were through work?"

"Yes, the overseers, the workers, the—"

"And outside of work?"

"He liked to meet with the Hebrew clan chiefs."

"What did they talk about?"

"We're a proud and touchy people. There have been stirrings of independence. A handful of zealots saw Moses as a potential leader. But the whole thing would have blown over once Pi-Ramses was finished."

"One of the workers you 'helped' told me that a stranger visited Moses and they talked for quite a while, alone, in his official residence."

"That's right. Nobody had ever seen him before—apparently some architect from the south who came to give Moses technical advice. Never went with him on site, though."

"Describe this man for me."

"Middle-aged, tall, thin, a hawk face with a hooked nose, high cheekbones, thin lips, a jutting chin."

"How was he dressed?"

"An ordinary tunic . . . an architect would have been better dressed, come to think of it. You would have sworn the stranger was trying to go unnoticed. He didn't talk to anyone but Moses."

"A Hebrew?"

"Certainly not."

"How many times did he come to Pi-Ramses?"

"At least twice."

"Since Moses left town, has this stranger been seen again?"

"No."

Still thirsty, Serramanna downed another beer. "I hope you're not hiding anything, Abner. It would really get on my nerves. I might lose control of myself."

"I've told you all I know about the man!"

"I'm not asking you to go straight, Abner; you'd never make it. Just try to stay out of trouble."

"Would you like . . . I could have some more of this beer delivered to you."

The Sard twisted the Hebrew's nose between his thumb and forefinger. "And I could rearrange your face if you pull any more tricks, Abner."

The brickmaker crumpled to the floor in pain.

Serramanna shrugged his shoulders, walked out of the brickmaker's quarters, and headed for the palace, deep in thought. His new line of inquiry had yielded a great deal of information.

Moses had been part of an active plot. He planned to head a Hebrew uprising, no doubt to improve his people's situation, perhaps even demanding an autonomous settlement in the Delta. What if the mystery man who visited him was a foreigner who had come to offer outside help? In that case, Moses could even be guilty of high treason.

Ramses would refuse to consider such an accusation.

Before he could say anything against the man who had been the king's closest friend, Serramanna would need solid proof.

All of a sudden he was playing with fire.

Iset the Fair, Ramses' secondary wife and the mother of Kha, his only son, had her own suite of apartments in the royal palace at Pi-Ramses. Although she and Nefertari got along beautifully, she preferred the social life in Memphis, where she was a reigning beauty with her green eyes, delicate nose, and sweet mouth.

Lively, charming Iset lived a glamorous but empty life. She felt too young to be living on her memories. She had been Ramses' first lover, had loved him to distraction, and still loved him with all her heart, but with no desire to try and win him back. For a while (in retrospect it seemed like seconds), she had hated Ramses for the very power she worshiped in him. How could he keep his hold on her while his soul belonged to Nefertari?

If only the Great Royal Wife had been ugly, stupid, and despicable . . . But Iset had succumbed to Nefertari's charm and acknowledged how special she was, a born queen and a match for Ramses.

What a strange fate, thought Iset, to see the man she loved in the arms of another woman and give the cruel situation her full approval.

If Ramses ever came to her, Iset the Fair would have no complaints. She would offer herself with the same abandon she felt on their first nights together, in a reed hut deep in the country. Her desire for him was so overpowering that for all she cared he could have been a shepherd or a fisherman. Iset had no taste for power. She would never have relished being Queen of Egypt and taking on the crushing obligations she watched Nefertari shoulder. Since it was not in her nature to be jealous, Iset the Fair thanked her lucky stars for the gift of a lifetime: loving Ramses.

As usual, it was a happy day. Iset was playing with Kha, now nine years old, and Meritamon, the only child of Ramses and Nefertari. The darling little girl would soon turn four. The two children were devoted to each other. Kha loved reading and writing more than ever. He was teaching his sister hieroglyphs now, guiding her tiny hand when she faltered. Today they were working on birds, which required a great deal of dexterity.

"Come for a swim, the water is wonderful," Iset called to them.

"I'd rather keep working."

"You should learn how to swim, too."

"I don't care about swimming."

"Your sister might like a break."

Meritamon, a miniature version of her beautiful mother, looked from one to the other, not wanting to take sides. Swimming was fun, but her brother was so big and so smart.

"Do you mind if I go in?" she asked him anxiously.

Kha thought for a moment.

"All right, but just for a while. You need to do that quail over again; the head isn't round enough."

The little girl ran over to Iset the Fair, and Iset thought once again how good Nefertari was to trust her with Meritamon's upbringing.

The two of them bobbed in the cool, pure water of the garden pool, shaded by a sycamore. Yes, as usual, it was a happy day.

TEN

In Memphis, the heat was almost stifling. The north wind had stopped blowing and what torrid gusts there were left man and beast with parched throats. Lengths of sturdy cloth had been stretched between housetops to shade the alleyways. The water bearers couldn't keep up with business.

In his secluded villa, the sorcerer Ofir remained comfortable. Slits high in the walls kept the air circulating. It was a quiet spot, restful, fostering the intense concentration his evil spells required.

Ofir was customarily calm, almost indifferent, as he worked his magic, but lately he had felt a creeping excitement. This ambitious new undertaking challenged his abilities. The prospect of revenge was tantalizing—revenge for his grandfather, Akhenaton's Libyan adviser.

His distinguished guest arrived in the mid-afternoon, when the city's streets and byways lay deserted. The secretary of state used a chariot belonging to his associate Meba, driven by a mute coachman.

The sorcerer greeted Shaanar deferentially. As on their previous meeting, the prince felt ill at ease; the hawk-faced Libyan wore such an icy expression. With his dark green eyes, prominent nose, thin lips, he looked more like a demon than a man. Yet his voice and manner were both so mild that at times you might feel you were chatting with some kindly old priest.

"Why did you send for me, Ofir? I don't appreciate being caught off guard."

"Because I've been working for our cause, Your Highness. You won't be disappointed."

"I hope not, for your sake."

"Please step this way. The ladies are waiting."

Shaanar had set the sorcerer up in this villa, calculating that the more support he gave to Ofir's black magic, the swifter his own rise to power would be. Naturally, the house had been put in the name of his sister, Dolora. Such useful allies, and so willing . . . Ahsha, the king's boyhood friend and a master plotter; the Syrian merchant Raia, a deft Hittite agent; and now Ofir, thanks to that old fool Meba. The prince smiled, remembering how he had talked Ramses into giving him Meba's job, then persuaded the old diplomat that it was all the king's idea. Ofir represented a strange and dangerous world that both worried and intrigued him. There was no denying the sorcerer's potential to do harm.

Ofir was supposedly spearheading a political movement to revive Akhenaton's heresy and the worship of a single deity, Aton, the sun god. The mad king's feeble great-granddaughter was to replace Ramses. Shaanar had encouraged the sorcerer to expand his activities, hoping the sect would attract Moses. The sorcerer had been trying to enlist the Hebrew in what he claimed was their common quest.

Shaanar reasoned that internal strife, even on a small scale, would be one more obstacle in Ramses' path. When the time came, he planned to get rid of everyone no longer of use to him, for a man of power can have no past.

Unfortunately, Moses had committed murder and fled the country. Without the Hebrews, Ofir's movement would never gain enough strength to topple Ramses. Ofir had given a convincing demonstration of his magical powers, nearly killing Nefertari in childbirth and weakening Meritamon in the process. Even so, they had both survived, and while the queen could never bear another child, the Pharaoh's magic had proved stronger than the Libyan's.

Ofir was becoming less useful, even a bother. In fact, when he received the magician's summons to Memphis, Shaanar had considered eliminating him.

"Our guest is here," Ofir announced to the two seated women holding hands in the shadows. One was Dolora, Shaanar's sister; the other, blond and shapely, was Lita, Akhenaton's great-granddaughter (or so Ofir claimed). She appeared to Shaanar to be mentally deficient and completely under the sorcerer's sway.

"How are you, sister dear?"

"Glad to see you, Shaanar. The fact that you're here shows we're still moving forward."

Dolora and Sary, her late husband, had vainly sought favors from Ramses when he was Seti's co-regent. When their hopes were dashed, they plotted against him. Only the combined influence of the Queen Mother Tuya and Nefertari, the Great Royal Wife, had convinced Ramses to spare their lives. Sary, who had once been the king's private tutor, then head of the royal academy, was forced to work as a brickyard overseer. Broken and bitter, he had taken his resentment out on the Hebrew workmen, blatantly abusing them until a furious Moses came to their defense and killed him. As for the dark and ungainly Dolora, she had fallen under the spell of Ofir and Lita. Immersed in the cult of Aton, the One God, she put her limited energies into reviving his religion and banishing Ramses, the unbeliever.

Shaanar was determined to make the most of Dolora's misguided passion. Promising her an important role when he came to power, he manipulated her hatred of Ramses, planning to do away with her eventually if she remained a fanatic.

"Any news of Moses?" asked Dolora.

"He's vanished," replied Shaanar. "No doubt his fellow Hebrews have killed him and buried him out in the desert."

"We've lost a valuable ally," Ofir acknowledged, "but the will of the One God must be done. Our numbers are still on the rise, are they not?"

"We must proceed with care," Shaanar insisted.

"Aton will help us!" Dolora said fervently.

"I haven't lost sight of my initial plan," the sorcerer continued. "Weakening Ramses' magical forces will eliminate the only real obstacle in our path."

"Your first attempt was not an unqualified success," Shaanar pointed out.

"But not a total failure, either."

"That's not good enough."

"I agree, Your Highness. That's why I've decided to use a different technique."

"What technique?"

With his right hand, the sorcerer gestured toward the tag on a large earthenware vessel.

"Would you read that for me?"

" 'House of Life, Heliopolis. Four fish: Mullet,' " he read. "Why dried fish?"

"Not just any fish: they were specially consecrated as an offering, they're already magic. I also acquired this piece of cloth." Ofir held out a tattered shawl.

"That looks like—"

"Yes, Your Highness, it belongs to the Great Royal Wife, Nefertari. Her favorite shawl."

"You stole it?"

"My followers are everywhere, as I said."

Shaanar was astonished. Did the Libyan have sources inside the palace?

"The combination of consecrated food and cloth that has touched the queen's person is essential. Thanks to these magical objects, and your continued support, Aton will once again reign supreme. Lita will represent him as our queen, and you will be Pharaoh."

Lita lifted her dreamy eyes toward Shaanar. She was not at all bad-looking, he thought, considering her as a bedmate.

"Still, there's Ramses."

"He's only human," declared Ofir. "Not even he can resist black magic forever. But if I'm to succeed, I need help."

"You know you can count on mine!" exclaimed Dolora, clutching Lita's hands as the wide-eyed princess focused on Ofir.

"Tell us your plan," Shaanar demanded.

Ofir held his arms crossed on his chest. "Your help is indispensable as well, Highness."

"Mine? But . . ."

"All four of us wish the king and queen dead. And the four of us symbolize the cardinal directions, the quadrants of time, the entire world. If one of these four forces came to be missing, the spell would be broken."

"I'm not a sorcerer!"

"Your simple acceptance will do."

"Say yes!" begged Dolora.

"What will I have to do?"

"Nothing complicated," Ofir assured him. "But your hand will play an important part in destroying Ramses."

"Let's get started."

The sorcerer opened the vessel and removed the four dried

and salted fish. Lita, as if in a trance, broke loose from Dolora and lay down on her back. Ofir spread Nefertari's shawl over her bosom.

"Take one of the fish by the tail," he ordered Dolora.

She passively obeyed. From a pocket in his tunic, Ofir withdrew a tiny figurine of Ramses and stuck it down the mullet's throat.

"The next fish, Dolora." He repeated the procedure until each of the four fish had swallowed a tiny effigy of Ramses.

"Either the king will die in battle," prophesied Ofir, "or else fall prey to us when he returns from the war. This cuts him off from the queen forever."

Ofir went into a smaller room, followed by Dolora, carrying the four fish, and Shaanar, whose desire to harm Ramses won out over his fear.

In the middle of the room was a small charcoal grill.

"Throw the fish in the fire, Your Highness. Your wish will be granted."

Shaanar did as he was told.

As the fourth and final fish went up in smoke, a cry startled him. The trio retraced their steps to the front parlor.

Nefertari's shawl had spontaneously burst into flames, burning Lita until she was nearly unconscious.

Ofir lifted the cloth, which put out the fire.

"Once we burn the rest of the shawl," he explained, "our demons will be unleashed upon Ramses and Nefertari."

"Will Lita still have to suffer?"

"Lita accepted this sacrifice. She must remain conscious for the duration of the experiment. As soon as her burns are healed, we'll try again, until every last bit of the shawl is gone. It will take time, Your Highness. But it will work."

ELEVEN

The chief physician of upper and lower Egypt and head of the palace medical service, Dr. Pariamaku was in his fifties, brisk of manner, with long, slender, manicured hands. Rich, married to a Memphis noblewoman who had given him three fine children, his long and distinguished career had taken him to the top of his profession.

Yet that summer morning he was cooling his heels outside Ramses' office and growing angrier by the minute. The king wasn't ill—he was never ill—and he'd kept the famous doctor waiting for more than two hours.

Finally a chamberlain showed him in.

"Your Majesty, I am your humble servant, but—"

"How are you, my dear Doctor?"

"Disturbed, Your Majesty, very disturbed. At court they're saying that you've chosen me as surgeon general for your northern campaign and—"

"That would be quite an honor, don't you think?"

"Of course, Your Majesty, of course, but wouldn't I be of more use to you here at the palace?"

"I suppose I ought to take that under consideration."

Pariamaku was visibly distressed. "Your Majesty, if you would be so good as to inform me—"

"Yes, you're right, Doctor. The palace can't do without you."

He could barely contain a sigh of relief. "I have complete confidence in my associates, Your Majesty. Any of the court physicians you choose will give satisfaction."

"I've already made my selection. You remember my friend Setau, I believe?"

A dark, thickset, square-jawed man stepped forward. He was hard-eyed, unshaven, without a wig, and wearing an antelope-skin tunic studded with pockets. The distinguished physician recoiled.

"Doctor, glad to see you, I know I don't belong to the medical establishment, but I do get along with snakes. Would you like to have a look at the viper I captured yesterday?"

Pariamaku took another step backward and looked toward the king in bewilderment. "Your Majesty, there are certain requirements that a military surgeon general—"

"I want you to be particularly vigilant during my absence, Doctor. I hold you personally responsible for the health of the royal family."

Setau stuck a hand into one of his pockets. Afraid he might pull out a snake, Pariamaku quickly bid his farewell to the king and retreated.

"Why do you put up with clowns like him?" asked the snake charmer.

"Don't be too hard on him. Sometimes he even cures his patients. By the way, did I hear you say you agree to become my surgeon general?"

"I have no interest in the position, but I can't let you march north alone."

A vessel of dried fish missing from the House of Life in Heliopolis. Then Queen Nefertari's shawl. Two thefts, and only one suspect. Serramanna was sure he knew who had done it: Romay, the king's chief steward. The Sard had been watching him for some time. Behind his jovial facade was a traitor. He'd even tried to assassinate the Pharaoh.

For once, Ramses had chosen the wrong man for the job.

Serramanna knew, however, that if he revealed his suspicions about Romay, the king might not take it kindly. The same for Moses. He saw no way to get the steward arrested or cast doubt on the Hebrew's loyalty—unless maybe Ahmeni could help. Ramses' private secretary was nobody's fool. He would listen.

Serramanna walked past the two soldiers flanking the corridor leading to Ahmeni's office. The tireless secretary directed a staff of twenty scribes to deal with the day-to-day business of government. Each morning, Ahmeni briefed Ramses on important matters.

At the giant's heels came the sound of rapid footsteps. He wheeled around in surprise. A clutch of foot soldiers was coming at him.

"What's going on here?"

"We have orders."

"I'm the one who gives you orders!"

"We've been told to arrest you."

"Preposterous!" raged Serramanna.

"We're obeying orders."

"Back off, if you know what's good for you!"

Ahmeni's office door opened and the scribe appeared.

"Tell these morons to leave me alone, Ahmeni!"

"I can't, Serramanna. I had the warrant drawn up for your arrest."

For a moment, the old pirate felt he was back on a sinking ship. As he stood there, stunned, the guards moved quickly to disarm him and tie his hands behind his back.

"What's going on here?"

At a sign from Ahmeni, the guards hustled Serramanna into his office. The secretary consulted a scroll on his desk.

"Are you acquainted with a certain Lilia?"

"A lady friend of mine. The latest, to be precise."

"Did you have a fight with her?"

"She threw herself at me, but that was in bed."

"Did you assault her?"

"I gave her my best shot, you might say. All in good fun."

"So you have no quarrel with this young woman?"

"I do! She nearly wore me out. A Sard has his pride, you know."

Ahmeni remained stone-faced. "This Lilia has made grave accusations against you."

"But she consented, I swear it!"

"It has nothing to do with your sexual escapades. I'm talking about treason."

"What? Did I hear you say treason?"

"Lilia claims you're a Hittite spy."

"The hell I am!"

"She's a patriotic young woman. When she noticed some strange-looking wooden tablets in your linen chest, she decided to turn them in. Do you recognize these?"

Ahmeni handed the tablets to the Sard. "They don't belong to me!" he protested.

"They're proof of your crime. The writing is rather crude, but in essence you tell your Hittite contact you'll make sure that your elite commandos will never see battle."

"Ridiculous!"

"Your girlfriend has given a sworn statement before a magistrate and witnesses."

"It's an attempt to discredit me and undermine Ramses."

"According to the dates on the tablets, you've been spying for the last eight months. The Hittite emperor has promised you a fortune once Egypt is defeated."

"I've been Ramses' man ever since the day he spared my life."

"Then why are you corresponding with the Hittites?"

"You know me better than that, Ahmeni! Yes, I was a pirate, but I'm a loyal friend!"

"I thought I knew you, but maybe you're like everyone else at court, only thinking how you can line your pockets. Don't mercenaries work for the highest bidder?"

Hurt to the quick, Serramanna stiffened.

"If Pharaoh named me head of his personal guard troops, then gave me an elite command in his army, it must mean he trusts me."

"But should he?"

"I deny your accusations."

"Untie him."

Serramanna was immensely relieved. Ahmeni's interrogation had been thorough, as usual, but the point was to let him prove his innocence.

The secretary handed the Sard a sharpened reed, dipping the tip in black ink, and a smooth slab of limestone.

"Write your name and title."

Uneasily, the Sard did as he was told.

"The handwriting is the same as on the tablets in question.

This sample will also be submitted as evidence. You're guilty, Serramanna."

Blind with fury, the pirate rushed at the slender scribe. Instantly, four spears pricked at his ribs, drawing blood.

"That's as good as admitting it," said Ahmeni.

"Let me see the girl! I'll make her take it back!"

"You'll see her at your trial."

"I'm being framed, Ahmeni."

"Start working on your defense, Serramanna. For traitors like you, the only punishment is death. And don't expect Ramses to let you off."

"Let me speak to him. I've made some breakthroughs in my investigation."

"The army is marching out tomorrow. Your Hittite friends will miss you."

"Let me talk to Ramses, please!"

"Throw him in jail and guard him closely," ordered Ahmeni.

TWELVE

Shaanar's spirits were excellent and his appetite ravenous. His breakfast, "the cleansing of the mouth," consisted of barley porridge, two roast quail, goat cheese, and round honey cakes. Since Ramses was marching north with his army that morning, he decided to celebrate with grilled goose rubbed with rosemary, cumin, and chervil.

Serramanna had been arrested and thrown in jail, significantly compromising the elite force's effectiveness.

The prince had just touched his lips to a cup full of cold milk when Ramses strode into his private suite.

"May your face be protected," said Shaanar, rising to employ this traditional morning greeting.

The king wore a white kilt and a short-sleeved surplice. Silver bracelets adorned his wrists.

"You don't look ready to travel, beloved brother," he said.

"I didn't hear you were planning to take me with you, Ramses."

"You don't seem to have the fighting spirit."

"No. You were always the brave one."

"Here are my instructions: while I'm gone, you're to gather

information from abroad and submit your reports to Nefertari, Tuya, and Ahmeni. They're my ruling council, authorized to act in my name. I'll be at the front with Ahsha."

"He's going with you?"

"I need his expertise. He has firsthand knowledge of the region."

"Our diplomacy hasn't helped the situation this time, I'm afraid."

"No, Shaanar, but we can't drag our feet any longer."

"What will be your strategy?"

"To regain control of the border provinces, regroup, and then march on Kadesh for a direct confrontation with the Hittites. When the second phase begins, I may call for you."

"Taking part in the final victory will be an honor."

"One more challenge Egypt will survive."

"Be careful, Ramses. Our country needs you."

Ramses took a boat across the canal separating the warehouse district from the oldest part of Pi-Ramses. This was the site of Avaris, onetime capital of the Hyksos, Asian invaders whose sinister memory still lingered. Here stood the temple of Set, the terrifying god of thunder and celestial disturbances, keeper of the most powerful force in the universe, and patron of Ramses' father, Seti, the only pharaoh who had ever dared to bear his name.

Ramses had rebuilt the temple in a larger and grander form, for it was here that his father, secretly grooming him to become pharaoh, had tested him against the mighty Set.

Fear and the strength to overcome it had struggled within the young prince's heart. When the combat ended, Ramses was touched with the power of Set's fire. As Seti had summed up his patron's lesson: "Believing in human goodness is a mistake no pharaoh should ever make."

In the covered forecourt of the temple stood a pink granite stela. A carving of a bizarre creature, part dog, with large upright ears and a long curved snout, sat atop it. This was the animal incarnation of Set, which no man had ever seen or ever would. Carved into the tablet was Set's human form, with a cone-shaped crown, a solar disk, and two horns. His right hand held the ankh, or key of life, his left the scepter of power.

The text was dated to the fourth day of the fourth month of summer of the year 400; the number four represented the organizing principle of the cosmos. The hieroglyphs began with an invocation:

> *Hail to thee, Set, son of the goddess of heaven,*
> *You, whose power is great in the bark of millions of years.*
> *You stand at the prow of the bark of light, repelling its foes,*
> *Yours is the voice of thunder!*
> *Permit Pharaoh to follow your ka.*

Ramses entered the sanctuary and prayed before the statue of Set. He would need the god's energy in the fight ahead. And Set, who could change four years on the throne into four hundred years set in stone, would be his strongest ally.

Ahmeni's office was crammed with papyrus scrolls, stuffed into leather cases, standing upright in earthenware jars, or piled into wooden chests, tagged with the documents' date and contents. No one was allowed to interfere with his system of organization; he even cleaned the room himself, with the utmost care.

"I wish that I could go with you," he confided to Ramses.

"Your place is here, my friend. Every day you'll consult with the queen and Queen Mother. And no matter how Shaanar tries to worm his way in, be sure he's granted no decision-making power."

"Don't stay away too long."

"I intend to strike quickly and hard."

"You'll have to do it without Serramanna."

"Why?"

Ahmeni related the circumstances surrounding the bodyguard's arrest. Ramses seemed disheartened.

"Prepare the indictment carefully," the king demanded. "When I return, I'll question him; I'm sure he'll be able to explain his actions."

"Once a pirate, always a pirate."

"If so, his trial and sentencing will serve as an example."

"You could use his sword arm in battle," said the scribe regretfully.

"Not if he'd stab me in the back."

"Are our troops really ready for combat?"

"They have no choice but to be."

"Does Your Majesty believe we have a real chance of winning?"

"We should be able to quell the unrest in the provinces, but after that . . ."

"Before the push to Kadesh, will you let me join you?"

"No, my friend. You're of more use to me here in Pi-Ramses. If I were to die, Nefertari would need your help."

"I'll keep the war effort going," Ahmeni promised. "We won't stop manufacturing arms. And, well, I've asked Setau and Ahsha to keep an eye on you. With Serramanna out of commission, you might take more chances than you should."

"Unless I march at the head of my army, the war is lost before we take the first step."

Her hair was darker than the dark of night, sweeter than the fruit of the fig tree; her teeth were whiter than gypsum powder, her breasts round and firm as love apples.

Nefertari, his wife.

Nefertari, the Queen of Egypt, whose luminous gaze was the joy of the Two Lands.

"After my visit to Set," Ramses told her, "I stopped in to see my mother."

"What did she say?"

"She talked about Seti, how long he would meditate before launching any battle, how he managed to husband his energy on the march."

"Your father's soul lives on in you. He'll fight at your side."

"I leave the kingdom in your hands, Nefertari. Tuya and Ahmeni will be your faithful allies. Serramanna has been jailed on suspicion of treason. Shaanar will certainly try to assert himself. It's up to you to hold the ship of state on a steady course."

"Rely on yourself alone, Ramses."

Two waist-length bands of pleated linen hung from the blue crown; Ramses wore a padded leather garment, a combination doublet and kilt, forming a sort of breastplate covered with metal scales. A long filmy robe completed the majestic outfit.

When Homer saw the Pharaoh approach in full war regalia, he put down his pipe and rose. Hector, the black and white cat, ran under a chair.

"So the time has come, Majesty."

"I wanted to say my farewell to you before we head north."

"Listen to the verses I wrote today: *'To his chariot he hitches his two horses, swift and bronze-shod, with manes of gold. He is dressed in a dazzling tunic, he takes his whip in hand and with a snap of the wrist sends them galloping heavenward.'* "

"My two horses do deserve your praise. For several days now I've been grooming them for the trials ahead."

"Too bad you're leaving. I've just made an interesting discovery. If I mix barley meal with pitted dates—I pit them myself—it makes quite a tasty brew, once it ferments. I wish you could try it."

"That's an old Egyptian recipe, Homer."

"In a new edition from a Greek poet, it might have a different taste."

"We'll have a glass when I come home."

"I may be a grouchy old hermit, but I do hate to drink alone. A good friend improves the best drink in the world. You'll do me a favor if you hurry back."

"I intend to. Besides, I want to read your *Iliad*."

"It will be years before I'm finished. That's why I'm aging slowly, to buy more time. I hope I won't need to buy extra for you."

"I'll be back, Homer."

Outside, Ramses climbed into his chariot, hitched to his two finest horses: Victory in Thebes and the Goddess Mut Is Satisfied. Young, strong, alert, they strained toward the open road, toward a new adventure.

The king had left his dog, Watcher, with Nefertari. Fighter, the mammoth Nubian lion, ran alongside the royal chariot, at Ramses' right hand. Stupendously strong and handsome, the beast was also eager to prove himself in war.

Pharaoh raised his right arm.

The chariot moved forward, the wheels began to turn, the lion kept pace with his master. And thousands of foot soldiers, flanked by the cavalry, followed Ramses.

THIRTEEN

Though the early summer heat was even more intense than usual, the Egyptian army marched as though they were on a country outing. Crossing the northeastern Delta was a delight. Farmworkers, unaware of the looming threat of war, were harvesting spelt with their sickles. A light sea breeze ruffled the stalks of grain; the fields shimmered green and gold. The king had set a fast pace, but the foot soldiers still enjoyed watching the lush scenery and the herons, pelicans, and pink flamingos flying overhead.

Maintaining discipline, they stopped to eat fruits and vegetables, drink the local wine diluted with water, sample the beer. It was a far cry from the tale of the starving soldier, dying of thirst and sagging under the weight of his gear.

Ramses was supreme commander of an army divided into four divisions of five thousand foot soldiers each, placed under the protection of the gods Ra, Amon, Set, and Ptah. There were also reserve troops, some remaining behind in

Egypt, as well as the elite cavalry unit. To make these mighty numbers easier to maneuver, the king had organized each division into companies of two hundred men under the command of a standard-bearer.

The general in charge of the cavalry, the division commanders, the scribes, and the head of the Supply Corps followed strict orders and consulted Ramses when any difficulty arose. Fortunately, Ahsha was available with his superior problem-solving skills, and the bulk of the commanding officers respected him.

As for Setau, he had demanded a chariot to haul what he considered necessary for housekeeping in the forbidding lands of the north: five bronze razors, pots of salves and balms, a whetstone, a wooden comb, pestles, a hatchet, sandals, reed mats, a cloak, kilts, tunics, canes, several dozen containers full of lead oxide, asphalt, red ocher, and alum, plus jars of honey, sacks of cumin, bryony, castor oil seed, valerian. A second chariot carried his medicines, potions, and remedies, under the care of his wife, Lotus, the lone female participant in the expedition. Since she was known to handle poisonous snakes like weapons, however, no one bothered the shapely Nubian beauty.

Setau wore five cloves of garlic strung around his neck to ward off vapors and protect his teeth. Many of the soldiers did the same, as the virtues of the aromatic bulb were well known. Garlic had supposedly saved the god Horus's baby teeth as he hid in the Delta marshlands with his mother, Isis, attempting to escape the wrath of Set, who was intent on destroying Osiris's son and heir.

At the first night's camp, Ramses had retired to his tent with Ahsha and Setau.

"Serramanna has been working for the Hittites," he revealed.

"Surprising," Ahsha appraised. "I consider myself a fair judge of character, and I would have bet he was loyal to you."

"Ahmeni has gathered evidence against him."

"Bizarre," commented Setau.

"There's no love lost between the two of you," Ramses pointed out.

"We clashed, it's true, but it gave me the chance to size him up. Your pirate captain is a man of his word—and he gave it to you, on his honor."

"What about the evidence?"

"Ahmeni could be wrong."

"That would be a first."

"Not even Ahmeni is infallible. My guess is that someone framed Serramanna to keep him away from the fighting."

"What do you think, Ahsha?"

"Setau's hypothesis seems reasonable enough."

"Once we've brought the protectorates back in line," declared the king, "and the Hittites have asked for mercy, we'll investigate further. Either Serramanna is a traitor or else he was brought in on trumped-up charges. No matter which, I want to find out the whole truth."

"I've given up hope of that," admitted Setau. "The world of men is too full of lies."

"A pharaoh fights for the truth."

"Better you than me. At least with my snakes I know they'll never bite me in the back."

"Unless you're running away from them," added Ahsha.

"Then you'd deserve it," Setau concluded.

Ramses sensed that his two friends were coming to grips with the same awful suspicion he was feeling. They could have spent hours building a case against the conclusion that Ahmeni himself could have planted the evidence. Ahmeni, the devoted scribe, entrusted with the day-to-day business of government; Ahmeni, who had been left in charge because Ramses trusted him completely? Neither of the two men dared accuse him openly, but the king sensed their unspoken doubts.

"Why would Ahmeni do such a thing?"

Setau and Ahsha exchanged a glance and said nothing.

"If Serramanna had noticed Ahmeni acting suspicious, he would have informed me."

"Unless Ahmeni threw him in jail to keep him quiet."

"Unlikely," said Setau. "Look, this is all just speculation. When we get back to Pi-Ramses, we'll set things straight."

"That makes sense," agreed Ahsha.

"I don't like this wind," Setau added. "It's not what you usually see in summer. An ill wind, as if the year might die in its prime. Watch out, Ramses. I tell you, it's not a good sign."

"A rapid strike is our best guarantee of success. No wind will slow us down."

Strung along the northwestern border of Egypt, the forts that made up the king's great wall communicated with each other by signals and sent regular reports back to court. In peacetime, their role was to regulate immigration. Now that they had been put on alert, archers and scouts scanned the horizon from atop their walls. Centuries earlier, Sesostris I had built the line of fortifications to stop the Bedouins from raiding livestock and to check any attempt at invasion.

Whoever crosses this border becomes the son of Pharaoh, proclaimed a marker in front of each fully manned and well-supplied garrison. The forts were also home to customs officers who collected duties on goods crossing into Egypt.

The Wall of the King, built up over the centuries, kept the people feeling safe. It was a proven system for preventing surprise attacks and barring invading hordes from the rich lands of the Delta.

Ramses' army marched serenely onward. The veterans were reminded of the routine inspection tours that each pharaoh carried out from time to time, displaying Egypt's military might.

When the battlements of the first fortress came into sight, bristling with archers, the mood grew a bit more subdued. But the huge doors parted to let Ramses pass, and his chariot had barely braked before a portly figure rushed forward, followed by a servant holding a parasol.

"Glory to you, O Majesty! Your presence is a gift from the gods."

Ahsha had given Ramses a detailed report on the governor general of the Wall of the King. A rich landowner, graduate of the royal academy in Memphis, and father of four, he loved good food and hated the military mind-set. He was eager for his prestigious though boring appointment to come to an end so that he could return to Pi-Ramses and an upper-level government post. The governor general had no army training and dreaded the sight of blood, but his accounts were flawless and there was no denying that under his leadership the garrisons were well supplied with food.

The king stepped down from his chariot and patted his two horses. They whinnied softly.

"I've ordered a banquet, Your Majesty. You'll have all the comforts of home here. Your bedchamber may not be quite as comfortable, but I hope you'll like it and find it restful."

"I'm not here to rest. We have an insurrection on our hands!"

"Of course, Your Majesty. But you'll deal with that in a matter of days."

"How can you be so sure?"

"The reports from our sites in Canaan are promising. There's so much infighting among the rebels that the movement is falling apart."

"Have our positions been attacked?"

"Far from it, Your Majesty. Here's the latest dispatch; it arrived this morning by carrier pigeon."

Ramses scanned the document, written without undue haste. It did indeed appear that bringing Canaan back into the fold would be fairly straightforward.

"See that my horses are well cared for," the monarch ordered.

"Clean stalls and special forage," promised the governor.

"Where is the map room?"

"Right this way, Your Majesty."

Determined not to waste a second of the king's time, the governor walked much faster than usual. At this rate, he'd soon slim down. His servant even had trouble keeping him in the shade.

Ramses called for Ahsha, Setau, and his generals.

"Starting tomorrow," he announced, tracing the route on the map spread out on a low table, "we head due north, passing west of Jerusalem, along the coast, until we encounter the first rebel position and subdue Canaan. Then we stop at Megiddo until I decide to advance."

The generals murmured their agreement. Ahsha remained silent.

Setau left the room, looked at the sky, and returned to Ramses' side.

"What's the matter?"

"I've told you. There's something wrong with the wind."

FOURTEEN

The pace was lively, the discipline somewhat relaxed. Entering Canaan, long controlled by Egypt and paying tribute to the pharaoh, the army had no sense of straying into foreign territory, no sense of danger. Perhaps it was only a local incident, and Ramses had taken it too seriously.

Egypt was responding with such a show of force that the rebels would soon be on their knees, begging the king's mercy. It would be one more peacekeeping mission, unmarked by deaths or serious injuries.

On the march, the soldiers noted that one small outpost had been destroyed. Its staff of three had kept track of herd migrations. No one paid much attention.

Setau continued to brood. Driving his chariot single-handed, bareheaded in the blazing sun, he hardly spoke to Lotus, though every lucky soldier who passed her by made sure to take a good look.

The sea breeze was a godsend, the road was level, the water bearers came by at regular intervals. You had to be in shape, you had to walk for hours, but even so, it wasn't such a bad life, nothing like the scribes claimed, but then they were quick to sneer at other occupations.

To his master's right loped Ramses' lion. No one tried to approach him, but everyone was cheered by his presence. He was a walking symbol of the Pharaoh's supernatural strength. With Serramanna gone, the lion was Ramses' best protection.

The first fortress in Canaan came into view. It was an impressive structure with tall, sloping brick walls, thick parapets, sturdy ramparts, watchtowers, and crenellations.

"Who's in charge here?" Ramses inquired of Ahsha.

"An experienced commander, born in Jericho but raised in Egypt, who underwent extensive training and served several tours of duty in Palestine before his appointment here. I've met him. A good man, highly professional."

"Wasn't he the one who sent the initial dispatches alerting us to a revolt in Canaan?"

"Yes, Your Majesty. This fortress is a strategic information-gathering point for the region."

"Would this commander be a good candidate for governor?"

"I'm sure he would."

"In the future, we won't make the same mistakes. The more efficiently we run the province, the less we run the risk of rebellion."

"There's only one way to control it effectively," Ahsha suggested. "Eliminating Hittite influence."

"Precisely what I intend," said Ramses.

A scout galloped up to the fortress gate. An archer waved from the ramparts.

The scout headed back. A standard-bearer ordered the lead detachment to advance. The weary soldiers looked forward to a drink, a meal, a good night's sleep.

A flurry of arrows pinned them to the ground.

Dozens of archers had appeared on the wall walk, firing point blank at their helpless targets. Arrows through the head, chest, or stomach mowed the Egyptians down. The standard-bearer leading the charge pressed defiantly forward, determined to take the fort with the handful of surviving soldiers.

The archers' deadly precision left them no chance. The standard-bearer took a shot to the neck and collapsed at the foot of the ramparts.

Within a few minutes, many of the army's most seasoned veterans lost their lives.

A new wave of troops was surging forward to avenge their comrades when Ramses stopped them.

"Retreat!"

"Majesty," said a lieutenant, "let us at the traitors!"

"Rush the fort and you'll end up like they did. I said retreat."

The men obeyed him.

A new volley of arrows landed ten paces from the king, who was soon surrounded by his panic-stricken commanders.

"Have your troops form a ring around the fortress, out of firing range, archers in front, then foot soldiers, followed by the chariots."

The king's icy calm helped restore the men to order. Falling back on their training, the men formed their ranks.

"We need to tend to the wounded," interjected Setau.

"Impossible. The enemy sharpshooters would cut you down."

"I told you the wind was wrong."

"I can't understand it," said Ahsha. "None of my agents gave any indication that the rebels had captured this fort."

"They must have taken it from inside," offered Setau.

"Even so, the commander would have had time to send an emergency message by carrier pigeon. They always have some on hand, already drawn up."

"The facts are simple and disastrous," concluded Ramses. "The commander was killed, his garrison wiped out, and then the insurgents sent us fake messages. If I'd sent my divisions to the different forts instead of coming here first, we would have suffered heavy casualties. The revolt is much more widespread than we thought. Only Hittite commandos could have orchestrated an effort like this."

"Do you think they're still in the area?"

"Whether they are or not, we'd better get back to our positions as fast as we can."

"This fortress can't withstand our attack for long," Ahsha calculated. "Why not give them a chance to surrender? If there are Hittites inside, we'll make them talk."

"Take a squadron in there, Ahsha, and negotiate with them yourself."

"I'll go with him," said Setau.

"Let him show off his diplomatic talents. At least he can bring back the wounded while you get the infirmary set up, Setau."

Neither of Ramses' friends questioned his orders. Even the sharp-tongued snake charmer bowed to Pharaoh's authority.

Five chariots, under Ahsha's command, made their way toward the fort. At the diplomat's side, a charioteer held a lance with a white flag tied to its tip.

The chariots never got close. As soon as they were within firing range, the marksmen began to shoot again. The lead charioteer was hit twice in the throat, while another arrow grazed Ahsha's left arm, leaving a bloody gash.

"Turn around!" he shouted.

"Don't move," ordered Setau. "Or that honey compress will slide right off."

"You're not the one who feels the sting."

"Toughen up, Ahsha!"

"I don't find war wounds glamorous, and I prefer Lotus's bedside manner."

"Yes, but I get all the tough cases. Since I used my best honey, you ought to mend. The cut will heal quickly, without infection."

"What savages. I couldn't even get a look at their defenses."

"Don't bother trying to cut any deals for the insurgents when the time comes. Ramses doesn't take kindly to people who try to mow down his friends, even the ones who've strayed into the Foreign Service."

Ahsha winced in pain.

"At least this is a good excuse for staying on the sidelines," Setau commented.

"Sounds like you wish the arrow had hit its mark."

"Stop talking nonsense and try to rest. If we do get our hands on any Hittites, we'll need to use you as a translator."

Setau left the spacious tent that served as the field hospital. Ahsha would be the first patient to stay there. The snake charmer hurried off to deliver some bad news to Ramses.

With his lion in tow, Ramses had ridden the perimeter of the fortress, studying the massive brick structure dominating the plain. What had once been a symbol of peace and security was now a deadly threat that must be eliminated.

From atop the ramparts, Canaanite lookouts observed the Pharaoh, refraining from shouts or jeers.

One hope remained: that the Egyptian army might not try to recapture the fort, instead dividing up to march through the province and assess the situation. If so, the ambushes the rebels had planned with their Hittite mentors might still be able to force a retreat.

Setau, convinced he understood the enemy strategy, wondered if it might not be better to have a look around first, rather than attacking a well-prepared fortress and suffering heavy losses.

The generals considered the same angles; the consensus was that a small contingent should be left to hold the main fort under siege, while the rest of the army marched north to reconnoiter.

When they approached Ramses, he was lost in thought, stroking his lion's noble mane. The connection between man and beast was so direct, so powerful, that they felt uneasy intruding.

The senior general, who had served in Syria under Seti, finally dared to break the silence.

"Your Majesty . . . may I have a word with you?"

"Go ahead."

"My fellow officers and I have had lengthy discussions. We believe that it would be wise to gauge how widespread this revolt is. Due to the false information we received, our view of the situation is unclear."

"And how do you propose to rectify it?"

"By launching a reconnaissance mission before we undertake a full-scale attack on this fortress."

"An interesting viewpoint."

The old general was relieved. Perhaps Ramses would listen to the voice of moderation after all.

"Shall we convene to hear Your Majesty's directives?"

"No need," replied the king. "My directives can be

summed up in a few words: prepare to attack this fort at once."

FIFTEEN

R amses fired the first arrow. He alone had the strength to shoot with the acacia bow he used. The bowstring was made from a bull's tendon, demanding a storm god's power to pull it back.

When the Canaanite lookouts saw the King of Egypt take a shooting stance, nearly a thousand paces from the fortress, they smiled. It was only a symbolic gesture to give his troops courage, they thought.

The reed arrow, with its bronze-covered hardwood tip and notched tail, arched through the bright sky and dove into the heart of the nearest lookout. With a horror-stricken glance at the blood spurting out of him, he fell headfirst from the battlements. The next man felt a thud on the head, staggered, and followed suit. The third managed to call for help, but as he turned an arrow pierced his back. He landed in the courtyard. Meanwhile, a regiment of Egyptian archers moved in.

The rebels tried to spread out along the battlements, but their attackers had them outnumbered. With deadly accuracy, they felled half the sentries with their first salvo. Their replacements suffered the same fate. As soon as the enemy numbers were no longer sufficient to defend the fort, Ramses ordered the sappers to bring up their ladders. Fighter, the gigantic lion, surveyed the scene calmly.

Their ladders positioned against the walls, the soldiers began to climb. The men on the ramparts, realizing the Egyptians would give them no quarter, fought with desperate energy. Pulling stones from the walls, they pelted their assailants, some of whom broke bones as they hit the ground. Nevertheless, the Pharaoh's archers made short work of the rebels.

Hundreds of foot soldiers stormed the walls and took control of the wall walk. The archers followed, firing down at the enemy gathered in the courtyard below.

Setau and his medics removed the wounded on stretchers, carrying them to the Egyptian camp. Lotus joined the edges of clean wounds, crisscrossing them with adhesive bandages. Occasionally she had recourse to suturing. Fresh meat was used to stop bleeding; after a few hours, the site was dressed with an antibiotic mixture of honey, astringent herbs, and moldy bread. Setau dipped into his stock of pharmaceuticals, which included extracts, pellets of anesthetic, lozenges, salves, and potions. He relieved pain, put the seriously wounded to sleep and made them as comfortable as possible in the field hospital. Those who seemed fit enough to travel would be sent home to Egypt, along with the dead, not one of whom would be buried on foreign soil. Their families, if they had any, would receive a pension for life.

Inside the fortress, the Canaanites offered feeble resistance. Outnumbered ten to one, there was little they could do. To avoid what he knew would be a merciless interrogation, their chief slit his throat with his own dagger.

The gates were opened. Pharaoh entered the recaptured fortress.

"Burn the corpses," he ordered, "and purify the site."

The soldiers sprinkled the walls with natron, a substance that dried and purified any surface, and fumigated the living quarters, storerooms, and weapons rooms. Sweet scents filled the victors' nostrils.

By the time dinner was served in the commander's private dining room, every trace of bloodshed had been removed.

The generals applauded Ramses' decisiveness and cheered the outcome of his initiative. Setau, still tending the wounded, was missing from the party. Ahsha seemed preoccupied.

"Aren't you happy with our victory?" the king inquired.

"Yes, but how many more battles like this one will there be?"

"We'll take the forts back one by one, and Canaan will be pacified. Since we won't be caught by surprise again, our losses shouldn't be so heavy."

"Fifty dead and more than a hundred wounded . . ."

"Only because they sprung a trap on us. There was no way we could have known."

"I should have seen it coming," Ahsha admitted. "The Hittites love intrigue as much as bloodletting."

"Any Hittites among the enemy dead?"

"None."

"Their raiders have headed home, it seems."

"Leaving a trail of surprises behind them, I'm sure."

"We'll take them one at a time. Get some rest, Ahsha. We're marching out tomorrow."

Ramses left an adequate garrison in place, restocking the fort as well. Several messengers were already on the way to Pi-Ramses with orders for Ahmeni to dispatch convoys to the main fort.

The king led his army north, heading a detachment of a hundred chariots.

Ten times, the same scenario unfolded. A thousand paces from the rebel stronghold, Ramses sowed panic by picking off the archers posted on the ramparts. Covered by a constant stream of Egyptian arrows that kept the Canaanites from returning fire, the soldiers raised their ladders, climbed with their shields in front of them, and took control of the wall walk. No attempt was ever made to enter a fortress through its main gates.

In less than a month, Ramses was once again the master of Canaan. Since the insurgents had massacred every inhabitant of the forts, including women and children, they knew there was no point in surrendering and throwing themselves on the king's mercy. Pharaoh's reputation had the rebel leaders terrified from the moment they learned of his initial victory. By the time the army reached the northernmost fortress, recapturing it was a mere formality.

Galilee, the valley north of Jordan, and the trade routes were restored to Egyptian control. Everyone along the way cheered the Pharaoh, swearing eternal allegiance to him.

Yet not one Hittite had been captured.

The governor of Gaza, the capital of Canaan, laid on a splendid banquet for the Egyptian high command. He and his people had bent over backward to supply Pharaoh's army, feed and stable the horses and donkeys. The brief campaign to restore order was now ending on a note of friendship and celebration.

The governor had made a speech denouncing the Hittites in the strongest terms. These Asian barbarians, he said, had made an unsuccessful attempt to shatter the indestructible ties between his country and Egypt. The gods had sent Pharaoh to the rescue, knowing that the monarch would never abandon his faithful allies. They mourned the tragic loss of Egyptian soldiers and civilians. But Ramses had fulfilled the law of Ma'at, restoring order to Canaan.

"This hypocrite is making me lose my appetite," the king said to Ahsha.

"You can't change human nature."

"No, but I can change governors."

"Replace this one with another? You could, of course. But as soon as the next one finds an advantage in betraying you, he'll go right ahead. At least we know what manner of man this governor is—corrupt, greedy, a liar. Controlling him poses no problems."

"You're forgetting that he turned his back while Hittite raiders took over our forts."

"As I said, any governor in his position would do the same."

"So you're advising me to stick with the known evil?"

"Tell him he's out if he makes one more false move. That ought to keep him in line for a few months."

"Are you this cynical about everyone?"

"As a diplomat, I deal with reality. Men will do anything to keep what power they have or grab some more. If I allowed myself to trust politicians, I wouldn't last long."

"You haven't answered my question. Is there anyone you respect?"

"I admire you, Ramses, which is an exception for me. But aren't you also a man of power?"

"I'm the servant of Ma'at and of my people."

"What if one day you forgot that?"

"That would be the day my magic deserted me—the beginning of the end."

"May the gods protect you from any such eventuality."

"Enough, Ahsha. Tell me what intelligence you've gathered."

"The local merchants were willing to talk, as were a few officials, for a consideration. They confirmed that Hittite commandos stirred up the revolt and told the rebels how to take over the forts."

"So how did they do it?"

"They arranged deliveries of local produce, except that the wagons were really carrying armed rebels. All the forts were attacked at the same time. Women and children were taken hostage, forcing the commanders to surrender—a fatal error, as we now know.

"The Hittites assured their allies that Egypt's response would be too little, too late. The rebels thought they had nothing to fear if they wiped out our garrisons, even though they were on excellent terms with the natives."

Ramses was satisfied that his response had been appropriate. The craven rebels deserved their fate.

"Any word of Moses?"

"No serious leads."

The commanders met in the royal tent. Ramses presided from his gilded folding throne, with the Nubian lion dozing at his feet.

The monarch asked Ahsha and each of the officers to speak. The senior general was the last to take the floor.

"The army's morale is high. Supplies and equipment are excellent. Your Majesty has won a resounding victory which will have its place in the royal annals."

"That may be going too far."

"Your Majesty, we are proud to have taken part in these battles, and—"

"Battles? Save that word for later. We can use it when we encounter some real resistance."

"Pi-Ramses is ready to give you a hero's welcome."

"Pi-Ramses will wait."

"We've regained control of Palestine and put down the rebellion in Canaan. Isn't it time to go home?"

"Our most difficult challenge lies ahead: retaking the province of Amurru."

"The Hittites may be amassing their troops in the region."

"Do I sense that you're afraid of fighting, General?"

"We need time to develop our strategy, Your Majesty."

"We already have one. We're heading straight for the north."

SIXTEEN

Wearing a short wig tied in place around her forehead— the ends of the ribbon dangling to her shoulders—and a form-fitting tunic with a red sash, Nefertari purified her hands with water from the sacred lake. She then entered the inner sanctum of the temple of Amon, the naos, to nourish the divine presence with delectable offerings from the evening meal. In her role as the wife of the god, she was acting as the Daughter of Light, issuing forth from the creative source of the universe.

The queen closed the doors of the sanctuary behind her, sealed them, went out of the temple, and followed the priests toward the House of Life at Pi-Ramses. As the incarnation of the distant goddess, mother of life and death, she would attempt to repel the forces of evil. If the sun's eye became as her own, she would be able to perpetuate life and continue the eternal cycles of nature. The tranquil flow of days depended on her ability to counter the forces of destruction.

A priest handed a bow to the queen. A priestess held out four arrows.

Nefertari pulled on the bow, aiming the first arrow east, the second north, the third south, and the fourth to the west. Ramses' invisible enemies were once again held at bay.

Tuya's chamberlain was waiting for Nefertari.

"The Queen Mother wishes to see you as soon as possible, Your Majesty." A litter was waiting to transport the Great Royal Wife.

Slender in her long, tucked linen tunic and sash with striped panels, adorned with gold bracelets and six strands of lapis lazuli around her neck, Tuya was supremely elegant.

"Don't fret, Nefertari. A messenger has just arrived with wonderful news from Canaan. Ramses has the province back in hand, and order has been restored."

"When is he coming back?"

"He doesn't say."

"Meaning they're heading farther north."

"Probably."

"Is that what you'd do?"

"Absolutely," replied Tuya.

"North of Canaan lies the province of Amurru, the buffer zone between our territory and the Hittite sphere of influence."

"Seti hoped that establishing it would decrease the possibility of conflict."

"If the Hittites have taken over . . ."

"It will mean war, Nefertari."

"I shot the four arrows this evening."

"Then what do have we to fear?"

Shaanar detested Ahmeni. To be forced to meet with the pretentious pipsqueak of a scribe every morning was torture, but it was his only means of keeping informed about Ramses' northern campaign. "Once I'm in charge," Shaanar reassured himself, "Ahmeni will be sent to some faraway military base and forced to haul manure until his health breaks."

His sole satisfaction was watching Ahmeni's expression grow more downcast by the day, a sure sign that the campaign's progress was stalled. The king's brother put on a sympathetic face and promised he'd pray for the tide to turn in Egypt's favor.

Shaanar had much less to do at the State Department than he claimed. He also avoided any overt contact with the Syrian merchant Raia. In these troubled times, it would be unseemly for a figure of Shaanar's stature to focus on his collection of rare imported vases. He therefore had to make do with cryptic messages from Raia, the contents of which were encouraging.

According to Syrian "observers" in Canaan, the rebels' trap had worked to perfection. Headstrong as ever, Ramses had forged eagerly ahead, forgetting that his enemies might have a surprise or two in store.

In his spare time, Shaanar had solved the mystery on everyone's mind at court—the theft of Nefertari's shawl and the dried fish from the House of Life in Heliopolis. It had to be Romay, the chief steward of the royal household. Shaanar had summoned the fat man on some lame pretext, and they were to meet that very morning, before his regular briefing with Ahmeni.

Romay looked like the former chef he was, with his big belly, round cheeks, and multiple chins. His performance as chief steward had been flawless. Handpicked by the Pharaoh, he had quickly silenced his critics. While admittedly slow moving, he was a stickler for cleanliness and for detail. He tasted every dish served to the royal family and maintained strict discipline among his staff. Failure to follow his orders resulted in instant dismissal.

"How may I be of service, Your Highness?" Romay asked Shaanar.

"Didn't my steward explain the problem to you?"

"He mentioned a scheduling conflict for an upcoming banquet, but I'm not aware—"

"What if we discussed the theft from the House of Life in Heliopolis instead? I'm sure you've heard about the missing vessel of fish."

"Fish? I know nothing about it."

"And Queen Nefertari's shawl?"

"I've been informed of that, of course, and I was appalled, but—"

"Did you look into it?"

"It's not my place to conduct investigations, Your Highness!"

"You'd be in the ideal position, though."

"No, I don't think—"

"Just think about it—you're the key man in the palace. Nothing gets by you, I hear!"

"You overestimate me."

"Why did you do it, Romay?"

"Me? You aren't insinuating—"

"No, I'm not insinuating. I'm positive. What did you do with the queen's shawl and the missing fish?"

"Your accusations are completely unfounded!"

"I know what men are like, Romay. And I have proof."

"No!"

"Why would you take such a risk?"

Romay's flustered expression, the unhealthy flush spreading upward from his neck, the way his whole body suddenly sagged, were proof enough. Shaanar was right again.

"Was it a bribe, or do you simply hate the Pharaoh? Either way, it's a serious offense."

"Your Highness, I—" The fat man's distress was almost touching.

"Considering your record, I'm inclined to overlook this incident. But if I need your help in the future, you'd better be prepared to do as I ask."

Ahmeni was composing his daily report to Ramses in his quick, sure hand.

"Can you spare a moment?" Shaanar asked affably.

"You know I always have time for you. We're meeting at the king's request, after all." He set down his writing kit.

"You look exhausted, Ahmeni."

"Only outwardly."

"Shouldn't you be taking better care of your health?"

"The health of our nation is my sole concern."

"Don't tell me you have bad news!"

"Quite the contrary."

"Could you be more specific?"

"I've wanted to tell you about Ramses' triumphs in Canaan, but I thought it was best to wait until the information was confirmed. Since we were fed some false reports recently via carrier pigeon, I've learned to be more careful."

"A Hittite scheme, I suppose?"

"Yes, and it almost cost us dearly! Our garrisons in Canaan had fallen into rebel hands without our even knowing. If Ramses had split up the forces, our losses would have been disastrous."

"But fortunately that didn't happen."

"The province of Canaan is once again under our control, with free access to the coast. The governor has sworn his loyalty to Ramses."

"In such a short time! Quite an accomplishment for my brother. Since he's answered the Hittite challenge, I suppose they're marching home now."

"That's classified information."

"What do you mean, classified? I'm secretary of state, remember?"

"I have no further information."

"Impossible!"

"But true."

Shaanar stormed out.

Ahmeni was alone again with his regrets—not over his attitude toward Shaanar, but because he'd been so hasty in detaining Serramanna. The evidence had certainly been stacked against the bodyguard, but perhaps it had deserved closer attention. With the pressure of impending war, Ahmeni had been a bit more lax than usual. He'd feel better if he double-checked all the evidence, as was his habit.

Irritated with himself, he got up to locate Serramanna's file.

SEVENTEEN

Guarding the main point of entry to Syria, the fortress of Megiddo sat on a hilltop above a lush plain. It looked forbidding with its stone walls, battlements, high square towers, wooden hoardings, and thick gates.

The garrison included both Egyptians and Syrians loyal to the Pharaoh, but who could trust the official messages asserting that the fort had not fallen into rebel hands?

Ramses found the scenery unsettling: high wooded hills, gnarled oak trees, muddy rivers, dank wetlands, sandy soil . . . a hard land, hostile and closed, so very different from the beauty of the Nile and the sweeping vistas of Egypt.

Twice his scouts had been attacked by wild boars intent on protecting their sows and young. His horsemen had trouble negotiating the overgrown forest trails and tight passages between tree trunks. On the other hand, the easy availability of water and the abundance of game were distinct advantages.

Ramses gave the order to halt, but not to pitch the tents. Eyes fixed on the fortress in the distance, he waited for the scouts' return.

Setau was glad of the extra time in his infirmary. The seriously wounded had been sent home, so the remaining troops were able-bodied except for men suffering from colds and stomach complaints. A little byrony, cumin, or castor oil cleared up their ailments. He still distributed garlic and onions as a preventive measure, including the special variety he had brought along.

Lotus had just saved a donkey bitten on the leg by a snake which she had managed to capture. The expedition was finally getting interesting. Now that they were near Syria, she was encountering species that were new to her. The one she was now examining hadn't yielded much venom but was quite interesting.

Two foot soldiers made an appeal to the talents of the beautiful Nubian, under the pretext that they, too, were victims of snakebite. Hearty slaps across the face were their antidote, and when Lotus pulled a hissing viper out of a bag, they turned tail and hid amongst their comrades.

More than two hours had passed since the troops had halted. The cavalry had been given permission to dismount, the infantry had broken ranks, with several lookouts on duty.

"The scouts are taking their time," said Ahsha.

"I agree," said Ramses. "How is your arm, by the way?"

"Completely healed. Setau really is a wizard."

"How do you like this country?"

"I don't. The way looks clear, but the ground is swampy. All those big oaks, hedges, grasses—our troops are getting separated."

"The scouts aren't coming back," asserted Ramses. "They've either been killed or taken prisoner."

"That means Megiddo is under enemy control, as we feared, and not likely to surrender."

"Megiddo is the key to southern Syria," Ramses countered. "Even if the Hittites have taken up residence, it's our duty to fight for control."

"That wouldn't amount to a declaration of war," said Ahsha. "We'd only be reclaiming territory within our zone of influence. We can therefore attack at any time and without prior warning. In the context of international law, we're dealing with a local rebellion, not a conflict between major states."

The diplomat's argument would be sure to have relevance for the surrounding states.

"Inform the generals they should prepare to attack."

Before Ahsha even had time to ride away, a troop of horsemen came thundering out of the oak grove to the king's left, heading straight for the dismounted Egyptian cavalry. Many of Ramses' men were pinned by short lances; several horses had their legs or throats slashed. The survivors defended themselves with pike and sword; a few managed to climb into their chariots and retreat toward the infantry position, where foot soldiers stood behind their shields.

The raiders had pulled off a deadly strike. They were easy to identify as Syrians by their goatees, fringed ankle-length robes, brightly striped sashes and scarves.

Ramses remained strangely calm. Ahsha was agitated.

"They're going to charge the infantry!"

"Success has gone to their heads."

The Syrian advance was quickly checked as the infantry pushed the raiders toward the archers, who took deadly aim.

Fighter gave a throaty growl.

"It's not over yet," said Ramses ominously.

From the cover of the oak grove rushed hundreds of hatchet-wielding Syrians, straight for the backs of the Egyptian marksmen.

"Let's go!" the king urged his horses. Their master's tone of

voice told the two noble steeds they must fly. Fighter sprang
forward. Ahsha and another fifty chariots followed.

The melee was wild and gory, with the lion clawing at
anyone bold enough to attack Ramses' chariot, while the king
fired arrow after arrow into enemy hearts, necks, heads.
Chariots ran over the wounded. Foot soldiers running to the
rescue sent the Syrians fleeing.

Ramses noticed a strange-looking warrior running back
toward the oak grove.

"Stop him," he yelled to Fighter.

The lion wiped out two stragglers along the way, then
knocked the man over. Though the beast had tried to exercise
restraint, the fallen man lay critically injured, blood pouring
from his back. Ramses examined the raider. He had long hair
and a scruffy beard; his red and black striped robe was in shreds.

"Send for Setau," the monarch demanded.

The fighting was nearly finished. The Syrians had been
wiped out to the last man, inflicting only slight damage on the
Egyptian forces.

Setau arrived at Ramses' side, breathless.

"Save him," the king requested. "This man is no Syrian;
he's a desert nomad. We need to find out what he's doing
here."

The sight of a Bedouin, so far outside his normal range—
the Sinai caravan routes he would normally haunt— intrigued
Setau.

"Your lion did some serious damage."

The man's face ran with sweat, blood poured from his nostrils, his neck was stiff. Setau took his pulse and listened to the
"voice of his heart." It was so weak that the diagnosis was
simple: the man was dying.

"Can he speak?" asked the king.

"His jaw is locked. There may be one last chance, though."

Setau worked a cloth-covered wooden tube into the man's mouth; through this he poured a preparation made from cypress root.

"That should ease his pain. If he's as strong as he looks, he may hang on for a few hours."

The nomad seemed to recognize his captor. Awestruck, he struggled to get up, broke the wooden tube with his teeth, flapped his arms like a grounded bird.

"Calm down now," soothed Setau. "We're trying to help you."

"Ramses . . ."

"Yes. The Pharaoh of Egypt, and he wants to talk to you."

The Bedouin stared at the blue crown.

"Are you from Sinai?" inquired the king.

"Yes," he said hoarsely.

"Why are you fighting with these Syrians?"

"Gold—they promised me gold."

"Have you met any Hittites?"

"They gave us a battle plan and then they left."

"Were there other Bedouins with you?"

"They ran away."

"Have you ever seen a Hebrew by the name of Moses?"

"I don't think so."

Ramses described his friend.

"No, I've never come across him."

"Have you heard of a man like him anywhere in the desert?"

"No, I don't think so."

"How many men are there inside the fort over there?"

"I don't know," he stammered.

"Don't lie."

In a sudden burst of energy, the Bedouin sat up, pulled out his dagger, and flailed at the king. Setau knocked the knife from his hand.

It was too much for the wounded raider. His face con-
tracted, his body arched, and he fell back dead.

"The Syrians tried to recruit the Bedouins," commented
Setau. "What stupidity! They would never get along."

Setau returned to his field hospital, where Lotus and their
assistants were already at work on the wounded. The dead had
been rolled up in reed mats and loaded onto wagons. A convoy
would take them home for a proper burial.

Ramses patted his horses and stroked Fighter. The lion's
muffled growls sounded almost like purring. Soldiers clus-
tered around their king, raising their weapons on high and
hailing the Pharaoh who had just led them to victory with the
flair of a true commander.

The generals pushed their way through the crowd and
added their congratulations.

"Any more Syrians lurking in the woods?"

"No, Your Majesty. Shall we camp for the night?"

"We have better things to do. On to Megiddo!"

EIGHTEEN

Revived by a huge dish of lentils that wouldn't add an
ounce to his meager frame, Ahmeni spent the night at
his desk, planning to get a head start on the next day's work.

That way he'd be able to spend some time on Serramanna's file. Whenever his back started to hurt, he'd touch his gilded scribe's palette in the graceful shape of a lotus column, a gift from Ramses on the day he had made Ahmeni his private secretary. His energy was instantly renewed.

Since their school days, a mysterious bond had linked Ahmeni to Ramses. He knew instinctively when his friend was in danger. On several occasions, he had sensed death hovering close to the king, too close for a man without his magical powers. If Ramses' special barrier of divine protection was ever breached, his habitual risk taking could lead to disaster.

And if Serramanna was one of the stones in that magical barrier, Ahmeni had made a grave mistake in relieving the Sard of his duties. He simply wasn't sure.

The accusations relied heavily on the testimony of Serramanna's girlfriend Lilia. Ahmeni had asked to have her brought to him for further questioning. He'd get the truth out of her.

At seven o'clock, the police officer heading the investigation appeared at his door. He was a no-nonsense public servant in his fifties.

"Lilia won't be coming today," he announced.

"Did she refuse to see me?"

"No. We can't find her."

"Doesn't she live at the address she gave?"

"She did, but according to the neighbors, she moved out a few days ago."

"Without telling anyone where she was going?"

"Right."

"Did you search the house?"

"It was completely stripped. Even the linen chests were empty, as if the woman wanted to wipe out every trace of her existence."

"What kind of girl are we talking about?"

"A woman of easy virtue, the neighbors say. Her face was her fortune."

"She worked in a tavern, then?"

"Not that we could discover."

"Did she bring men home?"

"Apparently not, but she went out a lot, mostly at night."

"We have to find her and identify her patrons."

"We will."

"Then hurry."

When the policeman left, Ahmeni took another look at the wooden tablets covered with Serramanna's alleged secret message to the Hittites.

In his quiet office, in the clear light of early morning, a theory began to take shape in Ahmeni's mind. To test it, he'd have to wait until Ahsha was back.

High on a rocky spur, the fortress of Megiddo daunted the Egyptian soldiers staring up from the plain. Its towers were so high that new ladders had been built, and even so, the walls hardly looked easy to scale. Arrows and stones from above could decimate the assault teams.

With Ahsha at his side, Ramses drove his chariot around the fortress, keeping up his speed to make them a swiftly moving target.

Not a single arrow was fired. Not a single sharpshooter peeked above the battlements.

"They'll stay under cover until the last minute," assessed Ahsha. "That saves them ammunition. The smartest tactic would be to starve them out."

"A fortress this big could withstand a siege for months. Would our morale survive that long?"

"An attack would cost us a great many lives."

"Do you believe I'm so hard-hearted that all I think about is winning?"

"Egypt comes first, before individual lives."

"I hold all life precious, Ahsha."

"What's your plan, then?"

"We'll circle our chariots around the fort, at shooting distance, and our marksmen will pick off the lookouts on the wall walk. Three squads of volunteers will raise the ladders and climb up with their shields in front of them."

"What if Megiddo's defenses are too strong for us?"

"First let's try to take the fort. We can't go into battle with a defeatist attitude."

Ramses' forcefulness energized the soldiers. A crowd of volunteers pressed forward, archers vied for a place on the chariots that would ring the fort, which stood there like a silent and menacing beast.

Hoisting the long ladders over their shoulders, the columns of foot soldiers advanced warily toward the fortifications. Once the ladders went up, Syrian archers could be seen on the highest tower, pulling their bowstrings. None of them had the time to take aim; Ramses and the Egyptian marksmen shot them down. A second wave of Syrian archers stepped up, all dark goatees and headbands around their flowing hair. This time a few of them launched their arrows, but not one Egyptian was hit. Again, the king and his sharpshooters mowed them down.

"They aren't putting up much of a fight," the old general remarked to Setau. "You'd swear these people have never seen combat before."

"Good," Setau replied curtly. "It will make less work for me. I may even be able to devote a whole night to my wife. These battles are wearing me out."

The foot soldiers had just begun scaling the walls when some fifty women suddenly appeared.

The Egyptians did not customarily massacre women and children. They were instead taken prisoner and brought back to Egypt, where they were put to work on great agricultural estates. Their names were changed and they were fully assimilated into society.

The old general was confounded. "I thought I'd seen everything. The creatures must be mad!"

Two women hoisted a brazier to the edge of the wall and dumped it on the climbing soldiers. Burning coals bounced off them as they gripped the rungs of the ladder. The archers' shafts pierced the women's eyes and they fell over the edge. The same fate befell the next group of women that came forward with a fresh brazier. One bold girl put hot coals in her slingshot, wound up, and let them fly.

One of the coals hit the old general in the thigh. He went down slapping his reddening skin.

"Don't touch it," cautioned Setau. "Hold still and let me take care of it."

Lifting his kilt, the snake charmer urinated on the burn. His patient knew as well as he that urine was more sanitary than river or well water and cleansed open wounds without risk of infection. Setau hailed a stretcher to carry him off to the hospital tent.

The foot soldiers overran the ramparts, now completely undefended. A few minutes later, the main gate of the fortress of Megiddo swung open.

Inside, only a few women and terror-stricken children remained.

"The Syrians decided to put all their manpower into keeping us from ever reaching the fortress," Ahsha summed up.

"It might have worked," assessed Ramses.

"They don't know you."

"Who can say he does, my friend?"

A dozen soldiers were looting the fortress, full of alabaster vessels and silver statuettes. A roar from the lion broke up their party.

"Place those men under arrest," decreed Ramses. "See that the living quarters are purified and fumigated."

The king named a governor to remain behind with a garrison of his own selection.

There was several weeks' worth of food already in storage, and men had already been sent out to hunt game and round up livestock.

Ramses, Ahsha, and the new governor established a plan for the local economy. Because of the shifting allegiances in the region, farmers had stopped working their fields. Before the week was out, they began to view the Egyptian occupation as a stabilizing force.

The king had several small outposts built to the north of Megiddo, each with room for a handful of lookouts and horses. In case of Hittite attack, the main fortress would be forewarned.

From the main watchtower, Ramses surveyed the unfamiliar scenery. Being so far from the Nile, the palm groves, the broad, green fields, the desert, was painful. In the hush of evening, Nefertari would be celebrating the evening rituals. How he missed her!

Ahsha interrupted the king's meditation.

"As you asked, I've held discussions with the officers and representatives from the enlisted men."

"What's the consensus?"

"They have complete trust in you, but they long to go home."

"Do you like Syria, Ahsha?"

"It's a dangerous country, full of pitfalls. Hard to understand unless you spend a great deal of time here."

"Is this what it's like in Hatti?"

"It's even wilder and harsher. In the Anatolian highlands, the winters are freezing."

"Do you think it will appeal to me?"

"You are Egypt, Ramses. No other land will find a place in your heart."

"The province of Amurru is close by now."

"So is the enemy."

"Do you think the Hittite army has invaded Amurru?"

"We have no reliable information."

"I asked your opinion."

"I think we'll find them waiting for us there."

NINETEEN

Stretching along the sea between the coastal villages of Tyre and Byblos, the province of Amurru lay to the east of Mount Hermon and the trade center of Damascus. It was the northernmost Egyptian protectorate, bordering the Hittite sphere of influence.

Far from home now, the Pharaoh's soldiers marched with a heavy tread. Against his generals' recommendations, Ramses had opted not to follow the coastal route, taking the high road instead. The rocky trail was proving difficult for man and beast alike. There was no more chatting or laughter; armed confrontation with the Hittites was too close for comfort. Their enemy's fierce reputation was enough to frighten the most courageous soldier.

Ahsha contended that reclaiming Amurru would not be an overt act of war in diplomatic terms, but where would the bloodletting end? The troops had been hopeful that the king would be satisfied with Megiddo and head for home. But after the briefest of stops in Syria, Ramses was back on the march.

A scout came galloping to the head of the column and reined hard in front of the Pharaoh.

"They're straight ahead, at the end of the trail, between the cliffs and the sea."

"How many?"

"Several hundred men armed with spears and bows, hiding in the brush. They're watching the shore road, so we'll catch them unawares."

"Hittites?"

"No, Your Majesty. They're local men."

Ramses was puzzled. What kind of trap was this?

"Show me the place."

The general heading the chariot division intervened. "Pharaoh must not expose himself to such a risk."

Ramses' eyes blazed.

"I need to see for myself and make a decision."

The king rode out after the scout. Eventually the two men dismounted and walked down a steep path strewn with loose boulders.

Ramses froze.

The sea, the trail alongside it, the thick brush, the enemy

lying in ambush . . . nowhere to conceal the Hittites' massed troops here. Yet opposite stood a cliff that blocked his view. Dozens of chariots could be massed behind it, ready to spring into action.

Ramses had his soldiers' lives in his hands. His army was what kept Egypt safe from harm.

"Let's move into position," he murmured.

The Prince of Amurru's foot soldiers had been lulled by the long wait for the first Egyptians to appear along on the shore road.

Prince Benteshina was applying the strategy devised by his Hittite "observers." They doubted Ramses would ever make it this far north, given the number of traps laid for him along the way. And even if he did, he would be so battle-weary that one last ambush would make quick work of him.

A paunchy despot of fifty with a handsome black mustache, Benteshina had no love for the Hittites, but he was afraid of them. Amurru was so close to their sphere of influence that he would be a fool not to stay on their good side. Yes, he was a vassal of Egypt and paid tribute to the Pharaoh, but the Hittites had other plans for him. He was supposed to join the uprising and deal the final blow to what remained of the Egyptian army.

His throat was dry. The prince, in the shelter of a cave, ordered his valet to go and fetch some cool wine.

The servant advanced only a few steps.

"Your Highness . . . Look!"

"Get going, man. I need a drink."

"Look, on the cliffs! Hundreds, thousands of Egyptians!"

Benteshina rose in astonishment. The servant was right.

A tall man wearing a crown of blue and a gold-trimmed kilt advanced down the path. At his side loped an enormous lion.

One by one, then in unison, the Lebanese soldiers turned to take in the spectacle that had greeted their leader. Those napping were shaken to attention.

"Come out, Benteshina, wherever you are," Ramses called in his deep and powerful voice.

Trembling, the Prince of Amurru approached the Pharaoh.

"You are my vassal, are you not?"

"Your Majesty, I have always served Egypt faithfully."

"Then why is your army lying in ambush for me?"

"We thought . . . for the safety of our province . . ."

A dull roar reached his ears. Ramses looked toward the cliffs that he suspected were concealing Hittite chariots. This was the moment of truth.

"You're a traitor, Benteshina."

"No, Your Majesty! The Hittites forced me to obey them. If I refused, they threatened to kill me and massacre my people. We've been hoping you'd come to our rescue."

"Where are the Hittites?"

"They're gone. They doubted that your army would ever reach here, with everything you'd been through."

"What's that strange noise I'm hearing?"

"The breakers crashing against the cliffs."

"Your men were prepared to attack me. My army is ready to fight."

Benteshina knelt down. "How sad it is, Your Majesty, to descend into the silent kingdom of death! To swoon and to sleep forever! The voices of those who depart are heard no more, for there are no doors or windows. No ray of sunlight pierces it, no breeze arrives to refresh the dead. No one wishes to enter the land of the dead! I beg Pharaoh's pardon, that my people may be spared and that I may continue to serve you!"

Seeing their master prostrate, the Lebanese soldiers threw down their arms.

When Ramses bent to help Benteshina up, his soldiers and their Egyptian counterparts cheered with joy.

Shaanar's head was swimming as he left Ahmeni's office.

The outcome of Ramses' incredibly swift campaign was that he had reclaimed the province of Amurru, wresting it from direct Hittite control. How had this inexperienced young sovereign, leading his first foray into hostile territory, navigated a host of obstacles and pulled off such a stunning victory?

It was years since Shaanar had put any faith in the gods, but it was clear to him that Ramses had magical powers, perhaps a legacy from Seti, handed down in some secret ritual. Some force was certainly guiding him.

Shaanar composed a memo to Ahmeni. In his official capacity as secretary of state, he planned to depart for Memphis and personally announce this remarkable news to the notables there.

"Where is your sorcerer?" Shaanar asked his sister, Dolora.

The tall and languid brunette was sheltering Lita from the prince's rage as Akhenaton's fragile, blond great-grand-daughter trembled with fear.

"He's busy."

"I demand to see him at once."

"He needs to concentrate. He's working on another way to use Nefertari's shawl."

"For all the good it does us! Ramses has recaptured every fort from here to Amurru, bringing the protectorates back in line. Our losses have been minimal, and not a scratch on our darling little brother! The soldiers have decided he's a god."

"Are you sure?"

"Ahmeni is an excellent source of information. In fact, I'm sure he errs on the side of caution. Canaan, Amurru, and southern Syria are no longer under Hittite control. Count on Ramses to make them a well-fortified base and a buffer zone the enemy will no longer dare to cross. This campaign was supposed to be our little brother's downfall; instead, it's reinforced his defenses," fumed Shaanar.

Lita's blank stare was fixed on him.

"We aren't one step closer to the throne, my lady. Perhaps you and your wizard friend are even toying with me?"

Shaanar ripped the top of Lita's dress from her shapely bosom. Her chest was scored with deep burns.

The lost princess began to sob, clutching at Dolora.

"Don't torture the girl, Shaanar. She and Ofir still represent our best hope."

"Hope!" he spat. "Is that all they have to offer?"

"No, Your Highness," came a low and measured voice. "There's so much more that I can give you."

Shaanar wheeled around.

The sorcerer's hawk face once again made its impression. His dark green gaze seemed fully capable of flattening any opponent within seconds.

"I'm unhappy with our progress, Ofir."

"Lita and I have done our utmost, as you can see for yourself. Ramses is no ordinary target, and weakening his defenses will take time, as I already explained. Until the last scrap of Nefertari's shawl has been burned, the spell will be incomplete. Unfortunately, if we proceed too quickly, Lita will die. That would compromise our legitimate claim to the throne."

"How long, Ofir?"

"Lita is fragile because she's an excellent medium. Between sessions, Dolora and I tend her wounds. They need to heal before my next attempt to break through the force field."

"Couldn't you experiment with someone else?"

"Lita is no mere medium. She's the future Queen of Egypt—your future wife. She's been training for years to serve this purpose. She's determined, and no one could take her place."

"All right. But the longer we wait, the more Ramses grows in stature."

"We can snuff him out in an instant."

"My brother has unusual powers. Exceptional powers."

"I know that, Your Highness. That's why I'm drawing on the deepest recesses of my magic. Haste would ruin everything. Still, perhaps . . ."

Shaanar hung on Ofir's every word.

"In the meantime, I could try something tailored to the situation. War heroes tend to let down their guard. Even Ramses may have a moment of weakness. We'll turn it to our advantage."

TWENTY

Amurru was celebrating. Prince Benteshina was determined to show how greatly he honored Ramses and how much he valued the province's newfound peace. Solemn declarations of allegiance had been drawn up on papyrus. The prince agreed to donate a supply of cedar flagstaffs that would be erected in front of Egypt's great temples. These, he vowed, would be shipped without delay. Likewise, the Lebanese soldiers extended their warmest hospitality to their Egyptian counterparts. Wine flowed like water; women gave ample demonstrations of their gratitude.

Setau and Lotus saw through the forced gaiety, but they were content to take part in the festivities. They had the good fortune to meet a local wise man who was also a snake lover. Although the northern species were less spectacular than those found in Egypt, they enjoyed talking shop with him and picked up a few trade secrets.

Ramses remained formal and sober, despite his host's obsequious attentions. Benteshina concluded that as the world's most powerful ruler, Pharaoh must naturally have a great deal on his mind.

But Ahsha knew he was far more pensive than usual.

At the end of a banquet for the high command of the two armies, Ramses had retired alone to the balcony of the palace Benteshina had lent him.

The king was staring hard at the northern sky.

"Excuse me for intruding on your thoughts."

"What can I do for you, Ahsha?"

"You don't seem too thrilled with the prince's hospitality."

"Once a traitor, always a traitor. But I'm following your advice to stick with the known evil."

"What has you so preoccupied? I know it's not Benteshina."

"So you're a mind reader now?"

"You're looking toward Kadesh."

"Kadesh, the pride of the Hittites, the symbol of their dominance in northern Syria, of the unrelenting threat to Egypt. Yes, I've been thinking about it."

"Attacking Kadesh would mean trespassing on the Hittite sphere of influence. That would require a formal declaration of war."

"Did the Hittites declare their intentions before they stirred up trouble in our protectorates?"

"No, but that was a covert action. Attacking Kadesh would require us to cross the border between our territory and their empire. Full-scale war, in other words—a conflict that could last months and end up destroying us."

"We're ready."

"We aren't, Ramses. Don't let success go to your head."

"You aren't giving me much credit."

"You've won a string of real victories, but over weak opponents. Benteshina folded before the first shot was fired. It won't be like that with the Hittites. What's more, your men are tired and homesick. Heading into a major conflict at this point could only lead to disaster."

"Is our army as weak as all that?"

"The men were physically and mentally prepared to put out some fires in our own protectorates. They aren't prepared to attack the greatest military power in the world."

"Won't waiting be just as dangerous?"

"The battle of Kadesh will take place, if you so will it. Just be sure you're ready."

"I'll make my decision tonight."

The festivities were over.

The order was given at dawn and spread quickly through the ranks: report for duty. Two hours later, Ramses arrived on the scene, dressed in full battle regalia, his two faithful horses hitched to his chariot.

There were butterflies in more than a few stomachs. Could there be any truth to the rumor that they were about to attack Kadesh? Were they really going to march on an indestructible Hittite citadel? Come face to face with the world's fiercest warriors? No, the Pharaoh wouldn't do anything so rash. He was his father's son. He'd never challenge his enemies in their own territory. He'd negotiate first.

The monarch inspected his troops. They were tense and silent. From the greenest recruit to the most experienced veteran, the men stood stiffly, almost painfully, at attention. Their lives depended on what their pharaoh said next.

Never fond of military pomp, Setau lay prone in his wagon as Lotus massaged his back, her bare breasts grazing his shoulder blades.

Prince Benteshina was holed up in his palace, unable to tolerate his usual breakfast of rich pastries. If Ramses declared war on the Hittites, Amurru would be the Egyptian army's fallback position. His subjects would be drafted into the war. And if Ramses lost, the Hittites would ravage the province.

Ahsha attempted to guess the king's intentions, but Ramses' face remained unreadable.

Once he'd reviewed the troops, Ramses did an about-face with his chariot. For an instant, the horses seemed to be heading north, toward Kadesh. Then Pharaoh circled south, toward Egypt.

Setau shaved with his bronze razor, combed his hair with a jagged-toothed wooden comb, coated his face with insect repellent, dusted his sandals, and rolled up his mat. He could never be suave like Ahsha, but he was making an effort to look his best, despite peals of laughter from his lovely wife.

Since the army had headed happily home, Setau and Lotus finally had some time alone in their wagon. The soldiers made up songs about Ramses' exploits and sang them as they marched. The charioteers, more restrained, merely hummed along. They agreed on one thing: the soldier's life was a wonderful life, as long as he wasn't fighting. They kept up a brisk pace through Amurru, Galilee, and Palestine. The local people cheered them and offered food. Before the last stage of their journey to the Delta, they camped to the north of the Sinai desert, to the west of the Negev, a sun-baked region where the Egyptian desert patrol guided caravans and policed nomadic tribes. Setau was delighted. The area was crawling with vipers and cobras, bigger and more lethal than normal. Lotus, lightning-quick as ever, had already caught several as she walked the perimeter of the camp. She smiled to see how the soldiers steered clear of her.

Ramses looked out at the desert. He was looking north, toward Kadesh.

"Your decision was lucid and wise," declared Ahsha.

"If wisdom means retreating in the face of the enemy."

"It certainly doesn't mean leading your men to slaughter or attempting the impossible."

"Wrong, Ahsha. The impossible is the test of true courage."

"For the first time, Ramses, you frighten me. Where will you lead your country?"

"Kadesh isn't simply going to disappear."

"Diplomacy resolves conflicts that appear to have no solution."

"Can your diplomacy pacify the Hittites?"

"Why not?"

"Give me the peace I desire, Ahsha, a true peace. Or else I'll have to achieve it in my own way."

They numbered a hundred fifty.

A hundred fifty men, nomads, Bedouins and Hebrews, trolling the desert for weeks at a time in search of errant caravans. Their acknowledged leader was a squint-eyed man in his forties, rumored to have escaped from a military prison on the eve of his execution. With thirty caravan raids and twenty-three murders (of Egyptian merchants and assorted foreign traders) under his belt, Vargoz was a hero to his band.

When the Egyptian army appeared on the horizon, they thought at first they were seeing a mirage. The chariots, the horsemen, the rows of foot soldiers . . . Vargoz and his men found a grotto where they could hide out until the enemy moved on.

That night in his dreams Vargoz saw a face, the hawk face of a Libyan he had known long ago. He heard the measured voice of the sorcerer who had taught him to read and write in a remote oasis somewhere between Libya and Egypt. Ofir had also used him as a medium.

The imperious face, the persuasive voice from his past now gave him new orders that echoed in his brain.

Wild-eyed, haggard, he roused his band of raiders.

"Our biggest job yet," he told them. "Follow me!"

As usual, they did as he said. Vargoz had a nose for plunder.

When they reached the outskirts of the Egyptian encampment, several of the bandits balked.

"What are we after?" they asked him.

"The big tent over that way—full of treasure."

"We don't stand a chance."

"There aren't very many sentinels and they don't expect an attack. Move quickly and we'll be rich."

"It's the Pharaoh's army," one objected. "Even if we pull it off, they'll never rest till they catch us."

"Imbecile! You think we'll hang around the desert? With all the gold we steal, we'll be richer than princes!"

"Gold?"

"Pharaoh never travels without a supply of it. Gold and precious stones are what he uses to bribe his vassals."

"How do you know?"

"I had a dream."

The bandit stared at Vargoz, wide-eyed. "You expect me to believe that?"

"Trust me."

"Risk my neck for a dream? You're out of your mind, man."

With a quick blow from his hatchet, Vargoz cut the raider's head halfway off. Knocking the man to the ground, he finished the job.

"Anyone else have a question?"

The hundred forty-nine raiders crept toward Pharaoh's tent.

Vargoz had to accomplish what Ofir told him in the dream: cut off one of Ramses' legs and cripple him.

TWENTY-ONE

Several of the Egyptian sentinels dozed. Others were lost in their thoughts of home and family. Only one noticed the strange form creeping toward him, but Vargoz overpowered the guard before he had time to cry out. The outlaw band was forced to admit that their leader was right once again. There would be no problem approaching the royal tent.

Vargoz had no idea whether Ramses was really carrying a treasure with him. He was not looking forward to the moment when his cohorts realized he'd deceived them. But his head was full of Ofir. He had to get rid of the sorcerer's face, his voice.

Recklessly, he rammed the officer lying by the entrance to the royal tent, leaving the guard no time to draw his sword. Winded by his attacker's butting head, he was trampled into unconsciousness.

The way was clear.

Even if Pharaoh were a god, a frenzied attack could kill him in his sleep.

A hatchet ripped through the tent flap.

Awakening with a jolt, Ramses leapt to his feet. Vargoz was rushing at him, waving his weapon.

An enormous weight crushed the raider. Intense pain sheared through his back.

Glancing back, he caught a fleeting glimpse of a gigantic lion closing its jaws around his head in the moment before it shattered like a ripe melon.

The terrified shriek of the bandit following on Vargoz's heels warned the rest of the band. Without their chief, disoriented, unsure whether to attack or retreat, the robbers were felled by the sentinels' arrows. Fighter alone took five of them. Then, seeing that the archers had the situation under control, he curled up in his spot behind his master's bed.

Furious over the death of the sentinels, the Egyptians took revenge on the outlaw band.

A plea from one of the wounded men intrigued an officer, who alerted the king.

"A Hebrew, Your Majesty."

The bandit was close to death, two arrows protruding from his stomach.

"Have you lived in Egypt, Hebrew?"

"It hurts," he moaned.

"Talk, and we'll help you."

"No, not in Egypt. I've always lived here."

"Did your tribe ever shelter a man called Moses?"

"No."

"Why did you attack us?"

The Hebrew said a few garbled words, then died.

Ahsha ran up to Ramses, exclaiming, "You're still in one piece!"

"Fighter takes care of me."

"Who are these bandits?"

"Bedouins, nomads, and at least one Hebrew."

"Their attack was suicidal."

"An insane idea. They must have been given a strong incentive."

"By the Hittites?"

"Perhaps."

"Are you thinking of someone else?"

"There are too many demons lurking in the shadows."

"I couldn't get to sleep tonight," confessed Ahsha.

"What's the trouble?"

"I'm worried about the Hittites' lack of reaction. They won't remain passive for long."

"Are you blaming me now for not attacking Kadesh?"

"Our top priority should be consolidating the defense system in our protectorates."

"That will be your next mission, Ahsha."

Ahmeni frugally scoured an old wooden tablet to reuse it as a writing surface. His staff was well aware that the king's private secretary did not tolerate waste and set great store in caring for equipment.

Ramses' triumph in the protectorates and the perfect level of the floodwaters were cause for rejoicing as Pi-Ramses prepared to welcome home the victors. Boats delivered quantities of food and drink for the monumental banquet to which all the city's inhabitants, rich and poor alike, were invited.

Unable to work in the fields during the inundation, the peasants rested or rowed out to visit their near or distant relatives. The Nile Delta had become a sea dotted with islands where the villages were built. Ramses' capital was like a ship anchored in the heart of this watery vastness.

Yet Ahmeni's soul was uneasy. If he had thrown an innocent man in prison, a man who was also one of Ramses' most faithful defenders, this injustice would count heavily against him in the Judgment Hall of the Dead. The scribe had been reluctant to visit Serramanna, who continued to proclaim his innocence.

The police officer Ahmeni had put in charge of investigating Lilia, the principal witness for the prosecution, reported to the secretary's office late in the evening.

"Anything new?"

The detective spoke deliberately. "Aye, sir."

Ahmeni felt relieved. The breakthrough had finally come.

"Lilia?"

"I found her."

"Why didn't you bring her with you?"

"Because she's dead."

"Accidentally?"

"According to the physician who examined her corpse for me, it was murder. Lilia was strangled."

"Murder . . . then someone wanted to silence her. But

why? Because she'd lied or because there was more she knew?"

"With all due respect, sir, this new twist seems to cast some doubt on Serramanna's guilt."

Ahmeni turned even paler than usual.

"I had due cause for detaining him."

"There's no disputing the evidence," agreed the detective.

"Of course there is! Suppose this Lilia was paid to implicate Serramanna, but she panicked at the thought of appearing in court, lying under oath, defying the law of Ma'at. Whoever hired her would be forced to make sure she wouldn't talk. There's still the physical evidence to consider, but suppose the incriminating tablets are only forgeries? Then our case is hardly as solid as it seemed."

"It would be easy to get a sample of Serramanna's handwriting," the detective admitted. "He posted a weekly bulletin on the door of the royal bodyguard barracks."

"Serramanna was framed . . . isn't that what you think?"

The detective nodded.

"As soon as Ahsha gets back," said Ahmeni, "I'll be able to clear Serramanna without waiting for the real culprit to be arrested. Do you have any leads?"

"There were no signs of struggle at the murder scene. Lilia probably knew her attacker."

"Where did you find her?"

"In a house at the edge of the warehouse district."

"Who owns it?"

"It was unoccupied and the neighbors couldn't tell me anything."

"I can probably trace it through the tax rolls. Didn't the neighbors notice anything suspicious?"

"One half-blind old lady claims to have seen a man leave

the house in the middle of the night, but she can't give a description other than that he was short."

"Do we have a list of Lilia's men friends?"

"No hope of finding out. It's even possible that Serramanna was the first big fish she'd landed."

Nefertari was savoring a long, warm shower. Her eyes closed, she sensed the moment of Ramses' return growing nearer and nearer. His absence had felt like torture.

The maidservants gently rubbed her with purifying ashes and natron. After a final rinse, the queen stretched out on a platform of heated tiles and a masseuse kneaded her with a pomade of turpentine, oil, and lemon juice, which would keep her body smelling sweet all day long.

Dreamily, Nefertari watched the beauticians give her a manicure and a pedicure. Next came the makeup artist, rimming her eyes with a soft green paint that both enhanced and protected them. Since Ramses was due to arrive shortly, the queen's magnificent hair was treated with special oil scented with rare balsamic resins. Then the beautician offered Nefertari a polished bronze mirror, its handle in the shape of a naked woman, the earthly representation of Hathor's celestial beauty.

All that remained was to put on her human hair wig, curled in back and with two large plaits reaching all the way down to her breasts. Once again, Nefertari looked in the mirror and was pleased.

"If I may say so," murmured the hairdresser, "Your Majesty has never been lovelier."

The handmaidens dressed her in an immaculate linen dress, fresh from the palace weavers.

The queen had barely had time to sit down, testing the seams of the delicate garment, when a yellow dog with a short and powerful build, floppy ears, corkscrew tail, and short black muzzle jumped on her lap—a dog bounding in from the just-watered garden, splattering mud on the queen's new dress.

Horrified, a lady-in-waiting grabbed a flyswatter and made toward the animal.

"Don't touch him," ordered Nefertari. "It's Watcher, Ramses' dog. He's trying to tell me something."

A velvety pink tongue slobbered kisses on the queen's cheeks, smearing her makeup. Watcher's trusting eyes gave her a look full of indescribable joy.

"Ramses will be home tomorrow, won't he?"

Watcher put his paws on the straps of her dress and wagged his tail for all he was worth.

TWENTY-TWO

Lookouts at the border forts and outposts flashed the message: Ramses was on his way.

Pi-Ramses was full of commotion. From the area around the temple of Ra to the workshops near the port, from the villas of government officials to the dwellings of ordinary folk, from the palace to the warehouses, everyone scurried to complete preparations for the sovereign's much-awaited return.

Romay, the chief steward, wore a short wig to conceal his increasing baldness. Forty-eight hours without sleep had done nothing for his temper. His subordinates were all too slow and too sloppy. For the royal table alone, he would need hundreds of roasted quarters of beef, several dozen grilled geese, two hundred baskets of bread and dried fish, fifty vats of cream, and a hundred platters of pickled fish, not to mention side dishes. The wine must be of the highest quality, and beers would be brewed especially for the occasion. A thousand banquets would have to be organized in the city's various neighborhoods so that on this day of days even the humblest would share in the king's glory and Egypt's good fortune. The slightest hitch, and fingers would be pointed at Romay.

He reread the scroll with details of the latest shipment: a thousand loaves of bread in fancy shapes, made from finely milled flour; two thousand crusty golden rolls; twenty thousand pastries dripping with honey and carob juice, studded with raisins; three hundred fifty-two sacks of grapes to be set out in dishes; a hundred twelve crates of pomegranates; ditto for figs.

"Here he is!" exclaimed the wine steward.

Standing on the kitchen roof, a scullion waved broadly.

"It can't be!"

"Yes, it's him!"

The scullion jumped down from the roof, the wine steward ran toward the capital's main thoroughfare.

"Stay here," bellowed Romay.

In less than a minute, the palace kitchens and storerooms

were deserted. Romay collapsed on a three-legged stool. No
one was left to arrange all those grapes artistically.

He shone.

His titles proclaimed him the sun, the powerful bull, the
protector of Egypt and conqueror of foreign lands, the king
of resounding victories, the chosen son of the divine light.

He was Ramses.

In a golden crown, wearing silver armor and a gold-
trimmed kilt, holding a bow in his left hand and a sword in
his right, he stood erect on the platform of a lily-trimmed
chariot, driven by Ahsha. Fighter, the Nubian lion with his
blazing mane, kept pace with the horses.

Ramses' beauty combined both might and radiance. He
was the ultimate expression of what a pharaoh should be.

The crowd squeezed along either side of the long pro-
cessional route leading to the temple of Amon. Laden with
flowers, scented with perfumed oils, musicians and singers
celebrated the king's return with a hymn of welcome. "The
heart rejoices at the sight of Ramses," they sang. People jos-
tled against one another, competing for even the briefest
glimpse of the monarch.

On the threshold of the holy place stood Nefertari, the
Great Royal Wife, Light of Egypt, Sweet of Voice, Lady of
the Two Lands. She wore a twin-plumed crown and a
golden collar complete with a lapis lazuli scarab inscribed
with the secrets of resurrection. She held a cubit rule,
symbol of Ma'at, the goddess of justice.

When Ramses stepped down from his chariot, a hush
fell over the crowd.

The king walked slowly toward the queen, stopping ten paces in front of her. Letting go of his bow and sword, he placed his right hand over his heart, fist tight.

"Who are you," came the ritual question, "who dare to contemplate Ma'at?"

"I am the Son of Light, heir to the testament of the gods. It is I who vouchsafe justice and level the inequities between the weak and the strong. It is I who shield Egypt from harm, from within as well from without."

"Have you observed the law of Ma'at while journeying far from the land she rules?"

"I have, and I lay my acts before her, that she may judge me. Thus may my country be solidly grounded in truth."

"Let the goddess acknowledge your rectitude."

Nefertari raised the golden cubit, glinting in the sun.

A long cheer went up from the crowd. Even Shaanar, captivated, could not help murmuring his brother's name.

In the open forecourt of the temple of Amon, only the notables of Pi-Ramses were admitted, anxious for the ceremony to begin. Medals would be awarded, the Gold of Valor. Whom would Pharaoh decorate, what promotions would he grant? Several names were circulating. A few bets had even been placed.

When the king and queen were seen in the Window of Appearance, the assembled dignitaries held their breath. The generals occupied the front row, eyeing one another suspiciously.

Two fan bearers were on hand to accompany the chosen few to the Window of Appearance. For once, no one knew what to expect. Even the court insiders were out of the loop.

"The first to be honored is the bravest member of my armed forces," declared Ramses. "He was always ready to risk his life for his pharaoh's. Step forward, Fighter."

The crowd parted in terror, letting the lion through. He actually seemed to enjoy having all eyes on him as he loped toward the Window. Ramses leaned forward, patted the beast's great head, and placed a thin gold chain around his neck, establishing the lion as a high-ranking court personality. Sphinx-like, Fighter lay down.

The king whispered two more names in the fan bearers' ears. Walking gingerly around the lion, they marched past the row of generals, then the ranking officers, then the scribes, and asked Setau and Lotus to follow them. The snake charmer balked, but his wife took him by the hand.

The glowing Nubian beauty turned every head, while Setau, in his working attire of an antelope-skin overall, made a less favorable impression.

"I now honor those who cared for the wounded and saved countless lives," said Ramses. "Thanks to the efforts of these two, brave men survived their suffering and returned home alive."

Bending forward once again, the king placed several golden bracelets around his friends' wrists. Lotus was thrilled, while her husband muttered protests.

"I entrust the directorship of the palace laboratory to Setau and Lotus," added Ramses. "Their mission will be to develop remedies from snake venom and provide for their nationwide distribution."

"I'd rather keep my place in the desert," grumbled the snake charmer.

"Are you sorry you'll see us more often?" inquired Nefertari.

The queen's smile melted his defenses. "Your Majesty..."

"Your presence at the palace, Setau, will be an honor for the court."

Setau flushed in embarrassment. "As Your Majesty wishes."

The generals, somewhat shocked, carefully refrained from critical remarks. They had all had occasion to consult Setau or his wife for help with poor digestion, labored breathing, or some other minor problem. The pair had fulfilled their duties correctly during the campaign. And although the ranking officers viewed their reward as excessive, they had to admit it was not undeserved.

It remained to be seen which of the generals would be singled out for the post of commander-in-chief of the Egyptian army, answering directly to Ramses. The stakes were high, for the choice of appointee would indicate the king's political intentions. Selecting the senior general would be a sign of passivity and retreat, while naming the head of the cavalry would mean war was still brewing.

The two fan bearers now flanked Ahsha. Well bred, well dressed, and supremely at ease, the young diplomat looked respectfully up at the royal couple.

"I honor you, my noble and faithful friend," declared Ramses, "because your advice has been invaluable. You, too, were always prepared to face danger. You convinced me to alter my plans when the situation required. Our country is once again at peace, but the peace remains tenuous. We surprised the rebels with the swiftness of our response, but we have yet to deal with the Hittites, the real instigators. Yes, we have reorganized the garrisons of our fortresses in Canaan and left troops in the province of Amurru, most vulnerable to enemy reprisals. We still must coordinate defense efforts in our protectorates to forestall any future sedition. I entrust this mission to Ahsha. Henceforth, Egypt's security is largely in his hands."

Ahsha bowed. Ramses draped three golden collars around his neck. The young diplomat had achieved the status of elder statesman.

The generals were unanimously bitter. An inexperienced bureaucrat had no business taking on such a difficult assignment. The king was making a grave mistake. His lack of faith in the military establishment was unpardonable.

Shaanar would be losing his right-hand man at the Finance Ministry, but he would gain a precious ally with broad powers. Naming his friend to this post would be Ramses' undoing. As far as Shaanar was concerned, the high point of the ceremony was the knowing look he exchanged with Ahsha.

Ramses had a promise to keep. He left the temple, taking Watcher and Fighter along in his chariot. The old playmates were delighted to be back together.

Homer seemed rejuvenated. In the shade of his lemon tree, he was pitting dates, as Hector, his meat-loving black and white cat, looked on disdainfully.

"Sorry I didn't make it to the ceremony, Your Majesty. My old legs won't hold me up for long anymore. Glad to find you looking so healthy, though."

"I came to find that flask of date beer with my name on it."

In the hush of evening, the two men sipped Homer's delectable brew.

"You don't know what a rare pleasure this is for me, Homer—believing for a moment that I'm an ordinary man, enjoying a quiet drink without a care in the world. How is your *Iliad* coming?"

"Like my memory, it's strewn with slaughter, corpses, lost friendships, and bickering gods. The lives of men are shaped by human folly."

"The war my people feared has not broken out after all. Our protectorates are once again under our wing, and I hope to hammer a permanent wedge between us and the Hittites."

"Wise words from a ruler as young and impetuous as you! Could you possibly combine the political skills of a Priam with the valor of an Achilles?"

"I'm convinced that the Hittites are sick over my victory. This peace is only a truce. Tomorrow, the fate of the world will be played out at Kadesh."

"How can such a fine evening contain the promise of such a tomorrow? The gods are cruel."

"Will you be my guest at the banquet tonight?"

"As long as you get me home early. At my age, sleep is the best medicine."

"Have you ever dreamed there was no more war?"

"My aim in writing the *Iliad* is to depict war in its true colors, to show how repulsive man's destructive urges really are. But will generals listen to the voice of a poet?"

TWENTY-THREE

Tuya's huge, almond-shaped eyes, stern and piercing, softened at the sight of Ramses. Proud and striking in her perfectly cut linen gown, belted with a striped sash reaching almost to her ankles, she took a long look at the Pharaoh.

"Not a scratch on you, really?"

"Do you think I'd be able to hide it from you if I was wounded? You look wonderful, Mother."

"Even the best makeup artists can't hide the wrinkles on my forehead and neck anymore."

"You still seem younger than your years."

"Seti's strength is still with me, perhaps. But my youth is only a memory, a foreign land with me as its sole inhabitant. Why dwell on the past when tonight is a joyful occasion? I'll take my place at your banquet, you can be sure."

The king held his mother in his arms. "You're the soul of Egypt."

"No, Ramses, I'm only its conscience, the reflection of a past you must honor. Egypt's soul is you and Nefertari. Have you made a lasting peace, my son?"

"Peace, yes; lasting, no. I reasserted our authority over the provinces, including Amurru, but the Hittite backlash promises to be violent."

"You considered attacking Kadesh, did you not?"

"Yes, but Ahsha talked me out of it."

"He was right. It was one war your father decided not to fight, knowing how heavy our losses would be."

"But haven't times changed? Kadesh is a threat we can't tolerate much longer."

"Our guests are waiting, Ramses."

Not one false note marred the sumptuous banquet. Ramses, Nefertari, and Tuya presided, while Romay scurried from the banquet hall to the kitchens, the kitchens to the banquet hall, checking each dish, tasting each sauce, and taking a swig of every wine.

Ahsha, Setau, and Lotus were at the head table. The young diplomat's brilliant conversation had won over two crusty generals. Lotus collected compliments, while Setau concentrated on the alabaster plate continually refilled with tasty dishes. The aristocracy and the fighting class shared an evening of relaxation, safe from storms brewing on the horizon.

Finally, Ramses and Nefertari were alone in their bedchamber, a vast palace room filled with the scent of a dozen bouquets. The fragrance of jasmine and galingale dominated.

"Is this what it means to be king, having to steal a few hours with the woman you love?"

"You were away so long—too long."

They lay down on the huge bed, shoulder to shoulder, hand in hand, savoring the pleasure of being together again.

"It's strange," she said. "It was torture having you gone from me, but I thought your thoughts. Each day when I went to celebrate the morning rites, your image came out of the wall and your hand guided me."

"During the worst moments of this campaign, your face never left me. I felt you around me, like the wind in the wings of Isis when she brings Osiris back to life."

"Magic brought us together, and nothing should be able to keep us apart."

"Do you have any doubts?"

"Sometimes I feel a cold shadow . . . it comes close, recedes, comes back again, and fades."

"If there is such a shadow, I'll destroy it. For now, let me look in your eyes, at that sweet light burning for me."

Ramses shifted onto his side and admired Nefertari's perfect body. He undid her hair, slipped the straps of her gown off her shoulders, and undressed her slowly, so slowly that she shivered.

"Are you cold, my darling?"

"You're still too far from me."

He turned her and melded his form with hers, merging their desire.

At six o'clock in the morning, after showering and rinsing his mouth with natron, Ahmeni headed for his office and ordered a breakfast of barley porridge, yogurt, farmer's cheese, and figs. Ramses' secretary ate quickly, his eyes glued to a scroll. The sound of leather sandals on the tile floor startled him. His staff was instructed not to arrive so early. Ahmeni wiped his mouth and prepared to investigate.

"Ramses!"

"Why weren't you at the banquet last night?"

"Just look! I've been swamped. My files seem to be reproducing in captivity. And then I don't much care for society, as you know. I planned to ask for an audience with you this morning to fill you in on the interim measures I've taken."

"I'm sure they're excellent."

A smile flickered across Ahmeni's serious face. Ramses' trust was what he treasured most in the world.

"Tell me . . . why are you here so early?"

"Because of Serramanna."

"That was the first thing I intended to discuss with you."

"We missed him in the field. You were the one who first accused him of treason, weren't you?"

"The evidence seemed indisputable, but . . ."

"Yes?"

"I've reopened the investigation."

"Why?"

"I have the feeling I was manipulated. And the evidence against Serramanna looks less and less solid. The girlfriend who accused him, a strumpet by the name of Lilia, was murdered recently. As for his alleged correspondence with the Hittites, I've been itching to have Ahsha take a look at it."

"Then why don't we go wake him up?"

Ahsha's suspicions regarding Ahmeni had been laid to rest—one satisfaction that the king planned on keeping to himself.

Cool milk sweetened with honey awakened Ahsha, who packed his bedmate off to enjoy the ministrations of his masseur and hairdresser.

"If it wasn't Your Majesty here in person," confessed the diplomat, "I wouldn't have the courage to open my eyes."

"Open your ears, too," urged Ramses.

"Don't you and your secretary ever sleep?"

"Wouldn't you get up early to save a man rotting in jail for a crime he may not have committed?" countered Ahmeni.

"Who are you talking about?"

"Serramanna."

"But weren't you the one—"

"Take a look at these tablets, please."

Ahsha rubbed his eyes and read the messages Serramanna had supposedly written to his Hittite contact, promising to keep his elite commandos away from the enemy if ever they met in battle.

"Is this a joke?"

"Why do you say that?"

"Because all the luminaries at the Hittite court are sticklers for procedure, even in secret correspondence. There would have to be an exchange of formalities before letters like these could reach Hattusa. Serramanna would have no idea how to go about it."

"So someone must have imitated his handwriting."

"It wouldn't be difficult; he's hardly a scribe like you. And I'm convinced that these letters were never even sent."

Ramses took a turn examining the tablets.

"Isn't one clue obvious?"

Ahsha and Ahmeni stared at the evidence.

"For graduates of the royal academy, you aren't especially observant."

"It's just that it's so early," Ahsha said lamely. "But I do see what you mean. Whoever wrote this must be a Syrian. Fluent in Egyptian, of course, but the phrasing here"—he pointed—"and here is typically Syrian."

"I agree," said Ahmeni. "I'm sure it's the same man who paid Lilia to make her accusations. He was afraid she might talk and decided he'd have to get rid of her."

"What kind of man would kill a woman?" asked Ahsha in disgust.

"There are hundreds of Syrians in Egypt," Ramses pointed out.

"Let's hope he's made a mistake, one simple little mistake," said Ahmeni. "I'm investigating, and if there's a lead, I'll find it."

"This criminal may be more than a murderer," suggested Ramses.

"What do you mean?" asked Ahsha.

"A Syrian with links to the Hittites . . . does this mean a spy network is operating within our borders?"

"Nothing demonstrates a direct link between the Hittites and whoever tried to frame Serramanna."

Ahmeni lit into Ahsha. "You're only saying that because your pride is wounded. You're the head of our intelligence services and you've just learned something you'd rather not have to admit."

"Today isn't getting off to a good start," said the diplomat, "and the next few days are bound to be crucial."

"Find this Syrian as fast as you can," ordered Ramses.

In his cell, Serramanna followed his personal drill, loudly maintaining his innocence and pounding on the wall with his fists. When he was brought to trial, he'd bash in the heads of his accusers, whoever they might be. His rage so terrified the jailers that they kept clear of him, handing food through the thick wooden bars of his cell.

When the cell door finally swung open, the giant's first impulse was to charge the intruder.

"Your Majesty!"

"A few months behind bars haven't done you much harm, Serramanna."

"I never betrayed your trust!"

"It was all a mistake, and I've come to free you."

"I'm really going to get out of this cage?"

"Do you doubt the word of your king?"

"You still . . . trust me?"

"You're the head of my bodyguard."

"Then, Your Majesty, I'll tell you everything. All I've learned, all I suspect, and all the reasons that someone needed to have me locked up."

TWENTY-FOUR

As Ramses, Ahmeni, and Ahsha looked on, Serramanna wolfed down his meal. Comfortably seated in the palace dining room, he worked his way through pigeon pie, grilled beef, beans simmered with goose fat, cucumbers in sour cream, watermelon, and goat cheese. He ate steadily, barely pausing to gulp down the strong red wine he drank straight.

Full at last, he glared at Ahmeni. "Why did you throw me in jail, scribe?"

"My deepest apologies. Not only was I deceived, I also made the mistake of acting in haste, because of the army's imminent departure. My only intention was to protect the king."

"Apologies . . . wait until you're locked up, and you'll see what they count for. Tell me, what's happened to Lilia?"

"Dead," replied Ahmeni. "Murdered."

"Can't say I'm sorry. Who paid her to put me out of commission?"

"We don't know, but we plan to find out."

"I know." The Sard took another swallow of wine and dabbed at his curling mustache. "Your Majesty, I tried to warn you," he said sententiously. "When Ahmeni arrested me, I was preparing to make a certain number of revelations I feared might displease you."

"We're listening, Serramanna."

"The man who wanted me out of the way, Your Majesty, was Romay, your new steward. When the scorpion turned up in your stateroom,* I suspected Setau, but I was wrong. Your friend cared for me when I was sick, and I found out then what manner of man he is. There's not a dishonest bone in his body. Romay, on the other hand, is a sneak. Who else would have had the opportunity to steal Nefertari's shawl? And he must have been responsible for the dried fish disappearing from the House of Life as well."

"But what was his motive?"

"I have no idea."

---

*Ramses, Volume II: The Eternal Temple.

"Ahmeni insists I have nothing to fear from Romay."

"Ahmeni isn't infallible," the Sard retorted sharply. "He was wrong about me, and he's making a mistake about your chief steward as well."

"I'll question Romay myself," announced Ramses. "Do you still want to take his part, Ahmeni?"

The scribe shook his head to say no.

"Any more revelations, Serramanna?"

"Yes, Your Majesty."

"Concerning whom?"

"Your friend Moses. There's no room for doubt about him. Since I'm still in charge of your security, I might as well be the one to tell you."

The grim expression on Ramses' face would have been enough to silence most men. Steeling himself with another gulp of wine, Serramanna forged ahead.

"To me, Moses is a turncoat and an instigator. His goal was to lead his people and found an independent Hebrew state in the Delta. He may still have some friendship for you, but in the end, if he's still alive, he'll be your most ruthless enemy."

Ahmeni was prepared for an outburst from Ramses, but the king remained strangely calm.

"Is this guesswork or the result of an investigation?"

"As thorough an investigation as I could manage. Furthermore, I learned that Moses had several contacts with a foreigner posing as an architect. This man came to encourage him, even offer his aid. Your Hebrew friend was at the heart of a plot against Egypt."

"Have you identified this mysterious architect?"

"Ahmeni didn't leave me time."

"Let's put that behind us, Serramanna. You were treated unfairly, but now we need to join forces."

Ahmeni and Serramanna eyed each other reluctantly. After a long pause, they shook hands, and Ahmeni thought he might never write again.

"I can't think of a worse scenario," the king resumed. "Moses is a stubborn man; if your information is correct, Serramanna, he'll never give up. But today who knows what ideal he worships? Does he even know himself? Before we accuse him of high treason, we need to find him."

"This so-called architect seems highly suspect," said Ahsha, intrigued. "I'd like to know who's behind him."

"We need to shed light on a number of questionable areas before reaching any conclusions," recommended Ahmeni.

Ramses laid a hand on the Sard's broad shoulder. "Your frankness is a rare quality, Serramanna. Don't ever lose it."

In the week that followed Ramses' triumphant return, Shaanar, as secretary of state, had nothing but good news to report to his brother. The Hittites had lodged no official protest and seemed to be taking the situation lying down. The Egyptian army's show of force made them decide to keep observing the pact of nonaggression imposed by Seti.

Before Ahsha left on his tour of the protectorates, he was the guest of honor at one of Shaanar's famous banquets. Seated to the right of his host, the young diplomat was enjoying the entertainment—three dancing girls, naked except for colored wisps of cloth around their waists that did nothing to hide the jet-black triangle below.

They moved gracefully to the changing rhythms their pretty accompanists played on a harp, three flutes, and an oboe.

"Which one would you like for the night, Ahsha?" Shaanar inquired unctuously.

"This may shock you, Shaanar, but I've spent an exhausting week with a sex-starved widow. All I want tonight is twelve hours' sleep before I head out for Canaan and Amurru."

"Thanks to the music and my talkative guests, you and I can say anything we want."

"I no longer work for the State Department, but I don't suppose you're disappointed with my new mission."

"It couldn't have turned out better if we'd planned it ourselves."

"Oh yes, Shaanar. Ramses could have been killed, maimed, or dishonored."

"I've always known he was a born warrior, but I had no idea that he was such a strategist. When you think about it, this was only a relative victory. Besides taking back the provinces, what has he accomplished? The Hittites' failure to respond has me puzzled."

"They're taking stock of the situation. Once the shock has passed, they'll strike back."

"How do you plan to proceed, Ahsha?"

"By giving me carte blanche in the protectorates, Ramses has played into our hands. While I'm supposedly reorganizing our defensive system, I'll really be dismantling it bit by bit."

"What if you're exposed?"

"I've already persuaded Ramses to keep the princes of Canaan and Amurru where they are. They're both crooked characters who'll sell themselves to the highest bidder. It will be easy for me to nudge them into the Hittite camp, eliminating the buffer Ramses is always talking about."

"Be careful, Ahsha. You're playing for very high stakes."

"We'll never win if we aren't prepared to take risks. The hardest part will be anticipating the Hittites' strategy. Fortunately, that's my specialty."

An immense empire stretching from Nubia to Anatolia, an empire that he would rule—Shaanar could scarcely conceive of it, but his dream was little by little becoming reality. Ramses' choice of friends was his downfall. There was Moses, a murderer and instigator; Ahsha, a traitor; and Setau, a limited eccentric. That left Ahmeni, loyal and straight as an arrow but without ambition.

"We'll have to drag Ramses into a war he can't win," continued Ahsha. "He'll be the shame of Egypt, and you'll appear as the savior. That's our mandate, and we mustn't forget you."

"Has Ramses given you any other instructions?"

"Yes, he wants me to find Moses for him. You know how greatly he values friendship. Even if the Sard thinks the Hebrew is guilty of high treason, Pharaoh won't believe it until he hears it straight from Moses' own mouth."

"Has anyone found a trace of him?"

"No definite sightings. Either he's died of thirst in the desert, or else he's hiding out with one of the tribes roaming the Sinai and Negev deserts. There are hundreds of them. But if he turns up in Canaan or Amurru, I'll catch him in the end."

"If he turns up as the head of a rebel faction, he could be of use to us."

"One thing bothers me," revealed Ahsha. "According to Serramanna, Moses was in contact with a mysterious stranger."

"Here, in Pi-Ramses?"

"Yes, here."

"Does anyone know who this man was?"

"Only that he looked like a foreigner and was passing himself off as an architect."

Shaanar tried to hide his alarm. Ofir had been spotted! The sorcerer remained an unknown quantity, of course, a mere shadow, but he was becoming a potential threat. Even the hint of a connection to him would be fatal, since practicing black magic against the Pharaoh was a capital offense.

"Ramses is adamant about finding this stranger," added Ahsha.

"Probably some illegal Hebrew immigrant. He could be the one who led Moses into exile. I'll wager that both of them are gone for good."

"I agree. Ahmeni is pursuing the matter, though, and he'll give it his best try, especially after his fiasco with Serramanna."

"Do you think Serramanna will forgive him?"

"He seems more likely to hold a grudge."

"They say he was framed?" Shaanar ventured.

"Some Syrian paid a prostitute to plant the evidence, apparently. Later he killed her to keep her quiet. It's also certain that a Syrian forged Serramanna's handwriting on the tablets that were supposed to prove he was a Hittite spy. A clever ploy, though rather too easy to see through."

Shaanar was finding it difficult to stay cool. "Which means . . ." he said blandly.

"Which means there's a flourishing spy ring here in Egypt."

Raia, the Syrian merchant, Shaanar's key contact, was also in danger. And Ahsha, his other major partner, was intent on tracking Raia down!

"I'll have the State Department pursue the investigation, if you like," he offered smoothly.

"Ahmeni and I will take care of it. It's better to move cautiously so as not to alarm our prey."

Shaanar took a healthy swallow of white Delta wine. Ahsha would never know what a valuable service he was providing.

"I can tell you about one major figure that's in for some serious trouble," the young diplomat told him, amused.

"Who?"

"Romay, that big man who runs the palace with an iron hand. Serramanna has been watching him, and he's convinced that Romay should be in prison."

Shaanar felt punch-drunk, like a fighter who'd suffered one blow too many, yet he managed a blithe smile.

He'd have to move quickly, very quickly, to stay out of the gathering storm.

TWENTY-FIVE

The end of the annual inundation was fast approaching. The peasants had refurbished the plows they would hitch to a pair of oxen and use to dig shallow furrows in the loose river silt. Since this year's flood level had been ideal, neither too high nor too low, the irrigation experts had plenty of water in reserve for the dry season. The gods smiled on Ramses. Once again this year, the granaries were bursting and the Pharaoh's people would eat their fill.

Romay, the palace steward, could not appreciate the mild late October weather, cooled by an occasional squall. The more he fretted, the more he ate. With his troubles growing by leaps and bounds, Romay's increasing girth made it difficult to keep up his frantic pace. From time to time he was forced to sit down and catch his breath.

Serramanna was keeping him under constant surveillance. When he couldn't tail Romay personally, he sent one of his brawny henchmen. They were easy enough to pick out in the palace corridors or around the market stalls where the chief steward still insisted on selecting all the ingredients for the royal kitchens.

Once Romay would have taken pleasure in composing a new recipe from lotus root, bitter lupine boiled in several changes of water, zucchini, garbanzo beans, garlic, almonds, and tidbits of grilled perch; now even this delightful prospect failed to make him forget he was a hunted man.

Since his acquittal, the giant bodyguard had been overstepping his bounds. But Romay could not protest. When your heart is heavy and your conscience troubled, peace of mind is a rare commodity.

Serramanna had a pirate's patience, waiting to pounce on the first false move from the puffy, black-hearted steward. His instincts hadn't failed him: for months he had suspected the man of spinelessness, the fatal flaw that leads to the worst betrayals. Although he had gained a high position, Romay had not proved immune to greed. He craved riches as well as the small measure of power he wielded.

The constant surveillance was taking its toll on the steward's nerves. Eventually he'd crack under pressure, perhaps even come forward of his own accord.

As Serramanna expected, Romay hadn't gone to the king with complaints about being watched. If he were innocent, he wouldn't hesitate to do so, a fact the Sard stressed in his daily reports to Ramses.

After several days of this treatment, the bodyguard would ask his men to take over Romay's surveillance, but remain out of sight. In his relief, Romay might rush to confide in his partner in crime—the one who had bribed him to steal in the first place.

The bodyguard reported to Ahmeni's office well after nightfall. The secretary was putting away the day's scrolls in a large sycamore cabinet.

"Anything new, Serramanna?"

"Not yet. Romay is tougher than I would have thought."

"Are you still mad at me, Serramanna?"

"Well . . . what you put me through is hard to forget."

"It would do no good to offer my apologies again, so let me offer you something better. Come have a look at the tax rolls with me."

"Are you officially involving me in your investigation?"

"Exactly."

"My anger is melting away like a bad dream. Let's get going."

The bureaucrats in charge of the Pi-Ramses tax rolls were so meticulous that it had taken them several months to reach the same production levels as the Memphis branch. Getting used to a new capital, making a record of properties and buildings, and identifying the owners and tenants all demanded a great deal of verification. That was why Ahmeni's request, though classified as urgent, had taken so long to fulfill.

Serramanna noted that the director of the department, a thin, bald man over sixty, looked even more sickly than Ahmeni. His pasty complexion was proof that he was a stranger to sunshine and fresh air. The bureaucrat welcomed them with chilly formality and led them through a maze of stacked wooden tablets and pigeonholed papyrus scrolls.

"Thank you for seeing us at this late hour," said Ahmeni.

"I guessed you'd require the strictest secrecy."

"You were right."

"I hope you don't mind my admitting that your request made extra work for us, but we finally did identify the owner of the property in question."

"Who is it?"

"A merchant from Memphis called Renouf."

"Do you know his home address?"

"He lives in a villa south of the old town."

Pedestrians scattered in every direction as Serramanna's two-horse chariot sped through the streets. Ahmeni, feeling queasy, squeezed his eyes shut. The vehicle clattered on to the newly built bridge from Ramses' capital to the old city of Avaris. The wheels creaked, the carriage rattled, but the chariot made it across.

It was a neighborhood where handsome villas set in elaborate gardens stood next to modest two-story houses. Some inhabitants, feeling the chill of the autumn evening, had lit a fire of kindling or dried mud.

"Here it is," said Serramanna.

Ahmeni had trouble letting go of the leather strap he'd been clutching on the ride.

"Are you feeling all right?"

"Fine, fine."

"Let's go, then! We may be able to wrap the investigation up tonight, if our man's at home."

Ahmeni clambered out and followed the Sard, weak-kneed.

Renouf's doorman was sitting by the gateway in a rough brick wall trimmed with flowering vines. He was eating some bread and cheese.

"We're here to see the merchant Renouf," said Serramanna.

"He's not at home."

"Where can we find him?"

"He's left for the south."

"When do you expect him back?"

"Don't know."

"Is there anyone here who could tell us?"

"Don't think so."

"Send for us as soon as he returns."

"Why should I?"

Glowering, Serramanna grabbed the doorman under the arms and dragged him to his feet.

"Because we have orders from Pharaoh. And if you delay even one minute, you'll answer to me."

Shaanar was suffering from insomnia and heartburn. He needed to go to Memphis as soon as possible to catch up with Raia and confer with Ofir. The secretary of state could not make a trip to the former capital without a valid reason; as it happened, there were several administrative matters requiring his attention in Memphis. It was therefore in the name of Pharaoh that Shaanar began an official voyage on a boat much slower than he would have liked.

Either Ofir would have to silence Romay, or else Shaanar would be forced to sever his ties with the sorcerer prematurely, before his spell was complete.

Shaanar was glad he'd kept his allies compartmentalized, a strategy that was paying off at present. A wily diplomat like Ahsha would hardly appreciate uncovering the prince's links to a pro-Hittite spy network. A professional agent like Raia, convinced he was manipulating the Pharaoh's brother, would surely be offended to find that Shaanar was only using the Hittites. As for Ofir, it was preferable that he remain ensconced in the occult.

Ahsha, Raia, Ofir. Three balls Shaanar could juggle in the air until his future was assured—providing they never collided.

On the first day of his stay in Memphis, Shaanar held audiences with the officials he needed to consult with; in the evening, he planned to give one of his famous banquets. He also asked his steward to send for Raia, who might be able to supply him with some new collectible vases.

As the sun went down in the prince's garden, his guests drifted back into the mansion.

"The vase merchant is here," announced his steward.

If he'd been a religious man, Shaanar would have thanked the gods. Feigning indifference, he headed toward the gatehouse.

The man who greeted him there was not Raia.

"Who are you?"

"The manager of Raia's shop in Memphis."

"Ah. The owner usually comes himself."

"He's left for Thebes and Elephantine to arrange for a shipment of fine victuals, but I do have some items that might interest you in the meantime."

"Show me what you brought."

Shaanar studied the vases. "I've seen better. Still, I'll take these two, I suppose."

"The price is very reasonable, Your Highness."

Shaanar did the customary bargaining and let his steward pay for the vases. Returning to his guests, he smiled and chatted with practiced ease, though his mind was elsewhere.

"You're looking lovely," he greeted his sister, Dolora.

The languid brunette was enjoying the attentions of a group of empty-headed young noblemen.

"And you've outdone yourself, Shaanar."

He gave her his arm and led her out to the covered walkway adjoining the banquet hall.

"I must see Ofir tomorrow morning. And tell him not to go out on any account. He's in danger."

TWENTY-SIX

Dolora herself answered the door to her villa.
Shaanar looked behind him. No, he hadn't been followed.

"Come in, Shaanar."

"All quiet?"

"Yes, don't worry. Ofir's experiment is moving forward,"
his sister assured him. "Lita is giving her all, but her health
is fragile and we mustn't hurry the process. What's so
urgent?"

"Is your wizard awake?"

"I'll go get him."

"Watch out for yourself with Ofir, little sister."

"He's a wonderful man who serves the One God, and
he's sure you're the key to the future."

"Please tell him I'm waiting. There's not much time."

Dressed in a flowing black robe, the Libyan sorcerer
bowed to the prince.

"You must leave this place today, Ofir."

"What's happened, Your Highness?"

"You were seen talking with Moses in Pi-Ramses."

"Could the witnesses give a description?"

"Nothing too detailed, but now the investigators are on the lookout for a foreigner who was posing as an architect."

"That's not much to go on, Your Highness. I can blend in when it's necessary."

"You took an unnecessary risk."

"Personal contact with Moses was indispensable. It may still bring results in the long run."

"Ramses came back safe and sound from his expedition in the protectorates. He wants to find Moses and the man who spoke with him. If you can be identified, you'll be brought in for questioning."

Ofir's smile made Shaanar's blood run cold.

"Do you think a man like me can be arrested?"

"You may have made one fatal error," the prince said ominously.

"What was that?"

"Trusting Romay."

"Why do you think we're connected in any way?"

"On your orders, he stole Nefertari's shawl and the fish from the House of Life in Heliopolis—the material you needed for your spell."

"Remarkable deduction, Your Highness. But you have one thing wrong: Romay did take the shawl, but a friend of his, a Memphis delivery man, brought me the fish."

"A delivery man? What if he talks?"

"The poor soul just passed away of a heart attack."

"Was it a . . . natural death?"

"All deaths are natural in the end, Your Highness, when the heart stops."

"That still leaves Romay. Serramanna is convinced of his guilt and is hounding him mercilessly. If Romay talks, the trail will lead back to you. And practicing black magic is a capital offense, especially casting spells on the royal person."

Ofir's slight smile never wavered. "Let's go into my laboratory."

The cavernous room was full of scrolls, bits of carved ivory, goblets full of colored substances and cords. Order prevailed, and there was a pleasant smell of incense. It felt more like a craftsman's studio or a scribe's office than a sorcerer's den.

Ofir stretched his hands out above a copper mirror on a three-legged stand. He poured water over the surface and beckoned Shaanar closer.

Slowly, a face appeared in the mirror.

"Romay!" exclaimed Shaanar.

"Romay the steward is a good man, but weak, greedy, and easily influenced. It took no special magic to work a spell on him. The theft he committed in spite of himself is eating away at him like acid."

"If Ramses questions him, Romay will talk."

"No, Your Highness."

Ofir's left hand traced a broad circle above the mirror. The water bubbled and a deep crack appeared in the copper.

Shaanar backed away in astonishment.

"Will that be enough to silence him?"

"Consider the problem solved. I doubt that there's any call for me to leave Memphis. This house is in your sister's name, is it not?"

"Yes."

"Everyone sees her come and go. Lita and I are her devoted servants and prefer to stay close to home. Until we've broken through the royal defenses, neither the girl nor I will leave this place."

"And your congregation?"

"Your sister serves as my liaison. For the time being, they're staying underground, awaiting a sign from Aton."

Shaanar departed, somewhat reassured. He had no use for religious fanatics and wished he could see Romay eliminated with his own eyes. He could only hope this mumbo jumbo worked.

Still, it was better to err on the side of caution.

The Nile was a marvelous river. Thanks to the strong current, Shaanar covered the distance between Memphis and Pi-Ramses in less than two days.

The king's older brother stopped at his office and called a quick meeting of his key staffers in which he was briefed on dispatches from abroad and reports from diplomats stationed in the protectorates. Then a litter took him to the palace as rain clouds gathered.

Pi-Ramses was a fine city, though without Memphis's patina and old-fashioned charm. When he took the throne, Shaanar would strip it of its status as capital, especially since it was Ramses' creation. For now, a cheerful bustle filled the streets, as if peace were eternal, as if the vast Hittite empire had disappeared into a bottomless pit. Shaanar momentarily acknowledged the attraction of this simple existence, in tune with the rhythm of the seasons. Perhaps he, like the entire population of Egypt, should let go and accept Ramses as his ruler.

But Shaanar was not a follower.

He had the makings of a king who would go down in history, a monarch with a vision far broader than that of

Ramses and his Hittite counterpart. His brainchild would be a new world, with him as its master.

Pharaoh did not keep his brother waiting. Ramses had just been conferring with Ahmeni, whose face had been lovingly washed by Watcher. The king's private secretary and the prince nodded coldly at each other. The yellow dog lay down in a patch of sunlight.

"Good trip, Shaanar?"

"Excellent. If you don't mind my saying so, I'm awfully fond of Memphis."

"Who could blame you? It's a special place, and Pi-Ramses will never be its equal. If the Hittite threat hadn't reached such proportions, I wouldn't have needed to create a new capital."

"The Memphis government remains a model of professionalism."

"The civil service is efficiently run here as well. Isn't your State Department a case in point?"

"I spare no effort, believe me. But there have been no disturbing messages, either official or officious. The Hittites are silent."

"What are our diplomats saying off the record?"

"That the enemy was stunned by your rapid strike. They had no idea the Egyptian army was so powerful and decisive."

"Hmm."

"Why doubt it? If the Hittites were so sure of their overwhelming superiority, they should have responded by now."

"I can't believe they plan to stay within the boundaries Seti established."

"Are you becoming a pessimist, Your Majesty?"

"The territorial imperative is the only thing the Hittites understand."

"But wouldn't Egypt be a bit much to handle, even for them?"

"I doubt they think so. Hatti lives to fight."

"Then we'll have to fight fire with fire."

"Are you suggesting intensive rearmament, Shaanar, and an increase in troop size?"

"What better solution?"

The patch of sunlight had vanished. Watcher jumped onto his master's knees.

"That would be tantamount to a dare," worried Ramses.

"There's only one language these people understand: the language of force. That's what you really think, too, if I'm not mistaken."

"I also want to consolidate our defenses in the north."

"Make our protectorates a buffer zone, I know . . . a tall order for your friend Ahsha, ambitious as he is."

"Am I expecting too much of him?"

"Ahsha is young. You've just decorated him and made him one of the most important figures in your administration. Such a rapid rise may go to his head. No one denies his talent, but shouldn't you be cautious?"

"The generals did feel passed over, I realize. But Ahsha is the man for the job."

"There's one minor detail I think I should mention. You know how the palace servants gossip. Most of it is just rumors, but once in a while I hear something of interest. Now, my steward is on very close terms with one of the queen's chambermaids, and he tells me this girl saw Romay leave the palace with that shawl of Nefertari's."

"Will she testify against him?"

"She's terrified of Romay, afraid of the repercussions if she accuses him."

"But this is Egypt. The goddess of justice rules."

"Perhaps you should try to make Romay confess first. Then the girl will corroborate his story."

Shaanar was taking chances, and he knew it. Criticizing Ahsha was dangerous; reporting Romay might lead Ramses too close to the truth. On the other hand, Shaanar was gaining credibility with the Pharaoh.

If Ofir's black magic failed to produce results, Shaanar would strangle him with his own hands.

TWENTY-SEVEN

Romay had found only one way to calm his mounting anxiety: inventing a new marinade recipe he'd name after Ramses, a recipe that would be handed down from master chef to apprentice. The steward shut himself up in the huge palace kitchen, where he could be alone. He had personally selected the mild garlic, top-quality onions, red oasis wine from a special vintage, vinegar spiced with the best salt from the land of Set, several kinds of aromatic herbs, fillets of tender Nile perch, and beef that was fit for the gods. The marinade would give the mixture an inimitable flavor that would delight the king. Then he just might remember how valuable his chief steward was to him.

Despite his request for the strictest privacy, someone was opening the kitchen door.

"I thought I said . . . Your Majesty! You don't belong in the kitchen!"

"Is any corner of my kingdom off limits to me?"

"That's not what I meant. Forgive me, I—"

"Am I allowed to taste this?"

"I'm still testing it. I want my marinade to be a recipe that goes down in the palace annals."

"Do you have a taste for secrecy, Romay?"

"No, no," he laughed. "But good cooking demands discretion. And I guard my creations closely, I'll admit that much."

"Is that all?"

Ramses loomed over Romay. The steward felt himself shrivel and lowered his gaze. "There's nothing mysterious about what I do, Your Majesty. My life is devoted to serving you, only to serving you."

"Are you so sure? Every man has his weaknesses, they say. What are yours?"

"I, well, I don't know. Overeating, certainly."

"Are you unhappy with your salary?"

"No, certainly not!"

"The office of chief steward is enviable and sought after, but it won't make a rich man of you."

"That's not my goal, I assure you."

"Who could resist a sizable reward in exchange for a few small favors?"

"I'd rather seek favor with you, Your Majesty."

"Don't lie to me, Romay. Do you recall that unfortunate incident when a scorpion was left under my pillow?"

"Thank goodness it never bit you!"

"You were promised that it wouldn't be fatal and that you could never be caught. Am I right?"

"No, Your Majesty. That's wrong, all wrong."

"You shouldn't have given in to temptation, Romay. Then you gave in again when you agreed to steal the queen's favorite old shawl. And it wouldn't surprise me to learn you were involved with the disappearance of the fish from Heliopolis."

"No, Your Majesty!"

"Someone saw you."

Romay couldn't breathe. Huge beads of sweat popped out on his forehead.

"That can't be . . ."

"Are you wicked, Romay, or merely the victim of circumstance?"

The steward felt a sharp pain in his chest. He wanted to tell the king everything, free himself of the nagging remorse.

He knelt, bumping his head on the edge of the table where his ingredients were laid out. "No, I'm not bad. I was weak, too weak. Forgive me, Your Majesty, I beg you."

"Only if you tell me the truth now, Romay."

Through a fog of pain, the fat man saw Ofir's face. The face of a vulture, with a hooked beak, digging through his skin and gnawing at his heart.

"Who ordered you to commit these evil deeds?"

Romay wanted to talk, but Ofir's name couldn't cross his lips. A sticky web of fear was smothering him, beckoning him to escape, to slip into nothingness.

Romay looked up at Ramses imploringly. His right hand clutched at the dish of marinade experiment, upending it. The spicy sauce trickled over the steward's face as he fell to the floor, stone dead.

"He's so big," said Kha, looking at Fighter, his father's lion.

"Are you afraid of him?"

At the age of nine, the Pharaoh's son with Iset the Fair was as serious as an old scribe. Childish pastimes bored him. All he wanted to do was read and write, spending the greater part of his time in the palace library.

"He scares me a little."

"You should be scared, Kha. Fighter is a very dangerous animal."

"But you're not afraid of him, because you're Pharaoh."

"This lion and I are old friends. When he was just a baby in Nubia, a snake bit him. I found him, my friend Setau helped him get better, and we've been together ever since. Not long ago, it was Fighter's turn to save my life."

"Is your lion always nice to you?"

"Yes, but only to me."

"Does he talk to you?"

"Yes, with his eyes, his tail, the sounds he makes . . . and he understands what I say to him."

"Can I pet his mane?"

Lying like a sphinx, the enormous lion observed the man and boy. He gave a throaty roar, making Kha cling tight to his father.

"Is he angry?"

"No, he'll let you touch him."

Emboldened by his father's reassurances, Kha approached the beast. His small hand stroked the thick mane haltingly at first, then steadily. The lion purred.

"Can I sit on his back?"

"No, Kha. Fighter is a proud, proud warrior. He's already granted you a special privilege. Don't ask too much of him."

"I'll write his story and tell it to my sister, Meritamon. It's a good thing she stayed in the palace garden with the queen. A little girl like her would be scared of such a tremendous lion."

Ramses gave his son a new scribe's palette and brush case. The boy was enchanted with the present and eager to try the new implements at once. Soon he was lost in his writing. The king did nothing to disturb his son. To Ramses, these quiet moments were a gift, especially since he was haunted by the still-fresh memory of his steward's frightful death. The skin on Romay's face had instantly puckered, like an old man's. The traitor had died of fright, without revealing who had set him on the road to self-destruction.

Shadowy forces were at work against Pharaoh. And whoever was mustering them was an enemy no less fearful than the Hittites.

Shaanar was jubilant.

Romay was dead of cardiac arrest, effectively sealing off the trail that led back to Ofir. The sorcerer took no credit, but his black magic had certainly killed the big steward when Ramses pressed him for answers. At the palace, no one seemed shocked by his sudden demise. The man had become obsessed with food, growing fatter and more fretful by the day. His heart had finally given out.

Satisfying as it was to be rid of the thorny problem Romay had represented, Shaanar also had another cause for rejoicing. Raia, the Syrian merchant, was back in Pi-Ramses. He sent to say he had a remarkable vase to show the prince. They met late one mild and sunny November morning.

"How was your trip to the south?"

"Tiring, Sir Prince, but well worth the effort."

The Syrian's goatee was neatly trimmed. His small and lively brown eyes absorbed the details of the column-lined reception room where Shaanar displayed his masterpieces. Raia whisked the wrapping off a potbellied bronze vase trimmed with grapevines and stylized grape leaves.

"The provenance is Crete; I acquired it in a trade with a rich Theban lady. You won't find this style anymore."

"Say no more. You've sold me, friend."

"Very well, Sir Prince, but . . ."

"Is the lady imposing conditions?"

"No, it's only that the price is rather high. It's a unique piece, truly unique."

"Let's set this little gem on a stand and go into my office. I'm sure we can reach an agreement."

The thick sycamore door closed behind them. No one could overhear their conversation.

"One of my assistants told me you were in Memphis asking to buy a vase from me. I cut my trip short and came straight back to Pi-Ramses."

"Exactly as I hoped."

"What's going on?"

"Serramanna is out of prison, cleared of all charges, and back at work for Ramses."

"Awkward," Raia said tersely.

"That damned little snoop Ahmeni started questioning the evidence. Then Ahsha got into the act."

"I'd watch my step around Ahsha. He's clever and understands the Near East."

"Fortunately, he's not assigned to the State Department

any longer. Ramses decorated him and sent him to shore up the defenses in our protectorates."

"Tricky, if not impossible."

"Ahsha and Ahmeni have reached some rather alarming conclusions. They think someone forged Serramanna's alleged correspondence with the Hittites, and they believe that someone was a Syrian."

"Very awkward," Raia said darkly.

"Then Serramanna's girlfriend turned up dead. Lilia, the one you paid to plant the tablets."

"I had to get rid of her. The imbecile was threatening to talk."

"Of course you had to, but you ought to have been more careful."

"How so?"

"Choosing the scene of the crime."

"I didn't choose it. She was about to sound the alarm. I had to act quickly and get out of town."

"Ahmeni is trying to find the owner of the building where she was killed and bring him in for questioning."

"He's a merchant, on the road most of the time. In fact, I ran into him in Thebes."

"Will he give your name?"

"I'm afraid so, since I am his tenant."

"It's not a pretty picture, Raia! Ahmeni is convinced that a Hittite spy ring is operating on Egyptian soil. Even though he personally had Serramanna locked up, the two of them seem to be working hand in glove now. The search for the man who framed the Sard and murdered his former girlfriend has become an affair of state. And they have several clues that point in your direction."

"They haven't found me yet."

"What's your plan?"

"I'll need to make sure my landlord doesn't talk."

"How?"

"The usual way, Sir Prince."

TWENTY-EIGHT

With the approach of winter, the days grew shorter, the sun grew dimmer. Ramses preferred the intensity of summer, the full heat of his heavenly father the sun. He alone of mortal men could stare the heavenly body in the face without being blinded. But this delightfully mild autumn day offered him a rare pleasure: a late afternoon in the palace gardens with Nefertari, their daughter, Meritamon, and her half-brother, Kha.

Sitting on folding chairs by a shallow pond, the king and queen observed the siblings' play. Kha wanted his sister to study a scroll with him, a difficult text on the moral precepts a scribe should follow, while she insisted that he should learn the backstroke. Despite his single-mindedness, the boy gave in, though not without complaining that the water was freezing and he'd catch a cold.

"Meritamon is a force to be reckoned with. She can charm anyone alive, just like you."

"Kha is a budding magician . . . look, he's getting out the

scroll now. His sister will read it with him whether she wants to or not."

"How are they doing in school?"

"Kha is exceptional, of course. Nedjem, your agriculture secretary, is still informally supervising his education. He tells me Kha could already pass the entry-level scribe exam."

"Would he want to take it?"

"He only wants to learn."

"Let's give him the nourishment he needs to develop his talent. He may be in for a rough time, since lesser men will always try to stifle genius. I hope Meritamon will have an easier life."

"She only has eyes for her father."

"And I have so little time for her . . ."

"Egypt must come before our children, as Ma'at decrees."

The king's pet lion and yellow dog lay near the garden gate. The moment anyone approached, Watcher would rouse his partner.

"Come, Nefertari."

The young queen, her hair undone, sat on Ramses' lap and leaned her head on his shoulder.

"You're the light of my life. We could be a normal couple, spend all our afternoons together . . ."

"This garden is a beautiful dream, but the gods and your father made you Pharaoh. You've given your life to your people, and offered it up for good."

"Right now my life is the sweet-smelling hair of the woman I love to distraction, her soft hair dancing in the evening breeze and brushing my cheek."

Their lips met in the eager kiss of two young lovers.

It was time for Raia to act.

He headed for the Pi-Ramses waterfront. It was a smaller port than Memphis, therefore not quite so busy, though the loading and unloading of boats was still strictly regulated by port authority officials.

Raia would take his fellow merchant Renouf off to a hearty lunch at a good inn, with many witnesses to vouch that they had enjoyed themselves immensely. That night, Raia would sneak into Renouf's house and strangle him. If a servant got in the way, he'd meet the same fate. Hittite training camps in northern Syria had taught Raia how to kill. Of course, this latest crime would be attributed to Lilia's murderer. But what did it matter? With Renouf out of the way, Raia would be safe.

The waterfront was lined with stands selling fruits, vegetables, sandals, fabric, trinkets. Since no purchase was considered satisfactory unless both parties drove a hard bargain, there was a considerable racket. If it were up to him, Raia would reorganize this free-for-all to make it more profitable.

The Syrian approached a uniformed official.

"Has Renouf's boat docked yet?"

"Pier 5, next to the barge there."

Raia hurried forward.

On the bridge of Raia's boat, a sailor dozed. The Syrian walked up the gangplank and woke the guard.

"Where is your boss?"

"Renouf? I have no idea."

"When did you get in?"

"Just after dawn."

"You sailed at night?"

"We had special permission because we were hauling fresh cheese from the main Memphis dairy. Some of the nobles here can't do without it."

"Once he signed off the cargo, your boss would have headed home, don't you think?"

"I doubt it."

"Why?"

"Because that big bodyguard of the king's—you know, the Sard with the whiskers—took Renouf off in his chariot. Not the kind of guy you want to argue with, eh?"

The sky had just fallen on Raia's head.

Renouf was a cheerful, comfortably built man, the father of three, who had inherited his family's shipping business. When Serramanna met him at the pier, the merchant was bewildered, but judging from the Sard's expression it seemed wiser to go along with him and clear up the misunderstanding.

The giant sped him off to the palace and escorted him to Ahmeni's office. Renouf had never met the king's private secretary, but knew him by reputation. The scribe was supposed to be serious, hardworking, and loyal to a fault, a silent power who handled government business with exemplary integrity, shunning honors and invitations.

The first thing that struck him was Ahmeni's pallor. Rumor had it that the scribe hardly ever left his office.

"It's an honor to meet you," said Renouf, "though I would have appreciated some advance warning. Being hauled off my boat the moment we docked in Pi-Ramses was quite a surprise."

"Please forgive me," Ahmeni replied. "We're investigating a very grave matter."

"A matter concerning me?"

"Perhaps."

"How can I help you?"

"I need honest answers to a few questions."

"Fire away."

"Are you acquainted with a certain Lilia?"

"A fairly common name. I must know ten!"

"The one I'm talking about is a local resident, young, single, and very pretty. She sells her charms to the highest bidder."

"A prostitute?"

"In a manner of speaking."

"I love my wife, Ahmeni. As much as I travel, I've never been unfaithful to her. I can assure you that we have a solid relationship. Ask my friends and neighbors, if you don't believe me."

"Will you swear by the law of Ma'at that you've never met the aforementioned Lilia?"

"I solemnly swear," said Renouf.

The merchant's earnestness impressed Shaanar, who looked on silently.

"Strange," Ahmeni said ruefully.

"Why strange? We merchants may not enjoy the best reputation, but I pride myself on being an honest man. I pay my employees well, I maintain my boats, I feed my family, I pay my bills, my taxes have never been audited . . . is that what you call strange?"

"Men such as you are all too rare, Renouf."

"Unfortunately so."

"Well. The strange thing is where they found Lilia's body."

The merchant looked up, startled.

"Her body . . . do you mean . . ."

"She was murdered."

"How awful!"

"She may have led a criminal life, but any murder is a capital offense. The strange part is that she was found in a house in Pi-Ramses that belongs to you."

"In my house?" Renouf asked, the color draining from his face.

"Not in your villa," Serramanna interjected. "A property right here." His touched his index finger to the map of Pi-Ramses that Ahmeni had unrolled in front of them.

"I don't understand."

"Does this house belong to you or not?"

"Yes, but it's not a house."

Ahmeni and Serramanna exchanged glances. Was Renouf on the level?

"No one lives there," he explained. "It's a warehouse. I thought I might need more storage space for my merchandise, which is why I bought the property. But my eyes were bigger than my stomach; at my age, I no longer feel like expanding my business. I plan to retire to my farm outside Memphis at the earliest opportunity."

"And you're planning to sell this property?"

"For the moment, I've rented the warehouse."

Hope glimmered in Ahmeni's eyes.

"To whom?"

"A merchant I know named Raia. A rich man, very active in business, with several barges and shops all over the country."

"What does he sell?"

"He specializes in high-quality conserves. Also sells collectible vases to an upper-crust clientele."

"Where is he from, do you know?"

"He's Syrian, but he's lived in Egypt for years."

"Thank you, Renouf. You've been very helpful."

"Are you done with me?"

"I think so. And please don't mention our conversation to anyone."

"You have my word."

Raia, a Syrian . . . if Ahsha had been there, he would have seen how right he had been. Before Ahmeni even got to his feet, the Sard was bolting out the door toward his chariot.

"Serramanna, wait for me!"

TWENTY-NINE

Despite the cold, Uri-Teshoop wore only a coarse woolen kilt. Bare-chested, he rode at a gallop, forcing the horsemen he commanded to push their mounts to the limit. Tall and muscular, with fleecy red hair all over his body and flowing locks, Uri-Teshoop, son of the Hittite emperor Muwattali, was the proud new commander of the army after the failed uprising in the Egyptian protectorates.

Ramses' swift and energetic response had taken Muwattali by surprise. And yet Baduk, the prince's predecessor as commanding general, had insisted that staging the insurrection would present no particular difficulty; nor would occupying the territory, once the revolt succeeded.

The Syrian spy he'd been using in Egypt for years was less convinced. He insisted that Ramses was a great pharaoh, a strong and decisive leader. Baduk retorted that the Hittites had nothing to fear from an inexperienced king and an army of mercenaries, jittery recruits, and bunglers. The peace agreement with Seti had been convenient in that it gave Muwattali time to consolidate his authority, ridding himself of any parties eyeing the throne too hungrily. At this point, he reigned supreme.

The expansion policy could be resumed. And if there was one country the Anatolian emperor wished to dominate, one country that would make his people the masters of the known world, it was Egypt.

According to General Baduk, the fruit was ripe for the picking. With Amurru and Canaan in Hittite hands, it would be simple to press into the Delta, lay waste to the fortresses that made up the King's Wall, and invade lower Egypt.

A magnificent plan, which the Hittite high command had been eager to execute.

Except that they had failed to reckon with Ramses.

In Hattusa, the Hittite capital, everyone was wondering why the wrath of the gods had fallen upon their empire. Uri-Teshoop, however, knew exactly what the problem was: he attributed the fiasco directly to General Baduk's stupidity and incompetence. The emperor's son was now touring the country not only to inspect the fortifications, but also to ferret out Baduk, who had failed to reappear in Hattusa.

He thought he might find him at Gavur Kalesi, a hilltop fort at the edge of the Anatolian plateau. Three giant statues of armed soldiers flanked it, announcing the Hittite nation's warlike nature. "Submit or be slain," they seemed to proclaim. Along the roads, on the rock walls of riverbanks, on freestanding boulders in the middle of fields, sculptors had carved military scenes—marching foot soldiers, each with a javelin in the right hand and a bow slung over the left shoulder. In Hittite country, the love of war conquered all.

Uri-Teshoop had swiftly covered the fertile, well-watered plains with their rows of nut trees. The swamp-studded maple forests hadn't slowed him down a bit. Driving his men and horses hard, the emperor's son was headed as fast as he could for the fortress of Mashat, the only place left where General Baduk could be hiding.

Despite their endurance and constant drilling, the Hittite cavalry arrived at Mashat exhausted. The fort sat on a rise in the middle of an open plain between two mountain ranges, an excellent vantage point for surveying the environs. Night and day, archers were posted in the watchtower's crenellations. The officers, scions of noble families, maintained an iron discipline.

Uri-Teshoop was frozen some three hundred paces in front of the fortress. A javelin had just landed deep in the ground in front of his horse.

The emperor's son dismounted and advanced. "Open up!" he shouted. "Don't you recognize me?"

The fortress gate opened. Ten soldiers stood in the doorway, brandishing their lances. Uri-Teshoop walked straight through them.

"The emperor's son demands to see the governor."

The commander instantly descended from the ramparts at breakneck speed. "Prince, what an honor!" The soldiers raised their lances in salute.

"Is General Baduk in residence here?"

"Yes, I've given him my own quarters."

"Take me to him."

The two men climbed a stone stairway with steep, slippery steps.

Atop the hill, the wind blew. The commandant's residence was of roughly hewn stone, the inner walls blackened from the thick smoke of oil lamps.

The moment he spied Uri-Teshoop, the middle-aged man within rose ponderously.

"Prince Uri-Teshoop . . ."

"How are you, Baduk?"

"Still wondering where my plan went wrong. If the Egyptian army hadn't reacted so swiftly, the insurgents in Canaan and Amurru would have been better organized. But I wouldn't say all is lost. The Egyptians have taken over, yes, but their hold on the region is superficial. Even though the local princes are back in Pharaoh's fold, their hearts are still with us."

"Why didn't you order our troops stationed at Kadesh to attack the Egyptians once they reached Amurru?"

General Baduk registered shock. "That would have required a formal declaration of war . . . well beyond the powers vested in me! Only the emperor could make such a decision."

Once as bloodthirsty and domineering as Uri-Teshoop, Baduk had become a shell of a man. His hair and beard were grizzled.

"Have you analyzed your failure?"

"That's what I've been doing here in Mashat. My report will spare no one, including myself."

"May I be excused, Your Highness?" asked the fort commander, aware that he shouldn't be privy to high-level military secrets.

"No," replied the prince.

The commander was embarrassed to watch the prince humiliate General Baduk. He was a great soldier and devoted to his country. But obedience was the prime Hittite virtue, and the word of the emperor's son was law. Any insubordination was punishable by death on the spot, since there was no other way to maintain cohesion in an army perpetually on the brink of war.

"The fortresses in Canaan offered a strong resistance to the Egyptian attacks," offered Baduk. "The garrisons we trained refused to surrender."

"That doesn't change the outcome," Uri-Teshoop said bluntly. "The insurgents were exterminated. Canaan is back under Egyptian control. The same holds true for Megiddo."

"Unfortunately true, even though our commandos had prepared things brilliantly. But the emperor wanted them back in Kadesh before the fighting started, so that no trace of the Hittite presence could be detected in Canaan or Amurru."

"Let's talk about Amurru! How many times did you assure us that you had the prince eating out of your hand, that he'd never go back to Ramses?"

"That was my biggest mistake," Baduk conceded. "The Egyptians threw us off completely. Instead of following the coastal route that would have led them straight into an ambush, they cut through the interior. The Prince of Amurru was caught unawares, and surrender was his only viable option."

"Surrender!" spat Uri-Teshoop. "I don't want to hear about surrender! As I understand it, the point of your strategy was to weaken the Egyptian army, crippling the infantry and chariot divisions. Instead, the Pharaoh's losses were light, his troops gained confidence, and he chalked up a major victory!"

"I won't try to deny how wrong I was. I should never have trusted the Prince of Amurru; he'd rather face dishonor than fight."

"Defeat has no place in a Hittite general's career."

"It's not that my men were defeated, Your Highness; it was only an incorrectly executed attempt to destabilize the Egyptian protectorates."

"You were afraid of Ramses, weren't you?"

"His forces were much larger than we'd imagined, and my mission had been to foment rebellion, not to confront the Egyptians."

"Sometimes, Baduk, you have to be able to improvise."

"I'm only a soldier, Your Highness, trained to obey my superiors."

"Why did you hole up here instead of reporting to Hattusa?"

"I told you, I needed to gain perspective. And I have some good news: our allies in Amurru are ready to take up the cause again."

"You're dreaming, Baduk."

"No, Prince. Give me a little more time, and I'll show you."

"You're no longer the commander of the Hittite army. The emperor has named me to replace you."

Baduk walked a few paces toward the massive fireplace where oak logs burned. "Congratulations, Uri-Teshoop. You'll lead us to victory."

"I have another message for you, Baduk."

The former general warmed his hands by the fire, turning his back to the emperor's son. "Yes, Your Highness?"

"You're a coward."

Unsheathing his sword, Uri-Teshoop plunged it into Baduk's bulky torso.

The commandant stood petrified.

"A traitor as well as a coward," Uri-Teshoop sneered. "He refused to acknowledge his wrongdoing and then attacked me. You're my witness."

The commandant bowed.

"Hoist the body on your shoulders, carry it down to the yard, and burn it without the funeral rites reserved for warriors. So perish defeated generals."

As Baduk's corpse burned with the garrison looking on, Uri-Teshoop personally greased the axles of his chariot with mutton fat. His war chariot, he mused. For, once he returned to the capital, he planned to advocate total war on Egypt.

THIRTY

A finer capital was nowhere to be found. Uri-Teshoop admired it as he rode toward the central Anatolian plateau, where gorges and ravines cut through arid steppes. Hattusa was the heart of the Hittite empire. The climate was dramatic, with sweltering summers and frigid winters. The city sprawled up an uneven mountain-side, requiring heroic efforts of its builders. At the top stood a citadel housing the imperial palace. To the untrained eye, Hattusa looked like a jumble of building blocks piled on rocky outcroppings. The surrounding peaks sheltered it from potential attackers. Within the city walls, the foundations were also made of stone, the walls of rough brick and wood.

Hattusa, proud and unbowed. Hattusa, fierce and untamed, where the name of Uri-Teshoop would soon win renown.

The five miles of ramparts, bristling with towers and battlements, were enough to warm a soldier's heart. They snaked up the side of the plateau, overlooked dizzying gorges. Here man dominated nature, stealing the secret of its strength.

Passing the lower town's two gates, then the upper town's Lion's Gate and King's Gate, Uri-Teshoop headed for the ultimate point of entry, the Sphinx Gate leading to the citadel.

The lower town did have its own distinguishing feature, of course: the temple of the Storm God and the Sun Goddess, a complex of no fewer than twenty-one shrines of varying sizes. But Uri-Teshoop preferred the upper town and the palace. He liked to gaze out at the slopes studded haphazardly with government buildings and fine mansions.

Entering the city, the emperor's son had broken the three ritual pieces of bread and poured wine on a huge stone slab, repeating the time-honored blessing: "May this rock be eternal." Around it lay votive offerings of oil and honey.

The palace was set on an imposing rocky summit with

three peaks. Stout walls with permanently manned watch-towers isolated the imperial dwelling from the rest of the capital and protected it from attack. Muwattali, cautious and wily, was mindful of the sudden reversals and desperate power struggles common in Hittite history. Disputes often ended in stabbing or poisoning, and it was the rare Great Chief who died a natural death. The Great Fortress, as the people dubbed it, was therefore designed with three blind sides. Visitors were screened at the single, closely guarded entrance.

Uri-Teshoop submitted to the regulation search. The men frisking him, like most other soldiers, were glad he'd been named to head the army. Young and valiant, the emperor's son would be far more decisive than old Baduk had been.

Within the palace walls were several reservoirs, essential in summer. Stables, armory, and guardrooms opened onto a paved yard. The plan of the imperial quarters was in most regards similar to that of other Hittite dwellings, great or small, consisting of a square space in the center with rooms arranged around the four sides.

An officer saluted Uri-Teshoop and showed him into a hall with thick pillars where the emperor received visitors. Stone lions and sphinxes guarded the entrance, as well as the doorway to the adjacent archives storing the records of Hittite military victories. Here, in the empire's invincible core, Uri-Teshoop felt utterly confident in his mission.

Two men entered the room. The first was the emperor Muwattali, a robust fifty, of medium height, with a barrel chest and stubby legs. Easily chilled, he was draped in a long mantle of red and black wool. His eyes were dark and alert.

The second was Hattusili, the emperor's younger brother. Short and slight, his hair tied back, wearing a silver chain around his neck and a silver cuff at his left elbow, he was draped in a length of multicolored fabric that left his shoulders bare. He was the high priest of the Sun God, married to the lovely Puduhepa, the intelligent and influential daughter of a respected religious leader. Uri-Teshoop hated them both with a passion, but the emperor seemed to value their advice. In the eyes of the new commander, Hattusili was simply playing a waiting game.

Uri-Teshoop knelt before his father and kissed his hand.

"Did you catch up with General Baduk?"

"Yes, Father, in the fort at Mashat."

"What did he have to say for himself?"

"He attacked me, so I killed him. The commander of the fort was my witness."

Muwattali turned to his brother.

"Regrettable," commented Hattusili, "but no one can bring that unfortunate general back to life. The gods were displeased with him, it would appear."

Uri-Teshoop found it hard to conceal his surprise. For the first time, his uncle was taking his side!

"Wise words," the emperor appraised. "The Hittite people dislike defeat."

"I'm in favor of invading Amurru and Canaan at once," ventured Uri-Teshoop, "then attacking Egypt."

"The King's Wall bars the way into the Delta," objected Hattusili.

"It isn't as impenetrable as it looks. The forts are too far apart. We'll isolate them and capture them all in a single coordinated attack."

"I find that overly optimistic, considering the Egyptian army's recent performance."

"But look at the enemies they were facing! When they meet up with us, it will be a different story."

"Have you forgotten Ramses?"

The emperor's question silenced his son.

"You'll lead us to victory, Uri-Teshoop, but not without preparation. Launching an attack so far from our home base would be a mistake."

"Then where will we start?"

"We'll lure the Egyptian forces north once more."

"Do you mean . . ."

"Yes, Kadesh. Kadesh will be the site of the great battle sealing Ramses' defeat."

"Why not take Egypt's protectorates in the bargain?"

"I've studied our informants' reports with care and drawn conclusions from Baduk's fiasco. Ramses is a true warrior, much more dangerous than we ever supposed he would be. We must be thoroughly prepared when we meet him in battle."

"We'll waste too much time!"

"No, my son. Our attack must be deadly and accurate."

"Our army is years ahead of a bunch of Egyptian recruits and mercenaries! We're already deadly, and my battle plans will show you how accurate I can be. I have it all figured out. Why delay? All I need to do is whip my troops into a frenzy, and I'm off!"

"I'm still in charge, Uri-Teshoop. You will act on my orders, and my orders alone. For now, go clean yourself up. I'm addressing the court in less than an hour."

The emperor exited the reception room.

Uri-Teshoop stared defiantly at Hattusili.

"You're the one who's trying to undermine me."

"I have nothing to do with the army."

"Don't make me laugh. Sometimes I wonder who's really ruling here."

"Show some respect for your father, Uri-Teshoop. Muwattali is the emperor. I serve him as best I can."

"While waiting for him to die!"

"You're going too far."

"The court is seething with plots, and you're behind most of them, Uncle. But believe me, you won't win out in the end."

"You misread me completely. Or perhaps a life of service is a concept beyond your comprehension."

"You're more ambitious than that, Hattusili."

"Your mind is made up, I see."

"Yes."

"The emperor has made you his commander-in-chief, as well he should. You're an excellent soldier and our troops trust you. But you're a fool if you think you can go your own way."

"You're forgetting one essential fact, Hattusili. In this empire, the army is the law."

"Do you know what most of our people value? Their house, their fields, their vineyards, their livestock . . ."

"You're preaching peace?"

"No war has been declared, as far as I know."

"Anyone speaking in favor of peace with Egypt might as well be a traitor."

"I forbid you to twist my words."

"Don't stand in my way, Hattusili, or you'll regret it."

"Threat is the weapon of the weak, Uri-Teshoop."

The emperor's son reached a hand to the pommel of his sword. Hattusili gazed at him steadily.

"You dare to raise your sword against the brother of Muwattali?"

Uri-Teshoop gave a strangled cry of rage and stormed out of the huge, cold room.

THIRTY-ONE

Uri-Teshoop, Hattusili, Puduhepa, along with the high priests of the Storm God and the Sun Goddess, the head of imperial construction, the inspector of markets, and all the empire's other dignitaries, were gathering to hear the emperor's speech.

The failure of the campaign to destabilize Egypt's protectorates had been troubling. Clearly, the blame lay with General Baduk—the late General Baduk—but what did it mean in terms of Muwattali's foreign policy? The military establishment, roused by Uri-Teshoop, was pressing for a direct and rapid strike against Egypt. The merchants, whose financial power was considerable, were tired of having trade relations disrupted; they favored peace, however tentative. Hattusili had met with the trade delegation and advised the emperor not to dismiss their concerns. The caravans traversing Hatti paid hefty taxes to the government, an important source of revenue for military operations, considering that the average donkey carried more than a hundred pounds of trade goods, over a hundred fifty of textiles. The merchants had transformed towns and villages into thriving trade centers. They established an efficient economic system through the use of inventories, written orders, shipping contracts, discharge of debts, and specific legal regulations. If, for instance, a merchant was accused of murder, he could avoid trial and conviction by paying a sizable fine instead.

Military might and a thriving economy were the two mainstays of the emperor's power. He needed them both to survive. Since Uri-Teshoop was becoming the military hero of the day, Hattusili positioned himself as the merchants' special representative, leaving his well-connected wife, Puduhepa, to control the clergy.

Muwattali was too shrewd not to have noticed the intense clandestine rivalry pitting his son against his brother. Granting each of them a limited sphere of influence, he had acknowledged their ambition while keeping the upper hand, but for how long? Soon he would be forced to act.

Hattusili would not object to the conquest of Egypt, except for the fact that it was liable to promote Uri-Teshoop as a war hero and future emperor. He therefore needed to cultivate his relationships with the military establishment, undermining his nephew's authority. For an emperor's son, what could be more desirable than a glorious death on the battlefield? Hattusili recognized Muwattali's skill as a leader and would have been content merely to serve him, had Uri-Teshoop not emerged as a threat to the empire's stability.

Muwattali did not assume his son would show him respect or gratitude; Hittite culture placed no great emphasis on family ties. The legal code deemed incest an acceptable practice as long as it caused no harm to the parties involved. The penalties for rape were light and were waived if the least presumption of consent was found to exist. Thus, for a son to assassinate his father in a takeover attempt would hardly be considered an outrage.

Putting Uri-Teshoop in command of the army had been a master stroke; it would take the young man's mind off eliminating his father, at least for the time being. Sooner or later, however, the danger would resurface. The challenge for Hattusili was to take advantage of the present situation and minimize his nephew's ability to do harm.

A chill wind raced through the upper town, heralding an early winter. The dignitaries were shown into the reception room, heated for the occasion with braziers.

The atmosphere was heavy and tense. Muwattali disliked speeches and public appearances; he preferred to work behind the scenes, manipulating his subordinates one by one, without a cabinet to get in his way.

In the front row, Uri-Teshoop's resplendent new armor contrasted with Hattusili's unassuming dress. Puduhepa, his wife, shone with the dignity of a queen in her red gown. She was covered with jewels, including gold bracelets from Egypt.

Muwattali sat down on his throne, a crude stone seat without ornamentation. His rare appearances caused everyone to wonder how this insignificant-looking man could be the emperor of a proud and mighty nation; but the attentive observer would note the aggression in his eyes and body language, liable to flare into the most extreme violence. Muwattali was as quick as he was brutal; he could strike like a scorpion.

"The Storm God and Sun Goddess," declared the emperor, "have placed this country, her capital and cities, in the care of none other than myself. I, the emperor, will protect Hatti, for power and the instruments of war have been placed in none other than my hands."

With these time-honored phrases, Muwattali drove home the fact that he alone wielded power; that his son and brother, however influential they might become, owed him their unquestioning obedience. One false move and they would be mercilessly purged. The emperor's decisions were without appeal.

"On the north, south, east, and west," Muwattali continued, "the Anatolian plateau is ringed with mountains. Our borders are inviolable, yet our people refuse to remain confined by natural boundaries. My predecessors determined that Hittite territory should stretch from sea to sea. I now declare that it must expand to include the banks of the Nile."

Muwattali rose. His speech was over.

His words were few. His people were now at war.

The party Uri-Teshoop threw to celebrate his new command was lavish and well attended. Commanders, chiefs of staff, and high-ranking officers discussed past exploits and future victories. The emperor's son outlined his plans for the cavalry, including a host of new chariots.

The air was rife with the scent of war to come, brutal and intense.

Hattusili and his wife took their leave when a hundred slave girls appeared on the scene, an after-dinner treat Uri-

Teshoop had arranged for his guests. The girls had a choice, either of granting whatever favors were demanded of them that night, or of being flogged and shipped off to the salt mines that were one of Hatti's greatest resources.

"Leaving so soon?" their nephew said in mock astonishment.

"We have a busy day tomorrow," answered Puduhepa.

"Uncle Hattusili should relax more. There are sixteen-year-olds from Asia in this lot, proud little fillies. The trader promised exceptional performance. Go along home, Aunt Puduhepa, and let your husband have a good time for once."

"Not all men are swine," she said sharply. "In the future, spare us such invitations."

Hattusili and Puduhepa returned to their own wing of the palace. Only a few woven carpets brightened the barren rooms. On the walls were hunting trophies and crossed lances.

Puduhepa, still keyed up, dismissed her maid and prepared for bed on her own.

"Uri-Teshoop is a dangerous madman," she fumed.

"He's still the emperor's son."

"But you're his brother!"

"Most people see him as Muwattali's designated successor."

"Designated . . . the emperor wouldn't make that mistake, would he?"

"It's only a rumor at this stage."

"Why not put a stop to it?"

"Because I'm not overly concerned."

"How can you be so cool?"

"If you look at the facts, there's no cause at all for alarm."

"Would you be so good as to enlighten me?"

"Uri-Teshoop has landed exactly where he's always hoped to be. He no longer has any need to plot against his father."

"Don't be a fool. The throne is what he's after."

"Obviously, Puduhepa, but is he capable of taking it?"

The priestess studied her husband attentively. Physically he was unremarkable, yet from the start his intelligence and foresight had attracted her. Hattusili had the makings of a great statesman.

"Uri-Teshoop is short-sighted," he declared. "He doesn't realize what an overwhelming task he's facing. Commanding the Hittite army requires skills far beyond his scope."

"He's a fearless warrior, though, they say."

"Yes, but a commanding general needs to be a leader of men, resolving diverse and even contradictory viewpoints. That requires experience and patience."

"You're right. I don't recognize our nephew in your description."

"What could be better? He'll come crashing out of the gate and offend his generals. The present infighting will only get worse, and soon they'll be at his throat."

"But Muwattali declared war, and he thought enough of his son to hand him a leading role."

"Appearances can be deceiving."

"Are you sure?"

"I'll say it again: Uri-Teshoop overestimates himself. The challenges he'll have to meet are tough and complex. His dreams of war will shatter against the foot soldiers' shields and be crushed beneath the wheels of chariots. But that's not all . . ."

"Don't tease me, darling."

"Muwattali is a great emperor."

"He plans to exploit his son's weaknesses?"

Hattusili smiled. "The empire is both strong and fragile—strong in terms of its military muscle, fragile because we're surrounded by envious neighbors, ready to pounce at the first sign of weakness. Conquering Egypt is a worthy ambition, but an ill-considered attack would lead to disaster. The vultures are out there, waiting to feed on our spoils."

"Can Muwattali restrain a hothead like your nephew?"

"Uri-Teshoop doesn't know about his father's true intentions or his plans for carrying them out. The emperor has given him inside information, but not the key piece."

"But Muwattali told you everything?"

"He did me that honor, Puduhepa. And the emperor also entrusted me with a mission: putting his plan into action while keeping Uri-Teshoop in the dark."

From the balcony of his quarters in the palace complex, Uri-Teshoop gazed at the new moon. There dwelt the secret of the future, his future. He spoke to her at length, confessing his desire to lead the Hittite army to victory, slaughtering anyone who stood in his way.

The emperor's son raised a loving cup toward the heavenly body. The water it contained would reflect her secrets. All Hittites practiced the art of divination, but appealing directly to the moon was a risk that few dared take.

Her silence violated, the moon became a scimitar that could slash an attacker's throat, hurling his body over the ramparts. Those who met with favor, however, were granted luck in battle.

Uri-Teshoop prayed to her, the insolent, fickle queen of the night. For more than an hour, she was silent.

Then the water rippled and began to bubble. The cup grew burning hot, but Uri-Teshoop held on.

The water stopped boiling. On the flat surface a man's face appeared, topped with the twin crowns of upper and lower Egypt.

Ramses.

So this was Uri-Teshoop's destiny! He would kill Ramses and make Egypt a docile slave.

THIRTY-TWO

His goatee trimmed to perfection, clad in a heavy tunic, the Syrian merchant Raia made his way to Ahmeni's office. The king's private secretary saw him at once.

"I hear you've been looking for me all over town," Raia said uneasily.

"Quite right. Serramanna was ordered to have you report to me, by force if necessary."

"By force? But why?"

"Circumstances surrounding you have aroused grave suspicions."

The Syrian looked shaken. "Suspicions?"

"Where have you been hiding?"

"I haven't been hiding! I was down at the docks, in my warehouse, arranging a special shipment. As soon as I got wind of this incredible rumor, I came running. I'm an honest trader, established in Egypt for years, with a clean record. Just ask my staff, my customers! My business is expanding and I'm about to invest in another barge. My foodstuffs are served in the finest homes and my imported vases grace the mansions of Thebes, Memphis, and Pi-Ramses. I even supply the palace!" Raia's voice rose nervously throughout his recitation.

"I'm not questioning your business practices," said Ahmeni.

"Then what am I accused of?"

"Are you acquainted with a certain Lilia, a woman of easy virtue residing here in Pi-Ramses?"

"No."

"You're not a married man?"

"My work doesn't leave me time for a wife and family."

"You must have relationships."

"My private life is my own business."

"It's in your interest to answer."

Raia hesitated. "I have women friends, here and there around the country . . . To be honest, I work so hard that when I have time off, I prefer to catch up on my sleep."

"Then you deny knowing this Lilia?"

"I do."

"But you do acknowledge that you dispose of a warehouse in Pi-Ramses."

"Of course! I rent a large space on the waterfront, but I'll soon outgrow it. That's why I took another place in town. I'll start to use it at the beginning of the month."

"Who's your landlord?"

"An Egyptian named Renouf, a business acquaintance of mine. A good man and an honest merchant who bought the place but decided not to use it. He offered me very good terms."

"For the moment, the building is vacant, then."

"Yes."

"Do you go there often?"

"I've only been once, with Renouf, to sign the lease."

"Lilia's body was found in that warehouse, Raia."

The merchant seemed stunned by this revelation.

"The poor girl was strangled," Ahmeni continued, "because she was about to denounce the person who'd forced her to bear false witness."

Raia's hands trembled. His lips went white. "A murder . . . a murder, here, in the capital! How dreadful . . . violence . . . I'm appalled."

"Where are you from, Raia?"

"Syria, originally."

"The evidence has led us to believe that the man we're seeking is Syrian."

"There are thousands of us in Egypt!"

"You're Syrian, and you hold the lease on the property where Lilia was murdered. A disturbing coincidence, don't you think?"

"Pure coincidence!"

"This crime is linked to another extremely serious offense. That's why the king asked me to expedite the investigation."

"I'm only a merchant, a simple merchant! There's always resentment against a successful foreigner, I know. But everything I have, I've earned the hard way. I've never stolen from anyone!"

"If he is the man we're looking for," thought Ahmeni, "this Raia is quite an actor."

"Look at this," the scribe demanded, handing the Syrian a dated copy of the police report on the discovery of Lilia's body.

"Where were you on the day and night in question?"

"Let me think. I travel so much that it's hard to remember . . . yes . . . I must have been in Bubastis, restocking my shop there."

Bubastis, the charming home of the cat goddess Bastet, was some distance south of Pi-Ramses. With a fast boat and a strong current, however, it was only five or six hours from the capital.

"Can anyone vouch for you?"

"Yes, my manager and my regional representative."

"How long were you in Bubastis?"

"Only that day. I left the next morning for Memphis."

"A perfect alibi, Raia."

"It's not an alibi! It's the truth."

"Give me the names of your men there."

Raia scribbled them on a scrap of papyrus.

"I'll check," promised Ahmeni.

"It will prove my innocence!"

"I request that you remain in Pi-Ramses until further notice."

"Am I under arrest?" he asked shakily.

"There may be more questions for you to answer."

"But my business! There are vases I need to deliver personally . . ."

"Your customers will wait."

"I may lose some of them. I always deliver on the day I promise."

"Circumstances beyond your control, you can tell them. Where are you staying?"

"In a little place behind my warehouse on the waterfront. How long are you planning to keep me in suspense?"

"Don't worry. It will all be settled soon."

The third full cup of strong beer barely took the edge off Serramanna's anger. He had been to Bubastis and back in record time.

"I questioned Raia's employees," he told Ahmeni.

"Do they confirm his alibi?"

"Of course."

"Will they swear it in court?"

"They're Syrians, Ahmeni! The Judgment Hall of the Dead doesn't faze them. They'll lie through their teeth if the price is high enough! They couldn't care less about the law of Ma'at. If you'd let me use my methods on them, though . . ."

"You're not a pirate anymore, and justice is Egypt's most precious commodity. Torture is unthinkable."

"What about letting a criminal go free—a criminal and a spy?"

The arrival of an orderly ended their sparring. Ahmeni and Serramanna were escorted into Ramses' vast office.

"What's the latest report?" asked the king.

"Serramanna is convinced that the Syrian merchant, Raia, is a spy and a murderer."

"What about you?"

"I agree."

The Sard looked at Ahmeni with unspoken gratitude. Every trace of dissension between them had long since vanished.

"Can you prove it?"

"No, Your Majesty," confessed Serramanna.

"If we hold him for probable cause, Raia will demand a trial, and he'll be acquitted," said the king.

"We know that," sighed Ahmeni.

"Let me take over, Your Majesty," the giant Sard begged.

"We've covered this subject before, Serramanna."

The bodyguard hung his head.

"We've reached an impasse," admitted Ahmeni. "In all probability, Raia is a member of a Hittite spy ring, perhaps even the head of it. The man is clever, slippery, and an excellent actor. He controls his reactions, knows when to break into tears and when to bluster. He's quite convincing as an honest, hardworking merchant who lives only for his business. The fact remains that he travels the length of the country, from town to town, meeting a great many people. Could there be any better setup for espionage?"

"Raia was sleeping with Lilia," Serramanna asserted, "and he paid her to frame me. He thought she'd keep quiet; that was his mistake. She tried to blackmail him, and he killed her."

"According to your report," Ramses noted, "the Syrian strangled the girl in the warehouse he rented. Why take such a chance?"

"The property isn't even in his name," Ahmeni pointed out. "It was no easy task to trace the owner, who had nothing to do with the case, and then finger Raia."

"Raia was probably planning to kill his landlord to keep him from talking," added Serramanna, "but we got to him first. Otherwise, the connection would never have come to light. In my opinion, Raia didn't plan to murder Lilia. Meeting her in an out-of-the-way place, where no one knew him, was perfectly safe. He probably thought he could scare her into silence. But things turned sour. The girl asked too high a price, said she'd go to the authorities. Raia throttled her and ran before he could move the body. Fortunately, his Syrian subordinates could furnish an alibi."

"We're on the brink of open conflict with the Hittites," replied Ramses, "and it doesn't help to have a spy ring operating freely within our borders. You make a convincing case, but the key element is finding out how Raia transmits his messages to the enemy."

"A good interrogation . . ." suggested Serramanna.

"A spy will never talk."

"What does Your Majesty suggest?" Ahmeni asked finally.

"Question him again, and release him. Try to convince him we're dropping the investigation."

"He'll never fall for it!"

"Of course not," the king acknowledged. "But if he feels we're closing in on him, he'll be forced to alert his contacts. I want to see how he goes about it."

THIRTY-THREE

The end of the month of November was when seedlings began to poke through the soil. The new growth proclaimed the triumph of life over death and the promise of nourishment for the people of Egypt.

Ramses helped Homer down from his litter. A laden table awaited them in a palm grove on the banks of the canal. Nearby, cattle crossed at a ford. The faint sun of the first days of winter warmed the poet's venerable head.

"I thought you might like a picnic," the king explained.

"Splendid," said Homer. "The gods have showered blessings on your country."

"And Pharaoh provides the gods with places of worship."

"This land is a mystery, Your Majesty, and so are you. This peaceful countryside, the beautiful palm trees, the shimmering light, the exquisite food . . . there's something supernatural about it. You Egyptians have created a miracle. You live in a magical world. But how much longer can it last?"

"As long as the law of Ma'at is here to guide us."

"You forget the world beyond your borders, Ramses, the world that cares nothing for your law. Do you think Ma'at will stop the Hittite army?"

"Righteousness will be our strongest defense."

"I've seen war with my own failing eyes: the cruelty, the fury, the frenzy that overtakes men who seemed sensible. War lurks in the human heart, waiting to spring out and break the bonds of civilization. Egypt will be no exception."

"It will, Homer. Our country is a miracle, you're right, but a miracle we build on every day. I'll turn back any invasion, no matter where it comes from."

The poet closed his eyes. "I'm no longer in exile, Your Majesty. I'll never forget Greece and its own rough magic, but this is my home now. This is where I commune with the heavens—and I sense that soon they will ring with the clash of weapons."

"What makes you think so?"

"The Hittites are obsessed with conquest. They live to fight, like so many of my compatriots. Your last campaign won't deter them."

"My army will be ready to fight."

"You're like a wild beast, Your Majesty. A panther confronting a hunter never trembles but keeps a calm heart, even when it hears the hounds baying; even when wounded by a spear, the panther keeps fighting and attacks to live or die."

Nefertari read the astonishing missive Shaanar had just passed on to her. Hittite couriers had delivered it to southern Syria, and the State Department's messengers had taken it from there.

> *To my sister and dearest Queen of Egypt, Nefertari,*
>
> *I, Puduhepa, wife to Hattusili, brother of the emperor of the Hittites, send my friendly greetings. We are far apart, our lands and peoples are very different, but do not they aspire to the selfsame peace? If you and I encourage understanding between our peoples, would we not be doing a good deed? For my part, I will endeavor to do so. May I ask my esteemed sister to act likewise?*
>
> *The favor of your reply would be an honor. May the gods protect you.*

"What could this curious document mean?" the queen asked Ramses.

"Well, it's completely authentic. The two dried mud seals and the handwriting leave no doubt."

"Should I answer Puduhepa?"

"She's not a reigning queen, but since the death of Muwattali's wife she's considered the first lady of the land."

"Will her husband, Hattusili, be emperor?"

"Muwattali seems to be leaning toward his son, Uri-Teshoop, who burns to fight against Egypt."

"This letter has no real meaning, then."

"It shows there's another way of thinking, supported by the clergy and business interests, who can exert considerable pressure, according to Ahsha. They're afraid that war will hurt them financially."

"Is their influence strong enough to keep us out of war?"

"Certainly not."

"If Puduhepa is sincere, why shouldn't I respond? There's still a slim hope we may prevent thousands of deaths."

The Syrian merchant Raia toyed nervously with his beard.

"We've verified your alibi," declared Ahmeni.

"Glad to hear it."

"You should be. Your staff backed up every detail."

"I told the truth. I have nothing to hide."

Ahmeni was fiddling with a brush. "I'm forced to admit that we may have been wrong about you."

"Finally, the voice of reason!"

"You must concede that the circumstantial evidence was against you. Still, I hope you accept my apologies."

"Egyptian justice deserves its reputation," said Raia.

"May the gods preserve it."

"Am I free to go?"

"Yes. You can resume your normal activities and travel as you wish."

"I'm cleared of all suspicion?"

"You are, Raia."

"I appreciate your honesty and hope you soon find out who murdered that poor girl."

Supposedly checking invoices, Raia paced the docks between his warehouse and his boat.

Ahmeni's charade hadn't fooled him for a moment. Why would the secretary let him off the hook with only a flimsy alibi from his two Syrian assistants? Because he obviously hoped Raia would resume his covert activities and lead Serramanna straight to the spy ring.

The more he thought, the more Raia saw how serious his situation had become. No matter what he did, his intelligence network seemed doomed. Ahmeni would soon determine that the vast majority of the Syrian's associates also worked for the Hittites and formed a fearsomely efficient underground army. A wave of arrests would destroy it.

He could play for time and go about his business as usual, but not for long.

He needed to get word to Shaanar as quickly as possible, but without arousing the slightest suspicion.

Raia delivered precious vases to several Pi-Ramses notables. Shaanar, a regular customer, was on the list. In due time, the Syrian arrived at the prince's house and spoke to his steward.

"His Royal Highness is not at home."

"Ah . . . Will he be back soon?"

"I have no idea."

"Unfortunately, I can't wait for his return. I have urgent business in Memphis, and events of the last few days have prevented me from leaving town. Would you be so good as to see that the prince receives this vase?"

"Of course."

"Please give him my best regards. Oh, I forgot . . . the price is rather high, but a vase of this quality is hard to find. We'll settle up when I return."

Raia called on three more customers before embarking on his southward journey. He knew what he had to do: get in touch with the chief of the Egyptian operation, once he managed to shake off anyone Serramanna might have set on his trail.

The secretary of state's personal scribe ran into Shaanar's office, forgetting his wig and the dignity of his position, to his colleagues' horror. Self-control was the mark of the literate man, they believed.

Shaanar was not to be found.

The scribe was in a terrible bind. Should he wait until the secretary returned or go over his head and alert the king? Though a reprimand was certain to follow, the scribe opted for the latter course.

Flabbergasted, his colleagues watched him leave the building without explanation, still without his wig, and jump into the official chariot, which would carry him to the palace within minutes.

Ahmeni greeted the scribe, quickly discerning the reason for his agitation.

The letter, transmitted by diplomatic representatives in southern Syria, bore the seal of Muwattali, emperor of the Hittites.

"The secretary of state is out of the office. I thought it would be better if—"

"You did right. You needn't fear any repercussions. The king will appreciate your initiative."

Ahmeni tested the weight of the missive, a wooden tablet wrapped in cloth and sealed in several places with typical Hittite dried mud stamps.

He closed his eyes, hoping that it was only a bad dream. When he opened them again, the message was still there, burning into his fingers.

His throat was dry as he walked very slowly toward Ramses' office. After spending a day with the secretary of agriculture and irrigation officials, the king was alone, preparing a decree aimed at improving the upkeep of the dikes.

"You look upset, Ahmeni."

The secretary stiffly presented him with the official-looking document direct from the emperor of the Hatti.

"The declaration of war," murmured Ramses.

THIRTY-FOUR

Without haste, Ramses broke the seals, tore off the protective cloth, and scanned the message.

Once again, Ahmeni closed his eyes, savoring the final moments before all hell broke loose, before the Pharaoh dictated his reply, marking Egypt's entry into war with Hatti.

"Are you sober as ever, Ahmeni?"

The question surprised him. "You know I am."

"Too bad. We could drink some special wine to mark the occasion. Read this."

Ahmeni deciphered the tablet:

> From the emperor of the Hatti, Muwattali, to his brother Ramses, Son of Light, Pharaoh of Egypt,
>
> I hope this finds you well and that your mother, Tuya, your wife, Nefertari, and your children are also in good health. Your reputation continues to grow, along with your wife's, and your valor is known throughout Hatti.
>
> How are your horses? Here, we set great store by ours. They are splendid animals, the most wonderful in all creation.
>
> May the gods protect Hatti and the Twin Kingdoms.

A broad smile lit Ahmeni's face. "This is wonderful!"

"I'm not so sure," said Ramses.

"But it's a typical diplomatic overture, nothing like a declaration of war."

"Only Ahsha can tell us that."

"You have no faith at all in Muwattali . . ."

"His power is based on a combination of brutality and deception. Diplomacy is only one more weapon in his stockpile; he's not really seeking peace."

"What if he's sick of war? The way you took back Canaan and Amurru showed him that he has to take the Egyptian army seriously."

"Oh, he does. That's why he's preparing for the conflict and trying to ease our fears with a few friendly gestures. Homer sees no hope of lasting peace, and he ought to know."

"What if he's wrong and Muwattali has changed? What if the merchant class has won out over the generals? Puduhepa's letter points in that direction."

"The military fuels the economy, and the Hittites are warriors at heart. The more widespread the conflict, the bigger the profits for the merchants."

"So you think war is inevitable."

"I hope I'm wrong. If Ahsha can find no sign of maneuvers, rearmament, or mobilization of troops, I'll feel better."

Ahmeni was troubled. A preposterous idea had just occurred to him. "Ahsha's official mission is to reorganize the defense systems in our protectorates. To get the information you need, won't he have to penetrate Hittite territory?"

"He will," admitted Ramses.

"That's madness! If he's ever captured . . ."

"Ahsha was free to turn down the assignment."

"He's our friend, Ramses, we were boys together. He's as loyal to you as I am, he—"

"I know, Ahmeni. That's why I'm relying on his courage."

"He has no chance whatever of coming back alive! Even if he can get a few messages back to us, they're bound to catch him."

For the first time, the scribe found himself questioning the Pharaoh's judgment. He was right, of course, to put the good of Egypt before all else. But he was sacrificing a friend, a man in a million, who deserved to live to one hundred ten, the age of the sages.

"I need to dictate a reply, Ahmeni. Let's assure our brother the Emperor of Hatti that all is well in my house and my stables."

Nibbling on an apple, Shaanar studied the vase his steward had just brought in to him.

"You're sure it was Raia himself who delivered it?"

"Yes, Your Highness."

"Tell me exactly what he said to you."

"He mentioned the high price of the vase and said you could work things out when he gets back to town."

"Bring me another apple and see that no one disturbs me."

"About the companion you requested for tonight . . ."

"Reschedule her."

Shaanar's eyes were riveted on the vase. A copy, he thought—a rough and ugly copy, so bad that it couldn't be bartered for a pair of shoddy sandals, so bad that it wouldn't play in the provinces.

Raia's meaning was clear. The spy had been exposed and was warning the prince to avoid all contact. His grand strategy was falling to pieces. Without being able to contact the Hittite, how could he function?

Still, he could see two bright spots.

First, at this crucial juncture, the Hittites would be unwilling to dismantle their Egypt spy network. They'd simply remove Raia, and his replacement would contact Shaanar.

Second, Ahsha was in an ideal position. He would further disrupt defenses in the protectorates, make valuable contacts with the enemy, and smooth the way for him.

And he mustn't forget Ofir, whose magic still had a chance to work against Ramses.

All in all, Raia's slip couldn't have been that serious. The Syrian would soon find his way out of this predicament.

A warm golden light bathed the temples of Pi-Ramses. After celebrating the evening rituals, Ramses and Nefertari met at the temple of Amon, which was still under construction. The capital grew more beautiful by the day, a happy and peaceful place. The royal pair walked in the temple gardens. Perseas, sycamores, and jojoba trees grew among clumps of oleander. Gardeners were watering the young trees, talking gently to them. It was common knowledge that plants needed encouragement as well as water.

"What do you think of our letters from the north?" asked Ramses.

"They worry me," replied Nefertari. "The Hittites are dangling the prospect of a lasting peace, trying to confuse us."

"I was hoping you'd see it in a more positive light."

"Hiding the facts as I see them would be a disservice to our love. I owe you the truth, even when storm clouds are brewing."

"It's hard to imagine a war, to think of so many young lives lost, when we're here in this peaceful garden."

"We have nowhere to hide, Ramses."

"Will my army be able to withstand Hittite attacks? There are too many veterans trying to coast toward retirement, too many inexperienced young soldiers, too many mercenaries focused on their wage . . . the enemy knows our weaknesses."

"Don't we know theirs?"

"Our intelligence-gathering network in their territory is still in its infancy. We thought Muwattali would stay within the boundaries my father established when he spared Kadesh. But Muwattali is bent on expanding his empire, and there's no sweeter prize than Egypt."

"Has Ahsha submitted any reports yet?"

"I haven't heard a word from him."

"You fear for his life, don't you?"

"I've sent him behind enemy lines. Ahmeni can't forgive me."

"Whose idea was it?"

"I can't lie to you, Nefertari. It was my idea, not Ahsha's."

"He could have said no."

"A pharaoh's request isn't easy to refuse."

"Still, Ahsha knows his own mind."

"If he's captured, I'll be responsible. If he dies . . ."

"Ahsha lives for Egypt, just as you do. He must hope his mission will save our country."

"Yes, that's what we discussed before he left. We talked the whole night long about pinpointing Hittite strategy. If he can do it, we may be able to prevent an invasion."

"What if you attack first?"

"I'm considering it . . . but not without Ahsha's input."

"The letters from Hattusa show that the emperor and his camp are trying to buy time, probably because of internal disagreements. A first strike may be the opportunity you're seeking."

Nefertari's melodious voice belied the iron will of a true queen. Like Tuya, she stood by her husband, feeding his strength.

"I think about Moses constantly," Ramses confessed. "How would he act now that Egypt is under threat? Despite his religious obsessions, I'm convinced that he'd join our fight to save the land of the pharaohs."

The sun had set. Nefertari began to shiver. "I miss my old shawl," she sighed. "It kept me so warm."

THIRTY-FIVE

The region called Midian was out of the way, east of the Gulf of Aqaba and south of Edom. The peace and quiet was broken only occasionally by nomads roaming the Sinai peninsula, and the Midianites liked it that way. They had been shepherds for centuries, sidestepping the squabbles so prevalent among Arab tribes in the land of Moab.

An old priest, father of seven daughters, reigned over the

small community that staunchly bore their hard existence in a rugged climate.

The old man was treating a lamb's hoof when he heard a strange sound in the distance.

"Horses," he thought. "Horses and chariots, traveling fast."

An Egyptian army patrol . . . yet they never wasted their time here. The Midianites possessed no weapons, nor did they care to fight. With their meager standard of living, they paid no taxes; they knew better than to harbor Bedouin pillagers, lest the desert patrol destroy their oasis and drive them off.

When the Egyptian chariots reached their camp, the women and children huddled inside their primitive tents. The elder rose and faced the intruders.

"Who are you?" barked the young officer in charge of the patrol.

"The priest of Midian."

"You're the leader of this sorry bunch?"

"I am."

"What do you live on out here?"

"We raise sheep, gather dates, drink water from our well. We grow a few vegetables."

"Have any weapons?"

"It's not our custom."

"I've been ordered to search your tents."

"Do as you please. We have nothing to hide."

"We've heard that you're harboring Bedouin outlaws."

"We'd be mad to provoke the wrath of Pharaoh. Remote and barren as this land may be, it's our home. Breaking the law would be our downfall."

"Wise words, old man, but I'll still have to do the search."

"I told you, search all you like. Before you do, may we invite you to share our meal? One of my daughters has just given birth to a son. We'll eat some lamb and drink palm wine in celebration."

The Egyptian officer was caught off guard. "It's not in the regulations . . ."

"While your soldiers go through the tents, come sit by the fire."

His panic-stricken flock huddled around the holy man, who reassured them and urged them to cooperate with the soldiers.

The officer accepted the invitation to sit down and share in the humble feast. The mother was still resting, but the father, an old, hunched, bearded man with chiseled features, rocked the newborn in his arms.

"A shepherd who married late," explained the elder. "This child will be the light of his old age."

The soldiers uncovered no hidden weapons or outlaws.

"Continue to observe the law," the officer told the priest of Midian, "and your people will be safe from harm."

The chariots disappeared into the distance.

When the sand settled, the new father stood up. The officer would have been surprised to see how the stunted shepherd transformed into a broad-shouldered giant.

"We're safe, Moses," the holy man said to his son-in-law. "They won't be back."

On the West Bank of Thebes, architects, stone carvers, and sculptors were hard at work on the Ramesseum, the Pharaoh's Eternal Temple. In accordance with the law of

Ma'at, the naos or inner sanctum was built first, to house the hidden god whose form would never be revealed to mortal men. A huge quantity of blocks of sandstone, gray granite, and basalt had been stockpiled at the highly organized construction site. The walls of the hypostyle hall, with its great rows of columns, were already going up. Work on the adjacent palace complex was also under way. As Ramses planned, his Temple of Millions of Years would be a fabled monument where his father's memory was honored for all time, his wife and his mother celebrated. It would be the wellspring of the invisible energy without which he could never rule in justice.

Nebu, the high priest of Karnak, was smiling. When the tired, arthritic old man had been put in charge of the largest and richest of Egyptian temples, the court viewed it as a purely political move. Nebu would totter toward senility doing Pharaoh's bidding, only to be replaced by another equally aged and servile royal pawn.

No one had expected that Nebu would age like granite. Bald and slow-moving, he ruled his vast domain with a steady hand. He was loyal to his king, unlike certain of his predecessors who had challenged the Pharaoh's authority. Serving Ramses was Nebu's fountain of youth.

But today Nebu gave no thought to Karnak, the immense temple, the huge staff, the hierarchy, the estates, the villages. He bent over the acacia Ramses had planted on the future site of his Eternal Temple, in the second year of his reign. The high priest of Karnak had promised the monarch he would care for the sapling, which was now a thriving young tree. In this magical spot, it grew much faster than normal.

"How is my acacia doing, Nebu?"

The high priest looked slowly around. "Your Majesty! No one told me you were expected."

"A surprise visit. Your staff couldn't have known. This tree is magnificent."

"I've never seen anything like it. You seem to have endowed it with your strength. It will be my privilege to nurture it; you'll live to see it full-grown."

"I wanted to see Thebes again, my tomb in the Valley of the Kings, my Eternal Temple, and this acacia before the storm breaks."

"Is war inevitable, Your Majesty?"

"The Hittites are trying to pretend it isn't, but who can trust their attempts at conciliation?"

"Everything is in order at Karnak, I can assure you. Its riches belong to you, and under my stewardship the estates have prospered."

"How's your health, Nebu?"

"As long as the blood flows through my heart, I'll serve you. Nevertheless, if Your Majesty wanted to replace me, I wouldn't argue. Sitting beside the sacred lake and watching the swallows is what I'd most like to do."

"Sorry to disappoint you, but I'm not prepared to let you go yet."

"My legs are giving out, my hearing isn't what it used to be, my bones ache . . ."

"But your mind is as quick as a falcon on the wing and as straight as an ibis. Keep up the good work, Nebu, and take care of this acacia. If I don't come back, you'll be its sole support."

"You'll come back. You have to come back."

Ramses visited the work site, recalling his days with the quarrymen at Aswan. He was building Egypt day by day, but it was the stoneworkers who raised the temples and Houses of Eternity. They were what kept the Two Lands from sinking into the anarchy and baseness inherent in human nature. Worshiping the power of light and following the law of Ma'at meant setting humanity on the straight and narrow path, overcoming the tendency toward selfishness and vanity.

The monarch's dream was becoming reality. The Temple of Millions of Years was taking shape, the awesome source of magical energy was beginning to function on its own, fueled by the hieroglyphs and images carved into the temple walls. Walking through the rooms that had been roughed out, praying in the future chapels, Ramses drew on the *ka* produced by this merging of heaven and earth. He drew on it not for his personal ends, but to gather the strength for his coming confrontation with the Hittites. He would chase away the storm clouds gathering over his sacred land.

Ramses felt that he carried within him all the dynasties that had gone before, the line of pharaohs who had created Egypt in the image of the cosmos.

For a moment, the twenty-seven-year-old monarch stumbled under the burden. Then he felt the past more clearly— not an unbearable weight but a guiding force. In this Eternal Temple, his ancestors were showing him the way.

Raia delivered vases to the upper crust of Memphis. If the men tailing him interrogated his employees, they would learn that the Syrian merchant was continuing to supply his select clientele. He was careful to display his usual sales tactics, consisting of direct contacts, showings, and heavy doses of flattery.

Then he headed for the famous harem at Merur, which he had last visited two years earlier. He could just picture

Ahmeni and Serramanna's henchmen scratching their heads in wonder. They would think he must have accomplices in this venerable institution. They would waste time and energy barking up the wrong tree.

Raia misled them further with a brief stay in a village near the harem. He held long discussions with local people who were complete strangers to him. To the men on his trail, though, they would obviously be involved in the spy ring.

Finally, the merchant ended his little game and went back to Memphis to check on his shipments of preserved meats destined for Pi-Ramses and Thebes.

Serramanna ranted.

"This spy is laughing in our faces! He knows we're having him followed, and he's deliberately misleading us."

"Calm down," Ahmeni recommended. "Sooner or later he'll make a mistake."

"What kind of mistake?"

"The messages he gets from Hatti must be hidden in his food shipments or inside the vases. My guess is that it's the vases, since most of them come from southern Syria and the Near East."

"Let's have a look at them, then!"

"That would be a shot in the dark. What we really need to find out is how he transmits the messages and what net-work he uses. Given the situation, he at least needs to let the Hittites know we suspect him. Let's be ready when he ships anything at all to Syria."

"I have another idea," Serramanna confessed.

"Legal, I hope?"

"If I promise not to make waves and furnish you with a legitimate reason to arrest Raia, can I go ahead?"

"How much time will you need?"

"I'll be done by tomorrow."

THIRTY-SIX

In Bubastis, the festival of the Intoxication of Bastet was being celebrated. She was the cat goddess, the goddess of pleasure, and for a week young men and maidens tasted the first stirrings of love. There was revelry and drinking. In the country, boys competed in wrestling tournaments to show off their strength and win the lovely spectators with their fighting spirit.

Raia's employees had been given two days off. The thin, stooped Syrian who ran the warehouse had checked the dozen or so moderately valued vases and bolted the door. He was not averse to joining in the fun and trying his luck with the ladies, even the more mature variety. Raia was a demanding boss. When he offered you a break, it was best to take it.

Humming as he pictured the pleasures awaiting him, the warehouse man headed down the narrow street leading to a square where merrymakers were already gathering.

A meaty hand grabbed him by the hair, dragging him backward, while its mate stifled his cry of pain.

"Hold still," Serramanna ordered, "or I'll strangle you."

Terrified, the Syrian let the giant steer him into a storeroom piled with wicker baskets.

"How long have you been working for Raia?"

"Four years."

"Is the pay good?"

"Not very."

"Are you afraid of him?"

"More or less."

"Raia is going to be arrested," Serramanna told him flatly. "He'll be sentenced to death as a spy for the Hittites. His accomplices will be next."

"But I only work for him!"

"Perjury is a serious offense."

"I'm a warehouse worker, not a spy."

"It was wrong of you to claim he was here in Bubastis when he was in Pi-Ramses committing a murder."

"A murder . . . no, that's not possible . . . I didn't know!"

"Now you do. Will you give another statement?"

"Yes . . . no, he'll kill me!"

"You leave me no choice, my friend. If you won't agree to come clean, I'll smash your head against the wall."

"You wouldn't dare!"

"I've killed more than my share of your kind, you lily-livered—"

"Raia will get me!"

"You'll never see him again."

"Promise?"

"I do."

"All right, then. He paid me to say he was here in Bubastis."

"Do you know how to write?"

"Not too well."

"We're going to the public scribe's office together. He'll take your statement. Then you can have your night on the town."

With her sparkling green eyes and delicately painted lips, Iset the Fair was young, attractive, and vivacious as ever. The winter evening was cool, so she slipped a shawl around her shoulders.

The wind blew hard through the outskirts of Thebes, yet Iset made her way toward the meeting place specified in the disturbing note she had lately received: "The reed hut, just like Memphis. On the West Bank, across from the temple of Luxor, at the edge of a wheat field."

His handwriting . . . there was no mistaking it. But why the curious invitation? Why the sudden reminder of their past closeness?

Iset walked along an irrigation ditch, saw the field of wheat gleaming gold in the sunset, and finally spied the hut. She was about to enter it when a gust of wind made the hem of her dress catch on a thorn bush.

As she bent over to keep the fine fabric from tearing, a hand suddenly freed it and lifted her upright.

"You're as lovely as ever, Iset. Thank you for coming."

"Your message surprised me, to say the least."

"I wanted to see you outside the palace."

The king fascinated her. His athletic body, noble bearing, and powerful gaze elicited an instant response, as always. She had never stopped loving him, although she knew there was no competing with Nefertari. The Great Royal Wife had captured Ramses' heart; it belonged to her entirely. Iset the Fair was neither jealous nor envious. She accepted her fate and was proud she had given the king a son. Already, Kha's star shone brightly.

Yes, she had been hurt when Ramses married Nefertari, but her resentment at the time was only a twisted form of love. Iset had refused to take part in the plots against him. She would never betray the man who had given her so much happiness, filling her heart and her body with his light.

"Why the secrecy . . . and why the same setting as our first nights together?"

"It was Nefertari's idea."

"Nefertari? I don't understand."

"She wants us to have another son to carry on the royal line, just in case anything happens to Kha."

Iset staggered and fell into Ramses' arms.

"This must be a dream," she murmured, "a marvelous dream. You're not the king, I'm not Iset, we're not in Thebes, we aren't going to try and make a brother for Kha. It's only a dream, but I want to live it to the fullest and keep it fresh for all eternity."

Ramses removed his tunic and laid it on the ground. Iset was feverish as he undressed her.

Then her body went wild with joy as it created a child for Ramses, a blinding flash she had never expected to feel again.

On the boat taking him back to Pi-Ramses, the king sat alone, staring at the Nile. Nefertari's face never left him. Yes,

Iset's love was true and her attraction intact, yet for her he did not have the feeling that had swept over him the moment he met Nefertari, a feeling imperious as the sun and vast as the desert, a love that grew stronger with each passing day. The same energy that built the Ramesseum and his capital went into his passion for his wife.

The king had neglected to tell Iset about Nefertari's true demands: that Iset become his secondary wife in more than name only, giving him several more offspring, since his vigor and overpowering personality might prove too much for some of his potential successors. There had been a serious precedent. Pepi II had outlived all his children, and when he died, aged over one hundred, he left a void that developed into a crisis. If Ramses lived a long life, what would befall the kingdom if Kha or Meritamon, for whatever reason, were unable to succeed him?

It was impossible for a pharaoh to lead the life of an ordinary man. Even his love life and his family were at the service of the royal line.

But there was Nefertari, his ideal among women, and the sublime love she offered him. Ramses was torn, wishing neither to neglect his duties nor to have any other lover, even Iset the Fair.

His answer came from the Nile, the river that gave new life each year through the inundation, with boundless generosity.

The court was assembled in the great audience chamber at Pi-Ramses, and the rumors were flying. Following his father's example, Ramses was rather sparing with such ceremonies. He preferred small work sessions with his advisers to pointless group discussions with courtiers whose only preoccupation was currying favor.

When Pharaoh appeared, many a heart skipped a beat at the sight of the staff he grasped in his right hand. It indicated that Ramses was about to make a decree immediately carrying the force of law. The staff symbolized the Word; the cord twined around it was the link with reality the king would bring into being when he announced the terms of a decision reached through careful deliberation.

The room was charged with emotion. No one doubted for a moment that Ramses was about to declare war on the Hittites. An ambassador would be sent to Hatti to deliver Pharaoh's message to the emperor, specifying when the hostilities were to begin.

"What I am about to say has the effect of a royal decree," declared Ramses. "It will be engraved on stelae, the heralds will proclaim it in towns and villages, and every inhabitant of the Two Lands will be informed. From this day forward and until I draw my last breath, I will confer the status of 'royal son' or 'royal daughter' on children who will be educated in the palace and receive the same instruction as my son, Kha, and my daughter, Meritamon. There is no limit to how many may receive this honor, and from their ranks I may choose my successor at random."

The crowd was amazed and delighted. Every father and mother secretly hoped their child would be among the lucky few. Some were already mentally drawing up the list of their progeny's outstanding qualifications, the better to impress Ramses and Nefertari.

Ramses wrapped a large shawl around Nefertari's shoulders. She was just recovering from a cold.

"It comes from the finest workshop in Sais. The high priestess herself wove it for you."

The queen's smile lit up the gloomy Delta sky.

"I would have loved to go south for the winter, but I know it's impossible."

"I'm sorry, Nefertari, but I have to stay here while the troops are being trained."

"Iset will bear you another son, won't she?"

"If the gods are willing."

"Good. When do you see her again?"

"I don't know."

"But you promised . . ."

"I've just made a decree."

"What does that have to do with Iset?"

"You'll have your wish, Nefertari. We'll end up with more than a hundred sons and daughters, and one of them will succeed me."

THIRTY-SEVEN

I can prove Raia lied," Serramanna reported enthusiastically.

Ahmeni sat stone-faced.

"Did you hear what I said?"

"Yes, yes," replied the king's private secretary.

The Sard understood why Ahmeni was so unresponsive. Once again, the scribe was operating on only two or three hours of sleep.

"I have in my possession the sworn statement of the man who heads Raia's Bubastis warehouse, clearly indicating that the merchant was not in that city on the day of Lilia's murder and that he paid his employee to lie for him."

"Congratulations, Serramanna. Nice work. Is your warehouse man still in one piece?"

"He left the scribe's office eager to join in the local festivities—the Feast of the Intoxication of Bastet, I believe. I think he was hoping to try his luck with the fair sex."

"Nice work. I mean it."

"You don't get it. We've destroyed Raia's alibi. He can finally be brought in and interrogated!"

"Impossible."

"Impossible? What's standing in our way?"

"Raia shook off the men we had tailing him and disappeared down a back street in Memphis."

With Shaanar alerted and out of danger, it was time for Raia to make his break. Since he was sure Ahmeni would be examining every shipment to southern Syria, even if it was only preserved meat, he could no longer communicate with the Hittites. Sending a message through one of the members of his network seemed risky; it was too easy to turn in a fugitive sought by Pharaoh's police. The only solution, Raia realized the moment he knew he was under suspicion, was to contact the head of the Egyptian network, despite strict orders to the contrary.

Losing the policemen on his trail had been no easy task. Thanks to an evening visitation from the Storm God, he sneaked into a workshop and out the back door.

Walking on the rooftops, he reached the spy chief's residence at the height of the storm, as lightning flashed and heavy winds whipped up clouds of dust in the deserted streets.

The house was plunged into darkness and looked abandoned. Raia's eyes grew accustomed to the gloom as he painstakingly made his way through the main room in total silence. He heard a muffled moan.

The merchant advanced, uneasy now.

There came another cry of intense but stifled pain. A ray of light was visible at the bottom of a nearby door.

Had the chief been caught? Was he being tortured? No, it wasn't possible. No one but Raia even knew his identity.

The door flew open and torchlight blinded the Syrian. He recoiled, shielding his eyes with his hands.

"Raia . . . what are you doing here?"

"Forgive me, Chief, but I had no alternative."

The Syrian merchant had met his chief only once, at Muwattali's court, but he made a lasting impression. Tall, thin, with prominent cheekbones, dark green eyes, he looked like a bird of prey.

Suddenly, Raia was afraid that Ofir would kill him on the spot. But the tall Libyan remained eerily calm.

In the laboratory beyond, a young blond woman continued to moan.

"I was preparing her for an experiment," explained Ofir, shutting the door.

The darkened room alarmed Raia. Black magic, it looked like to him.

"We can speak privately here, though you realize this is strictly against regulations."

"I know, but I was about to be arrested by Serramanna's henchmen."

"They're still searching Memphis for you, I imagine."

"Yes, but I shook them."

"If they followed you here, they'll break down the door before long. In that case, I'll be forced to kill you and claim I was attacked by a burglar."

Dolora, dozing away upstairs under the influence of a sleeping draught, would confirm Ofir's story.

"I know what I'm doing, Chief. They've lost my trail."

"Let's hope so, Raia. How did this happen?"

"A run of bad luck."

"Or perhaps a combination of mistakes?"

The Syrian told his story, filling in every detail. No use in lying to Ofir, who could read men's thoughts!

A long silence followed Raia's explanation. Ofir was thinking before handing down his verdict.

"You were unlucky, it's true; but we have to face the fact that the network is doomed."

"But my stores, my stock, the fortune I made . . ."

"You'll get them back once Hatti has conquered Egypt."

"May the gods of war grant it."

"Have you any doubt that we'll win?"

"None at all! The Egyptian army is unprepared. According to the latest reports, the rearmament effort is still lagging. The commanding officers dread facing the Hittites in combat, and a positive attitude is half the battle."

"Beware of overconfidence," cautioned Ofir. "We'll need every available tactic to bring about Ramses' downfall."

"Will you keep using Shaanar?"

"Does the Pharaoh suspect him?"

"He doesn't trust his brother, but he can't suppose that Shaanar is in league with us. Who could imagine that a member of the Egyptian royal family—a secretary of state—would be such a traitor? I still consider Shaanar a crucial pawn in our game. By the way, how do you plan to replace me?"

"That's not for you to know, Raia."

"You'll have to write a report on me, Ofir."

"It will be full of praise. You've served Hatti faithfully. The emperor will certainly be grateful."

"What will my next mission be?"

"I'll submit a proposal to Muwattali. He'll decide."

"This business about Aton . . . is it serious?"

"I couldn't care less about any religion, but there are advantages to leading a congregation. Since I have them eating out of my hand, why not take advantage of their gullibility?"

"The girl in your workshop . . ."

"A dim-witted mystic, but an excellent medium. She's helped me gain access to precious information that I never could have obtained otherwise. I soon hope to break through Ramses' magical defenses."

Ofir thought of Moses, a potential ally whom he regretted losing. Interrogating Lita in her trance state had convinced him that the Hebrew was still alive.

"Could I perhaps rest here for a few days?" asked Raia. "This ordeal has been hard on my nerves."

"Too risky. Go straight to the port, the southern end, and take the first barge departing for Pi-Ramses."

Ofir gave the Syrian the passwords and instructions that would get him safely out of Egypt, across Canaan and southern Syria, and into the Hittite sphere of influence.

As soon as Raia was gone, the sorcerer checked to make sure Lita was sleeping soundly and slipped out of the villa.

The unrelenting storm suited his purposes. He would go unnoticed and would quickly return to his lair after alerting Raia's replacement.

Shaanar was eating like mad. Although rationally he knew there was nothing to worry about, he needed to soothe his nerves with food. He was polishing off a roast quail when his steward announced a visit from Meba, his predecessor at the State Department, whom he had maneuvered into believing that Ramses was the cause of all his troubles.

Meba was a typical elder statesman, stiff and formal, from a long line of scribes accustomed to navigating the corridors of power, avoiding conflict and focusing on promotions. When he became secretary of state, Meba had attained the peak of his career and had counted on remaining there until his retirement. Then Shaanar had brought about his sudden ouster (though Meba would never know it). With time on his hands, the career diplomat had retired to his vast landholdings outside Memphis, appearing only rarely at court in the new capital.

Shaanar washed his hands and mouth, reapplied scent, and smoothed his hair. Meba was fastidious and the prince had no wish to suffer by comparison.

"My dear Meba! What a pleasure to see you here in Pi-Ramses. Will you be my guest at dinner tomorrow evening?"

"Gladly."

"I realize that we're living in serious times, but we must put our best face forward. The king is trying to keep up the normal routine at the palace."

Meba's broad, appealing face was part of his charm, as were his neat gestures and cultured voice.

"Are you happy with your position, Shaanar?"

"It's not easy, but I'm giving it my best, for the good of the country."

"Are you acquainted with Raia, a Syrian merchant?"

The prince stiffened. "I've bought vases from him. Remarkable pieces, though somewhat overpriced."

"Have you ever discussed anything besides objets d'art?"

"What's come over you, Meba?"

"You have nothing to fear from me, Your Highness. Quite the contrary."

"To fear . . . what do you mean?"

"You've been expecting a visit from Raia's replacement, haven't you? Here I am."

"You, Meba?"

"I need to keep busy. When the Hittite network contacted me, I saw it as an opportunity to get my revenge on Ramses. I can live with the fact that the enemy is backing you as his successor, provided that you give me back the State Department when you come to power."

The king's older brother looked defeated.

"Give me your word, Shaanar."

"You have it, Meba. You have it."

"I'll bring you the directives from our friends. If you have a message to send to them, you'll go through me as well. Since you're going to appoint me your assistant in Ahsha's absence—starting today, let's assume—we'll see each other often enough. No one will suspect me."

THIRTY-EIGHT

Freezing drizzle fell on Hattusa, the capital of the Hittite empire. The temperature plummeted, the inhabitants huddled around turf or wood fires. It was the time of year when infant mortality was at its highest. The boys who survived would make excellent soldiers. As for the girls, who were barred from any inheritance, their only hope was a suitable marriage.

Despite the harsh weather, Uri-Teshoop, the emperor's son and newly appointed army commander, had stepped up the pace of training. He was unhappy with the foot soldiers' physical conditioning, so they were forced to march for several hours every day, fully outfitted, as if departing for a long campaign. Several men had succumbed to exhaustion. Uri-Teshoop left them on the side of the road, figuring that their incompetence hadn't earned them a decent burial. The vultures would dispose of the cadavers.

The emperor's son was no more lenient with the cavalry, urging them to push their horses and chariots to the limit. The number of fatal accidents convinced him that certain charioteers had not mastered the new equipment and had grown sloppy during the extended truce.

No protest arose from the ranks of the military. Everyone sensed that Uri-Teshoop was preparing the troops for war, and preparing them well. While pleased with his growing popularity, the general bore in mind that Muwattali remained the supreme commander. There was one major disadvantage to leading maneuvers in remote corners of Anatolia, however: he was far from the center of activity. Uri-Teshoop therefore considered it worth his while to employ a number of courtiers to keep him up to date on his father's doings—and Hattusili's.

When he heard that his uncle had left on a tour of neighboring countries, Uri-Teshoop was at once astonished and reassured. Astonished because Hattusili rarely left the capital, and reassured because his absence would keep him from exerting undue influence over the merchant class.

Uri-Teshoop detested the merchants. After his victory over Ramses, he planned to depose Muwattali, banish Hattusili to the salt mines, and send Puduhepa, his arrogant, treacherous wife, to a provincial brothel. As for the merchants, they would all be forced to join the army.

Hatti's future was clear in his mind. It would be a military dictatorship and he, Uri-Teshoop, would be absolute master of the country.

Right now it would be folly to attack the emperor, at the height of his powers after ruling the country for years with a skilled and merciless hand. Impetuous as he was, Uri-Teshoop was determined to be patient and wait for his father to slip. Then Muwattali would either agree to abdicate or his son would eliminate him.

Swathed in a thick woolen mantle, the emperor stayed close to the fire, which barely warmed him. The older he got, the harder the winters seemed; yet he could never live without the uplifting sight of the snow-covered mountains. At times he was tempted to give up his expansionist policies and concentrate on exploiting his country's natural riches. But the notion was quickly dispelled, for his people's survival depended on the conquest of new territory. Taking Egypt would give them an inexhaustible horn of plenty. He would put Ramses' ambitious older brother, Shaanar, in charge of an interim administration. Then he would replace the traitor with a Hittite government that would snuff out the slightest hint of revolt.

The main danger, as he saw it, was his own son, Uri-Teshoop. The emperor needed him to get the troops back in order, to rekindle their fighting spirit. But Uri-Teshoop must not be allowed to turn victory to his advantage. He was an intrepid warrior, but had no talent for statecraft.

Hattusili was a different case. The emperor's brother might be physically unimposing, but he was an excellent administrator and knew how to stay in the background, without drawing attention to his true influence. What did he really want? Muwattali had no answer to the question, which made him all the more wary.

And here was Hattusili, back from his mission.

"Did you have a good journey, brother?"

"I think you'll be pleased with the results," Hattusili replied, then began sneezing.

"You've caught cold?"

"The inns are poorly heated. My wife has made me some mulled wine. I'll drink it while I soak my feet in hot water and I'll be good as new."

"Were our allies glad to see you?"

"They were surprised, and then they were afraid I was there to raise taxes."

"Good. They need to be reminded who's in charge."

"That's why I pointedly mentioned their leaders' past transgressions before discussing the matter at hand."

"You know how to handle the weapons of diplomacy, brother."

"It's a skill that requires constant practice, but well worth the effort. All of our vassals, without exception, said yes to our . . . invitation."

"I applaud your initiative, Hattusili. When will the preparations be complete?"

"Three or four months from now."

"Will official documents need to be drawn up?"

"We're better off without them," said Hattusili. "Our spies have infiltrated Egypt, so perhaps they have a network in place in our territory."

"Highly unlikely, but we can't be too careful."

"Our allies are eager to hasten the fall of Egypt. Giving their word to your official representative is tantamount to swearing before the emperor. They'll keep quiet until the action begins."

His eyes glazed with fever, Hattusili was grateful that the room was snug, its windows covered with cloth-lined wooden slats.

"How is the army shaping up?" he asked.

"Uri-Teshoop is doing an admirable job," replied Muwattali. "Our troops will soon reach the point of maximum efficiency."

"Do you think that Ramses and his wife will be fooled by the letters from you and Puduhepa?"

"The Pharaoh and the Great Royal Wife replied most amiably, and we have pursued the correspondence. At the very least, it will throw them off guard. What news of our spies in Egypt?"

"The Syrian merchant's network is out of commission, but our chief of intelligence, the Libyan Ofir, is still of great value."

"What's been done about this Syrian?"

"I thought he should be eliminated, but Ofir had a better suggestion."

"Go now and let that lovely wife of yours cure your cold."

Mulled wine helped Hattusili's fever and cleared his sinuses. The steaming footbath was heaven, after countless hours on the road. A servant girl massaged his neck and shoulders, and a barber shaved him under the watchful eye of Puduhepa.

"Mission accomplished?" she asked once they were alone.

"I believe so, my dear."

"I also accomplished things in your absence."

"What are you talking about?"

"It's not in my nature to be idle."

"Tell me what you mean!"

"I thought you'd be clever enough to guess."

"Don't tell me . . ."

"Yes, my dear diplomat. While you were on the emperor's errand, I decided to take care of your rival—your only rival."

"Uri-Teshoop?"

"Who else is holding you back and undermining your

influence with the emperor? His new appointment has turned his head. He thinks he's already on the throne!"

"Muwattali is manipulating him, not the reverse, I assure you."

"Both of you underestimate the danger."

"You're wrong, Puduhepa. The emperor is clearheaded. He put his son in charge of the army to energize the troops and make sure they're combat ready. But Muwattali doesn't consider Uri-Teshoop capable of running the country."

"Has he told you so?"

"No, but I can tell."

"That's not enough for me. Uri-Teshoop is violent and dangerous, he hates the two of us, and he'd love to get us out of the way. Since you're the emperor's brother, he doesn't dare attack you directly, but he'll stab you in the back."

"Just wait, Puduhepa, and Uri-Teshoop will trip himself up."

"We won't need to wait."

"Why not?"

"I've already taken steps."

Hattusili didn't want to believe his ears.

"A representative from the merchants' guild is on his way to General Uri-Teshoop's training camp. He'll ask for an audience, and to gain his trust he'll confide that his organization would welcome the end of Muwattali and the advent of his son. Then our man will take out his dagger, and that will be the end of the monster!"

"Hatti needs Uri-Teshoop . . . it's too soon, much too soon. He has to prepare our troops for battle first."

"Don't tell me you're going to save him," Puduhepa said in disbelief.

Aching, feverish, stiff-kneed, Hattusili stood up. "I'm on my way," he told her.

THIRTY-NINE

Ahsha was virtually unrecognizable in the guise of a courier riding the postal routes of northern Syria. In a coarse and tattered cloak, the formerly refined and elegant diplomat straddled a sturdy donkey. Two more donkeys trailed behind, each heavily laden with mailbags. Together they had just entered Hittite territory.

Ahsha had spent several weeks in Canaan and Amurru, examining the two protectorates' defense systems in detail. He had talked at length with Egyptian officers in charge of organizing resistance against an eventual enemy deployment. He had also added significantly to his list of feminine conquests.

Benteshina, the Prince of Amurru, had heartily approved of Ahsha. He was a model guest who enjoyed a good meal, made no unreasonable demands, and asked only that the prince alert Ramses at once if he noticed any unusual action from the Hittites.

Then Ahsha had headed home—or so he had led his hosts to believe. Obeying orders, the diplomat's escort rode south along the coastal route, while Ahsha destroyed his

Egyptian clothing, assumed his new identity (confirmed by expertly forged Hittite credentials), and traveled north.

Given the conflicting reports and unclear state of relations, it was impossible to assess Hatti's true intentions without firsthand knowledge. Since Ramses' needs meshed with his own, Ahsha had gladly accepted the challenge. This mission would put him ahead of the game.

The Hittites' great strength, it seemed to him, was their ability to make everyone believe they were invulnerable and ready to conquer the world. But were they? That was the crucial question he had to answer.

Thirty-odd soldiers, armed and sinister-looking, were guarding the Hittite border crossing. Four foot soldiers ringed Ahsha and his three donkeys. The would-be courier stood stunned and motionless.

A lance tip grazed Ahsha's left cheek.

"Your credentials?"

From beneath his cloak, Ahsha produced a tablet covered with Hittite writing. The soldier read it and handed it to a colleague, who also examined the document.

"Where are you going?"

"Hattusa, with letters and invoices for the merchants."

"Show me them."

"They're confidential."

"Nothing is confidential to the army."

"I don't want to have problems with the recipients."

"You'll have plenty of problems if you don't do as I say."

His fingers numb with the cold, Ahsha undid the string around the sacks full of tablets.

"It's got to be business," the soldier said as he examined the documents. "Can't make head nor tail of it. All right then, we'll search you."

The courier carried no arms. The Hittite border guard

gave up in frustration. "Before you go into any villages, report to the checkpoint first."

"Never had to before."

"You do now. Show your credentials at every checkpoint, or you'll be marked as an enemy and hunted down."

"There are no enemies in Hittite territory!"

"Just do as you're told."

"All right, all right."

"Now hit the road!"

Ahsha ambled off like a man with a clear conscience. Walking beside the lead donkey, he fell into a steady pace and took the road to Hattusa, in the heart of Anatolia.

Several times, he found himself looking for the Nile. The craggy northland was hard to get used to; it lacked the simple beauty of the great Valley with a river running through it. Ahsha missed the sharp divide between cultivated land and desert. He missed the spectacular sunsets. But he had to forget Egypt and think only of Hatti, this cold and hostile land whose secrets he was determined to learn.

The sky was low, unleashing violent downpours. The donkeys stepped around the puddles and stopped to munch on wet grass whenever they felt like it.

This was no country for peace. Its savagery made everyone living here see life as a struggle and view the future as survival of the fittest. How many generations would it take to turn these desolate valleys into farmland, to make soldiers into plowmen? Here men were born to fight, and fight they would.

The placement of checkpoints at the entry to every village intrigued Ahsha. Did the Hittites suspect there were spies within their country, tightly controlled as it was by the military? This unusual precaution was a clue in itself. The army might be conducting maneuvers that needed to be kept safe from prying eyes.

On two more occasions, roving patrols checked Ahsha's mailbags and questioned him regarding his destination. Each time he was allowed to go on his way. At the first village he came to, he found a checkpoint and was subjected to another thorough search. The soldiers were on their guard and irritable; the counterfeit postman did not protest.

After spending the night in a barn, he ate some bread and cheese and resumed his journey, secure in the knowledge that his disguise was completely believable. In mid-afternoon, he took a side road leading into some undergrowth. This was his chance to deposit a few tablets addressed to nonexistent merchants. As he approached the capital, he would gradually lighten his load.

The woodland overlooked a steep ravine. Huge boulders had rolled to the bottom, pried loose by rain and snow. Gnarled oak roots clung to the slope.

As he opened one of the sacks on the lead donkey, Ahsha had the feeling he was being watched. The animals were restless. Robins were flitting between the treetops.

He gathered up a stone and a piece of dried wood—a flimsy defense against a potential attacker. When he heard the unmistakable sound of horses approaching, Ahsha slunk behind a fallen trunk. Four men on horseback came out of the undergrowth and surrounded the donkeys. They were not soldiers, but bandits equipped with bows and daggers. Even in Hatti there were caravan robbers! When apprehended, they were executed on the spot.

Ahsha flattened himself on the ground. If the four bandits saw him, they were sure to slit his throat.

Their leader, bearded and pockmarked, sniffed the air like a hunting dog.

"Look," he said to one of his companions. "This is no prize. Nothing but tablets. You know how to read?"

"Never had time to learn."

"Is this stuff worth anything?"

"Not to us."

Furious, the outlaw shattered the tablets and threw the pieces into the ravine.

"Whoever owns these donkeys can't have gone far. And he has to have tin on him."

"Let's spread out," ordered the ringleader.

Numb with fear and chilled to the bone, Ahsha kept his wits about him. Only one bandit was heading in his direction. He crawled forward, hugging a tree root. The ringleader walked around him without even noticing.

Ahsha smashed the man's neck in with a rock. He fell forward, his mouth in the dirt.

"Over there!" cried one of his accomplices, who'd seen the attack.

Seizing his victim's dagger, Ahsha hurled it, hitting the man in his chest as he ran forward.

The two survivors readied their bows.

Ahsha's only option was to run. An arrow whizzed past his ear as he clambered down the ravine, aiming for a briar patch where he could take cover.

Another arrow grazed his right calf just as he plunged into his temporary shelter. Covered with scratches, his hands raw, he fought his way through the bramble, fell, got up, and began to run again.

He ran until he could run no more. If his pursuers caught up with him, he wouldn't have the strength to fight them. But the ravine was silent, save for the cawing of a flock of crows skirting black clouds.

Warily, Ahsha stayed put until nightfall. Then he climbed back up the slope to where he'd left his donkeys, edging along the ravine.

The animals were gone. Only the bodies of the two dead bandits remained.

Ahsha's own wounds were superficial but painful. He washed at a spring, rubbed his bruised skin with the herbs at hand, climbed to the top of a sturdy oak, and slept stretched out on two thick, almost parallel branches.

He dreamed of a comfortable bed in one of the plush villas Shaanar had provided in exchange for his services. He dreamed of a pool beneath tall palm trees, a cup of vintage wine, and a pretty lute player plucking a tune, then letting him stroke her body.

Cold rain woke him before dawn, and he headed north once more.

The loss of his donkeys and tablets would force him to change his identity. A courier without documents or beasts of burden would appear highly suspicious and soon be under arrest. He'd never make it past the next checkpoint.

If he stayed in the forest, he could steer clear of roving patrols, but what about the bears, wildcats, and bandits he might encounter? There was plenty of water, but what about food? With any luck, he might waylay a traveling salesman and assume his identity.

His situation was less than ideal, but nothing would keep him from reaching Hattusa and finding out for himself how strong the Hittite army really was.

FORTY

After a day on horseback directing cavalry maneuvers, Uri-Teshoop was taking a frigid shower. The intensive training was beginning to show results, but the emperor's son was still not satisfied. The Hittite army must leave no opening for the Egyptian troops, nor must it show any hesitation during the various phases of the attack.

As the general was drying off in the brisk wind, his aide-de-camp came to tell him that a merchant newly arrived from Hattusa desired an audience.

"Let him wait," said Uri-Teshoop. "I'll see him tomorrow at dawn. Merchants were born to obey. What manner of man is he?"

"Important, by the look of him."

"He can still wait. Put him in the least comfortable tent you can find."

"What if he protests?"

"Let him complain."

Hattusili and his escort had galloped at breakneck speed. The emperor's brother ignored his cold and his fever, obsessed with the need to reach Uri-Teshoop's headquarters before it was too late.

When he spotted the encampment in the middle of the night, it looked calm. Hattusili made himself known to the guards, who opened the wooden gates to him. Preceded by the chief security officer, the emperor's brother was shown into Uri-Teshoop's tent.

The general woke up unhappy. Seeing Hattusili was no pleasure under the best of circumstances.

"What's so important that it couldn't wait until morning?" grumbled Uri-Teshoop.

"Your life."

"What does that mean?"

"I've uncovered a plot against you."

"Are you serious?"

"I just returned from an exhausting journey, I'm ill, and my only desire is to rest. Do you think I would have ridden all night from Hattusa if it wasn't serious?"

"Who wants to kill me?"

"You know that I've worked closely with the merchants . . . While I was away, one of them confessed to my wife that his friend had gone over the edge and decided to kill you. He's afraid that a war with Egypt will wipe him out."

"What's the man's name?"

"I don't know, but I came here to warn you straightaway."

"You're no partisan of this war either, are you?"

"You're wrong, nephew. I see the necessity for it. Your victory will allow our empire to continue expanding. The emperor has appointed you to head his armed forces because he recognizes your abilities as a fighter and your capacity for leadership."

Hattusili's speech astonished Uri-Teshoop, though without allaying his suspicions. The emperor's brother was a master of the art of flattery.

Yet it was true a merchant had come seeking an audience with him. If Uri-Teshoop had consented to see the man at once, he might no longer be among the living. There was still one simple way to see whether Hattusili's story was true.

The merchant had spent a sleepless night, mentally rehearsing what he had to do. He would sink his dagger into Uri-Teshoop's throat to keep him from crying out, then exit at the leisurely pace of a dignified businessman. He would mount his horse and trot quietly out of the encampment, picking up speed, then jumping on the back of a faster mount concealed in the woods nearby.

The risk was considerable, but the merchant detested Uri-Teshoop. A year earlier, his two sons had taken part in one of the warmongering brute's senseless expeditions. They were among the twenty young men he drove to death in the course of it. When Puduhepa had planted the seeds of this plan, he had quickly consented. The reward she promised was almost beside the point. Even if he was arrested and executed, he would have the satisfaction of taking revenge for his sons and ridding the country of a monster.

At dawn, Uri-Teshoop's aide-de-camp went to fetch the merchant and escorted him to the general's tent. Controlling his nervousness, he spoke of his merchant friends who hoped to oust the emperor and help his son assume the throne.

The aide-de-camp frisked him and found no weapon. The short, double-edged dagger was concealed beneath the harmless-looking woolen hat most merchants favored during the winter.

"Go in. The general is waiting."

His back to the visitor, Uri-Teshoop was bent over a map.

"Thank you for seeing me, General."

"State your business."

"The merchant class is divided. Some wish to keep the truce, others lean toward war. I side with those who believe we should conquer Egypt."

"Go on."

It was the perfect chance: Uri-Teshoop was still concentrating on the map, drawing dots on it, his back turned.

The merchant whipped off his hat, gripped the handle of the dagger, and approached the prince, still talking calmly.

"My friends and I are convinced that the emperor will never be able to bring off such a conquest. But a general like you, a born warrior . . . Die, you cur, die like you killed my sons!"

Just as the merchant lunged, the general whirled around, his left hand also clutching a dagger. The attacker's blade plunged into his neck, while the general struck the merchant in the heart. Both fell down dead, their arms and legs tangled together.

The real Uri-Teshoop came out from behind a panel of his tent.

To learn the truth, he had sacrificed an enlisted man roughly the same build as himself. The idiot had moved too quickly and killed the merchant; questioning him would have been of value. Still, the prince had heard enough to corroborate his uncle's story.

Hattusili was a realist, and cautious, Uri-Teshoop calculated. He wanted to back the winner. He hoped that his nephew would return this important favor once he returned victorious, the future master of Hatti.

Hattusili was sadly mistaken.

Ahsha had no need to ambush a fellow traveler, for he happened upon far easier prey: a young widow by the name of Arinna, barely over twenty, childless and alone. Her soldier husband, stationed at Kadesh, had drowned when the army crossed the Orontes at flood stage. Now Arinna was struggling to eke a living from the meager farm he had left her.

Arriving on her doorstep in a state of exhaustion, Ahsha had explained that he had been robbed and escaped by crawling through a briar patch. He begged her to give him shelter for the night.

As soon as he began to wash in the water which she had heated on the hearth in an earthenware basin, Arinna's feelings changed. Her shyness was replaced by the overwhelming desire to touch his beautiful body. She had gone without love for months now. Acting on impulse, she undressed, slipped her arms around the stranger's neck, and pressed her ample bosom to his back. Ahsha did not resist.

For two days, the lovers didn't leave the farmhouse. Arinna was inexperienced, but ardent and giving; she was one of the rare lovers he would remember clearly.

Outside, it was raining.

Ahsha and Arinna lay naked by the hearth. His hand traced the young woman's furrows and valleys as she sighed with pleasure.

"Who are you really?"

"I told you, a traveling salesman robbed by bandits."

"I don't believe you."

"Why not?"

"You're too refined, too elegant. You don't act or talk like a salesman."

Ahsha took note. His disguise might not be as convincing as he thought.

"You're not brutal enough to be a Hittite. When you make love, you think of your partner. My husband only ever took his own pleasure. Who are you?"

"Can you keep a secret?"

"I swear by the Storm God!" The farm wife glowed with excitement.

"It isn't easy . . ."

"Trust me! Haven't I given you proof enough of my love?"

He kissed the tips of her breasts.

"I'm the son of a Syrian nobleman," explained Ahsha, "and my dream is to join the Hittite army. But my father won't let me because of the danger. He says some men don't even survive the training. I ran away to see Hatti on my own and prove myself so that I can be recruited."

"You're mad! Our soldiers will eat you alive."

"I want to fight against the Egyptians. If we don't push them back, they'll seize all my property in Syria and ruin me."

She laid her head on his chest. "I hate war."

"Is there any way around it?"

"Everyone thinks we're heading for war any day."

"Do you know where the army is training?"

"It's a secret."

"Have you seen any troops passing through?"

"Not here. It's the middle of nowhere."

"Will you come with me to Hattusa?"

"Well . . . I've never been there."

"Then it's time you went. In the capital, I can get to know some officers and convince them to sign me up."

"Why would you want to? You're too young to die!"

"If I don't act quickly, my province will be destroyed. Egypt has gotten too big."

"Hattusa is far away."

"I saw that you have pots stored out in the shed. Did your husband make them?"

"Yes, he was a potter before he was drafted."

"We can sell them and live in Hattusa. I hear it's an unforgettable city."

"But the farm . . ."

"There's not much to do here in winter. We'll leave tomorrow."

Arinna stretched out closer to the hearth and opened her arms to her heaven-sent lover.

FORTY-ONE

The House of Life in Heliopolis was the oldest center of learning in all of Egypt. As usual, ritualists were going over the texts to be used in the celebration of the mysteries of Osiris; state magicians were laboring to keep evil at bay; astrologers were charting their predictions for the following months; healers were formulating potions. Strangely, however, the library was off limits for the day—the library where millions of scrolls were stored, including

the original version of the Pyramid Texts and the prayers for
the pharaoh's rebirth in the heavens.

Today the library was reserved for a single reader:
Ramses.

Arriving during the night, the monarch had locked himself behind the great stone walls with their shelves preserving the essence of Egyptian knowledge, relating to the
known world and the afterlife as well. Ramses had come to
consult the archives because of his concern for Nefertari's
health.

The Great Royal Wife was wasting away. Neither the
palace physician nor Setau could determine why. The
Queen Mother, however, offered a disturbing diagnosis:
forces beyond the province of traditional medicine might be
causing Nefertari's sickness. Black magic, she felt, was at
work.

For ten hours or more, Ramses consulted the lore of his
ancestors. As soon as he found what he was looking for, he
headed back to his capital.

Nefertari had chaired a meeting of the Women Weavers'
Guild with representatives from every temple in the country.
She gave orders for the ritual vestments to be woven until
the next inundation. After making an offering of red, white,
green, and blue strips of cloth, the queen left the building,
supported by two priestesses. They helped her into a litter
that carried her back to the palace.

Dr. Pariamaku hurried to the Great Royal Wife's bedside and administered a stimulant, though without much
hope of alleviating the fatigue that had been slowly crip-

pling her. As soon as Ramses entered the room, the physician exited.

The king kissed Nefertari's hands and forehead.

"I'm so tired."

"You need to cut back on your duties."

"It's more than a passing weakness . . . I feel the life draining out of me like a stream, but now it's only a trickle."

"Tuya thinks it's something more than physical."

"She's right."

"Someone is using the forces of darkness against us."

"My shawl . . . my favorite shawl! It fell into the hands of a sorcerer."

"It must have, my darling. I've asked Serramanna to find out what happened."

"He'd better hurry, Ramses."

"There are other things we can try, Nefertari. But that means leaving Pi-Ramses tomorrow morning."

"Where are you taking me?"

"To a place where our secret enemy can't touch you."

Ramses met for hours with Ahmeni. Pharaoh's private secretary and sandal bearer had nothing out of the ordinary to report. As always when the king was about to leave for an extended period, he anxiously reviewed outstanding business in order to avoid potential pitfalls. The country's welfare was always his prime concern. Ramses noted how thoroughly Ahmeni studied each document, mentally filing away essential information and discarding the rest.

The king made a number of important decisions and gave Ahmeni the task of seeing that the various branches of government carried them out. Then he reviewed Serramanna's standing orders, not the least of which was overseeing the training of his elite commandos quartered in Pi-Ramses.

At the close of the day the monarch met his mother for a walk in the garden where she liked to meditate. Her shoulders covered with a shirred cape, she wore earrings in the shape of lotus blossoms and an amethyst necklace that softened her angular features.

"I'm leaving for the south with Nefertari, Mother. It's too dangerous for her here."

"You're right. Until we stop the dark forces at work against us, the queen must remain in seclusion."

"I'm leaving you in charge. If there's an emergency, Ahmeni will carry out your orders."

"What about this war on the horizon?"

"For the moment, everything's quiet. The Hittites are doing nothing. Muwattali keeps sending me meaningless letters."

"Couldn't that translate into domestic unrest? Muwattali eliminated quite a few rivals before he seized power. There must be factions still working against him."

"If so, that's hardly good news for us," commented Ramses. "What better way to unite his country than a new war?"

"In that case, the Hittites must be gearing up for a major confrontation."

"I hope I'm wrong . . . perhaps Muwattali has simply grown tired of bloodshed."

"Don't think like an Egyptian, my son. Peace is no virtue to the Hittites. An emperor has to preach conquest and expansion, or he's quickly toppled."

"If the attack comes while I'm out of reach, don't wait for my return to retaliate."

Tuya's small chin was square and determined.

"No Hittite will cross the border into the Delta."

The temple of the goddess Mut, the "Mother," contained three hundred sixty-five statues of Sekhmet, the lion goddess, for use in the morning offerings, and an equal number to be used each evening. This was where the kingdom's great physicians came to probe the secrets of illnesses and their cures.

Nefertari chanted the magic words that changed the lethal fury of the lioness into a life-giving force. Sekhmet's seven priestesses communed with the spirit of the queen as she offered herself to the goddess and brought light from the dark recesses of her chapel.

The high priestess poured water on the head of the lioness, sculpted in diorite, a hard, sparkling stone. The liquid ran over the goddess's body, which was human in form, and into a vessel held by an acolyte.

Nefertari drank the healing water, absorbing Sekhmet's magic. The goddess's ferocious energy helped her fight the creeping weakness. Then the Great Royal Wife remained alone with Sekhmet for a day and a night, in silence and total darkness.

When she crossed the Nile, tenderly leaning on Ramses' shoulder, Nefertari felt stronger than she had in weeks. The king's love gave rise to another kind of magic, as powerful as that of the goddess. A chariot took them to the rock-cut temple at Deir el-Bahri, Queen Hatshepsut's sublime achievement. The garden in front of it bloomed with frankincense trees imported from the land of Punt. This was the domain of the goddess Hathor, the patroness of love and beauty, Sekhmet's mirror image.

One of the temple buildings was a convalescent home where the patients were bathed several times a day and sometimes given a sleeping cure. The bases of the warm-water baths bore special hieroglyph texts to ward off illness.

"You need to rest, Nefertari."

"My royal duties . . ."

"Your first duty is to survive, so that our union may remain the cornerstone of Egypt. Those who wish us harm are trying to destroy the country by separating us."

The garden of Hatshepsut's temple seemed to be part of another world. The leaves of the frankincense trees gleamed in the soft winter sunlight. A network of shallow ditches provided constant irrigation, adjustable according to the weather.

Nefertari had the sensation that her love for Ramses was growing even stronger, as wide as the limitless sky. The way he looked at her showed that he felt the same. But their happiness was fragile, so fragile . . .

"Don't sacrifice Egypt for me, Ramses. Swear that Egypt alone will dictate your behavior. Your life belongs to your country, not to any mere human. The people's welfare depends on your commitment; so does the future of our civilization. Without our time-honored values, what will become of the world? I love you with all my strength, and my dying thought will be of our love; but I have no right to hold you back, for you are Pharaoh."

They sat down on a stone bench. Ramses held Nefertari close.

"You're my partner, Nefertari. Only you can see me as both Horus and Set, the warring brothers, using the magic formula handed down from the queens of the First

Dynasty. Through your eyes Pharaoh exists; your gaze holds his light and reflects it over the Twin Kingdoms. Every pharaoh that has gone before me drew strength from the law of Ma'at, but no two were alike, for the human spirit is ever changing. Your eyes are unique, Nefertari. Egypt and her pharaoh need your eyes."

In her darkest hour, Nefertari found a new love.

"In the library of the House of Life in Heliopolis, I discovered some measures we can take against our invisible enemy. The power of Sekhmet and Hathor, combined with the rest you will take in this temple, can renew your energy. But that won't be enough."

"Are you going back to Pi-Ramses?"

"No, Nefertari. I may have a cure for what ails you."

"A cure?"

"According to the ancient texts, there's a place in Nubia that's sacred to Hathor."

"Do you know where it is?"

"The exact site has been lost for centuries, but I'll find it."

"You can't stay away too long."

"Thanks to the current, the journey home will be short. If I find Hathor's magic stone without too much trouble, I'll be back soon enough."

"But the Hittites . . ."

"I've left my mother in charge. If they attack, she'll let you know at once. You're authorized to act."

They embraced in the shade of the frankincense trees. Nefertari wished she could cling to him forever, spend the rest of her days with him in this peaceful temple.

But she was the Great Royal Wife and he was the Pharaoh of Egypt.

FORTY-TWO

L ita looked pleadingly at the sorcerer Ofir.

"You must, my child."

"No, it hurts too much."

"That shows you the spell is working. We have to go on."

"My burns . . ."

"Dolora will dress them for you. They won't leave a trace."

Akhenaton's great-granddaughter turned her back to the sorcerer.

"No, I can't take any more!"

"Enough of your tantrums! Do as I say or I'll shut you up in the cellar."

"Not that, I beseech you, not that!"

Of all Ofir's punishments, the claustrophobic young woman feared the cellar most.

"Come into my workshop, strip to the waist, and lie down on your back."

Dolora, Ramses' sister, deplored the sorcerer's rough treatment of Lita, but understood its necessity. The latest news from court was gratifying: Nefertari, suffering from a mysterious and incurable disease, had departed for Thebes, retiring to the temple at Deir el-Bahri. Her lingering death would break Ramses' heart, and he wouldn't outlive her for long.

The path to power lay wide open for Shaanar.

As soon as Ramses left, Serramanna called at each of the four vast army bases in Pi-Ramses, demanding that the generals intensify their training efforts. The mercenaries immediately demanded a bonus, inciting the regular troops to make a similar request.

Faced with a problem beyond his capabilities, the Sard consulted Ahmeni, who took it to the Queen Mother. Her instantaneous reply was that the soldiers and mercenaries could choose between obeying orders and being replaced by fresh recruits. If they stayed, and Serramanna was satisfied with their progress the next time that he reviewed the troops, Tuya might consider a pay increase.

The troops gave in, leaving the Sard free to pursue his major preoccupation: finding the sorcerer who lured Romay, the late chief steward, into stealing Nefertari's shawl. Ramses had shared his suspicions freely with his security chief, citing Romay's strange death and the queen's even stranger illness.

If that stupid Romay had only survived, Serramanna would have had no trouble making him talk. Torture was not an accepted practice in Egypt, but using black magic against the royal couple must certainly qualify as an exception.

But Romay was dead, taking his secret with him to the demon-infested underworld, and the trail to the mastermind seemed to have gone cold. But had it really? Romay had once been jolly and talkative; perhaps he'd had an accomplice, some palace crony, an underling, a pretty maid-servant . . .

Questioning his peers and subordinates would certainly bring results, provided the questions were asked with a certain force of conviction . . . Serramanna hurried over to Ahmeni's office. He would convince the scribe that his methods were sound.

The entire domestic staff of the palace was assembled at the North Base. Linen maids, chambermaids, hairdressers, masseuses, kitchen boys, sweepers, and countless other servants gathered in a huge armory. Serramanna's stern-faced archers were there to keep order.

When the Sard appeared, in helmet and breastplate, there was a collective gasp.

"New incidents of theft have been reported at the palace," he revealed. "We know that the perpetrator is an accomplice of the late chief steward Romay, who angered the gods with his evil deeds. Today I will interrogate you one by one. Unless I get to the bottom of this today, you'll all be shipped off to a desert prison until the guilty party comes forward."

It had taken a great deal of arm-twisting before Ahmeni consented to let him use these blatantly illicit tactics. Any of the domestics might have stepped forward to challenge the Sard, and his baseless threats and assertions would never stand up in court.

However, the king's personal bodyguard was so fearsome-looking, his manner so commanding, and the cavernous armory so unnerving, they were completely cowed.

Serramanna was in luck: the third woman who came into the room where he was conducting the interviews had quite a bit to say.

"My job is keeping the flower arrangements fresh," she told him. "I hated that fat old Romay."

"Why?"

"He took advantage of me. He said if I didn't sleep with him, he'd have me fired."

"If you'd filed a grievance, you could have had him fired."

"I wasn't sure it would work . . . and then Romay kept saying he'd marry me and set me up for life."

"He told you he was rich?"

"He didn't like to talk about it, but I got him to tell me a little when he was, well, in the right mood."

"Go on."

"He said he'd be paid a fortune for a rare object."

"And how was he planning to get his hands on it?"

"Through a temporary helper in the queen's chambers."

"Do you know exactly what this priceless object was?"

"I'm not sure. But I do know that Romay never gave me a thing, not even an amulet. Will I get a reward for telling you all this?"

A temporary helper in the queen's chambers, Serramanna muttered to himself as he ran to see Ahmeni. A staff scribe located the palace payroll records for the week the queen's shawl had gone missing.

Indeed, a girl named Nani had filled in as a linen maid

that week, assisting in the queen's chambers. The head chambermaid gave a description and confirmed that the girl could well have participated in the theft of Her Majesty's shawl.

The chambermaid also recalled where Nani said she lived at the time.

"Question her," Ahmeni told Serramanna, "but don't lay a hand on her or do anything illegal."

"I wouldn't dream of it," the Sard replied without a hint of irony.

An old woman dozed on her doorstep on the east side of town. Serramanna shook her gently by the shoulder.

"Wake up, old woman."

She opened her eyes and brushed a fly away with a callused hand.

"And who might you be?"

"Serramanna, the Pharaoh's personal bodyguard."

"I've heard of you. Didn't you used to be a pirate?"

"It's hard to change, old woman. I'm as mean as ever, especially when people lie to me."

"Why would I lie to you?"

"Because I'm going to ask you some questions."

"It's a sin to talk too much."

"That depends on the circumstances. You could say that talking to me is an obligation."

"Be on your way, pirate. At my age, I'm obliged to no one."

"Are you related to a girl called Nani?"

"What makes you ask that?"

"This is her address."

"She doesn't live here anymore."

"When she had the good fortune to find a job at the palace, why would she run away?"

"I never said she ran away."

"Where did she go?"

"I wouldn't know."

"Remember, I hate being lied to."

"Would you strike an old grandmother, pirate?"

"Yes, to save Ramses."

The crone gazed anxiously up at him.

"I don't understand . . . is Pharaoh in danger?"

"Your granddaughter is a thief, perhaps worse. She may be involved in a plot against him. If you won't talk, you could be named as an accessory."

"I don't see how Nani could be mixed up in anything like that."

"She is, and I have proof."

The fly began buzzing around the old woman again. Serramanna swatted it.

"Death is a blessing, pirate, when it comes at the end of long suffering. I had a good husband and a good son, but my boy married a horrible woman who gave him a horrible child. My husband died, my son and his wife split up, and I was left to raise the brat. I fed her and cared for her, tried to teach her right from wrong . . . and now you're telling me she's a thief and a traitor?"

The old woman fell silent, wheezing. Serramanna said nothing, hoping she'd tell him more. If she didn't, he'd leave her alone.

"Nani left for Memphis. She kept boasting that she'd be living in a fine villa near the School of Medicine, and I'd be left to die in this poor excuse for a house."

Serramanna reported to Ahmeni at once.

"If you roughed up the old woman, she's bound to press charges against you."

"My men will back me up: I didn't touch her."

"What will you do next?"

"She gave me a detailed description of her grand-daughter; it matches the one we got from the palace chambermaid. It should be enough for me to identify her."

"But how will you find her?"

"With a house-to-house search of her Memphis neighborhood."

"What if the old woman was lying to protect this Nani?"

"It's a chance I'll have to take."

"Memphis isn't far away, but you're needed here."

"I won't be far away, as you said yourself. Suppose I do locate Nani and she leads me to the sorcerer: don't you think Ramses would approve?"

"Approve is far too weak a word."

"Then give me the authority to proceed."

FORTY-THREE

Ahsha and Arinna arrived at the gates to Hattusa, gaping. The capital of the Hittite empire bore the clear stamp of its military might. Since the three gates to the upper town—the King's Gate, Sphinx Gate, and Lion's Gate— were off limits to merchants, the young couple would have to enter through one of the lower town's two gates flanked by lance-wielding soldiers.

Ahsha displayed his earthenware pots, even offering one of the guards a bargain. The soldier shoved him roughly and ordered him on his way. The lovers walked slowly toward the part of town where craftsmen and shopkeepers sold their wares.

The rocky gorge, the zigzagging terraces, the boulders in the walls of the Storm God's temple . . . Arinna was impressed with Hattusa. But Ahsha deplored the lack of charm and elegance in this rugged city, topped by a citadel that made it virtually invulnerable, hewn out of the rough heart of Anatolia. Peace and comfort seemed to have no place here; every stone was steeped in violence.

The Egyptian looked for gardens, trees, fountains, but

found none. A chill wind whistled, making him miss the paradise he called home.

The couple was repeatedly forced to flatten themselves against a building when a patrol thundered by. Anyone in the way, including women, children, and old people, was pushed aside, even trampled by the hurrying foot soldiers.

The army's presence was everywhere. On every street corner, soldiers stood guard.

Ahsha displayed his wares to a seller of household goods. As was the custom in Hatti, Arinna stood behind him and kept silent.

"Nice work," said the shopkeeper. "How many do you make in a week?"

"I brought all I made in the country. I'm hoping to settle here."

"Do you have a place to stay?"

"Not yet."

"I have an empty shop in the lower town. I'll take the pots you have on hand in exchange for a month's rent. That will give you time to set up your workshop."

"All right, if you throw in three pieces of tin."

"You drive a hard bargain."

"I have to buy food."

"Agreed."

Ahsha and Arinna moved into a small, damp, windowless house with a dirt floor.

"I liked my farm better," the widow admitted. "At least we were warm there."

"We won't stay here long. Take one of these pieces of tin and go buy some blankets and groceries."

"And where are you going?"

"Don't worry, I'll be back later tonight."

In his flawless Hittite, Ahsha asked around the neighborhood and found a reputable tavern at the foot of a watchtower. The local craftsmen and tradesmen huddled in the smoke of oil lamps.

Ahsha entered into conversation with two bearded, affable men who sold spare parts for fighting chariots. They had begun as woodworkers but found their current line of work far more profitable than carving chairs.

"What an amazing city!" Ahsha said with enthusiasm. "I had no idea it was so grand."

"First time you've been here, then?"

"Yes, but I'm planning to start my own pottery business."

"Then try to supply the army. Otherwise you'll find slim pickings."

"They said back home that there might be a war . . ."

The carpenters howled. "You heard right, my friend! It's no secret here in the capital. Ever since the emperor put his son, Uri-Teshoop, in charge of the army, they've been drilling day and night. This is the big one, son. Egypt is going to get it."

"About time!"

"Not everyone's so sure, especially the big merchants. Hattusili, the emperor's brother, used to be their mouthpiece, but now he's thrown his lot in with Uri-Teshoop. For us, it only means more business. Times have never been better! At this rate, Hatti will have triple the number of fighting chariots in no time. Soon we'll have more chariots than men to drive them!"

Ahsha emptied his jar of coarse wine and swayed tipsily.

"To war! Hatti will make quick work of Egypt, and we'll dance in the streets!"

"Don't get carried away, man. The emperor doesn't seem in any hurry to launch the attack."

"So what's he waiting for?"

"How would we know? You'd better ask Captain Kenzor." The carpenters roared at their joke.

"Who is this Kenzor?"

"He's the military liaison between Muwattali and his son. And a handsome devil, believe you me! When he's in town, the ladies form a line. The most popular officer in the country, without a doubt."

"To war, I say! And to the ladies!"

The conversation turned toward the town's famed beauties and the local brothels. The carpenters bought their hilarious new friend more drinks.

Ahsha went to a different tavern every night. He made a great many contacts, but kept the conversation casual, throwing out Captain Kenzor's name from time to time.

It finally netted him some valuable information: the liaison officer had just returned to Hattusa.

A talk with the general's right-hand man would save him a great deal of time. He had to locate Kenzor, find a way to approach him, reel him in. Suddenly, Ahsha had an idea.

When he went home, he brought with him a dress, a cloak, and some sandals.

"For me?" Arinna asked tremulously.

"Is there another woman in my life?"

"They look so expensive!"

"I bargained."

She reached out to finger the fine cloth.

"Not yet!"

"But when?"

"I'm planning a special evening when I can take my time admiring you. Give me a while to work out the details."

"Whatever you say."

She threw her arms around his neck and kissed him fervently.

"You know, you look just fine to me wearing nothing at all . . ."

The farther south the royal flagship sailed, the younger Setau felt. As he held Lotus close, he was once again dazzled by the sight of Nubia, bathed in a light so pure that the Nile, reflecting it, seemed like a heavenly ribbon of blue.

With his hatchet, Setau had made a forked stick to capture a cobra or two, milking their venom into a copper flask. The lovely Lotus, bare-breasted and wearing only the briefest of skirts that fluttered in the breeze, took deep gulps of her native land's scented air.

Ramses steered the ship himself. With an expert crew, he kept to a swift and accurate course.

At mealtimes, the captain took over. In the central cabin, Ramses, Setau, and Lotus lunched on dried beef, tangy greens, and honeyed papyrus roots mixed with sweet onions.

"You're a true friend, Majesty," Setau acknowledged. "Bringing us on this trip is a wonderful reward."

"I can use your talents, and your wife's, too."

"We're out of touch in our palace laboratory, but we've been hearing unpleasant rumors. Is Egypt as close to war as everyone claims?"

"I'm afraid so."

"Isn't it dangerous to leave Pi-Ramses in these troubled times?"

"My first priority is to save Nefertari."

"I wasn't much more help than Dr. Pariamaku," Setau said glumly.

"You're looking for a miracle cure in Nubia, aren't you?" asked Lotus.

"From what I read in the library at the House of Life, there's one to be found here. A stone blessed by the goddess Hathor, hidden away in a secret spot."

"Any idea where?"

"All the text says is 'In the heart of Nubia, in a creek with golden sands, where the mountain cleaves and comes together.'"

"A creek . . . that must mean a backwater of the Nile."

"We have to find it fast," said Ramses. We've bought Nefertari a little time with the help of Sekhmet and her rest cure at the temple of Hathor. But we haven't broken the spell. Our only real hope is this magic stone."

Lotus looked into the distance. "You love Nubia, and it loves you back," she said. "Speak to this country and it will answer you."

All at once a pelican appeared above the royal vessel. The magnificent bird with its broad wingspan was one of the incarnations of Osiris, the god who returned from the dead.

FORTY-FOUR

Captain Kenzor was in his cups.

Three days' leave in the capital meant the chance to forget the rigors of military life in a wild blur of carousing. Tall, strapping, and husky-voiced, Kenzor had nothing but scorn for women, considering them only in terms of his own pleasure.

When he was drunk, Kenzor's sex drive was always heightened. Now, under the influence of a particularly heady wine, his need was pressing. He lurched out of the tavern toward the nearest brothel.

The captain didn't even feel the cold. He vaguely hoped a virgin might be available, a timid virgin. Her fear would add spice to the proceedings.

A man approached him deferentially.

"May I speak to you, Captain?"

"What do you want?" he slurred.

"I have something special to offer you," replied Ahsha.

Kenzor smiled. "Yes?"

"A young virgin."

Kenzor's eyes lit up. "How much?"

"Ten good pieces of tin."

"That's a lot."

"The merchandise is worth it."

"I need it right away."

"She's all yours."

"I only have five tin pieces on me."

"You can pay me the rest tomorrow."

"You trust me?"

"I'd like to keep doing business with you. She's not the only virgin in my stable."

"Good man. Come along now, I'm in a hurry."

Kenzor was in such a state that the two men nearly ran through the sleepy streets of the lower town.

Ahsha opened the door of his modest dwelling.

Arinna was dressed in her brand-new outfit, her hair carefully arranged. Captain Kenzor studied her hungrily.

"Looks old for a virgin," he muttered.

Without warning, Ahsha rammed the captain against a wall. As Kenzor slumped half conscious, the Egyptian nimbly relieved him of his short sword and held the tip to his throat.

"Who are you?" gasped the Hittite.

"It's not important. But you're the liaison between the army and the palace. Either you answer my questions or you die."

Kenzor struggled and the sword sliced his neck, drawing blood. Muddled with alcohol, he was at his captor's mercy.

Ahsha's terrified lover huddled in a corner of the room.

"When is the attack on Egypt planned?" asked Ahsha. "And why has the army ordered so many new chariots?"

Kenzor grimaced. The man already knew far more than he should.

"Attack . . . is classified information."

"Tell me, unless you want to be classified among the missing."

"You wouldn't dare."

"You're wrong, Kenzor. I'll kill you and work my way through a hundred officers, if I have to. I want the truth." He pushed the blade deeper, bringing a groan from the officer. The farm wife covered her eyes.

"Only the emperor knows. They don't tell me things like that."

"But you do know why the army has ordered so many chariots."

His neck hurt, his head felt fuzzy. Kenzor grunted something, as if talking to himself.

Ahsha's hearing was acute enough to pick it up. There was no need to make him repeat his appalling statement.

"Are you mad?" he shouted at Kenzor.

"No, it's the truth."

"Impossible."

"It's true, I tell you."

Ahsha was dumbfounded. He had just obtained a piece of information so important it could change the fate of the world.

Like lightning, he thrust the blade through Kenzor's neck, killing him instantly.

"Turn around," Ahsha said to the cowering woman in the corner.

"No, you go and leave me alone."

Sword drawn, he approached his lover. "I'm sorry, sweetheart, but I can't afford to let you live."

"I saw nothing, heard nothing!"

"Are you sure?"

"He was mumbling, I didn't hear a thing, I swear it!"

Arinna fell to her knees. "Don't kill me, I beg of you! I can help you get out of the city!"

Ahsha hesitated. She had a point. The gates to the capital were shut at night. He would have to wait until dawn before leaving town. With Arinna posing as his wife, he would be less conspicuous. Later, he could dispose of her along some country road.

Ahsha slumped next to Kenzor's body. He stayed awake all night, planning how best to make use of his startling discovery.

The Nubian winter, once the predawn chill lifted, was delightful. On the riverbank, Ramses sighted a pride of lions. Monkeys scampering in the tops of dum palms saluted the royal ship's passage with their shrill cries.

At a scheduled stop, the villagers offered the monarch and his retinue an impromptu feast of wild bananas and milk. Ramses sat next to the local chief, a white-haired shaman still presiding over his tribe at the age of ninety.

When they left, the old man attempted a deep bow to Pharaoh, but Ramses reached out an arm to check him.

"I thank the gods for blessing my old age with a visit from Pharaoh," the chief said, "may I not be allowed to pay my respects to him?"

"Old man, it is I who should bow to your wisdom."

"I'm only a village elder."

"A man who has lived a long life and followed the law of Ma'at is worth more than any temple priest with a hollow heart."

"You're Lord of the Two Lands, Majesty, as well as Nubia, while I have only my own little clan to care for."

"Even so, I must call on you for help. Will you lend me your memory?"

Pharaoh and the old shaman repaired to his accustomed seat in the shade of a palm tree.

"My memory . . ." the old man began. "It's full of blue skies, games I remember from childhood, the smiles of women, gazelles leaping in the distance, the return of the floodwaters. And all that belongs to you, my pharaoh. Without you, I'd have no memories, and future generations would have no heart."

"Do you recall anything about a sacred place where the goddess of love hid a sacred stone, somewhere deep in the heart of Nubia?"

With his walking stick, the shaman sketched a crude map in the sand. "My father's father brought such a stone back to the village. Our women were cured when they touched it. Sad to say, a band of nomads later made off with it."

"Where did it come from?"

His stick pointed to a spot farther down his map of the Nile. "There, where you enter the land of Kush. A place full of mystery."

"What would you like for your village?"

"Nothing other than what we have. But that's asking a lot, don't you think? Protect us, Pharaoh, and keep Nubia intact."

"Through you, old man, I have heard Nubia speaking. Through you I have understood."

The royal ship sailed out of Wawat and into Kush, where years earlier Seti and Ramses had quashed a rebellion and restored the shaky peace among warring factions.

It was a wild and dramatic land, kept alive by the Nile. There was only a narrow strip of cultivated land on either bank of the river, but date palms and dum palms provided some shade for farmers as they battled with the encroaching desert.

The cliffs came upon them suddenly.

Ramses sensed that any human presence was an intrusion here, that the Nile intended nature to stand alone in this majestic setting.

The enchanting scent of mimosa added to the otherworldly impression.

Two rocky ridges jutted out toward the river, almost parallel, with a sandy gorge between them. At the foot of the granite overhangs were flowering acacias. *In the heart of Nubia, in a creek with golden sands, where the mountain cleaves and comes together,* the ancient text went . . .

As if roused from a long sleep, or waking from a spell that had clouded his view, Ramses finally got his bearings. Why hadn't he thought of it sooner?

"We're landing," he ordered. "This is it, it can't be anywhere else."

Lotus dove naked into the river and swam to shore. Her body glistening with silvery droplets, she ran like a gazelle toward a native dozing in the acacia grove. She shook him awake, questioned him, ran off again toward the rock face, chipped off a piece of stone, and returned to the boat.

Ramses kept his eyes fixed on the cliff.

Abu Simbel . . . He was back at Abu Simbel, the magical place to which he had long ago been drawn, the spot where he had planned to build a temple, the realm of Hathor he had since neglected and then forgotten.

Setau helped Lotus board the ship again. She held a piece of sandstone in her right hand.

"It's Hathor's magic stone, all right. But these days no one knows how you make it work."

FORTY-FIVE

Dim light filtered through single slit in the wall of the dank little house. Arinna woke to the sound of a passing patrol. She squirmed when she saw Captain Kenzor's body.

"He's still here!"

"Come to your senses, woman," Ahsha scolded. "The officer can't incriminate us."

"But I didn't do anything!"

"You're posing as my wife. If I'm caught, you'll be executed, too."

Arinna threw herself at Ahsha, pounding his chest with her fists.

"I've had time to think tonight," he said calmly.

She stopped, inhaling sharply. In her lover's icy gaze, she saw her death. "No, you have no right . . ."

"I've been thinking," he said again. "Either I kill you on the spot, or you help me."

"Help you? But how?"

"I'm Egyptian."

The Hittite woman looked at him as if he was a creature from another world.

"I'm an Egyptian and I need to get home as soon as possible. If I don't make it out of here, I want you to cross the border and deliver a message for me."

"Why would I take such a risk?"

"I'll make it worth your while. The tablet I give you will entitle you to a town house, a servant, and an income for life. My employer is generous."

As a poor widow, it was more than she had ever imagined in her wildest dreams.

"All right," she said finally.

"Each of us will leave the city by a different gate," demanded Ahsha.

"What if you reach Egypt before me?"

"Don't worry about anything but getting there and delivering my message."

Ahsha wrote a short note in hieratic characters, a short-hand version of hieroglyphs, and handed the thin wooden tablet to his lover.

When he kissed her, Arinna didn't have the strength to resist.

"I'll see you in Pi-Ramses," he promised.

When Ahsha reached the edge of the lower town, he was swept up in a crowd of merchants on their way out of the capital.

All around, watchful soldiers paced.

It was impossible to backtrack. A squadron of archers was organizing the civilians into groups and checking their credentials.

There was probing, griping, jostling. Donkeys brayed in

protest. But nothing seemed to move the sentries guarding the gates.

"What's going on?" Ahsha asked a tradesman.

"They've sealed off the city because some officer is missing."

"What does that have to do with us?"

"Hittite officers don't go missing. Someone must have attacked him, even killed him. Palace intrigue is my guess. They won't rest until they solve this."

"Any leads?"

"Probably another officer . . . all this infighting between the emperor's brother and Uri-Teshoop. One of them is going to wind up dead."

"The sentries are searching everyone . . ."

"They're making sure that some armed soldier isn't trying to sneak out disguised as a merchant."

Ahsha relaxed.

The search was tedious and thorough. A man who looked about thirty was knocked roughly to the ground. His friends protested, saying that he was a cloth merchant who had never been in the army. The man was released.

Now it was Ahsha's turn.

A sharp-faced soldier laid a hand on his shoulder.

"Who are you?"

"A potter."

"Why are you leaving the city?"

"To stock up on pots at my farm."

The soldier frisked him.

"Am I done?"

The soldier gestured, brushing him off like a fly.

Just a few short paces away stood the gate to the city, the open road, the way to Egypt . . .

"Just a minute."

Someone had spoken to Ahsha's left.

A man of average build, with darting eyes and a trim goatee, dressed in a red and black striped woolen robe.

"Arrest this man," he ordered the sentry.

An officer intervened. "I'm in charge here," he blustered.

"My name is Raia," said the man with the goatee. "I'm with the palace police."

"What crime has this man committed? He's only a potter."

"He's no potter, not even Hittite. He's an Egyptian, his name is Ahsha, and he's one of the Pharaoh's closest advisers."

Thanks to the north-flowing current and the sleek design of his ship, Ramses covered the distance between Abu Simbel and Elephantine, the city at the southernmost tip of Egypt, in two days. It would take two more days to reach Thebes. The crew had been a model of efficiency, as if each man had grasped the seriousness of the mission.

During the voyage, Setau and Lotus had done countless experiments with samples of Hathor's magic stone. It was a unique variety of sandstone. As they prepared to land at Karnak, the frustration showed on their faces.

"I don't understand how this stone works," Setau admitted. "It doesn't behave the way it should. It resists acids, turns amazing colors, and seems to contain an energy I'm unable to measure. How can we cure the queen without any idea of how to use the stone in a formula?"

The monarch's arrival took the temple staff by surprise and upset the usual protocol. Ramses hurried to the temple laboratory along with Setau and Lotus, who explained the results of their initial testing to Karnak's chemists and pharmacists.

The king supervised the next phase of the research. The library's science collection yielded information that helped them draw up a list of substances to combine with the stone from Abu Simbel. The correct combination would cleanse the queen's blood of the demons sapping her life force.

The process of elimination, however, could take several months. The laboratory director was profoundly apologetic.

"Lay all the ingredients out on a stone table and leave me alone in here," demanded Ramses.

The king focused his thoughts, then reached for the divining rod his father had given him. He had been very young when Seti showed him how to find water in the desert.

Ramses held the rod over each ingredient. When it twitched, he set the substance aside. After rechecking his selections, he used the rod to determine the correct proportions.

Gum of acacia, anise, the pulp of scored sycamore fruits and crabapples, copper, and particles of the magic stone went into the final formula.

Carefully made up, Nefertari looked radiant. When Ramses entered the room, she was reading the famous story of Sinuhe the Sailor, in a version recorded by a particularly skillful scribe. She set down the scroll and melted into her husband's arms. Their embrace was long and passionate, punctuated by the calls of hoopoes and nightingales, adrift on the scent of frankincense.

"I found the magic stone of the goddess Hathor," said Ramses, "and the laboratory at Karnak helped me devise a formula."

"Will the prescription work?"

"I used my father's divining rod to put the ingredients together. The secret has been lost for centuries."

"Tell me how you found the stone in Nubia."

"A creek with golden sands, where two cliffs meet . . . Abu Simbel, where I planned to build a temple. A place I'd forgotten. Abu Simbel, where I plan to make sure that our love lives forever."

The warmth of Ramses' vibrant body restored the life that had been slowly ebbing from her.

"An architect and a team of stonemasons are leaving for the site this afternoon," the king continued. "The river cliffs will become twin temples, united for eternity, as you and I are."

"Am I going to see this wonder?"

"Of course you are."

"May Pharaoh's will be done."

"As it must, or I'm not worthy of the title."

Ramses and Nefertari crossed the Nile, heading toward Karnak. They performed their priestly duties in the hidden temple of Amon; then the queen prayed alone in Sekhmet's chapel. The stone goddess, half lion, half woman, now seemed to smile on her.

Pharaoh himself handed the Great Royal Wife the goblet containing the only possible antidote to the black magic working against her.

The potion was warm and sweet tasting.

Swooning, Nefertari lay down and closed her eyes. Ramses

remained at her bedside through the endless night, as her fragile body became a battleground where Hathor's magic clashed with the evil demons sucking the life from his queen.

FORTY-SIX

Haggard and wild-eyed, Ahmeni stumbled through a confused explanation.

"Calm down," the Queen Mother told him.

"But Your Majesty, this is war!"

"We've seen no official declaration."

"The generals are beside themselves, the barracks are in an uproar, and contradictory orders are flying in all directions."

"What's the cause of all this confusion?"

"I'm not sure, Your Majesty, but I've lost control of the situation. The military men won't listen to me anymore."

Tuya summoned the chief ritualist and two palace hairdressers. To emphasize the sacred nature of her duties, they fitted her with a wig resembling a vulture carcass; the two wings crossed over her forehead and hung down to her shoulders. The female vulture was seen as an attentive mother, and this symbol endowed Tuya with the power to protect the Two Lands.

Golden bangles adorned her wrists and ankles; around her neck she wore seven strands of semiprecious stones. In her long, tucked linen gown with a broad sash at the waist, she was the picture of supreme authority.

"Come with me to the North Base," she proposed.

"No, don't go there, Your Majesty! Wait until the situation's calmer."

"Trouble has a way of not dying down on its own. We'd better hurry."

Pi-Ramses was abuzz with rumors and arguments. Some insisted the Hittites were approaching the Delta. Others could already describe the battles. Still others were preparing their flight to the south.

No guard was posted at the North Base gate. The chariot carrying Ahmeni and the Queen Mother rode straight into the courtyard. Discipline had obviously broken down.

The horses stopped dead in the center of the huge yard.

A cavalry officer spied the Queen Mother and alerted his fellow officers, who summoned other soldiers. In less than ten minutes, hundreds of men were assembled to hear Tuya speak.

Tuya, small and frail, in the midst of these armed and hulking men, capable of trampling her in seconds . . . Ahmeni trembled, fearing that the Queen Mother's decision to intervene would prove suicidal. She should have stayed safe in the palace, guarded by Serramanna's security forces. Perhaps reassuring words would ease the tension somewhat, provided that Tuya was diplomatic.

The men fell silent.

The Queen Mother surveyed them disdainfully. "A fine collection of cowards," she said sharply, her voice ringing like thunder in Ahmeni's ears. "Cowards and imbeciles, unfit to defend their country because they fall apart at the first rumor of war."

Ahmeni shut his eyes. Neither he nor Tuya would make it out of there alive.

"Why insult us, Your Majesty?" asked a cavalry lieutenant.

"I'm only describing what I see going on here. Is that an insult? Your behavior is foolish and indefensible. The officers are more to blame than the enlisted men. Who determines when we engage in war with the Hittites, if not Pharaoh, or, in his absence, myself?"

The silence hung heavy. What the Queen Mother had to tell them would be no rumor. The fate of the entire nation depended upon it.

"I have received no declaration of war from the Emperor of Hatti," she affirmed.

The men broke out in cheers. Tuya had never lied to them. An appreciative murmur began.

Seti's widow stood motionless in her chariot. Finally the soldiers realized there was more to come. Again, they fell silent.

"I have no reason to believe, however, that the current truce will hold. In fact, it seems clear that our enemy would like nothing better than to force us into a decisive confrontation. Its outcome will depend on your efforts. When Ramses is back in the capital—and his return is near at hand—I want him to be proud of his army and confident of its ability to conquer the Hittites."

The cheers were even louder.

Ahmeni opened his eyes, spellbound as the men were.

The chariot began to move, and the crowd parted. The men were chanting the Queen Mother's name.

"Are we going back to the palace, Your Majesty?"

"No, Ahmeni. I suppose there have been problems at the foundry, too?"

The king's private secretary lowered his eyes.

With Tuya's encouragement, Pi-Ramses was soon producing weapons at full capacity again: spears, bows, arrowheads, swords, armor, harnesses, and chariot parts. There was no longer any doubt that the conflict was imminent, but there was a new sense of urgency to make sure that Egypt was better equipped than Hatti.

The Queen Mother visited the bases and spoke with both officers and enlisted men. She made a point of stopping to watch the chariots being assembled, with a kind word for the workmen.

The capital had shed its mantle of fear and welcomed the prospect of combat.

How soft it was, the elegant hand with long, incredibly slender fingers that Ramses kissed one by one before clasping them in his own hand, as if he could hold them forever. There was no part of Nefertari's body that failed to move her husband. The gods may have set a heavy burden on his shoulders, but they had also given him the most sublime of women.

"How are you this morning?"

"Better, much better. I feel my blood moving again."

"Would you like a ride in the country?"

"I've been longing for one."

Ramses chose two old, very steady horses, and yoked them himself to his chariot. They rode at a leisurely pace along the West Bank of Thebes, following the irrigation channels.

Nefertari drank in her fill of the sturdy palm trees and

tender green of spring fields. Communing with the forces of nature, she willed the last traces of evil from her body. When she alit from the chariot and walked on the river-bank, her hair in the wind, Ramses knew that the goddess's magic stone had saved the Great Royal Wife and that she would live to see the two temples at Abu Simbel, built to celebrate their eternal love.

Lita managed a pathetic smile as Dolora, Ramses' sister, removed the compress soaked in honey, acacia gum, and crabapple pulp. The burn marks had almost disappeared.

"It hurts," she moaned.

"Your wounds are healing."

"Don't lie to me, Dolora. They won't go away."

"You're wrong. The treatment is proven."

"Ask Ofir to find another medium. I can't go on."

"Thanks to you, we've almost driven a wedge between Nefertari and Ramses. Just hold on a while longer, and your trials will be over."

Lita gave up trying to convince Dolora. She was as much a fanatic as the Libyan sorcerer. Despite her superficial kindness, the king's sister lived only for revenge. Hatred had crowded out all her other feelings.

"All right," the fragile medium promised.

"I knew you'd be brave! Now rest before tonight's session. Nani will bring in your dinner."

Nani, the only servant allowed into Lita's room, was her last chance. When the girl appeared with a platter of fig puree and chunks of roast beef, Lita clutched at the sash of her dress.

"Help me, Nani!"

"What do you want?"

"I have to get away from here."

The girl made a face. "It would be dangerous."

"Leave the door open for me."

"I'll lose my job!"

"Nani, I'm begging you!"

"How much will you pay?"

"My supporters have gold . . . all the gold you want."

"Ofir will come after me."

"The congregation will hide us."

"I want a house and a herd of dairy cattle."

"Whatever you say."

Nani had already negotiated a good price for swiping Nefertari's shawl, but she was greedy, and Lita was offering the moon.

"When do you want to leave?"

"As soon as it's dark."

"I'll try."

"Make it work, Nani. Don't you want to be rich?"

"It won't be easy . . . I want twenty lengths of the finest linen, too."

"You have my word."

Since early that morning, Lita had been possessed by a vision: a woman of surpassing beauty, smiling and radiant, walked along the Nile, holding her hand out to a tall and powerful man.

The vision told her that Ofir's spell had failed and he was torturing her in vain.

Serramanna and his men were scouring the neighborhood behind the School of Medicine, questioning every inhabitant. The colossal Sard showed them a drawing of Nani's face and described in awful detail the penalties for lying. He needn't have bothered, since the mere sight of him inspired cooperation. Unfortunately, the search had been unsuccessful so far.

But Serramanna was stubborn, and his pirate's instincts told him that he was closing in on his quarry. When his men came back with a man who roamed the neighborhood selling bread and rolls, the giant felt a twinge in the pit of his stomach, the sign that something important was about to happen.

He waved the picture in front of the street vendor.

"Do you know this girl?"

"I've seen her around the neighborhood. She's somebody's servant. Moved here not long ago."

"Which villa does she work in?"

"One of the big ones, near the old well."

A hundred policemen surrounded the area, drawing the net tight.

The sorcerer using black magic against the Queen of Egypt was within Serramanna's reach, and the Sard was going to get him.

FORTY-SEVEN

The sun was low on the horizon.

Lita was running out of time to escape. Soon Ofir would lock her in his workshop. What was taking Nani so long?

A face still haunted the lost princess, the face of a lovely woman, happy and glowing—the Queen of Egypt. Lita felt she owed the woman something, a debt she must repay before breaking free from Ofir.

The young blond woman crept softly through the house. The sorcerer, as usual, was poring over stacks of old spells. Dolora was napping.

Lita lifted the lid of a wooden chest containing the last vestige of Nefertari's shawl. Two or three more sessions and it would be gone. Lita tried to tear it, but the cloth was too tightly woven and her fingers too weak.

A sharp noise. From the kitchen?

Lita stuffed the shred of cloth into the sleeve of her dress. Her skin burned instantly.

"Is that you, Nani?"

"Are you ready?"

"I'll just be a minute."

"Hurry, Lita!"

In the kitchen, Lita held the last piece of the shawl to the flame of an oil lamp.

A sputtering, then a final swirl of black smoke marked the end of the spell aimed at breaking through the royal couple's defenses.

"I'm free!" she said beneath her breath.

The lost princess raised her arms to the heavens, praying to Aton for a new life.

"Let's go," demanded Nani, who had spent the past hour gathering all the copper plate she could find in the house.

The two women ran out the back door and into the alleyway.

Nani collided with Ofir, standing still, his arms crossed.

"Where are you going?"

Nani backed away. Lita stood behind her, terrified.

"What's Lita doing with you?"

"She . . . she was feeling sick."

"Were the two of you running away?"

"It was Lita's idea, she made me."

"What did she tell you, Nani?"

"Nothing, nothing at all!"

"You're lying, girl."

Ofir's fingers hooked around the maidservant's neck, squeezing so tight that she had no chance to protest. Nani struggled to free herself from the sorcerer's grip, but it was too strong for her. Her eyes rolled back and she crumpled to the hem of the sorcerer's robe. He casually kicked her aside.

"Lita . . . what's happened to you, my child?"

Inside, Ofir saw the lamp and the blackened residue of fabric. Eyes blazing, he said, "What on earth have you done? You little . . ." he spat, grabbing a meat cleaver. "You burned Nefertari's shawl, you've ruined my work!"

Lita tried to run. Knocking into an oil lamp, she lost her balance. Quick as a bird of prey, the sorcerer pounced on her and caught her by the hair.

"You betrayed me, Lita. I can't trust you anymore."

"You're a monster!"

"I hate to lose you. You're a wonderful medium."

On her knees, Lita pleaded. "For the love of Aton . . ."

"Don't make me laugh, you fool. No one interferes with my plans."

With one well-aimed blow of the cleaver, Ofir slashed through Lita's throat.

Hair flying, face crumpled, Dolora burst into the room.

"The street is full of policemen—Oh, Lita! Lita!"

"She lost her mind and came at me with a knife," explained Ofir. "I had to defend myself. It was an accident. Police, you say?"

"I saw them from my bedroom window."

"Let's get out of this house."

Ofir led Dolora toward a trapdoor concealed beneath a reed mat. The secret passage beneath it tunneled to a warehouse.

From now on, Lita and Nani would tell no tales.

"There's only one villa left," a policeman reported to Serramanna. "We knocked, but no one answered."

"Let's break down the door."

"That's against the law!"

"We're investigating a threat to national security!"

"I still need to contact the owner and request permission."

"I'm giving you permission!" the giant bellowed.

"Without the owner's consent, I need a warrant. We have to follow procedures."

Serramanna wasted a good hour on police formalities. Finally, four husky policemen broke the bolts and forced their way into the villa.

The Sard was the first one inside. He found the lifeless body of a young blond woman, then the corpse of a servant girl he recognized as Nani.

"A massacre," murmured one of the policemen in disgust.

"Two crimes committed in cold blood," noted the security chief. "Search the premises."

The sorcerer's lair gave ample evidence that black magic had been practiced in the house. Although he'd arrived too late, there was one shred of evidence Serramanna found reassuring: charred remains of fabric that must have been part of the queen's old shawl.

Ramses and Nefertari made their entry into a capital that was as bustling as ever, though not as cheerful. The atmosphere was marked by the military presence, and most of the population was involved in the production of arms and chariots. The pleasure-loving city had been transformed into an efficient war machine.

The royal couple immediately called on Tuya, finding her immersed in tallies from the foundry.

"Have the Hittites sent any official word?"

"No, my son, but I'm sure their silence is no good omen. Nefertari . . . have you recovered?"

"My illness is nothing but a bad memory."

"Good. I'm tired of being in charge. I must be too old to run this great country of ours. You two need to straighten the army out right away, and the court needs some tending, too."

Ramses had a long conference with Ahmeni, then saw Serramanna, just back from Memphis. His report suggested that the threat of black magic had finally been countered. However, the king requested that his security chief pursue the investigation and identify the owner of the sinister villa. Who, he wanted to know, was the young blond woman who had died so violently?

The Pharaoh had other concerns. His desk was piled with alarmist dispatches from Canaan and Amurru. The commanders of the Egyptian outposts had no specific incidents to report, but the rumors of Hittite troop movements were too numerous to ignore.

Unfortunately, there had been no word from Ahsha to help him sort through the confusing information. The outcome of the conflict would depend on where the two armies engaged in combat. Without that knowledge, the king was forced to choose between reinforcing his defenses or else marching north to do battle. It was in his nature to take bold initiatives. But how could he risk men's lives so blindly?

It made the royal court feel better to see the queen plunge into her usual round of activities. Even those who had already buried Nefertari congratulated her on her recovery and assured her that surviving such a serious illness was a sure sign of longevity.

The Great Royal Wife cared nothing for gossip; she was

busy overseeing the production of uniforms and checking on the numerous rural initiatives she sponsored, with the help of Ahmeni's punctilious reports.

Shaanar saluted the king.

"You've put on some weight," observed Ramses.

"It's not from sitting around," protested the secretary of state. "I eat when I'm worried. The rumors of war, the hordes of soldiers everywhere . . . is this what Egypt has become?"

"The Hittites are bound to attack soon, Shaanar."

"You're probably right, but my department has received no official confirmation. Isn't Muwattali still sending you friendly letters?"

"A cover-up."

"If we can preserve the peace, millions of lives will be spared."

"Which, as you know, is my fondest wish."

"Moderation and caution should be our watchwords."

"Are you saying that we should be passive, brother?"

"Certainly not, but I fear that an overambitious general might do something rash."

"Rest easy, Shaanar. I have control of my army. Nothing of the kind will happen."

"I'm happy to hear you say so."

"How is Meba working out as your second-in-command?" asked Ramses.

"He's so happy to be back at the department that he's at my beck and call. I'm glad I brought him out of his forced retirement. Sometimes a solid professional deserves a fresh start. Generosity is the finest of virtues, don't you agree?"

FORTY-EIGHT

Shaanar was in conference with Meba. His distinguished assistant had taken care to bring an armful of scrolls, as he would for a typical work session.

"I've seen the king," declared Shaanar. "He's still unsure which course to pursue, given the lack of reliable information."

"Excellent," pronounced Meba.

Shaanar could not admit to his accomplice that Ahsha's silence surprised him. Why the delay in reporting on his mission, so crucial to Ramses' defeat? Something must have happened to him. His silence worried the prince, and left him as much at sea as Ramses.

"Exactly where are we, Meba?"

"Our spy network has been ordered to go dormant. In other words, the hour is near. No matter what initiatives Pharaoh takes, there's no way he can win."

"How can you be so sure?"

"The Hittite war machine is geared up to the maximum. Each passing hour brings you closer to the ultimate power, Your Highness. In the meantime, you may want to fine-tune your contacts in the various branches of government."

"Yes, except that Ahmeni has been watching me like a hawk. We have to be careful."

"Ahmeni could be taken care of."

"It's too soon for that, Meba. My brother would be furious."

"Listen to my advice. The weeks are going to fly by, and you must be ready to take the reins when our Hittite friends say the word."

"It's the moment I've been waiting for. Don't worry, Meba, I'll be ready."

In a daze, Dolora trailed after Ofir. The discovery of Lita's mutilated body, the police surrounding the house, this sudden flight out of Memphis . . . She could no longer think, no longer knew where she was going. When Ofir asked her to pose as his wife and continue the fight to reinstate Aton as the One God, Dolora eagerly accepted.

The couple stayed away from the harbor; it was crawling with police. Ofir shaved his beard; Dolora removed all trace of makeup. Donning peasant garb, they bought a donkey and headed south. The master spy knew that the search for them would center on the area north of Memphis and the border. It would be practically impossible to get through the roadblocks or evade the river patrols, unless they did the unexpected.

Now was the time to appeal to the fervent followers of Akhenaton, the heretic king. Most of them had settled close to his abandoned former capital in the middle of the country. Posing as the movement's new prophet had proved very useful; Ofir did not regret it in the least. If he made sure that Dolora still believed in him, Ofir could rely on her unqualified support and find shelter in the bosom of his congregation. Once the Hittites invaded, he could easily leave his followers behind.

Fortunately, just before the police closed in on him, the sorcerer had received a message of paramount importance and passed the word on to Meba. Muwattali's plan had been set in motion. It was only a matter of time before the two nations met on the battlefield. As soon as Ramses' death was announced, Shaanar would oust Nefertari and Tuya, then offer the Hittites a proper welcome. He didn't seem to realize that Muwattali was not in the habit of sharing power with anyone. His reign would be a short one. With Shaanar out of the way, the Two Lands would become no more than the Hittites' breadbasket.

Ofir relaxed and enjoyed the tranquil beauty of the Egyptian countryside.

Given his rank and position, Ahsha had been spared the dungeons of the lower town, where the average inmate lasted about a year. Instead, he was put in a stone building in the upper town reserved for important prisoners. The food was poor and the bedding worse, but the young diplomat adapted and stayed in shape by doing exercises several times a day.

Since his arrest, there had been no interrogation. His imprisonment might end any day in a brutal execution.

Finally, the door to his cell swung open.

"How are you feeling?" asked Raia.

"Very well."

"The gods were displeased with you, Ahsha. If I hadn't spotted you, you never would have been caught."

"I wasn't running away."

"It's hard to deny the facts."

"Appearances can be deceiving."

"I know you're Ahsha, a close friend of Ramses. I saw you in Memphis as well as in the new capital; I've even sold vases to some of your relatives. The king entrusted you with a dangerous mission, and you proved a resourceful spy, even a daring one."

"You're wrong about one thing. Ramses did send me here, but I serve another master. That's where I planned to send the information I gathered."

"What other master are you talking about?"

"Ramses' older brother, Shaanar, the future pharaoh of Egypt."

Raia fiddled with his goatee, wrecking the barber's artful arrangement. Could Ahsha really be a Hittite agent? No, there was something that didn't make sense. "In that case, why were you posing as a potter?"

The young diplomat smiled. "As if you didn't know!"

"I want to hear it from you."

"Muwattali is emperor, of course, but what's his base of support? How great is the true extent of his power? Are his son and brother still at each other's throats, or has the question already been settled?"

"Hold your tongue!"

"Those were the essential questions I was supposed to answer. You can understand why I went underground. Now perhaps you could furnish me with some answers?"

Raia slammed the door to the cell behind him.

Ahsha was taking a chance, and he knew it. Still, provoking the Syrian was the only way he could think of to save his neck.

In ceremonial dress, Emperor Muwattali left the palace with a swarm of bodyguards who put a distance between him and anyone in the streets, and also blocked him from any archer perched on a rooftop. Heralds preceded him, announcing that the Lord of Hatti was making his way to the great temple in the lower town, where he would make an offering to the Storm God.

There was no more solemn means of placing the country in a state of war than summoning the god's invincible energy.

From his cell, Ahsha heard the commotion greeting the emperor's passage. He, too, understood that a bridge was about to be crossed.

The Storm God ruled over the Hittites' lesser divinities. To keep the gods happy, the priests cleansed their statues. From now on no dissenting voice must be heard: it was time to act.

The priestess Puduhepa pronounced the words that turned the fertility goddesses into fearsome women warriors. Then she nailed seven iron nails, seven bronze nails, seven copper nails into a swine, to make the future conform to the emperor's wishes.

As the litanies were recited, Muwattali's eyes came to rest on his son, Uri-Teshoop, in his helmet and armor, overjoyed at the idea of waging war and slaughtering the enemy.

Hattusili remained calm and inscrutable.

The two of them had eliminated their competitors and now formed the emperor's inner circle, along with Puduhepa. But Uri-Teshoop detested his aunt and uncle, and they returned the favor.

The war against Egypt would permit Muwattali to solve domestic conflicts, extend his territory, and assert his control over the Near East before moving on to other conquests. Heaven had smiled upon him and would bless him again.

When the service was over, the emperor invited the generals and commanding officers to a banquet that began with the ritual offering of four portions of food. The palace steward placed the first one on the throne, the second near the fireplace, the third on the main table, and the fourth on the doorstep of the dining room. The guests then proceeded to eat and drink as if it was their last meal on earth.

At last Muwattali rose, and a hush fell over the gathering. The tipsiest among the party struggled to compose themselves.

There was only one more formality before the conflict began.

The emperor and his retinue filed out of the Sphinx Gate in the upper town, heading for a rocky crest, where Muwattali, Uri-Teshoop, and Puduhepa scrambled to the top.

They stood motionless, staring at the clouds.

"There they are!" shouted Uri-Teshoop.

The emperor's son drew his bow and took aim at one of the vultures soaring over the capital. His arrow went straight through the raptor's chest.

An officer retrieved the carcass for the commander-in-chief, who slit the bird's belly and pulled out its steaming entrails.

"Read them," Muwattali asked Puduhepa, "and tell us our destiny."

Struggling with the stench, the priestess fulfilled her duty.

"The omens are favorable."

The mountains shook with Uri-Teshoop's war cry.

FORTY-NINE

The meeting of Pharaoh's full council, expanded to include numerous high-ranking courtiers, was off to a rocky start. Cabinet members were grim-faced, department heads deplored the absence of clear directives, all omens pointed toward a military disaster. The buffer Ahmeni and his staff provided between Ramses and his government had broken down, and everyone wanted to hear what the king had to say for himself.

By the time he was seated on his throne, the reception room was packed. The speaker of the assembly was designated to relay their questions, in keeping with protocol. Barbarians might raise their voices and speak out of turn; proper Egyptians, with centuries of tradition behind them, did not.

"Majesty," said the speaker, "the country is concerned that a war with the Hittites is imminent."

"It is," answered Ramses.

A long silence followed this succinct and terrifying revelation.

"Is it unavoidable?"

"Yes."

"Is our army ready to fight?"

"The foundries have been working nonstop on new equipment. We could have used a few extra months, but we won't have them."

"Why, Your Majesty?"

"Because we have to march north on short notice. We'll meet the enemy far from Egyptian soil. Since Canaan and Amurru are back under our protection, we can pass through them without danger."

"Who will be appointed commander-in-chief?"

"I'll serve in that capacity myself. In my absence, the Great Royal Wife Nefertari will rule over the Two Lands, with the help of Queen Mother Tuya."

The speaker discarded the other questions. They were now completely beside the point.

Homer was smoking sage leaves stuffed into the oversized snail shell he used as a pipe bowl. Sitting beneath his lemon tree, he welcomed the warmth of springtime. It helped his aching joints. His flowing white beard, carefully groomed by the barber Ramses sent him, gave a noble air to his weather-beaten face. In the poet's lap lay Hector, his black and white cat, purring loudly.

"I was hoping to see you before you left, Your Majesty. This time it's really war, isn't it?"

"Egypt's survival is at stake, Homer."

"Listen to this passage of mine: *'Even in solitary places, man has tended the olive tree. It stands full of sap, well watered, bending in the wind, dense with white flowers. But a sudden gust can come up, uprooting the tree and crashing it to the ground.'*"

"And what if the tree withstands the storm?"

Homer offered the king a cup of red wine, flavored with anise and coriander, and took a hearty gulp from his own goblet.

"If it does, I'll write your epic, Ramses."

"Will your other work leave you time?"

"I was put on earth to sing of war and great journeys, and I like a hero. As a conqueror, you'll be immortal."

"And if I lose?"

"Can you imagine the Hittites invading my garden, cutting down my lemon tree, smashing my lap desk, frightening Hector? The gods would never stand for it. Where are you planning to fight the enemy?"

"It's a state secret, but I think I can trust you. We'll meet in Kadesh."

"The battle of Kadesh. Has a nice ring to it. Battles galore may be fought and forgotten, but my account will live on. I'll give it my best. Just one stipulation, Majesty: I'd prefer a happy ending."

"I'll try not to disappoint you, Homer."

Ahmeni was frantic. He had a thousand questions to ask Ramses, a hundred dossiers to show him, ten moral dilemmas to discuss . . . and only Pharaoh could make the final decisions. Pale, his breathing shallow, his hands trembling, the private secretary looked exhausted.

"You ought to take a rest," the king advised.

"But you're leaving! And who knows for how long? I might make mistakes that would harm the country."

"I trust you, Ahmeni, and the queen will be here to guide you."

"Tell me the truth, Your Majesty. Do you really have the slightest chance of defeating Hatti?"

"Would I lead my men into battle if I thought it was a lost cause?"

"They say that the Hittites are invincible."

"Once you've identified the enemy, nothing's impossible. Take care of Egypt for me, Ahmeni."

Shaanar was dining on lamb cutlets sautéed with parsley and celery—a bit too bland for his taste, so he sprinkled on more spices. The red wine, an excellent vintage, did nothing for him. The prince called for his butler, but instead an unexpected guest strode into his dining room.

"Ramses! Would you care to join me?"

"Frankly, no."

His curt reply ruined Shaanar's appetite. He rose.

"Shall we go out in the garden?"

"As you like."

Feeling slightly queasy, Shaanar sat down on a bench. Ramses remained standing, looking out at the Nile.

"Your Majesty seems irritated. The approaching conflict, perhaps?"

"There are other causes for my discontent."

"But surely they don't concern me?"

"They do, Shaanar."

"I thought you were happy with my work at the State Department."

"You've always hated me, haven't you?"

"Ramses! We've had our differences, I admit, but that's all in the past."

"Do you really think so?"

"You can be sure of it."

"Your only goal, Shaanar, is to replace me, no matter how low you have to stoop."

Shaanar felt as if the air had been knocked out of him. "Has someone been spreading lies about me?"

"I don't listen to gossip. My statements are based on facts."

"Impossible!"

"Serramanna recently raided a house in Memphis, where he found two murdered women and a magician's den—the workshop of the sorcerer who cast an evil spell over the queen."

"How could I be implicated in such a sordid affair?"

"Because the house belongs to you, although you took care to have it put in our sister Dolora's name. The tax rolls leave no doubt as to your ownership."

"I own so much property, especially in Memphis. I've lost count of all the houses I own there! I have no control over what goes on in them."

"Weren't you friendly with a Syrian merchant named Raia?"

"He's only someone who sold me imported vases."

"Raia was spying for the Hittites."

"That's . . . well, that's simply beyond belief! How could I have known? All the best people bought from him . . ."

"You're putting up a good defense, Shaanar, but it's no use. I know how your blind ambition led you to betray your country and collaborate with our enemies. The Hittites needed contacts inside our borders, and you were the answer to their prayers. You, my own brother."

"Have you lost your reason, Ramses? You think I'm a snake in the grass?"

"I know you are."

"You seem to enjoy insulting me for no reason."

"I'll tell you where you went wrong, Shaanar: thinking that every man has his price. You went straight for my closest friends, never dreaming that friendship can truly be as solid as granite. That's how you fell into my trap."

Shaanar's eyes rolled back.

"Ahsha has never been your man, Shaanar. He's reported back to me from the very beginning."

The king's older brother gripped the arms of his chair.

"I know everything you've been up to," Ramses continued. "You're evil, Shaanar, and you'll never change."

"I . . . I demand a trial!"

"You'll have one, and you'll be sentenced to death for high treason. Since it's wartime, you'll be held in the main jail in Memphis, then transferred to a desert outpost until your trial can begin. The law dictates that Pharaoh must deal with domestic threats before leaving for foreign wars."

Shaanar's mouth twisted into a sneer. "You don't dare kill me because I'm your brother . . . and the Hittites will slaughter you! When you're dead, they'll hand the country over to me!"

"A king must know how to look evil in the face," Ramses said calmly. "Thanks to you, Shaanar, I'll be a better warrior."

FIFTY

Arinna had told Ramses all about her adventures with Ahsha and her journey to Egypt. Once she had crossed the border and produced her message, she was promptly ushered in to see the Pharaoh.

In keeping with Ahsha's promises, Ramses had offered Arinna a modest home in Pi-Ramses and a stipend to cover her household expenses. Overcome with gratitude, she wished she could tell the king what had become of Ahsha, but she hadn't a clue.

Ramses faced the facts. His friend had been arrested and probably executed. Of course, Ahsha might have tried one final ploy: claiming that he was in league with Shaanar, on the side of the Hittites. But would he have even been allowed a chance to defend himself, much less convince them?

No matter how he had ended up, Ahsha had fulfilled his mission admirably. His message contained only three words, but they were enough to send Ramses marching off to war:

Kadesh. Fast. Danger.

He wrote no more for fear that his message might be inter-
cepted. He'd told his mistress nothing, unsure how far he
could trust her. But those three words said it all.

When Meba was notified of the council meeting, he
bolted for his bathroom and vomited. To cover his sour
breath, he rubbed on strong cologne made from attar of
damask rose. Since Shaanar's dramatic arrest, Meba, as his
right-hand man, was expecting to be collared at any
moment. Running away would be an admission of his guilt,
and Meba could no longer even contact Ofir, who'd gone
underground.

On his way to the palace, Meba tried to think. What if
Ramses didn't suspect him? The Pharaoh knew he was no
friend of Shaanar, who had replaced him as secretary of
state, kept him on the sidelines, and then reinstated him
with the sole and obvious intention of lording it over him.
That was how the court saw it, and perhaps the king did,
too. Meba was the innocent victim, gratified by his perse-
cutor's fall from grace.

The elder statesman decided to keep a low profile, not
offering to serve in his old position. The best course was
maintaining the composure of a dignified public servant,
blending in with the scenery, until war tipped the scales in
favor of either Ramses or the Hittites. If it turned out to
be the Hittites, he'd make his move.

The full complement of generals and commanding officers was present at the council meeting. Pharaoh and the Great Royal Wife took their place on their thrones, side by side.

"Due to information reaching us from the north," declared Ramses, "Egypt is declaring war on Hatti. Under my command, our troops will march forth from the city beginning tomorrow morning. We have just sent the emperor Muwattali a dispatch announcing our intentions. I pray that we may vanquish the forces of darkness and keep our land safe in the hands of the law of Ma'at."

It was the shortest council meeting since the beginning of the Pharaoh's reign. There was no discussion. Courtiers and generals filed out in silence.

Serramanna walked past Meba without so much as a glance.

Back in his office, the old diplomat downed a full jar of white oasis wine.

Ramses kissed his children, Kha and Meritamon, who were chasing around with Watcher, the king's dog. Under the tutelage of Nedjem, the onetime gardener whom the king had selected as his secretary of agriculture, they were making great strides in their study of hieroglyphs. They were also experts at the popular board game called Snake, the object of which was to keep from falling into the underworld and land in the realm of light. For the boy and his half-sister, this would be a day like any other. They cheerfully trailed after Nedjem until he agreed to read them a story.

Sitting on the grass, Ramses and Nefertari enjoyed one
of their rare private moments, contemplating the acacias,
the pomegranate and jojoba trees, willows and tamarisks,
which rose above the beds of cornflowers, irises, and lark-
spur. The king wore a simple kilt, the queen a skirt with
shoulder straps that left her breasts uncovered.

"Are you hurt by your brother's betrayal?" asked
Nefertari.

"I would have been more surprised to find out he was
loyal. Thank God for Ahsha! I'm afraid there's more to this
affair than meets the eye. The evil sorcerer is still at large,
and Shaanar probably had other allies, inside or outside the
country. Be very careful, Nefertari."

"I'll be thinking of Egypt, not myself, while you risk
your own existence to defend your country."

"I've ordered Serramanna to stay in Pi-Ramses and
watch over you. He was so primed for battle that he's
furious with me."

Nefertari laid her head on Ramses' shoulder. Her hair
was free, silken against the king's arm.

"I've barely recovered from the sorcerer's curse, and now
you're marching off to battle again. I wonder if we'll ever
know peace and quiet, the way your father and mother did."

"Perhaps, if we tame the Hittites. Avoiding this confrontation would be the end of Egypt. If I don't come back,
Nefertari, you become Pharaoh, and rule in the face of
adversity. Muwattali enslaves his conquered nations. I hope
our people will never be reduced to that."

"No matter what happens to us, we've been happy. We've
been touched with the gift of joy, fleeting as perfume or the
murmur of the wind in the treetops. I'm yours, Ramses, like
a wave on the sea, like a wildflower blooming in the sunshine."

The left strap of Nefertari's dress slipped off her shoulder. The king's lips grazed her warm and scented flesh as he slowly removed the remainder of the clothing from the queen's inviting and eager body.

A flock of wild geese flew over the palace gardens as Ramses and Nefertari became one fire.

Shortly before dawn, Ramses dressed in the "pure place" of the temple of Amon and prayed over the food and drink to be used in religious ceremonies. Then the Pharaoh left the sanctuary to witness the rebirth of the sun, his protector. Every night the sun disappeared to wrestle with the demons of darkness—the same battle he was about to launch against the fierce Anatolians. The dawning orb appeared between two hills on the horizon, where the legend said two huge turquoise trees stood, parting to let through the light.

Ramses said the words of the prayer said by every pharaoh through the ages: "Hail to you, light born of the primordial waters, filling the Two Lands with your beauty. You are the living soul that comes into being from nowhere. You fly through the sky like a falcon with many-colored plumage, banishing evil. The bark of night is on your right, the bark of day on your left; the crew of the bark of light rejoices."

Perhaps Ramses would never again perform this ceremony, if death awaited him at Kadesh. But another voice would follow his and the magical words would not be lost.

In the city's four bases, the troops were going over their final checklists. Thanks to the monarch's constant attention over the past few weeks, their morale was high even though the approaching encounter was expected to be bloody. They were glad to be well supplied with well-forged weapons.

As the troops marched out of the bases to meet at the city's main gate, Ramses drove his chariot from the temple of Amon to the temple of Set. It stood in the oldest part of town, which had long ago been the site of the Hyksos invaders' capital. To exorcise the evil, subsequent pharaohs had maintained a temple there, dedicated to the most powerful force in the universe. Ramses's father, Seti, had been named for the god Set. He had mastered the force and transmitted the secret to his son.

Today, Ramses had not come to challenge the angry god. He was there to attempt a feat of magic: linking Set to the Storm God worshiped by the Syrians and Hittites. He needed to make that mighty energy his own, to turn it against his enemies.

The confrontation was swift and intense.

Ramses' stare met the red eyes of Set's statue, a standing man with a canine head, a long muzzle, and drooping ears.

The pedestal shook. The god's legs appeared to move forward.

"O Mighty Set, you who embody power, let me join in your *ka*, let me share your strength."

The gleam in the red eyes softened. Set had granted the Pharaoh's petition.

The priest of Midian and his daughter were worried. Moses, who had led the tribe's main flock of sheep out to graze in the mountains, should have returned two days ago.

The old priest knew his son-in-law was a solitary man who liked to meditate in the wilderness, sometimes experiencing strange visions. Moses had also refused to answer his wife's questions and had shown little interest in the son born to him in exile.

The tribal leader knew that Moses was always thinking about Egypt, the bountiful country where he had been born and achieved high status.

"Do you think he'll go back there?" the old man's daughter asked him.

"I doubt it."

"Why is he hiding in Midian?"

"I don't know and I don't want to. Moses is an honest, hardworking man, a good husband; what more could you ask?"

"He seems so distant, so secretive . . ."

"Accept him as he is, my child. You'll be the happier for it."

"If he comes back, Father."

"Have faith and take care of the little one."

Moses did come back, but his face had changed. His brow was furrowed and his hair was white.

His wife threw her arms around his neck. "What happened, Moses?"

"I saw a bush burst into flame. It was on fire, but it didn't burn. From the middle of the bush, God called to me. He told me His name and gave me a mission. God is One, and I must obey Him."

"Obey Him? Does that mean you're going to leave us, me and your child?"

"I must fulfill my mission, for no one can disobey God. His commandments are far greater than you and I. What are we, if not instruments in the service of His will?"

"What is this mission you speak of, Moses?"

"You'll find out when the time comes."

The Hebrew sat alone in his tent, reliving his encounter with the angel of Yaweh, the god of Abraham, Isaac, and Jacob.

Shouts interrupted his meditation. A man on horseback had just galloped into the encampment and was breathlessly recounting how a huge army, with Pharaoh himself at its head, was marching north to attack the Hittites.

Moses thought of Ramses, his boyhood friend, and the amazing energy that drove him. In that instant, he wished him victory.

FIFTY-ONE

The Hittite army was massed in front of the capital's ramparts. From atop a watchtower, the priestess Puduhepa watched the chariots line up, then the archers and foot soldiers. Perfectly disciplined, they embodied the invincible power of an empire that would soon make Ramses' Egypt a province of Hatti.

According to form, Muwattali had responded to the Pharaoh's declaration of war with an identical letter in diplomatic terms.

Puduhepa would have preferred to keep her husband at her side, but the emperor had demanded that Hattusili, his chief adviser, be present at the front.

General Uri-Teshoop marched toward his soldiers, torch in hand. He lit a bonfire next to a never-used chariot. Swinging a sledgehammer, he smashed the chariot to pieces and threw them into the fire.

"Such is the fate of any soldier who runs from the enemy. The Storm God will unleash the fury of his fire upon you!"

By means of this magical ceremony, Uri-Teshoop endowed his troops with a cohesion that no confrontation, however intense, would weaken.

The general held his sword out to Muwattali as a sign of submission to the emperor.

The imperial chariot headed out toward Kadesh, the future burial ground of the Egyptian army.

Ramses' two splendid horses, Victory in Thebes and the Goddess Mut Is Satisfied, pulled the royal chariot, leading an army comprising four divisions of five thousand men each, placed under the protection of the gods Amon, Ra, Ptah, and Set. The four division commanders passed their orders on to unit commanders, lieutenant generals, and standard-bearers. As for the five hundred chariots, they were divided into five regiments. The soldiers' gear included tunics, shirts, breastplates, leather greaves, helmets, small two-sided axes, and a wealth of other weapons to be distributed by the supply corps as necessary.

Ramses' driver, Menna, was an experienced charioteer familiar with Syria. He was far from thrilled to have Fighter, the gigantic Nubian lion, keeping pace with the chariot, mane flaring in the wind.

Despite the king's attempts to dissuade them, Setau and Lotus had insisted on returning to run the medical unit and set up the field hospital. They also hoped to bring back some unusual snakes, since they had never traveled as far north as Kadesh.

The army left the capital at the end of the month of April in Year Five of Ramses' reign. The weather turned out to be mild, and nothing hindered their progress. After crossing the border at Sile, Ramses had followed the coastal route, studded with well-guarded watering places, then passed through Canaan and Amurru.

At the place called the Dwelling of the Valley of Cedars near Byblos, the king reviewed his reserve troops, three thousand men who were stationed there to seal off the protectorates. They were ordered to continue north to Kadesh, approaching the fortress from the northeast. The generals opposed this strategy, arguing that the reinforcements would encounter stiff resistance and be cut off on their way up the coastal route. Ramses ignored their protests.

The route the king himself was following cut through the Bekaa Valley, a flatland between two mountain ranges. The strange scenery had an unsettling effect on the Egyptian soldiers. Some of them were aware that the muddy streams were teeming with crocodiles and the thickly forested mountains crawling with bears, hyenas, wildcats, and wolves.

The cypresses, pines, and cedars grew so thick that when they crossed a wooded area the soldiers lost sight of the sun and panicked. A general had to reassure the men that the sky had not fallen.

The division of Amon was in the lead, followed by the Ra and Ptah divisions, with Set bringing up the rear. A month after leaving their home base, the Egyptian troops approached the colossal fortress of Kadesh, built on the left bank of the Orontes River, at the outlet of the Bekaa Valley. The fort marked the border to the Hittite empire and served as a base for the commandos sent to destabilize the provinces of Amurru and Canaan.

The weather turned rainy at the end of May and the soldiers complained about the dampness. The fact that their rations were plentiful and tasty went a long way toward easing the discomfort.

Ramses paused to reconnoiter a few miles outside Kadesh, at the edge of the gloomy forest of Labwi. It turned out to be a likely spot for an ambush. The chariots would be immobilized, the infantry unable to maneuver. Though Ahsha's scrawled message—Kadesh, Fast, Danger—was constantly on his mind, the king made sure to proceed with caution.

He called for a temporary halt, with a front line of archers and chariots keeping watch, and met with his war council. Setau sat in with them; as on their last expedition, the snake charmer and his wife had become very popular with the troops, treating their minor injuries and illnesses on the march.

Ramses summoned his charioteer, Menna. "Unroll the map."

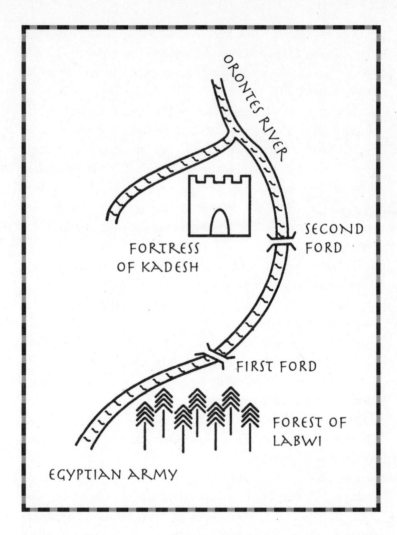

ORONTES RIVER

FORTRESS
OF KADESH

SECOND
FORD

FIRST FORD

FOREST OF
LABWI

EGYPTIAN ARMY

"We're here," Ramses said, pointing to the edge of the forest, "on the east bank of the Orontes. On the other side of the forest, there's a ford where we can cross the river, out of range of the archers on the fortress watchtowers. The second ford, just to the north, is much too close. We'll stay

clear of the fortress and camp to the northeast so we can
take it from behind. Do you all agree to my plan?"

The generals nodded in unison.

The king's eyes blazed. "Then have you all lost your
wits?"

"The forest could give us trouble," the general in charge
of the division of Amon offered.

"I was wondering when you'd notice. And do you think
the Hittites will stand idly by and let us ford the river, then
take our positions next to the fortress? This is the battle
plan devised by you—you, my own generals. Unfortunately,
you've neglected one minor detail: the Hittite army."

"The enemy will stay safe inside the fortress," objected
the general in charge of the Ptah division.

"If Muwattali was an ordinary commander, that might
be what he'd do. But he's the Emperor of Hatti. He'll attack
us in the forest, at the ford, and in front of his stronghold
at the same time. He'll isolate our units and keep us from
answering his fire. The Hittites will never make the mistake
of staying on the defensive. Why would they keep their
fighting potential walled up inside a fortress? You have to
admit it would be most out of character."

"The choice of terrain is decisive," argued the general in
charge of the division of Set.

"Fighting in forests is hardly our strong point; a flat,
open area would better suit our purposes. Let's cross the
Orontes before the forest of Labwi."

"Impossible, there's no ford anywhere around."

"Then let's torch the forest!"

"For one thing, the winds could turn against us. For
another, it would be slow going over burnt stumps and
fallen trees."

"We should have followed the coast road," the general of

the Ra division complained, not hesitating to contradict his own plan, "and attacked Kadesh from the north."

"Hopeless," commented the Ptah general. "With all due respect to Your Majesty, the reserve troops coming up from Amurru will be unable to rendezvous with us. The Hittites are on their guard, and they'll have a full contingent posted at the outlet of the coast road to repel a potential attack from that quarter. The strategy we proposed really is the best course of action."

"Of course it is," the Set general said ironically, "but there's one small problem: we can't advance! I suggest we send a thousand foot soldiers into the forest of Labwi and see how the Hittites react."

"What will we learn from a thousand casualties?"

The Set general was deflated.

"Shall we retreat before we've met the enemy? The Hittites will laugh at us, and Your Majesty's prestige will be seriously compromised."

"How glorious will I look if I lead my army to slaughter? I'm out to save Egypt, not my own reputation."

"What will you decide, Your Majesty?"

Setau emerged from his watchful silence. "As a snake charmer, I prefer to work alone or with my wife to help me. If I headed out with a hundred soldiers, I'd never see a single cobra."

"What is that supposed to mean?" demanded the Set division general.

"Let's send a small band of soldiers into the forest," proposed Setau. "If they get through, they can size up the enemy forces. Then we'll know what to do next."

Setau volunteered to head a commando force of a dozen young, highly trained soldiers, armed with slingshots, bows, and daggers. All of them knew how to move without making noise.

As soon as they entered the forest of Labwi, murky even in the brightest daylight, they scattered, often scanning the treetops for archers who might be lurking there.

Acutely aware of his surroundings, Setau sensed no hostile presence. He exited the forest first and crouched in the thick grass, soon joined by his companions, surprised at how uneventful their hike had been.

The first ford was in sight. No Hittite soldier was in the vicinity.

In the distance stood the fortress of Kadesh, built on a rise. The flats in front of it were deserted. The Egyptians looked at each other, gaping in amazement.

They watched for an hour or more, still disbelieving, before they could face the fact that the Hittite army was nowhere near Kadesh.

"Over there," said Setau, pointing toward three oak trees by the ford. "Something's moving."

The commandos moved quickly to surround the trees. One of the men stayed behind. If this turned out to be an ambush, he would run back to warn Ramses. But the operation went off without a hitch, netting the Egyptians two prisoners who looked to be Bedouin chieftains.

FIFTY-TWO

The two prisoners were terrified.

One was tall and thin, the other of average height, bald and bearded. Neither of them dared raise their eyes to the Pharaoh of Egypt,

"Your names?"

"I'm Amos," said the bald man. "My friend is called Keni."

"Who are you?"

"Bedouin chiefs."

"How do you explain your presence in these parts?"

"We're supposed to be meeting with a Hittite dignitary."

"Why is that?"

Amos bit his lip. Keni hung his head even lower.

"Answer!" demanded Ramses.

"The Hittites want us in league with them against Egypt, attacking caravans."

"And you've accepted, I suppose."

"No, we only wanted to discuss it."

"What was the outcome of your negotiations?"

"There were no negotiations, Your Majesty, since there

aren't any Hittite dignitaries around. Inside the fortress, there's nothing but Syrians."

"Where is the Hittite army?"

"They pulled out of Kadesh more than two weeks ago. According to the fortress commander, they were heading for Aleppo, several days north of here, for maneuvers with their hundreds of brand-new chariots. Keni and I were reluctant to make the journey."

"Weren't the Hittites expecting us here in Kadesh?"

"Yes, Your Majesty . . . but nomads like us had alerted them to the size of your forces. They hadn't been counting on such overwhelming numbers, and decided they'd rather draw you to more open terrain."

"You and your fellow Bedouins warned them that we were coming?"

"We beg your forgiveness, Majesty! We believed the stories about Hatti being so superior. And you know the Hittites don't offer us many alternatives. Either we cooperate or they slaughter us."

"How many men are still in the fortress?"

"A good thousand Syrians, convinced that Kadesh is impregnable."

The war council was reconvened. The generals regarded Setau with new respect. He deserved a medal.

"The Hittite army has retreated," the Ra commander proudly declared. "Can we call that a victory, Your Majesty?"

"Not much of one. The obvious question is whether we should lay siege to the fortress."

Opinion was divided, but the majority leaned toward a rapid advance toward Aleppo.

"If the emperor's forces decided against an engagement here," offered Setau, "it's only because they want to meet us on their own ground. Wouldn't it be wise to take hold of this fortress and use it a base for launching our attack, instead of sending all our divisions into battle and playing into the enemy's hands?"

"We may end up wasting precious time," objected the Amon general.

"I don't think we will. Since the Hittite army has stopped defending Kadesh, we can make quick work of it. We may even be able to persuade the Syrians to surrender, in exchange for their lives."

"We'll lay siege to Kadesh and take the fortress," Ramses pronounced. "Henceforth, this region will be placed under Pharaoh's authority."

Led by the king, the Amon division cut through the forest of Labwi, took the first ford, and crossed the flats. They halted northwest of the imposing fortress with crenellated walls and five towers where Syrian soldiers stood by as the Ra troops took up a position facing the fort. The Ptah division camped near the ford, while the Set division stayed at the edge of the woods. The next day, after a night and morning of rest, the Egyptian troops would join forces before encircling Kadesh and launching their initial attack upon the fort.

The engineers set up Pharaoh's camp with lightning swiftness. Forming a rectangle with tall shields, they raised the sovereign's spacious tent, which featured a bedroom, a study, and an audience chamber. A number of smaller tents were reserved for the officers. The ordinary soldiers would sleep under the stars or, in case of rain, under cloth shelters. At the entry to the camp, a wooden gate flanked with two statues of lions led into a central walkway. It ended at a chapel where the king would say prayers to Amon.

As soon as the division general gave the order to lay down arms, the soldiers went about a variety of tasks assigned to them by unit. The horses, donkeys, and oxen had to be tended to. Laundry was done, wheels were repaired, daggers and lances were sharpened, rations distributed, meals prepared. The aroma of cooking made the men forget Kadesh, the Hittites, and the war. They began to joke, tell stories, gamble their wages. A group of hotheads organized a wrestling tournament.

Ramses groomed his horses himself, then fed his lion; Fighter was as voracious as ever. The camp settled down, the stars took possession of the sky, the king's eyes were riveted on the hulking fortress that his father had judged wiser not to annex. If he could take it, he would deal a serious blow to the Hittite empire. Ramses would install an elite garrison, thwarting any future invasion of Egyptian territory.

He stretched out on his claw-footed bed and laid his head on a pillowcase in a papyrus and lotus print. The delicacy of the pattern brought a smile to his face. How far away the Two Lands seemed, with their good life!

When the king closed his eyes, he saw the sublime face of Nefertari.

"On your feet, Shaanar."

"Do you know who you're talking to, guard?"

"A traitor who should get the death penalty."

"I'm the king's older brother!"

"You're nobody now. Your name will vanish forever. Get up, or you'll feel the sting of my whip."

"You have no right to mistreat a prisoner."

Sensing the threat was serious, Shaanar now rose.

In the main jail in Memphis, he had suffered no special hardships. Unlike the other inmates, who did forced labor in the fields or repairing dikes, the prince was kept in a cell and fed twice a day.

The jailer muscled him into the hall. Shaanar thought he might be put in a chariot heading for a desert outpost, but instead the burly guards marched him into an office. Waiting for him was the man he hated most after Ramses and Ahsha: Ahmeni, the faithful scribe, the incorruptible.

"You've chosen to side with the losers, Ahmeni. Your triumph will be short-lived, believe me."

"You never did know when to give up, Shaanar."

"I'll have the last laugh when the Hittites crush Ramses and get me out of here."

"Your incarceration has evidently made you lose your mind, but perhaps your memory still serves you."

Shaanar scowled. "What do you want from me, Ahmeni?"

"The names of your accomplices."

"Accomplices? Why, the whole court, the whole country, my dear little man! When I take the throne, they'll worship at my feet, and I'll punish my enemies."

"I want names, Shaanar."

"You're much too curious, Ahmeni. And don't you believe I was strong enough to have acted alone?"

"You were manipulated, Shaanar, and your friends have abandoned you."

"You're wrong. Ramses is a doomed man."

"If you talk, Shaanar, the conditions of your imprisonment might be less harsh."

"I won't be a prisoner for long. If I were you, little scribe, I'd start running! I plan to settle every score, and you'll be at the top of my list."

"One last time, Shaanar: will you give me the names of your accomplices?"

"When demons slash your face and rip out your entrails!"

"Life in a penal colony will loose your tongue."

"You'll grovel at my feet, Ahmeni."

"Take him away," the secretary told the guards.

The prince was pushed into a chariot drawn by two oxen. A policeman was at the reins. Four mounted policemen would ride along to the desert penal colony.

Shaanar sat on a rough plank and felt every bump in the road. But the pain and rough treatment made no difference to him. Feeling the ultimate prize within his grasp, then seeing it slip away, had inspired an insatiable desire for revenge.

As the day wore on, Shaanar dozed, dreaming of triumphs to come.

Suddenly, grains of sand whipped his face. He fell to his knees in astonishment and looked around.

A huge tan-colored cloud hid the sky and filled the desert. The storm came from nowhere and hit with incredible speed.

In a panic, two of the horses threw their riders. As their comrades rushed to help them, Shaanar punched the driver, shoved him out of the chariot, grabbed the reins, and headed for the eye of the storm.

FIFTY-THREE

The morning was overcast and the fortress of Kadesh was slow to emerge from the fog. Its imposing mass continued to challenge the Egyptian army. Tucked between the river and the wooded hills, it seemed unassailable. From the height at which the king and the Amon division had positioned themselves, Ramses could see the Ra division on the flatland in front of the fort and the Ptah division between the forest of Labwi and the first ford. Soon they would cross the river, with the Set division following close behind. Then the four divisions would come together in a victorious attack on the fortress.

The soldiers checked their weapons. They were itching to use their daggers, spears, swords, short sabers, clubs, hatchets, and bows. As the battle approached, the horses grew skittish. On orders from the Supply Corps scribe, the campsite was cleaned and the kitchen gear washed and rinsed. The officers reviewed the troops and sent the ill-shaven to see the barber. They were just as picky about neat uniforms. Any infraction was worth several days' hard labor.

Shortly before noon, when the sun's heat finally made itself felt, Ramses had the signal corps give the go-ahead to the Ptah division. They advanced, beginning to ford the river. A messenger was dispatched to send the Set division on its way through the forest of Labwi.

Then came the sound of thunder.

Ramses raised his eyes to the heavens, but saw no cloud.

A clamor rose from the plain. Incredulous, the Pharaoh discovered the true cause of the terrifying roar filling the battle site.

Hundreds of Hittite chariots had just surged across the second ford, nearer the citadel, and were barreling toward the Ra division. Another gigantic wave was descending upon the Ptah division. Behind the chariots ran thousands of foot soldiers, swarming over the hills and valley like a plague of locusts.

This immense army had been concealed in the forest to the east of the fort and now caught the Egyptian troops at their most vulnerable.

The sheer numbers of the enemy force stunned Ramses. When Muwattali appeared, standing in his chariot, the Pharaoh understood.

The Emperor of Hatti was surrounded by the princes of Syria, Mittani, Aleppo, Ugarit, Carcemish, and Arzawa, as well as several lesser chieftains whom Hattusili had convinced (on the emperor's orders) to join the Hittites in their effort to crush the Egyptian army.

Muwattali had forged the broadest coalition that had ever existed, including every country along the coast, by handing out enormous quantities of gold and silver.

Forty thousand men and three thousand chariots bore down upon the Egyptians, still scattered and now frozen in their tracks.

Hundreds of the Ptah division's foot soldiers fell beneath the enemy arrows. Overturned chariots clogged the ford. The survivors ran for shelter in the forest of Labwi, blocking the Set division's advance. It hardly mattered, since the troops would be easy prey for the massed enemy marksmen if they emerged from the forest.

Virtually all of the Ptah division's chariots were destroyed. The Set division's were stuck in the woods. On the flatland, the situation was becoming catastrophic. The truncated Ra division was powerless; the soldiers began to scatter. The coalition troops were slaughtering the Egyptians, the iron of their weapons breaking bones and rending flesh, their daggers sinking into stomachs.

The coalition princes cheered Muwattali.

The emperor's strategy had been brilliant. Who would have supposed that Ramses' proud army could be exterminated before even having a chance to fight? The survivors were fleeing like frightened rabbits; their lives would depend on how fast they could run.

All that remained was to deal the death blow.

The Amon division and the Pharaoh's camp, still intact, could not hold out long against the clamoring enemy horde. Then Muwattali's victory would be complete. With Ramses' death, the Egypt of the pharaohs would finally bow its head and become Hatti's slave.

Seti had never fallen for the trap, but Kadesh had tempted Ramses, a mistake he would pay for with his life.

A wild-eyed warrior pushed aside two minor potentates and confronted the emperor.

"Father, what's going on?" asked Uri-Teshoop. "Why wasn't I told about the timing of the attack, when I'm commander-in-chief of your army?"

"I gave you a specific assignment: defending the fortress with our reserve battalions."

"But the fortress isn't in danger!"

"Those are my orders, Uri-Teshoop, and you're forgetting an important fact: I didn't put you in charge of the coalition forces."

"Then who . . ."

"Who else but my brother, Hattusili, could qualify? Since he's the one who led the long and patient negotiations with our allies, the honor goes to him."

Uri-Teshoop shot a hateful look his uncle's way and brought his hand to the hilt of his sword.

"Back to your post, General," Muwattali ordered curtly.

The Hittite horsemen overturned the hedge of shields protecting Pharaoh's camp. The few Egyptian soldiers who attempted to resist were showered with spears. A cavalry lieutenant screamed at the fleeing soldiers not to run. A Hittite arrow pinned him in the mouth, and he died gagging on the shaft.

More than two thousand chariots were preparing to overrun the royal tent.

"Master," exclaimed the driver Menna, "Protector of Egypt, Lord of the Battle, look! We'll soon be alone in a sea of enemies. Let's not stay here a moment longer. Let's go!"

Ramses gave his groom a withering look. "Out of my sight, man, since you've lost your courage."

"Majesty, I beg you! Standing your ground won't prove we're brave, only mad! The country needs you to stay alive."

"Egypt doesn't need a defeated pharaoh. I'll fight them, Menna."

Ramses put on his blue crown and fastened his battle gear, combining a kilt and a breastplate covered with small metal disks. On his wrists were golden bracelets with lapis lazuli clasps in the shape of ducks, with golden tails.

Calmly, as if it were an ordinary day, the monarch padded his two horses with red, blue, and green cotton blankets. Victory in Thebes, the stallion, and the Goddess Mut Is Satisfied, the mare, were adorned with magnificent plumes of red tipped with blue.

Ramses climbed into his gilded war chariot, ten feet long, its caisson resting on an axle and shaft. The pieces had been bent with heat, covered with gold leaf, and joined with tenons; at the fittings, leather protected the parts from friction. The caisson's frame, open at the back, was made from gold-plated planks. The bottom was of interlaced thongs.

On the side panels, Asian and Nubian warriors were depicted kneeling in submission. The dream of a kingdom that was being shattered, the final symbolic statement of Egypt's power, its domination over both the north and the south.

The chariot was equipped with two quivers, one for arrows, the other for bows and spears. With these paltry weapons, Pharaoh was preparing to combat an entire army.

Ramses wrapped the reins around his waist, leaving his hands free. His horses were brave and intelligent; they would head straight into the fray. A low growling sound gave him reassurance: his lion, Fighter, would be steadfast, striding by his side to the death.

A lion and a pair of horses were all the allies the King of

Egypt had left. The Amon division's cavalry and infantry were fleeing at the approach of the enemy.

"If you make a mistake," Seti had told his son, "blame no one but yourself and correct your error. Fight like a bull, a lion, and a falcon. Rage like the storm. Otherwise, you will be beaten."

With a deafening roar, raising a cloud of dust, the enemy hurtled up the rise where the Pharaoh of Egypt stood proud and alone in his golden chariot.

Ramses was filled with a profound sense of injustice. Why was his destiny turning against him, why must Egypt be trampled by the barbarians?

On the flat stretch in front of the fortress, the Ra division was in tatters, the few survivors having fled southward. The remains of the Ptah and Set divisions were trapped on the east bank of the Orontes. His own Amon division, though it boasted the cream of the charioteers, had behaved appallingly. The very first enemy charge had sent it running. There was not one commanding officer left, not one shield bearer or bowman ready to fight. No matter what their rank, his soldiers had thought only of saving their necks, forgetting their country. Menna, the king's personal driver, was on his knees, head in hands, so as not to witness the enemy charge.

Five years on the throne, five years during which Ramses had tried to be faithful to Seti's spirit and build on his heritage. Five years ending in disaster, on the heels of which Egypt would be invaded and her people enslaved. Nefertari and Tuya could offer only a token resistance to the swarm of predators spreading over the Delta, then devastating the Nile Valley.

As if they could read their master's thoughts, the two horses began to shed tears.

It was too much for Ramses.

Raising his eyes to the sun, he spoke to Amon, the god concealed in the light, whose true form no other being would ever know.

"I call on you, Amon! How can a father abandon his son in the midst of the enemy? What have I ever done to deserve such treatment? Every country around has joined against me; my soldiers, though great in number, have stranded me here, alone and helpless. And whom am I left to fight? Cruel barbarians, strangers to the law of Ma'at. For you, my father, I have built temples, to you made my daily offerings. The fragrance of my rarest flowers has wafted up to you. Great pillared halls have risen in your name. Banners bearing your name fly from towering flagstaffs to announce your holy presence. From the quarries of Elephantine I have hewn tall obelisks proclaiming your glory.

"I call on you, Amon, because I am alone, absolutely alone. I have acted for you with a loving heart. In my distress, Father, grant me your strength. Amon would do more for me than millions of soldiers and hundreds of thousands of chariots. A valiant army is nothing compared to the might of Amon."

The palisade protecting the entry to the center of the camp gave way, opening the way to the speeding chariots. In less than a minute, the young Pharaoh's life would be over.

"Father," cried Ramses, "why have you abandoned me?"

FIFTY-FOUR

Muwattali, Hattusili, and the assembled princes admired the Pharaoh's stance.

"He'll die a warrior," said the emperor, "like a Hittite, and that's no small compliment. Hattusili, I give you credit."

"Those Bedouins were perfect," replied his brother. "They convinced Ramses that our troops were days from Kadesh."

"Uri-Teshoop was mistaken to oppose your plan and recommend an engagement out on the level. I won't forget that."

"The important thing now is to bring off the final victory. Once we've conquered Egypt, Hatti will reign supreme."

"First let's finish with Ramses, when the last of his troops have gone."

The sun abruptly grew twice as bright, blinding the Hittites and their allies. The rumble of thunder cut through the cloudless sky.

It had to be a hallucination. The voice from the ends of the universe, reverberating through the blue vastness . . . a voice that spoke for Ramses' ears alone: "I am your father, Amon. Your hand is in mine. I am yours, the Father of Victories."

The Pharaoh was suddenly wrapped in light. His body grew dazzling as gold in the sun. Ramses, the son of Ra, took on the power of the heavenly body, hurling himself at his stunned opponents.

He was no longer a failed commander, overwhelmed and alone, but a king of unrivaled strength with a tireless sword arm. He was a devastating flame, a shooting star, a rushing wind, a wild bull on the rampage, a falcon with talons poised to strike. Ramses let fly arrow after arrow, killing the drivers of the Hittite chariots. Uncontrolled, the horses reared and collided. The chariots overturned, wreaking havoc.

Fighter, the massive Nubian lion, sprang into action, raking his claws over enemy soldiers, sinking his fangs into necks and skulls. His proud mane blazed as he attacked with deadly accuracy.

Ramses and Fighter turned the tide and broke through the enemy lines. The infantry commander raised his spear, but before he could throw it Pharaoh's shot hit him in the left eye, precisely as the lion's jaw closed over the terrified face of the emperor's lead charioteer.

Despite their superior numbers, the combined forces began to back away, scurrying down the rise toward the level ground.

Muwattali blanched. "That's not a man," he exclaimed. "That's Set himself, the only one with the power to overcome a force of thousands! Look, when you try to attack him, your hands won't work, you can't move, you forget how to use your weapons!"

Even the imperturbable Hattusili was awestruck. He could have sworn that he saw fire spurting out of Ramses.

A giant Hittite managed to scramble into the king's chariot and flail at him with a dagger, but his coat of mail went up in smoke and he died screaming in agony from his burns. Neither Ramses nor the lion slowed down. Pharaoh felt the hand of Amon guiding him. The Father of Victories was at his side, giving him the strength of an army. Like a whirlwind sweeping through a haystack, the King of Egypt scattered his opponents.

"We can't let this go on," Hattusili said angrily.

"Our men are panic-stricken," the Prince of Aleppo pointed out.

"Then get them under control," ordered Muwattali.

"Ramses is a god . . ."

"Ramses is a man, even if his courage seems super-human. Take action, Prince, encourage our soldiers, and this battle will soon be over."

The Prince of Aleppo reluctantly spurred his horse and rode down the knoll that served as the coalition leaders' command post. He was determined to put an end to Ramses' antics with his lion.

Hattusili, scanning the hills to the west, suddenly went rigid.

"Your Majesty, over there . . . it looks like Egyptian chariots heading this way."

"Which direction are they coming from?"

"It would have to be the coast road."

"But how would they get through?"

"Uri-Teshoop refused to set up roadblocks, claiming that no Egyptian would dare to try that approach."

The reinforcements were speeding forward, encountering no opposition, spreading out over the flatland and rushing into the breach Ramses had opened.

"Don't run," the Prince of Aleppo screamed at his troops. "Get Ramses!"

A few soldiers obeyed. The moment they did an about-face, the lion clawed them from head to chest.

When the Prince of Aleppo saw the Pharaoh's golden chariot bearing down on him, his heart sank. He took off at a gallop. In his attempt to escape, his mount trampled several Hittites. Alarmed, he let go of the reins. The horse bolted for the river, where a tangle of chariots was breaking apart—some sinking, others drifting off on the current. Soldiers were struggling in the mire, some drowning, others trying to swim. They all preferred to take their chances in the Orontes rather than face the demigod cutting through their ranks like wildfire.

The Egyptian reinforcements finished the job for Ramses, exterminating the enemy troops still in place, herding stragglers into the river. One charioteer fished out the sputtering Prince of Aleppo, feet first.

Ramses' chariot was approaching the knoll where the enemy command was stationed.

"Let's pull back," Hattusili advised the emperor.

"We still have units on the west bank."

"They won't be enough. Ramses may even take the ford and bring across his other two divisions."

The emperor wiped his forehead with the back of one hand.

"I don't understand, Hattusili. How can one man fight off an entire army?"

"If that man is Pharaoh, if he's Ramses . . ."

"I know. 'Rich in Armies, Powerful in Victories,' they say in Egyptian . . . but that's only his title, and this is a field of battle!"

"We're beaten, Your Majesty. Let's move to safety."

"A Hittite never retreats!"

"Consider the prospect of staying alive to fight another day."

"What are you suggesting, Hattusili?"

"Why not take cover inside the citadel?"

"We'll be trapped!"

"We have no choice," advised Hattusili. "If we go north, Ramses and his troops will pursue us."

"Let's hope Kadesh really is impregnable."

"It's not just any fortress. Even Seti decided not to storm it."

"But his son will."

"Let's hurry, Your Majesty!"

Grudgingly, Muwattali raised his right hand and held the pose for what seemed to him endless seconds, ordering the retreat.

Biting his lips until he drew blood, Uri-Teshoop watched the whole sorry spectacle. The battalion blocking access to the first ford on the east bank of the Orontes moved up to the second ford. What was left of the Ptah division refused to follow, fearing a second ambush. The commander decided instead to shore up the rear, dispatching a messenger to give the all clear to the Set division, bringing it out of the forest of Labwi.

The Prince of Aleppo came to his senses, escaped from his rescuer, swam across the river, and joined his allies retreating toward Kadesh. The Egyptian reinforcements fired volleys of arrows on them, killing hundreds.

The Egyptians marched through the cadavers, cutting one hand from each, to be used in a gruesome tally eventually entered in the royal archives.

No one dared approach the Pharaoh. Fighter lay sphinx-like in front of the weary steeds. Blood-spattered, Ramses climbed down from the golden chariot and stood for a long while stroking his lion, rubbing his pair of horses, not even glancing at the petrified soldiers who dreaded his reaction.

Menna was the first to approach him. The charioteer trembled, barely able to put one foot in front of the other.

Beyond the second ford, the Hittite army and the coalition forces were streaming toward the fortress of Kadesh and entering the main gate. The Egyptians had run out of time to prevent them from taking shelter.

"Your Majesty," Menna said haltingly, "we won."

Staring at the fortress in the distance, Ramses looked like a granite statue.

"The leader of the Hittites has withdrawn," continued Menna. "You alone killed thousands of men! Who will find the words to sing your praise?"

Ramses turned his stone face to the groom.

Menna fell to the ground, terrified that the Pharaoh's lightning power would strike him.

"Is that you, Menna?"

"Yes, Your Majesty, Menna, your driver and faithful servant. Forgive me, forgive your army. May your great victory help you forget our failings!"

"A pharaoh never pardons, faithful servant. A pharaoh governs and acts."

FIFTY-FIVE

The Amon and Ra divisions had been decimated, the Ptah considerably weakened. Only the Set division was intact. Thousands of Egyptians were dead; even more of the Hittites and coalition troops had perished. A single fact remained: Ramses had won the battle of Kadesh.

It was true that Muwattali, Hattusili, Uri-Teshoop, and certain of their coalition chieftains (even the half-drowned Prince of Aleppo) were alive and safe inside the fortress.

Yet the myth of Hittite invincibility had perished. A number of princes allied with the Emperor of Hatti had succumbed to Egyptian arrows or died in the river. Henceforth, the neighboring powers would know that Muwattali's shield was not enough to protect them from the wrath of Ramses.

The Pharaoh convened a meeting of all his surviving commanders, including the generals commanding the Ptah and Set divisions.

There was little joy in the victory. On his gilded throne, Ramses wore the face of an angry falcon.

"Every man here," he began, "was responsible for a command. All of you flaunted your rank before the battle. Yet when the time came, all of you acted like cowards! You were fed and clothed, exempt from taxes, respected and envied as the heads of divisions. All of you failed me and ran from battle."

The commander of the Set division took one step forward.

"Your Majesty . . ."

"Do you presume to contradict me?"

The general got back in line.

"I can no longer trust you. Tomorrow, you'll fail me again, scattering like sparrows at the first hint of danger. I'm demoting every last one of you. Consider yourselves fortunate to remain in the army as simple soldiers, serving your country, earning your pay and, in time, your pension."

There was no protest. Most had expected a harsher punishment.

Later that day, the king named new commanding officers, choosing from among the reinforcement units.

On the day following his upset, Ramses launched the first attack on the fortress of Kadesh, where Hittite banners fluttered on the towers.

The Egyptian archers shot volleys of arrows, but the shafts broke against the solid rock of the battlements. Unlike its Syrian counterparts, Kadesh had towers beyond their aim.

Eager to prove their valor, the infantry scaled the rocky base of the fortress and laid wooden ladders against the walls. But the Hittite sharpshooters picked off most of them, and those that remained were forced to abandon the effort. Three more attempts were made, each one ending in failure.

The next day, and the next, a few daring souls made it halfway up the walls before a stream of projectiles knocked them to their deaths.

Kadesh lived up to its legend.

A somber Ramses convened his new war council. His appointees tried hard to outdo each other in bravado, hoping to please the king. Weary of their chatter, he dismissed them, keeping only Setau at his side.

"Lotus and I will save dozens of lives," Setau told his old friend, "provided that we don't die of exhaustion. At the rate we're going, our hospital will soon run out of supplies."

"Don't beat around the bush, Setau."

"All right. Let's go home, Ramses."

"And forget about the fortress of Kadesh?"

"We have our victory."

"Until Kadesh is under Egyptian control, the Hittite menace persists."

"Taking Kadesh would waste too many resources and too many lives. Why not go back to Egypt? We need to take care of the wounded and rebuild our forces."

"This fortress must fall like the others we conquered."

"What if it doesn't, no matter how hard you try?"

"Nature is bountiful in these parts; you and Lotus can find what you need to prepare your own remedies."

"What if Ahsha was locked up inside that fort?"

"All the more reason to take it and free him."

The driver Menna ran up and bowed low to Ramses. "Your Majesty! They threw a lance from the ramparts, with this message tied to the tip!"

"Hand it over."

Ramses studied the text:

> To Ramses, Pharaoh of Egypt, from his brother Muwattali, Emperor of Hatti,
>
> Before continuing our confrontation, would it not be wise for us to hold discussions? Let a tent be erected on the level, halfway between your camp and the fortress.
>
> I will come there alone, tomorrow when the sun is at its highest, to meet you, my brother ruler, alone.

Inside the tent sat two folding thrones, face to face. Between them was a low table on which two goblets and a small jar of cool water had been placed.

The two sovereigns sat down at once, eyeing each other. Despite the heat, Muwattali was dressed in a long woolen mantle of red and black.

"I am happy to meet with my brother the Pharaoh of Egypt, whose glory is ever increasing."

"The Emperor of Hatti's reputation sows fear wherever it reaches."

"In that regard, my brother Ramses has now surpassed me. I formed an invincible coalition and you defeated it. Surely the gods lent you their protection?"

"Amon, the Father of Victories, seconded me with his power."

"I found it hard to believe that a mortal man could fight like that, pharaoh or not."

"You didn't mind resorting to deception."

"It's a weapon like any other. It would have beaten you, too, if you hadn't had the benefit of supernatural powers. The soul of your father, Seti, fed your incredible courage and made you oblivious to fear and defeat."

"Are you ready to surrender, my brother Muwattali?"

"Are you always so blunt, my brother Ramses?"

"Thousands of men are dead because of Hatti's expansionist politics. There's no more time for idle conversation. Are you ready to surrender?"

"Does my brother know who I am?"

"The Emperor of Hatti, cornered in the mighty fortress of Kadesh."

"I have with me my brother, Hattusili, my son, Uri-Teshoop, my vassals and my allies. Our surrender would cripple the empire."

"Such are the consequences of your defeat."

"I concede that you won the battle of Kadesh, but the fortress is still intact."

"Sooner or later, it will fall."

"You saw how far you got with your initial attempts. Keep going and you'll lose a great many men, without even putting a dent in the fortress walls."

"That's why I've decided to adopt another strategy."

"Since it's only the two of us, my brother, will you tell me your plans?"

"Haven't you guessed? It will require great patience. There are so many of you inside the fortress that soon you'll be short of rations. Which makes more sense, surrendering or being starved out?"

"My brother Ramses does not know the strength of this fortress. It has vast storerooms with months' worth of food. We will also have certain advantages over the Egyptian army."

"Preposterous," said the Pharaoh.

"Think again, my brother. You Egyptians are far from your bases. Conditions will grow more difficult by the day. Everyone knows that you hate staying away from your country for very long and that Egypt likes to have you near at hand. Before long autumn will be here. The cold brings disease as well as discomfort. Your men will grow weary and disenchanted. You can be sure, my brother Ramses, that my allies and I will be better off than you. And don't worry about us having enough water: the fort's cisterns are full, not to mention the well we've dug inside the walls."

Ramses took a sip of water, not because he was thirsty, but to pause and think. Muwattali's arguments were not without merit.

"Would my brother care for a drink?" the Pharaoh offered.

"No, I'm quite comfortable."

"You're not afraid of poison, are you? I hear it's common at the court in Hatti."

"Not any longer, though I do have my steward taste all my food for me. My brother Ramses should also know that one of his childhood friends, the young and brilliant diplomat Ahsha, was arrested in our capital while posing as a potter. As a spy, he'd be dead already if I hadn't intervened. It occurred to me that you might be willing to bargain for someone so close to you."

"You're wrong, Muwattali. I'm a pharaoh before I'm a man."

"Ahsha is not only your friend, but also the real head of your diplomatic service and your top Asia hand. Personal concerns aside, you might want to save a key adviser."

"What are you proposing?"

"Isn't an armistice, even a shaky one, preferable to a siege that would be disastrous for both of us?"

"An armistice? Impossible."

"Think about it, my brother. I didn't engage the entire Hittite army in this battle. Reinforcements will soon be on their way, and you'll have new battles to wage at the same time you keep up the siege. Do you have enough men, enough weapons, to prevent the tide from turning against you?"

"You lost the battle of Kadesh, Muwattali, and you dare ask me for a peace agreement?"

"I'm prepared to acknowledge my defeat in an official document. Once it's in your possession, you can lift the siege, and Kadesh will mark the limit of my empire. Never will my army march into Egypt."

FIFTY-SIX

The door to Ahsha's cell swung open.

Self-possessed as he was, the young diplomat jump-ed. The two guards were ominously stern-faced. Since his incarceration, Ahsha had expected daily to be executed. The Hittites showed no mercy when it came to spies.

An axe, a dagger, a forced jump off a cliff? The Egyptian hoped his death would be swift and brutal, not a long, drawn-out affair.

Ahsha was escorted to a cold, austere room decorated with shields and lances. As always, in Hatti, war made its presence felt.

"How are you feeling?" asked the priestess Puduhepa.

"I need more exercise and I don't like the food, but I'm still alive. Isn't that a miracle?"

"You might say so."

"I have the feeling that my luck is running out. However, I'm glad to see a woman here. Perhaps you won't be so hard on me."

"Don't count on special treatment from Hittite women."

"Have I lost my touch?"

The priestess's eyes blazed with fury. "Have you any idea how serious your situation is?"

"Egyptian diplomats prefer to die smiling."

Ahsha thought again about how he had failed Ramses, not managing to get out of Hatti and warn him about the coalition ambush. The Pharaoh's anger would pursue him even in the afterlife. Or had his farm wife gotten through with the three-word message? The chance was slim, but if she had delivered it, the quick-minded king would know what those three words meant.

Without that intelligence, by now the Egyptian army would have been wiped out at Kadesh and Shaanar would have claimed the throne. All things considered, he was better off dead than dealing with such a despot.

"You were never a traitor to Ramses," said Puduhepa, "and Shaanar never gave you orders."

"You be the judge."

"The battle of Kadesh is over," she revealed. "Ramses defeated the coalition troops."

Ahsha felt giddy. "Don't make me laugh."

"I'm in no mood for joking."

"Defeated the coalition . . ." Ahsha repeated in a daze.

"Our emperor is alive and free," added the priestess, "and the fortress of Kadesh is intact."

The prisoner grew somber. "What will you do with me?"

"I would gladly have you burnt at the stake as a spy, but you've become a pawn in the negotiations."

The Egyptian army was camped in front of the fortress. The walls of Kadesh remained gray, despite the warm June sun. Since the talks between Ramses and Muwattali, the Pharaoh's soldiers had launched no new attack. From atop the ramparts, Uri-Teshoop and the Hittite archers observed their opponents engaged in nonaggressive occupations: caring for their animals, playing games, holding wrestling tournaments. Cooks from the various regiments prepared their best dishes, flinging insults at each other.

Ramses had given his commanding officers only one order: to maintain discipline. None of them had been taken into his confidence about where matters stood with Muwattali.

The new Set division commander took the risk of inquiring. "Your Majesty, your generals are at a loss."

"Even though we've won a resounding victory?"

"We know that you alone won the day at Kadesh, Your Majesty. But why aren't we attacking the fortress?"

"Because we have no chance of taking it. We'd have to commit to losing at least half our troops, with no guarantee of success."

"How long do we have to sit here and stare at this pile of rock?"

"I reached an agreement with Muwattali."

"Do you mean a peace treaty?"

"If certain conditions are fulfilled. If not, we'll resume the hostilities."

"How soon will we know, Your Majesty?"

"I gave them until the end of the week. By then I'll find out what an emperor's word is worth."

In the distance, on the road coming down from the north, was a cloud of dust. Several Hittite chariots were approaching Kadesh, chariots that might represent the vanguard of Muwattali's reinforcements.

Ramses put an end to the excitement buzzing through the Egyptian camp. Climbing into his chariot behind Victory in Thebes and the Goddess Mut Is Satisfied, the king called his lion to his side and rode out to meet the enemy detachment.

The Hittite archers kept their hands on the reins. News of the Pharaoh's rampage with Fighter had already spread throughout Hatti.

A man climbed out of a chariot and walked with an easy grace toward the King of Egypt. He was slim, with a fine-boned face and a trim mustache.

Suddenly Ahsha forgot his protocol and broke into a run. Ramses opened his arms and the two old friends embraced.

"Was my message useful, Your Majesty?"

"Yes and no. I didn't know exactly what to expect, but the magic of destiny was on Egypt's side. Thanks to you, I was able to act quickly. Still, the victory belongs to Amon."

"I thought I'd never see Egypt again. Hittite prisons are sinister. I tried to convince my inquisitors that I was in league with Shaanar, and that must have saved my life. Then things started moving too quickly. Dying in the Hittite capital would have been in the worst possible taste."

"We need to decide whether to sign a truce or pursue the hostilities. I could use your advice."

Inside his tent, Ramses showed Ahsha the document the Hittite emperor had sent him:

> *I, Muwattali, am the faithful servant of Ramses, whom I recognize as the truly begotten Son of Light. My country is at your feet. But do not abuse your power!*
>
> *Your authority is absolute, as you proved in winning a victory against all odds. But why would you continue to exterminate your servant's people, why would you act unjustly?*
>
> *Since you are victorious, concede that peace is better than war, and give the Hittites respite.*

"Quite the rhetoric," commented Ahsha.

"Do you think this text is explicit enough concerning the region as a whole?"

"A masterpiece! A Hittite defeat is quite unprecedented, but for their emperor to admit his defeat is one more miracle we can attribute to you."

"I couldn't lay my hands on Kadesh."

"The fortress doesn't matter. You won a decisive battle. Muwattali the Invincible considers himself your vassal, at least in words. Taking Kadesh could hardly add to your acclaim."

Muwattali had kept his word, producing an acceptable admission of defeat and freeing Ahsha. Therefore, Ramses kept his, ordering the army to break camp and begin the long trek back to Egypt.

Before leaving the site where so many of his countrymen had perished, Ramses looked back at the fortress. Muwattali, his brother, his son, would march away as free men. The Pharaoh had not destroyed the prime symbol of Hittite power, but after the humiliating defeat of the coalition, how much of that power remained? Muwattali, in writing, declared himself Ramses' servant.

He had succeeded beyond his wildest dreams. Yet

Ramses would never forget that only with the aid of his celestial father, on whom he had relied in his hour of need, had he turned a potential disaster into a triumph.

"There's not one Egyptian left on the level in front of the fortress," declared the chief of the Kadesh lookouts.

"Send the scouts to the south, east, and west," Muwattali ordered his son, Uri-Teshoop. "Ramses may have learned his lesson and hidden his troops in the forest to attack us the minute we leave the fort."

"How long will he keep us running?"

"We need to go back to Hattusa," advised the emperor's brother. "It's time to rebuild our forces and reconsider our strategy."

"I'm not talking to a defeated general," flared Uri-Teshoop, "I'm addressing the emperor of the Hittites."

"Calm down, my son," soothed Muwattali. "I'm not ashamed of my performance at the head of the coalition army. All of us underestimated Ramses' personal power."

"If you'd taken my advice, we would have won!"

"You're wrong. The Egyptians were very well armed, and their chariots were as good or better than our own. A frontal attack in the open would never have gone in our favor. Our losses would have been very heavy."

"So you'll settle for a humiliating defeat . . ."

"We've kept a key fortress, Hatti has not been invaded, and the war with Egypt will go on."

"How can it go on after you've signed that disgusting document?"

"It wasn't a peace treaty," explained Hattusili, "but a

simple letter from one reigning monarch to another. The fact that Ramses accepted it at face value shows a woeful lack of experience."

"It says in black and white that Muwattali considers himself Pharaoh's vassal!"

Hattusili smiled. "When vassals have the necessary troops, nothing prevents them from rebelling."

Uri-Teshoop looked his father straight in the eye. "Don't listen to him, Father. He's a fool. Just let me take charge of the army. Diplomacy and deceit will get us nowhere, but I'll show you I can handle Ramses."

"Let's go back to Hattusa," the emperor said decisively. "The mountain air will help us think more clearly."

FIFTY-SEVEN

Springing high, Ramses plunged into the pool where Nefertari was bathing. The king swam underwater and grabbed his wife by the waist. Feigning surprise, she let him pull her under, and they rose to the surface in a slow embrace. Watcher, the yellow dog, ran barking around the pool, while Fighter dozed in the shade of a sycamore, a thin golden collar around his neck testifying to his valor in battle.

Ramses could never look at Nefertari without falling under the spell of her beauty. Beyond the sensual attraction and bodily communion, a mysterious link united them, stronger than time and death. The mild autumnal sun speckled their faces as they glided through the blue-green water. When they emerged, Watcher stopped barking and licked their legs. The king's old dog hated the pool and could never understand why his master seemed to enjoy getting wet. After he'd had his fill of petting, he cuddled up against the massive lion for a well-deserved nap.

Nefertari was so desirable that Ramses' hands grew bold. They stroked the young woman's restful body as eagerly as an explorer discovering an unknown country. At first passive and happy to be seduced, she was soon aroused to a quest of her own desire.

All over the country, Ramses had become Ramses the Great. Upon his return to the capital, a huge crowd had acclaimed the victor of Kadesh, the Pharaoh who had sent the Hittites running back into their own territory. This resounding victory was properly celebrated with several weeks of festivities, in town and village alike. Once the specter of imminent invasion receded, Egypt returned to its usual happy state, cheered even more by a bountiful inundation.

Year Five of the reign of Seti's son was closing with a triumph. The new military leadership was in awe of him and the court was captivated, bowing to his wishes. Ramses' youth was nearly over. The twenty-eight-year-old Lord of the Two Lands recalled the achievements of his greatest predecessors and had already put his indelible stamp on his own era.

Leaning on a cane, Homer walked out to meet Ramses.

"I'm finished, Your Majesty."

"Would you like to take my arm and go for a stroll, or shall we sit down by your lemon tree?"

"Let's walk. My head and my hand have been working hard lately. Now my legs need a turn."

"This new poem has interrupted your work on the *Iliad*, I'm afraid."

"Yes, but what material you've given me!"

"And what have you done with it?"

"I've stuck to the truth, Your Majesty. I've put it all in— your army's desertion, the appeal to your heavenly father, your single-handed fight. I found the story of your extraordinary victory so inspiring that I felt like a young poet writing his first ode! The verses brimmed on my lips, the scenes seemed to write themselves. Your friend Ahmeni helped me with the grammar. Egyptian isn't an easy language, but its flexibility and precision make it a joy to work with."

"Your account of the battle of Kadesh will be engraved on the exterior south wall of the great hypostyle hall at Karnak," Ramses revealed, "and on the exterior wall of the temple of Luxor's courtyard and the facade of the monumental gateway, the outer walls of the temple at Abydos, and eventually in the forecourt of my Eternal Temple."

"Then the memory of the battle of Kadesh will be written forever in stone."

"My intention is to honor Amon, the hidden god, and the victory of order over chaos, the stability handed down in the law of Ma'at."

"You astound me, Your Majesty, and your country surprises me more every day. I didn't believe that the law you so honor could help you overcome a determined foe."

"If it came to pass that Ma'at was not uppermost in my heart and mind, my kingship would be doomed, and Egypt would find another pharaoh to husband her."

Despite the huge quantities of food he consumed, Ahmeni stayed thin as a reed. Sickly-looking as ever, the king's private secretary never left his office, plowing through an impressive number of documents with his select staff. He stayed in close contact with the vizier and the cabinet, making sure he knew everything that was happening in the country and at the same time checking on their performance. In his opinion, sound management practices could be summed up in one simple precept: the higher and more influential the office, the harsher the punishment in case of mistakes or oversights. From the head of the department on down, each supervisor was held responsible for his subordinates' actions. Former top advisers and demoted government officials had learned the hard way that Ahmeni kept to the highest standard and never played favorites.

When the king was in residence at Pi-Ramses, he met with his éminence grise each day. When he left for a visit to Thebes or Memphis, Ahmeni prepared detailed reports that the king studied attentively before deciding matters.

The scribe had just presented his public works plan for the coming year when Serramanna was shown into the office. He towered among the shelves full of carefully organized papyri. The burly Sard made his bow to the monarch.

"I still sense a certain resentment," commented Ramses.

"Would I ever have let you fight a whole army single-handed?"

"Taking care of my wife and my mother was a high-priority assignment."

"I grant you that, but I wish I could have slaughtered some Hittites with you! They claim they're the world's greatest warriors, and then they hole up in a fortress!"

"Our time is limited," interrupted Ahmeni. "What's the latest on your investigation?"

"Nothing," replied a downcast Serramanna.

"No trace of him?"

"I found the chariot and the policemen's corpses, but not Shaanar's. According to some traveling merchants who'd taken shelter in a stone hut nearby, the sandstorm was extremely violent and lasted much longer than usual. I searched as far as the oasis of Kharga, and I can assure you that my men and I combed the desert."

"In a blinding storm," reasoned Ahmeni, "he'd most likely have stumbled into a wadi. Shaanar's body is probably lying in some dry riverbed, buried under a ton of sand."

"Yes, probably," admitted Serramanna.

"I don't agree," declared Ramses.

"He never could have made it out alive, Your Majesty. He left the main road, got lost, and succumbed to the wind, the sand, and thirst."

"His hatred is so intense that it could serve him as food and drink. Shaanar is not dead."

The king was praying before the statue of Thoth in the lobby of the State Department, after placing a bouquet of lilies and papyrus stems on the altar. The god of wisdom was represented as a baboon with a crescent moon as a headpiece. Thoth sat with his eyes raised to the heavens, far beyond earthly concerns.

High public servants rose and bowed at Ramses' passing. Ahsha, his new secretary of state, came out to greet him at his office door. The Pharaoh's old friend had been hailed as a hero by the court. The two embraced, and Ahsha knew that the Pharaoh's visit was a singular mark of his favor, confirming the young diplomat in his new role as head of Egypt's foreign affairs.

His office was quite different from Ahmeni's. Bouquets of Syrian roses, sprigs of narcissus and marigold, slender alabaster vases on graceful stands, floor lamps, acacia chests, and colorful wall hangings formed a decor that was inviting yet refined, less like a workspace than the private apartments in some plush villa.

His eyes gleaming with intelligence, elegant, wearing a simple perfumed wig, Ahsha looked like a sophisticated guest at a lavish banquet. Who would have guessed that this well-bred specimen was a master spy, able to assume the identity of a humble Hittite merchant? There was no clutter of documents in the new appointee's office; he preferred to keep crucial information filed away in his prodigious memory.

"I may be forced to hand in my resignation, Your Majesty."

"You've done something wrong already?"

"It's what I haven't been able to do. I've used every resource available, but there's still no sign of Moses. It's curious. By now someone should have run across him. The only possibility I can see is that he's gone to the middle of nowhere and simply stayed put. If he's changed his name and joined with a tribe of nomads, it could be very difficult to identify him, if not impossible."

"Keep looking. What can you tell me about the Hittite spy ring?"

"The young blond woman was buried; we never found out who she was. The sorcerer disappeared. We think he's left the country. Once again, no sightings, as if every member of the network simply vanished in a matter of days. The danger it represented was real enough, though."

"Are you sure we're safe now?"

"I wouldn't go that far," Ahsha acknowledged.

"Don't give up the search."

"I'm wondering what form the Hittite reaction will take," the statesman admitted. "Kadesh was humiliating, and the internal power struggle is unrelenting. I don't believe they'll stick with the truce, but it will be months, if not years, before they're ready to fight again."

"How is Meba working out?"

"My distinguished predecessor is a fine addition to the department, tireless and most respectful."

"Watch out for him. I'm convinced that he still holds a grudge. What do you hear from our outposts in southern Syria?"

"Dead calm, but my trust in their observations is somewhat limited. That's why I'm leaving tomorrow for Amurru. We need a force that's ready to react at the first sign of an invasion."

FIFTY-EIGHT

To calm her fury, the priestess Puduhepa locked herself up in the holiest site in the Hittite capital, the upper town's underground chamber, carved out of the rocky prominence on which the imperial palace was built. Muwattali, after the defeat at Kadesh, had decided to keep both his brother and son at a distance. He consolidated his personal power, maintaining that he alone was capable of holding the rival factions in check.

The underground sanctuary had an arched ceiling and walls covered with carvings that showed the emperor as a warrior and a priest, a winged solar disk hovering over him. Puduhepa made her way to the altar of the underworld, where a blood-spattered sword lay.

It was here that she came to find the inspiration she needed to save her husband from Muwattali's wrath and help him regain favor. Uri-Teshoop, for his part, still had the ear of the extremist wing of the military establishment. He would not be biding his time; he would try to get rid of Hattusili, if not eliminate the emperor outright.

Puduhepa meditated far into the night, thinking only of her husband.

The god of the underworld gave her the answer.

The meeting between Muwattali, his brother, and his son ended up in a violent clash of opinions.

"Hattusili is the one responsible for our defeat," Uri-Teshoop insisted. "If I'd been commanding the coalition troops, we would have crushed the Egyptian army."

"We did," Hattusili reminded him, "until Ramses came out of nowhere."

"I would have stopped him!"

"Don't be a braggart," interrupted the emperor. "No one could have overcome his superhuman power on the day of the battle. When the gods speak, man must heed them."

Muwattali's statement prevented his son from pursuing his argument. He therefore launched an offensive on another front. "What are your plans for the future, Father?"

"I'm thinking."

"There's no more time to think! Kadesh made us a laughingstock. We should wipe out the insult as soon as possible. Let me have what's left of the coalition army, and I'll invade Egypt."

"Absurd," Hattusili protested. "Our primary concern must be to rebuild our alliances. The coalition princes lost a great many men, and some of them may lose their thrones unless we support them financially."

"Excuses," retorted Uri-Teshoop. "Hattusili hopes that time will hide the fact that he's a loser and a coward."

"Watch your language," warned Muwattali. "It's no use calling names."

"I've waited long enough, Father. I want full control."

"I'm the emperor, Uri-Teshoop. Don't try to tell me what I should or shouldn't do."

"Stick with your brother's bad advice, if you want to. I'm not setting foot outside my rooms until you order me to lead our troops to victory."

Uri-Teshoop walked briskly out of the audience chamber.

"He's not entirely wrong," Hattusili admitted.

"What do you mean?"

"Puduhepa consulted the gods of the underworld."

"She did, did she?"

"They told her we have to make up for the loss of Kadesh."

"Do you have a plan?"

"A risky one, but I'll take full responsibility."

"You're my brother, Hattusili, and I don't want to lose you."

"I don't think I was wrong about Kadesh, and my sole aim in life is preserving the glory of the empire. The gods have spoken, and I vow to carry out their instructions."

The north wind blowing down through the Delta failed to disperse the dark, heavy rain clouds. Seated behind his father on the back of a splendid gray horse, the boy Kha shivered.

"I'm cold, Father. Couldn't we go a little slower?"

"We're in a hurry."

"Where are we going?"

"To see death."

"The beautiful Lady of the West, with her sweet smile?"

"No, that's the death of the just, and you're not one of them yet."

"That's what I want to be!"

"Then take this first step."

Kha clenched his teeth. He would never, ever disappoint his father.

Ramses stopped by the spot where a canal joined a branch of the Nile. A small granite shrine marked the site, which seemed harmless enough.

"Is this where death is?"

"Inside the shrine. If you're afraid, don't go in."

Kha jumped down, repeating the magic words he'd learned from stories, spells to protect him from danger. He glanced back at his father, but Ramses stood motionless. Kha comprehended that he could expect no help from Pharaoh. There was no way to go except toward the shrine.

A cloud hid the sun; the sky grew darker. The child walked haltingly, stopping in his tracks halfway to his destination. In the pathway was a cobra black as ink, very long, with a big head, poised to strike.

Petrified, the boy didn't dare run away. The cobra, emboldened, slithered closer.

Soon it would reach him. Muttering the ancient formulas, stumbling over the words, the boy squeezed his eyes shut as the cobra reared its head.

A forked stick pinned the snake to the ground.

"This death is not for you," declared Setau. "Go back to your father now, Kha."

Kha looked Ramses straight in the eye.

"I said the right words and the cobra didn't bite me. I'll become one of the just, Father, won't I?"

Settled into a comfortable armchair, savoring the pale winter sunshine that glazed the trees in her private garden with gold, Tuya was deep in conversation with a lanky dark-haired woman when Ramses arrived for a visit.

"Dolora!" the king said sharply, recognizing his sister.

"Don't be too hard on her," Tuya admonished. "She has a great deal to tell you."

Pale and tired-looking, Dolora threw herself at Ramses' feet. "Forgive me, I beg of you!"

"First tell me what you're guilty of, Dolora."

"That awful sorcerer misled me. I thought he was a righteous man. I must have been under a spell."

"Who is he?"

"A Libyan, skilled in black magic. He shut me up in a villa in Memphis, then dragged me along with him when he fled. He told me he'd slit my throat if I didn't go."

"Why would he threaten you?"

"Because . . . because . . ." Dolora broke out in sobs. Ramses helped her to her feet and into a chair.

"Tell me."

"The sorcerer . . . he killed a servant girl and the young woman that he'd used as a medium. They wouldn't follow his orders."

"Did you witness the murders?"

"No, I was locked in my room . . . but I saw their bodies when we escaped from the house."

"Why did this sorcerer hold you captive?"

"He thought I could be his next medium. Through me, he thought he could get to you. He drugged me and grilled me about you . . . but I was too far gone to talk. When he fled to Libya, he let me go. It was dreadful, Ramses. I was sure he was going to kill me."

"You should be more careful of the company you keep."

"I'm sorry. If you only knew how sorry I am!"

"You're under house arrest, Dolora."

FIFTY-NINE

Ahsha was on familiar terms with Benteshina, the prince of the province of Amurru. Little inclined to follow the ways of the gods, the prince was a slave to gold, wine, and women; a corrupt and venal man whose only aim in life was preserving his rank and privileges.

Since Amurru had a key strategic role to play, however, the new secretary of state had no qualms about using every available means to enlist the prince's cooperation. First of all, Ahsha would go to see him in person, in the name of Pharaoh, as a mark of respect. Furthermore, he would be laden with rich presents, notably fine fabrics, vintage wines, alabaster dinnerware, ceremonial weapons, and furniture fit for a king.

Most of the Egyptian troops stationed in Amurru had been mobilized as reinforcements in the battle of Kadesh. Since their valiant effort had largely saved the day, they were granted an extended home leave, and most still remained in Egypt. Ahsha therefore led a detachment of fifty officers who would recruit and train native soldiers. Eventually, a thousand foot soldiers and archers would arrive from Pi-Ramses, reestablishing a strong military base in Amurru.

Ahsha sailed north from Pelusium. It was a pleasant trip, with favorable winds, a calm sea, and a pretty Syrian to distract him.

When the Egyptian ship entered the Beirut harbor, Prince Benteshina was waiting on shore, along with a sizable retinue. Fiftyish, portly and affable, sporting a shiny black mustache, the prince kissed Ahsha on both cheeks and launched into a speech about the prodigious victory at Kadesh and how Ramses the Great had single-handedly shifted the balance of power.

"And you, my dear Ahsha! Such a brilliant career! So young, and already directing affairs of state for your mighty country! I bow to you, sir."

"No need, Your Highness. I come to you as a friend."

"You'll stay in the palace, of course. We'll see to your every need." There was a gleam in Benteshina's eye. "Perhaps you might like . . . a young virgin?"

"To refuse such a wonder would be presumptuous, surely. Now consider the modest presents I lay before you, Benteshina, and tell me if they please you."

The sailors unloaded their cargo.

The voluble prince could not hide his satisfaction. The sight of a bed with remarkably delicate carving produced an almost worshipful exclamation.

"You Egyptians know how to live. I can't wait to try this out," he said with a meaningful leer.

With the prince in such excellent spirits, Ahsha decided it was time to introduce the military contingent.

"These officers will train your subjects as soldiers. As a faithful ally of Egypt, you must help us build a defensive front to protect Amurru and discourage the Hittites from attacking you."

"That's my dearest wish," asserted Benteshina. "The constant fighting has disrupted our economy. My people want to be safe."

"In a few weeks, Ramses will send an army, and in the meantime these officers will set up a training camp."

"Excellent, excellent. Hatti suffered a serious setback, and Muwattali has been weakened by the power struggle between his son and brother."

"Which way do you think the military establishment is leaning?"

"It seems divided. Some of them support Uri-Teshoop, others Hattusili. For the moment, the emperor has a grip on the situation, but I wouldn't rule out the possibility of a coup. And then a number of the coalition members regret ever getting involved in a losing battle, so costly in human terms and a financial drain as well . . . Pharaoh's leadership might seem very attractive."

"It sounds promising."

"And I promise you an unforgettable welcome!"

The Lebanese girl, with her full breasts and ample thighs, lay down on top of Ahsha and softly rubbed her body back and forth against his. Every bit of her skin smelled sweet, and the blond thatch between her legs was enticing.

Although he had already gone several thrilling rounds, Ahsha responded. When the girl's massage produced the desired effect, he rolled her over on one side. Easily slipping into her intimate reaches, he once again found an intense and mutual pleasure. She was certainly far from a virgin, but her expert caresses more than made up for that failing. Neither of them had said a word.

"Go now," he said. "I'm sleepy."

She left him alone in the vast bedchamber overlooking a garden. Soon Ahsha forgot her and began to ponder Benteshina's revelations about the Hittite coalition and its potential unraveling. Making the right move would be difficult, but the thought was exciting.

What other power might sway the dissidents if they lost confidence in Muwattali? Certainly not Egypt. The land of the pharaohs was too far away, its culture foreign to the fractious Near Eastern princelings. Slowly it dawned on him, an idea so upsetting that he felt an immediate need to consult a map of the region.

The door to the bedchamber opened.

In walked a thin little man, his hair held in place with a headband, a slim silver chain around his neck, a silver cuff at his left elbow. He was dressed in a length of multicolored cloth that left his shoulders uncovered.

"My name is Hattusili. I'm the brother of Muwattali, Emperor of Hatti."

Ahsha felt light-headed. Perhaps, travel-weary and exhausted from lovemaking, he was having hallucinations.

"You're not dreaming, Ahsha. I'm delighted to meet the new chief of Egyptian diplomacy. I hear you're a very close friend of the Pharaoh."

"You, in Amurru?"

"You're my prisoner, Ahsha. Any attempt at escape will be futile. My men have captured your officers and taken your ship and crew. Hatti is once again master of the province of Amurru. Ramses should never have underestimated how quickly we might react to our defeat. Kadesh was a personal humiliation for me, as leader of the coalition. Without your king's wrath and his fearlessness, I would have exterminated the Egyptian army. That's why I need to reassert my leadership as soon as possible and gain the upper hand while Egypt is resting on its laurels."

"The Prince of Amurru has betrayed us once again."

"Benteshina sells to the highest bidder. But I'll make sure this province never falls under Egypt's control again."

"Aren't you forgetting the wrath of Ramses?"

"Oh, I fear it. I'm taking care not to provoke him."

"As soon as he learns that Hittite forces have occupied Amurru, he'll strike back. I'm certain you haven't had time to rebuild an army strong enough to resist him."

Hattusili smiled. "An expert analysis, but it will be of no use to Ramses. He won't learn the truth until it's much too late."

"My silence will speak volumes."

"There will be no silence, Ahsha, because you're going to write Ramses a reassuring letter, telling him your mission is going as planned and your officers are under way with the training."

"In other words, our army will march blindly into your trap."

"Yes, that's one part of my plan."

And the rest? Ahsha tried to read Hattusili's thoughts. He considered the people of the region, their good and bad qualities, their aspirations and frustrations. The answer struck him.

"Let me guess—the Bedouins!" Ahsha said with a sneer.

"It's worked before, and it will work again."

"They're cutthroats and pillagers."

"Unfortunately true. But they'll help me stir up trouble with Egypt's allies."

"If I were you, I wouldn't share all my secrets."

"Soon they won't be secrets; they'll be facts. Get dressed, Ahsha, and come with me. I want you to take down my letter."

"And if I refuse?"

"You'll die."

"I'm prepared for death."

"No, you're not. A man who enjoys making love as much as you do would rather keep living. I doubt you're prepared to give up your pleasures for a lost cause. You'll write the letter."

Ahsha hesitated. "And if I do?"

"We'll try to keep you comfortable in prison. You'll survive."

"Why not do away with me?"

"You may be instrumental if it ever comes to negotiations. You were a valuable bargaining chip at Kadesh, don't you agree?"

"You're asking me to betray Ramses."

"It isn't really treason. You're being coerced."

"You'll spare my life . . . it sounds too good to be true."

"By all the gods of Hatti, I give my word in the name of the emperor."

"Give me the pen, Hattusili."

SIXTY

T he seven daughters of the old priest of Midian, among them the wife of Moses, were drawing water from a well and filling troughs for their father's sheep when a small band of Bedouins on horseback burst into the oasis. Bearded, armed with bows and daggers, their appearance promised nothing good.

The sheep scattered, the womenfolk dove inside their tents, and the old man leaned on his cane to face the intruders.

"Are you in charge?"

"I am."

"How many able-bodied men do you have here?"

"Just me and a shepherd."

"Canaan is going to revolt against Pharaoh, with the help

of the Hittites. Thanks to them, this land will be ours. Every tribe must aid in the fight against Egypt."

"We're not a tribe, just a family living quietly in these parts for several generations."

"Show us your shepherd."

"He's up on the mountain."

The Bedouins conferred.

"We'll come back," said their spokesman. "On that day, we're taking your shepherd to fight with us. If he won't, we'll fill in your well and burn your tents."

Moses came back to his tent at nightfall. His wife and father-in-law leapt to their feet.

"Where were you?" she asked.

"On the holy mountain, where the God of our fathers reveals his presence. He spoke of the misery of Hebrews living in Egypt—my people oppressed by Pharaoh, my brothers lamenting their fate and longing for freedom."

"There's even worse news from here," the old priest of Midian told him. "Some Bedouins rode in today, saying that Canaan is going to break away from Egypt. They're drafting every able-bodied man they can find, and they say they'll be back for you."

"What a farce! Ramses will put down the rebellion in a minute."

"Even if the Hittites are behind the rebels?"

"The Hittites lost at Kadesh."

"That's what the caravan merchants told us," the priest agreed, "but can they be trusted? You have to hide, Moses."

"Did the Bedouins threaten you?"

"If you won't fight with them, they'll slaughter us."

The woman Zipporah clung to Moses. "You're leaving, aren't you?"

"God has ordered me to return to Egypt."

"You'll be tried and convicted!" the old man reminded him.

"I'll go with you," Zipporah said firmly, "and we'll bring our son."

"It may be a dangerous journey."

"I don't care. You're my husband, and I'm your wife."

The old priest sat down again, overcome.

"Don't worry," Moses told him. "God will watch over your oasis. The Bedouins won't return."

"What does that matter, when I'll never see the three of you again?"

"True, Father. Come bid us goodbye and ask the Lord's blessing on us."

In Pi-Ramses, the temples were preparing for the midwinter feasts, which included the reconsecration of statues and liturgical objects. The royal couple, their forces depleted, would commune with the light to draw on its holy energy and make offerings to Ma'at, who held the universe together in harmony.

The victory at Kadesh had reassured the Egyptian people. They no longer viewed the Hittites as invincible, and they knew that Ramses could handle any enemy. The peace they so loved would be preserved.

The capital looked better than ever. Stone carvers were embellishing the four main temples, dedicated to Amon,

Ptah, Ra, and Set. The noble mansions and villas were as fine as any in Thebes or Memphis. The port was bustling, the warehouses bulging with goods. The tile factory still turned out the blue faience that, found on almost every building, had earned Pi-Ramses its nickname, the Turquoise City.

One of the residents' favorite leisure activities was floating along the canals in fishing boats. Snacking on honey-sweet apples from local orchards, they drifted with the current, admiring flowering gardens on the banks, watching the ibises, flamingos, and pelicans, and often failing to notice that a fish was nibbling.

In his own small craft, Ramses was rowing his daughter, Meritamon, and son, Kha. The boy had told his sister all about his encounter with the cobra, speaking soberly, without exaggeration. After this brief interval of relaxation, Ramses would rejoin Nefertari and Iset the Fair, whom the Great Royal Wife had invited to dine with them.

At the landing, he found Ahmeni. For the scribe to leave his office, something serious had to happen.

"A letter from Ahsha."

"Problems?"

"See for yourself."

Ramses handed Kha and Meritamon over to Nedjem, who worried about outings in boats or even walks outside the palace gardens. The secretary of agriculture put a protective arm around each of the children as Ramses unrolled the papyrus Ahmeni proffered.

> *To the Pharaoh of Egypt, from Ahsha, Secretary of State,*
> *In accordance with Your Majesty's orders, I met with the*
> *Prince of Amurru, Benteshina, who extended the warmest*

welcome to me as well as our military contingent. The training officers, headed by a royal scribe who is one of our fellow alumni from the University of Thebes, have begun recruiting a Lebanese unit. As we assumed, the Hittites have retreated farther north after their defeat at Kadesh. Nevertheless, we must not relax our vigilance. The local forces will not be up to the challenge if an invasion is forthcoming. I therefore deem it necessary for you to dispatch a well-armed regiment to Amurru, to establish a defensive base that can safeguard our country and assure its lasting peace.

May this letter find the Pharaoh in excellent health, as always.

The king rolled up the document.

"It's Ahsha's handwriting."

"I agree, but . . ."

"If Ahsha wrote this letter, he was coerced."

"That's what I thought," Ahmeni said approvingly. "He never would have said that he studied with you in Thebes."

"Of course not, since we met at the royal academy in Memphis. There's nothing wrong with Ahsha's memory."

"Why did he put that in?"

"To show he's being held captive in Amurru."

"Has Benteshina gone mad?"

"No, I'm sure he was pressured, too, no doubt because he's sold his allegiance once more."

"Does that mean . . ."

"The Hittites have wasted no time," said Ramses. "They've taken back Amurru and set another trap for us. If Ahsha wasn't so clever, Muwattali would have had his revenge."

"Do you think Ahsha's still alive?"

"I have no idea, my friend. With Serramanna's help, I'll put together a strike force. If our friend is a prisoner, we'll get him out."

When Pharaoh gave the foundry foreman the order to resume arms production at full capacity, the news spread through the capital within hours and throughout the country in days.

Why hide from the facts? Kadesh had not been enough to break the Hittites' will to conquer. The four huge bases in Pi-Ramses were put on alert, and the soldiers realized they would soon be marching north to fight again.

Ramses spent one whole day and one whole night alone in his office. At daybreak, he went out on the palace roof to gaze at his heavenly counterpart, reborn after the nightly combat with the forces of evil.

At the eastern edge of the terrace stood Nefertari, pure and beautiful in the rosy blush of dawn.

Ramses held her close.

"I thought that Kadesh would open an era of peace, but I hoped for too much. Shadows are lurking all around us: Muwattali, Shaanar if he's still alive, the Libyan sorcerer who got away, my long-lost friend Moses, Ahsha stranded in Amurru, held captive or worse. Will we be able to weather the storm, Nefertari?"

"Your role is to hold the ship on course, no matter how strong the wind. You have neither the time nor the right to doubt. If the current is against you, you'll sail into it. The two of us will sail forward."

Breaking over the horizon, the first rays of sunlight shone upon the Great Royal Wife and Ramses, the Son of Light.

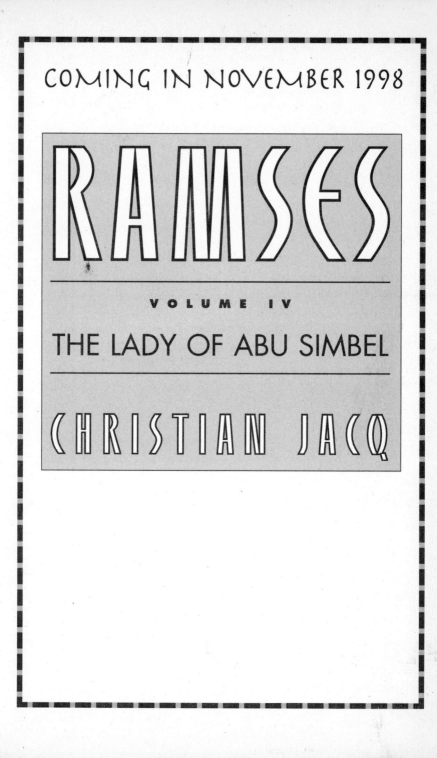

COMING IN NOVEMBER 1998

RAMSES

VOLUME IV

THE LADY OF ABU SIMBEL

CHRISTIAN JACQ